I Am Not Me

Excerpts from Chapter 1 and Chapter 14 in NO MAN IS AN ISLAND by Thomas Merton, copyright © 1955 by The Abbey of Our Lady of Gethsemani and renewed 1983 by the Trustees of the Merton Legacy Trust, reprinted by permission of Houghton Mifflin Harcourt Publishing Company.

Canadian Cataloguing in Publication Data

Sabo, Leslie G. (Leslie Gerald)
I Am Not Me

ISBN: 0-9813-5650-8
ISBN: 978-0-9813565-0-1

Printed and bound in U.S.A.

Summit Books
Mono Plaza, R.R. # 4
633419 Highway 10 North
Orangeville, ON L9W 2Z1

1 2 3 4 5 13 12 11 10

I Am Not Me

The Orangeville Novel

Leslie G. Sabo

Summit Books
Orangeville, Ontario
2010

Dedication

For Elsie. Now and always.

We ruin others and ourselves together not by entering into the sanctuary of their inner being—for no one can enter there except their Creator—but by drawing out of that sanctuary and teaching them to live as we live: centered upon themselves.

Thomas Merton
No Man Is an Island

The unexamined life is not worth living.

Socrates

Wrong is wrong even if everybody is doing it, and right is right even if nobody is doing it.

St. Augustine

1

Rodger Blackwell awakened with a queasy stomach, his head throbbing, both souvenirs of their tenth wedding anniversary celebration of the previous evening. He kept his eyes closed, fearing that opening them would only intensify the throbbing because he already knew that Claudia had opened the drapes wide, allowing the piercing July rays of the Orangeville sun to enter. Why had he drunk so damn much and gotten so stupidly drunk? Was it simply to celebrate ten years of marriage to a lovely woman, or something else? Deep down he knew that it *was* something else, like the disturbing knowledge that he had turned forty just a few weeks ago and had entered middle age. And he still saw no true, worthwhile achievement in his life. Thoughts of this failure were nothing new to him—he'd had them for weeks, months, years, only to push them repeatedly to the back of his mind.

But he just never became stupidly drunk. Actually, he felt that habitual drinking indicated a lack of character and rarely drank at all. Then why now? Why had he become stupidly drunk on his tenth anniversary when he hadn't become stupidly drunk on any of the previous nine? He knew the answer, knew that for him their tenth anniversary celebration had not been the joyous occasion it had been for Claudia, but nothing more than a persistent reminder that ten fruitless years had passed and he felt as empty and desolate as the Sahara Desert. Ten years. Ten celebrations. But did those ten years of marriage represent a milestone, or simply a millstone? After all, what had he achieved during those ten years? Nothing important. Nothing worthwhile. Merely a materialistic, pointless grasping for more and more possessions.

But now he knew that he could no longer do this. He couldn't go on like this. He refused to go on like this. Something unknown simmered inside him, demanding release. Their hedonistic lifestyle had become tedious, and this house, actually Claudia's house, meant little to him. Claudia could have the house her way, the furnishings her way, the decorations her way, but she wasn't going to have his life.

Not any longer.

Yet what was the alternative? What the *hell* was the alternative?

Yes, disregarding his ten-year marriage, he *had* reached a milestone last night, a milestone he wanted to avoid even thinking about which had assaulted his senses repeatedly as he drank one foolish drink after another, the two words hammering home their insistent, undeniable message.

I'm forty!

He refused to open his eyes yet, afraid that the light would invade them and make his headache even worse, but he felt Claudia's presence, knew that she sat before her vanity mirror brushing her long, blonde hair because he could hear every stroke. Brushing...brushing ..brushing...Sometimes a hundred times or more, until her hair took on a rich gloss.

He wanted her to believe that he still slept because he had no desire to talk to her. Not yet. But he knew that eventually he must talk to her because he wanted to voice his dissatisfaction, something he had rarely done before. Was it simply because he felt so lousy that he wanted to let it all out, or something else? Something even more insistent, even more important? Yes, and he knew why he had to finally voice his true feelings: because he felt his life slipping away with absolutely nothing vitally important being achieved.

I'm forty!

Brushing...brushing...brushing...

He pictured the large clutter of cosmetics spread out across the vanity top: the expensive welter of rejuvenating skin creams meant to forestall as long as possible the aging process which obsessed her, the blushes, the eye shadows, the false eyelashes, the lipsticks, the mascaras, the nail polishes, the false fingernails, the antiperspirants, the perfumes. And on and on and on. There were even a few blonde wigs on their stands, the exact colour of her own bleached hair, originally black, for those few occasions when she had a hurried appointment and simply lacked enough time to do her own hair properly.

At thirty-seven, the skin of her lovely face with its gray eyes, straight nose, full, tempting lips enclosing excellent teeth which she used whitening agents on daily, and a chin with a cute little cleft, still stood up fairly well under the almost daily onslaught of a heavy cosmetic mask, but he wondered what it would look like, even with the aid of the so-called age-defying creams and weekly facials, at forty-five, fifty-five, sixty-five.

Who would Claudia be today? He recalled watching Joan Rivers greeting actresses at the Academy Awards as they pranced along the red carpet and asking them, "Who are *you* tonight?" and meaning which designer's clothing are you wearing. And he longed for some brave, unique woman to reply, "I'm *me*, who do you think I am? I'm Marie Miller." Of course, Claudia had no Versace clothing, but her extensive wardrobe allowed her to dress well. Once, out of curiosity, he had counted her shoes and found twenty-four pairs, and when he had questioned her extravagance, she became angry and accused him of spying, then simply said, "I need them all. I work with the public. You can't expect me to wear the same thing every few days, can you?"

With her extensive wardrobe, and with an open house on her agenda that afternoon, who would she be today? What she wore depended on what type of client she would be meeting and what type of real estate sales pitch she planned to use. He had known her to wear three sets of clothing on the same day. Today, since she would be meeting potential buyers for the first time, she would probably dress conservatively, wearing either a slack suit or a dress or skirt which fell to just below her knees. For fear of offending wives who came with their husbands, or those women who came with their lovers or fiances, she would reveal no cleavage or thigh.

On her first meeting with any male client, she dressed conservatively, aware that some men would be suspicious or feel insulted if she portrayed a sexual image. One question she always asked a new male client during their first telephone conversation was whether he'd be bringing either his wife or a lady friend along to the showing. His answer told her what she wanted to know: that he was either attached or unattached. During warmer weather, when she met with a male client she'd previously met, and had determined by her seemingly innocent questions about his lifestyle that he would be interested in seeing a little skin, she pulled out all the stops, wearing low cut blouses, short skirts, or low cut dresses with high hemlines. She found it easy to secure such lifestyle information, for she knew that most people, both men and women, liked nothing better than to talk about themselves. And she was vain enough about her appearance to know that her shapely legs with their well-rounded thighs, which she remembered to cross and recross regularly, and her plump breasts encased in their uplift bra, which she remembered to make even more plump by bending forward regularly, combined with a faint scent of sultry perfume emanating from her body, would create exactly the sexual image she knew it would.

But there were also the stubborn ones, those who were all business and simply not interested in being distracted by sex. They knew that they had a large investment at stake and were determined to get the best deal possible. Yet she knew from experience that even these could sometimes be made to bend, or even break. When Claudia felt convinced that she had tried everything in her power with a stubborn client, without success, she called on reinforcements to accompany her to her next appointment. And these reinforcements took the formidable shape of her stepfather and boss, Gregory Gunderson, a pudgy, beer-bellied, loud-mouthed real estate broker and president of Supreme Real Estate Inc., who represented the very epitome of the hard sell by attempting to browbeat clients into submission, and often succeeded.

There was nothing Supreme about Supreme Real Estate Inc. when Gunderson entered the picture. His favourite targets were the elderly, either singles or couples. When Claudia's efforts failed, Gunderson stepped in and mercilessly browbeat his elderly victims until they usually gave in, often convincing them against their better judgment to accept precarious financing which would stretch their resources to the limit, his only goal being to collect a commission regardless of how severely his victims suffered. And many of them *did* suffer, losing the homes they could ill afford and being forced to retrench by seeking out smaller, less expensive accommodation. But they had learned their lesson and avoided ever calling Supreme Real Estate Inc. again and badmouthed the company to their friends.

Brushing...brushing...brushing...How many strokes would it be this morning? One-fifty? One-seventy-five? Two hundred?

Rodger's right side had become sore from lying on it too long, but he refused to turn over yet because he felt that Claudia would probably think him awake and begin talking to him. And he didn't want that. Not yet.

He recalled how he had also once become Gunderson's victim when Gunderson had convinced him to take the real estate salesman's course at Humber College and become one of his salesman. It was shortly after his engagement to Claudia, when he found himself at loose ends, having just given up a dead end job as a salesman for Webcor Products Ltd., a small company which manufactured, sold, and serviced their line of portable air purifiers. For the first time in years, he thought of the antics of Derek Hornsby, then single, thirty years old, and one of their gung ho salesman who firmly believed that his energy and extreme dedication to his job with Webcor would eventually make him quite wealthy. Hornsby never rested. Even when he sat he seemed to be activating springs implanted in his buttocks. Like a badge of honour, he proudly showed Rodger his cluttered appointment book jammed with half-hour appointments extending even into the evenings. Because of this, Hornsby never seemed to have enough time to do everything he wanted to do and was always in a hurry. "A half hour, that's all the time I give them," he often said. "If you can't make a sale in that time, forget it and move on. Maybe try a callback later on." To squeeze in as many appointments as he possibly could, he tried to shorten the time required to complete other activities and resented even spending time attending to his bodily functions. When he felt an urgent need to urinate, he started unzipping his fly while still ten feet from a washroom door, even a public washroom. As for bowel movements, Rodger sometimes wondered if Hornsby waited until he felt a turn edging dangerously from his rectum before frantic-ally searching for a toilet. Some day, Rodger suspected, if Hornsby rushed even more, he'd not only unzip his fly but actually expose his penis before entering a washroom, or pull down his slacks and underwear, and be arrested for indecent exposure. Either that, or end up with a heavy, smelly load in his underwear.

This incessant rushing also extended to Hornsby's eating habits. Once, while doing a few callbacks together to put more pressure on some stubborn leads, they had dropped into McDonald's for lunch. Amazed and concerned, Rodger watched anxiously as Hornsby wolfed down a quarter-pounder, large fries, and a large Coke in about ten minutes, afraid that the barely half chewed food would eventually lodge in Hornsby's throat, forcing Rodger to apply the Heimlich manoeuvre to prevent him from choking to death. But nothing happened. At the time, Rodger thought that Hornsby's gullet must be as wide as a piece of Kolbassa. The next thing Rodger knew, Hornsby was wiping his mouth and bounding to his feet, doubtless driven by his spring-implanted buttocks, and telling Rodger to bring his half eaten lunch with him to finish in the car, which he did.

Now, not having heard from or even seen Hornsby around Orangeville for several years, he wondered if indeed he had finally choked on his quarter-pounder, or had he simply given up on Webcor and moved away. But Rodger knew that if Hornsby had moved elsewhere and remained in sales, he'd no longer be carrying a crammed appointment book. Now he'd be the proud owner of a crammed Blackberry.

Yet in the final analysis what valid point did Hornsby's ceaseless rushing around make? What kind of life can it possibly be when you can't even relax long enough to enjoy a meal, a good leak, or a hefty shit? What kind of life can it possibly be when you're so obsessed with your work that you can't even squeeze out a drop of time to think of anything but the money it will bring in and the possessions that money will buy? What about the quality of your life itself? When do you begin to think of that? When do you begin to think of what you're actually *doing* with your life and what worthwhile goals you intend to achieve, not merely as a money machine but as a human being, as he, Rodger, was thinking now? And in the repugnant picture which came back to him he saw his ten-year marriage as nothing more than a hedonistic, self-seeking, barren wasteland.

Yes, he had asserted himself after discovering the truth about Webcor. In discussions with members of the swamped Webcor service department, he learned that the units were second rate and often barely survived the one-year warranty period before they began breaking down. Whenever that happened, the company started making money on service calls. This information prompted him to leave the job because he could no longer believe in the product.

And after that—what? After joining Supreme, he soon became disenchanted. "We'll be just one, big, happy family," Gunderson had promised, but when Rodger became aware of the hard sell company policy he soon realized that only two members of that family were happy—Gunderson and Claudia. After a year, when he could no longer stomach the lies, deceit, and constant browbeating, he quit and secured a position as a junior writer for Drummond & Waters, an advertising agency, for the past several years owned only by Bart Drummond after buying out Waters.

Once he left Supreme, his relationship with Gunderson had never been the same. From then on Gunderson considered him a gutless wimp who had jumped ship and deserted the company, and on the rare occasions when they met Gunderson invariably subjected him to the barbs from his acid tongue. Rodger hadn't minded—then. He realized that Gunderson's constant insults were his infantile way of expressing his reaction to his inability to control Rodger, as he controlled Claudia.

No, he hadn't minded then because he felt happy just being away from the hateful job and out of Gunderson's clutches. But now, after almost ten years of listening to Gunderson's insults, as he lay in bed on his aching side with his head pounding, he *did* mind. He minded very much and saw his year with Supreme as just another fruitless year of just another wasted, fruitless life.

I'm forty! Was this the reason why he vowed not to listen to Gunderson's insults any longer? Because half his life had probably already passed with nothing worthwhile achieved? He felt different this morning, and that difference made him yearn to pull his existing life up by its roots and transplant it into richer soil.

Brushing...brushing...brushing...Would it never end?

Now the ache in his right side had turned to pain. He had to turn onto his left side, turn so that his back would be facing Claudia. Maybe she'd continue to ignore him. But as he turned a stabbing pain shot through his head and he couldn't repress a groan. Still, he kept his eyes squeezed tightly shut.

The brushing stopped. " Are you awake, darling?"

He said nothing, hoping she'd believe that he was either still asleep or still unconscious from his heavy drinking of the previous night.

Brushing...brushing...brushing...

He'd been faithful to her from the start, and as far as he knew she'd always been faithful to him, in spite of the short skirts and low-cut necklines she sometimes wore to titillate her male clients. Not that he'd never wondered. It was natural for him to be jealous and want her to reserve even the sight of her sexual charms only for himself. He trusted her not to take the final sexual step. Yes, he trusted her—but not her male clients. She had often gone to lunch with them, sometimes even to dinner, and he knew that, because of her loveliness, these dinners were sometimes followed by invitations to join her clients for nightcaps at their homes. Yet Claudia looked upon these free drinks and meals as business meetings to further discuss and perhaps close a potential sale, for she usually brought along her briefcase which often contained a partially completed Offer To Purchase for the property in question. And when and if the nightcap suggestion came up, Claudia had repeatedly told Rodger that she always refused, never allowing sexuality with her clients to extend beyond the visual. "*Look,* but don't *touch!*" And, at least as far as he knew, none of her male clients had ever ended up in bed with her. Although quite willing to tease and soften up certain male clients by exposing some thigh or breast, she insisted that she always refused to go any further. Not even to sell a house.

And Rodger tried to believe her. But he also worried about her because she couldn't possibly always meet with male clients in the relative safety of public places. She had to either drive or be driven to a showing, where she'd be alone with the male client, offering him an opportunity to make sexual advances, or worse, and even Claudia's assurance that this had never happened failed to prevent him from wondering and brooding about it.

He knew exactly where and how he fitted into their marriage. Had known almost from the day they were married. He danced to Claudia's tune, and always had. When she wanted something, he occasionally protested, but weakly, and almost always surrendered in the end, mainly because what she wanted was usually only important to her, not him. Now, even with his eyes tightly closed, he knew exactly the decorations and furnishings of the bedroom: pink lace curtains, beige vertical blinds, floral wallpaper, thick, white pile carpeting, a white and gold Italian provincial bedroom suite comprised of a queen-sized bed flanked by two large bedside tables, a massive nine-foot vanity with a six-foot wide mirror, his five-drawer dresser, and two dressing valets. All selected by Claudia.

Nor did he need to go down into the basement rec room where they held their anniversary celebration last night to know exactly the furnishings there: the deep, brown pile carpeting, the home theatre equipment with surround sound, the forty-two-inch television set, the massive sofa and two La-z-boys in brown leather, the huge coffee table, the L-shaped bar with its black leather stools and mirrored back wall with plate glass shelves loaded with glasses and bottles, the hexagonal card table surrounded by six black leather swivel chairs. All selected by Claudia.

And he certainly had no need to go into the kitchen, living room, dining room, or Claudia's office to know what furnishings she had selected for these areas. Even the house itself—who had selected it? Claudia, of course. At times he identified with Richard in the British sitcom *Keeping Up Appearances*—just tagging along for the ride and making certain that he had the wallet and the Visa, MasterCard, or Interac card handy. Although Claudia certainly had more commendable attributes than the petty, greedy Hyacinth of the sitcom; she worked hard and earned a good living, and they generally shared expenses.

His den, housed in the basement, actually represented the only room in the house that he could call his own. Determined to have his way, although Claudia had tried diligently to influence him, here he had decorated to *his* taste. He had chosen restful browns: the large six-drawer pedestal desk which dominated the room, the leather manager's desk chair, the leather La-z-boy reading chair in the corner with its accompanying brass floor lamp with brown shade, the tan carpet, the panelled walls, the metal four-drawer filing cabinet, the laptop computer, even the short drapes on the casement window. The four Van Gogh and Gauguin prints which hung from the walls were his only concession to bright colours.

His world. His sanctuary.

But, as though Claudia simply couldn't bear the thought that nothing of herself existed in his sanctuary, she occasionally left him little reminders, like a crystal vase on his desk containing a single red rose, or a little tin of Scotch mints, or she brought him a cup of coffee in a floral mug, or sprayed the room with lavender scent. But he accepted these. At least he knew that he had decorated his den to his own taste, and Claudia's little "intrusions" did little to change that. He simply removed any flowers, transferred the Scotch mints to the living room, and sprayed the room with a masculine scent.

Now, for the first time since their marriage, he asked himself a surprising question: Would you rather have as a wife a beautiful but vain and selfish woman who gave you great sex but little more, or a homely woman who gave you everything?—and felt shocked when no definite answer came.

The brushing stopped. "Are you awake, darling? It's almost noon."

Groaning, he struggled to a sitting position, propped two pillows behind his back and leaned heavily against them, sighing deeply. "I'm awake," he said. "But it feels like my head's going to explode. It's throbbing like hell."

"I'll get you a Bromo." Rising and moving lightly toward the ensuite bathroom, she returned shortly with the foaming glass and handed it to him. "This will help."

"Thanks." Testing his stomach, he drank a little at a time, finishing the glass when the nauseousness receded.

After rinsing the glass in the bathroom, Claudia returned to the vanity and began applying her makeup. He watched as she smoothed on a pale red lipstick, and knew what would come next. After she had spread the lipstick, she rubbed her lips together to spread it more evenly, then, finished, she made a loud smacking sound. Over the years, he had heard this sound hundreds of times and it had never ceased to irritate him, but he had never mentioned it. But now, suddenly, he felt a rebellious urge to comment.

"Do you *have* to do that?" he grumbled.

She turned and gazed at him, perplexed. "Do what?"

"Make that loud smacking sound every time you finish applying your lipstick. I've been listening to it every since we got married, and it's irritating. Is it really necessary? Does it serve any purpose?"

"No, I suppose it doesn't, except that it gives me a feeling of satisfaction. It's just a habit, that's all. And you've never ever commented on it before, so I naturally assumed that it didn't bother you."

"Well, it *does* bother me. It's irritating."

"To you, perhaps, but not to me. Just think, darling, if you hadn't had so much to drink last night you'd have been up a long time ago and out of the bedroom and you wouldn't have had to listen to me smacking my lips. We all have our little foibles. Even you."

"Oh?" Rodger reflected on his meekness toward Claudia over the past ten years and saw little more than a continuous passive, non-irritating role. "What little foibles do I have?"

She smiled cryptically. "Well, I have an open house to go to soon and I haven't time to go into *that* subject now. But if you like, we can discuss it over dinner." She quickly changed the subject. "You're behaving very strangely this morning, Rodger. Was something bothering you last night? Was it just the celebration, or something else? I've never ever seen you drink like that."

"Did I make a complete idiot of myself? I can't remember even half of what I did."

"Well, I don't suppose you made any enemies. Not permanent ones anyway. Let's just say that you were the life of the party. Ten years of marriage should be a happy occasion, but you weren't a *happy* life of the party. You hardly smiled at all, and you kept picking arguments with people, and you've *never* behaved like *that* before." She turned to face him. "Is something wrong, darling?"

"Claudia, who am I?"

Bewildered, she stared at him. "What's the matter with you this morning?"

"Just answer the question," he snapped. "Who *am* I?"

She drew back a little, her forehead creasing in confusion, and he knew why. She had never seen this particular Rodger before. "Why...why, you're Rodger." She laughed nervously, trying to lighten the situation. "Rodger the Dodger."

"Don't call me that! Just because your father has called me that ever since I left Supreme. Just because I left a company that browbeats its clients and treats them like dirt. Just answer the question. Who the hell *am* I, Claudia?"

"You're Rodger Blackwell. And you're my husband. And I love you."

"I don't mean that. I don't mean my relationship with you. I mean who am I as a person, as a human being."

She looked concerned, and he could see that she disliked the direction the conversation had taken.

She said, "And who do *you* think you are as a person?"

"I...I don't know," he admitted. "I just feel...I just feel false. I am not me. I have no identity of my own. I am a product of the mercenary, materialistic, and obsessive society I live in. And do you know what that society represents, Claudia?"

"Of course I know. But we all have a choice. Either be part of the game or drop out. Go and hide in a corner somewhere, like my first father."

"A *game*. You think *life* is nothing more than a *game*?"

"Of course it is. We get up each morning and put on our costumes, and then we go out on stage. We play the game. And if we don't do that we're left behind to slave away at some crumby, third-rate job barely making ends meet, or even worse, to collect welfare and line up at the food bank."

"And just exactly what *is* the game, Claudia? Getting to the top no matter how many heads you trample on? Lying to trusting people in order to make a real estate sale? Wearing short skirts and low-cut blouses or tight sweaters in order to excite men so that they'll buy your houses? Is *that* what the game is all about?"

"Now you're just being insulting. Does it really matter how you get things? As long as you get them."

"What things?" He waved his arm to take in the room. "Do you mean things like this?"

"Of course. Nice things. Nice house, nice furnishings, nice clothes, nice car, and the money to buy what we want."

"And where do we go from here? To even *nicer* things? *Bigger* house, *bigger* car, *more* expensive clothes, *more* expensive furnishings. For what? Can't you see that we're on a treadmill, a treadmill to nowhere?"

"Well, I like the treadmill, and I like what the treadmill can give me." Confused, her eyes narrowed and her brow furrowed. "Rodger, what's this all about? What's the *matter* with you this morning? You never talk to me like this. I know you're hungover and aren't feeling well, but—"

"I'm forty, that's what's the matter."

She still looked confused. "And?"

Don't you understand, I'm forty. *Forty!* I'm middle-aged and probably half my life is gone and what the hell have I done with it? What have I achieved?"

Claudia nodded and smiled knowingly. "So *that's* it. Now I understand. You're simply suffering from mid-life crisis." She breathed a heavy sigh of relief. "And I thought it was something terribly serious the way you were carrying on. Don't worry, darling, you'll get over it and your life will be back to normal before you know it. Some day I may be in the same boat, with menopause and hot flashes, but that will also eventually pass." She laughed. "Do you remember the episode on *All in the Family* when Edith started to go through menopause and Archie said, 'You've got fifteen minutes to get through this and that's it! Finished!' Don't worry, darling, your mid-life crisis will soon pass."

"Don't you understand. I don't want this to pass…not until I've changed my life."

"Changed your life?" she said anxiously. "How? And why? I hope you don't intend to start looking for sweets in other candy stores."

"Meaning?"

"Meaning I hope you don't start exhibiting the classic symptoms of male menopause. Which is, of course, straying from the nest and looking for greener pastures. Starting relationships with other women. You wouldn't do anything *that* foolish, would you, darling?"

"You know as well as I do that I've never ever been unfaithful to you," he snapped. "Why would I start now?"

She laughed nervously. "Because that's the most common symptom exhibited by men going through male menopause. This is a whole new experience for you. And I don't want you to make a fool of yourself, as most men do when this happens to them. They feel that life is passing them by and that they've missed out on something, so they start looking. For another woman, maybe a flashy sports-car, maybe some flashy, juvenile clothes to go with it, maybe trying to move with a younger crowd, maybe drinking more, maybe starting to gamble for excitement. All sorts of crazy things. Things you'll never find because you're looking for something intangible, something which just isn't there." She faced him squarely. "What are *you* looking for, Rodger?

"I…I don't know. I know that I don't want a new sexual partner because I love you and I know that you're the best there is. And the other things you mentioned don't mean anything to me." He rubbed a hand across his aching eyes. "I just feel an emptiness inside me, like there's something missing which, if I had it, would make me whole, but I don't know what it is. I just feel like I'm not me. Not the real me. And I need to change so that I can find the real me."

"Don't be silly, darling. Why should you want to change anything. You're among the top writers in the creative department at Drummond. You earn an excellent salary, you receive bonuses every year, and you may soon be offered a partnership. You have no reason to feel false."

"You talk as though I've got the greatest job in the world. But what my job really entails is writing inane ads for pussy pads and asswipe. That's your father's favourite phrase, which he's been throwing at me for years, ever since I took the job at Drummond. Let's face it, I write ads for deodorants and lipstick and nail polish and hair colour. For cosmetics of every description. For toothpaste and tooth whitener. One woman, when interviewed on television, was actually stupid enough to say that she couldn't possibly feel confident about herself unless she used her tooth whitener *every* morning before venturing out into the world. Good God! We're consumed by cleanliness and the way we smell. And obsessed with ways of saving time. To do what? Sit on our fat asses and guzzle beer? Right now we're working on a commercial for a company that invented a soap called Shower Jolt. They claim that a morning shower with their soap supplies the caffeine equivalent of four cups of coffee because the caffeine is naturally absorbed through the skin and takes effect within ten minutes. What a load of crap! You can't rub caffeine onto your skin and expect it to act as a stimulant—you have to ingest it for it to work. But this company expects us to write a commercial which will make some gullible people believe that it *will* actually work. And the only reason this stuff is being put on the market is to tell people how much time they'll save by using it every time they take showers. But only foolish, naive people would buy it. And even if it did save time, which it won't because it won't work, who would be gullible enough to believe that washing with caffeine soap compares with actually *drinking* a good cup of Tim Horton coffee? But this is the kind of garbage we're expected to write."

The angry words he had kept bottled up for years flowed out of him, words he had always thought needed saying but had never seemed important enough to actually say, but now saying them had become crucial, even life sustaining, because of the changes he knew he had to make in his life. "We live in a mercenary world which is obsessed with outward appearances instead of internal qualities. When was the last time you saw a homely man or woman do a newscast or host a show on television? When was the last time you saw anyone but young, attractive women or young, handsome men do the weather on The Weather Network? How many senior citizens do you see working in front of the cameras on television?

"I read in a magazine article last week that in Canada the entire personal-care sector—including colour cosmetics, hair-care products, sun screens, toothpastes, fragrances, antiperspirants and deodorants, and skin-care products—is worth an estimated 5.3 billion dollars annually in retail sales. And that's only part of what we spend to feed our obsession with superficialities.

"Women stick on false fingernails. I went to the post office a few weeks ago to mail a parcel and the clerk was wearing these things. Instead of being rounded, the ends of the nails were almost blunt, and when she tried to separate the two parts of a form she had a hell of a time, and people were in line waiting. We spend far too much time worrying about outward *appearances*, and far too little time worrying about the inward *person*.

"You know as well as I do that today's advertising is meant to make us feel inadequate, meant to lower our self-esteem to convince us that we actually *need* the products that are being flogged. The proliferating ads for soaps, shampoos, deodorants, perfumes, and scented pussy pads are warning us again and again that we stink and will go on stinking unless we use their products every damn day of our lives."

Claudia said, "I know this is only your mid-life crisis talking, and you *will* get over this, but don't bite the hand that feeds you, darling. The advertising business has been very good to you over the years."

"Yes, it has, as far as money goes, but I've earned every cent of that money. Over the years I've brought in a lot of business for Drummond's. But that's another question. I'm talking about our obsession with outward appearances. Look at the way people wear jewellery today. Take rings. One finger isn't enough any more. Women, and even men, may have three or four rings on each hand.

We pierce the cap. out of our ears, sometimes putting three or four studs in each ear. Women pierce their navels and insert Playboy bunnies; they pierce their nipples and run metal rings through them. Young people pierce their eyebrows, noses, or tongues and run jewellery through them. Women now wear tattoos, something you never heard of before because women felt that a soft, clear skin added to their beauty. There's an absolute obsession in our society with superficial appearance."

"Don't get so wound up, darling. People simply want to look nice, that's all."

"But it's far better to *be* nice. To be a valuable, empathetic, productive member of society. When it comes right down to a person's true worth, what does it matter if a woman has a thirty-two-inch bust or a forty-two-inch bust, but thousands of plastic surgeons are out there making fortunes from women who want breast implants. What does it matter if a woman has a twenty-four-inch waist or a thirty-four-inch waist, or thirty-six-inch hips or forty-six-inch hips, but thousands of plastic surgeons are out there with their liposuction machines making fortunes from women who refuse to eat sensibly but want smaller asses and flatter bellies. What does it matter if a woman has fat lips or thin lips, but thousands of them, because of women like Angelina Jodie and others, are having their lips injected with fat to make them plumper. Facelifts, breast implants, neck lifts, buttlifts, tummytucks, nosejobs, you name it. The plastic surgeons have a goldmine business in Canada and the U.S.

"It's a conundrum, really. On the one hand, North Americans are obsessed with their superficial appearance, but on the other hand their superficial appearance goes all to hell because they continuously pig out on high calorie and high fat foods and refuse to control their gluttony. What's one of the biggest industries in North America? The diet industry. And why not when North America has the largest percentage of overweight and grossly obese people in the world. Over the years I've been with Drummond we've written dozens and dozens of commercials for diet products.

"And look at our sexual attitudes. Just look at an award show like the Academy Awards or the Emmys and what do you see. Tits! Nothing but tits drowning you on every side! And everyone trying to be like everyone else and afraid to be themselves. Nothing but a sheep mentality. No originality, no guts. Where are the women who come to the awards with their tits actually *covered*? If I were looking for a woman, *these* are the ones I'd be after. But where are they? All I see is a bunch of clones with their tits hanging out.

"And what about our youth? Instead of being themselves and asserting their own originality, they try to copy some practically naked teenaged performer who behaves like a sex symbol, can't sing, and shakes her tits and her ass all over the stage. And this is the smutty example they use for themselves! Good God! They even copy the way she dresses, wearing bare midriffs with their navels showing, just as she does. Look into a group of these teenaged girls and you'll see nothing but a bunch of clones without even a speck of originality. Same clothing, same bleached hair, same speech. Oh, sure, they will grow up, but what will they grow up *as*? Can you see any future business leaders in this bunch of silly teenagers? Hardly. Future business leaders, or teenagers who want to make some kind of positive difference in the world, are probably doing something constructive while the clones are wiggling their tits and asses at some teenaged dance.

"And what about today's films? The North American film industry is a desolate wasteland where most of the product is only fit to be burned because most of the product reeks with sex, foul language, and gratuitous violence. If you're looking for even a crumb of food for the mind or the soul, you'd be lucky to find it in one of fifty films made in North America today. Most of this trash is made for teenagers or young people, or even older people with little discernment. Do you need any discernment to watch films about comic book heroes like Batman or Spiderman? The special effects are very clever, and the films are very expensive to make, but they are nothing more than mindless entertainments loaded with tattered cliches, so don't expect to find even a sliver of meat in them.

"And if we wallow in and embrace mediocrity every day of our lives, can we ever expect to be anything but mediocre ourselves? And that's exactly how I feel right now. Mediocre, just like the rest of us. And that's exactly why I intend to do something about it."

Claudia said, "My, you *are* on a tear today, aren't you, darling. Thank goodness I'm not fat." She rose, undid the sash at her waist and pulled her pink satin dressing gown open. "Am I?"

Rodger gazed admiringly at her body, clad only in bikini panties and a brassiere, hands on her curvaceous hips, her long, shapely legs parted. At five-foot-four and weighing one-thirty, she had a soft, well-rounded figure which had tempted him countless times over the past ten years. He also appreciated that she'd avoided disfiguring her skin with body piercing or tattoos, all of which she found repugnant and demoralizing. One attribute he couldn't deny: Claudia was a great lover, by far the best he'd ever had, and she knew it. She knew exactly which buttons to press to bring him the greatest sexual pleasure. Whenever he wanted her, she was always there, ready, willing, and supremely able to drain his gonads, and to climax herself. But is even great sex enough? He doubted it—otherwise why would he still feel so hollow. There *had* to be more. There *must* be more!

"No, you certainly are not." he said finally. "Not too thin like those stick women on the fashion shows, and with just enough flesh on your bones to make you soft and desirable. If I didn't feel so rough I'd bring you to bed right now."

"And I'm afraid I'd have to refuse," she said coquettishly, closing her gown with a wide flourish and redoing the sash. "I've just finished applying my face and you'd make a terrible mess of it. Besides, I have an open house in Montgomery Village in less than two hours and still need to put out my signs and give the property a final check. Are you hungry? Would you like a little brunch before I go?"

"No, thanks. The Bromo has helped my headache a bit, but my stomach's still queasy. If I feel hungry later, I'll find something."

"You just relax then. I'll make you a delicious dinner when I get home."

He watched her as she opened a vanity drawer and removed a new pair of nylons. She quickly opened the package and pulled them on. They were knee highs, as he knew they would be, because she knew better than to wear a dress to an open house. She wanted to take no chance of losing a potential sale because some jealous wife saw her husband staring at Claudia's plump cleavage or shapely legs. Predictably, she slid open her wardrobe door and removed a conservative beige pantsuit and a plain white blouse. A business outfit, nothing more.

Once dressed, she attached a small gold stud to each of her pierced ears and a thin gold chain around her long, slender neck. She pulled on a pair of practical tan leather shoes with wedged two-inch heels, having realized years ago the foolishness of wearing high-heeled spikes when showing a home. Sometimes you had to escort clients around the grounds, and an earlier rain could cause the spiked heels to sink into the ground, possibly pulling the shoe off or even breaking a heel. She now reserved high-heeled spikes for indoor meetings with male clients where she wore either a skirt or a dress and wanted to show off her shapely legs to their best advantage.

She came to the side of the bed and stood over him. "I've got to be going now, darling." She gave him her prettiest smile, showing off her excellent, white teeth. "I know you're not feeling well yet, but you will try to get over this mid-life crisis business as soon as possible, won't you? Then we can get back to normal."

"I'm empty, Claudia. Empty and false. I need to change my life. I need to change my life and try to develop the interior man, and I will do that. Believe me, I *will*."

"And exactly how do you propose to do that?" she demanded, unable to hide her tenseness.

"I don't know," Rodger admitted, shaking his head. "I really don't know."

2

After Claudia had left for her open house, Rodger moved to the edge of the bed, sat up gingerly, pulled on his slippers and walked slowly to the wardrobe where he donned a maroon robe. In the kitchen, he found that Claudia had left the radio on, as usual, which greeted him with some dumb, noisy, hyper toothpaste commercial. He turned it off. He enjoyed silence, enjoyed listening to the sounds of his own thoughts and wondered again at the North American obsession with extraneous household noise. The TV or radio or both must be on every waking minute of every day. He knew a woman who kept radios on all day long, all tuned to the same station, in her bathroom, kitchen, and bedroom so that she would never be greeted by silence when leaving her living room TV and going into any of these rooms. Were people actually *afraid* of even a few seconds of silence, afraid of thinking their own thoughts, perhaps afraid of the emptiness they might find there?

He managed to force down a slice of toast, a half cup of coffee, and a few ounces of orange juice before returning to the bedroom. Deciding not to shave, he showered, saw the mirrored image of a younger edition of Matt, his father, as he vigorously brushed his teeth to rid his mouth of the clinging, previous night's bad taste, and, straightening to his full six feet, critiqued his face for signs of age as he ran a brush through his black, wavy hair which showed only a few strands of gray. The brown eyes, still slightly bloodshot from his anniversary binge, remained devoid of crow's feet at their outer edges; the complete set of straight, white teeth were still all his own with only a few fillings; the skin, deeply tanned from hours spent on tanning beds, still smooth except for the smile lines running from the edges of his straight nose to the corners of his thin lips. The boyishness, and the slightly receding chin, were the two elements of his face which he disliked. He'd been told more than once that his facial features resembled those of Robert Redford, a compliment he failed to appreciate. The boy-ish Robert Redford. No matter how old he became, Robert Red-ford always seemed to look boyish in his films. But Rodger disliked looking boyish; he would have much preferred to look more mas-culine, more rugged, more manly.

At the wardrobe, as he started to look over the rack of cloth-ing to make his selections for the day, he realized suddenly that most of the clothing hanging there had not been selected by him. Claudia knew his sizes and had the habit of buying clothes for him, sometimes bringing home shirts, slacks, socks, or underwear. She even bought ties for him, many of which he hated. Three of the sports jackets there were bought by Claudia. And she never both-ered asking him beforehand if he either liked or wanted these garments. She simply brought them home, and as she presented them to him, smiling her beautiful smile, insisted that he try them on immediately, and as he did so she crooned, "Oh, isn't that co-lour just lovely, and it looks so *perfect* on you!" or, "Doesn't it make you look terribly manly? Darling, I can hardly keep my hands off you!" All the while trying to convince him that he *had* to wear the clothes because *she* liked them. Although she pretended other-wise, the clothes were not bought for him—they were bought for her. And they represented just another way in which she attempted to infiltrate every aspect of his life.

I am not me! he thought. *Even my clothes are not me!*

Angry, he began searching through his shirts, sweaters, slacks, jackets, robes, ties, and belts to find those items which he had bought himself and found only two shirts and one pair of slacks. Until he dug deeper and examined the furthest end of the wardrobe hidden beyond the sliding doors and behind the wall. There he found numerous pieces of clothing, even ties and belts he had bought for himself over the years of their marriage and which he had conveniently, for Claudia, forgotten about. For Claudia had obviously culled his wardrobe, leaving a few scraps of his own selections in the forefront so that he wouldn't become too suspicious. And he hadn't, not persistently anyway. He recalled vaguely that a few times over the years he had mentioned to her that he thought he had other clothes, but she had insisted that everything was in his wardrobe, and he, partly because he trusted her and partly because his clothing had never been very important to him, had believed her and never bothered to examine the rest of the wardrobe.

But now, furious, he emptied the hidden end of the wardrobe of all the items he'd bought and moved them to the very centre of the opening made by the sliding door. He then went to his dresser and rummaged through it until he found a pair of boxer underwear and a pair of brown socks, *which he had bought*, and pulled them on. From the wardrobe, he selected a pair of dark brown polyester slacks and a tan polo shirt, *which he had bought*, and dressed himself. When Claudia returned home, she would see him in the same clothes, and she would know where they came from. Would she comment? Or simply ignore the obvious truth that she had lied to him, and that he knew that she had lied to him.

How often had she lied to him in the past?

When he came to the dinner table that evening, he felt much better and his appetite had returned. He decided to wait for Claudia's reaction to his clothing before saying anything, knowing that she knew exactly what he was wearing, and knowing also that she would bring up the subject once she knew that she had been found out. And she did, finally, and he sensed that she had been preparing her defence.

"I see that you're wearing some of your old things," she said. "They really don't do you justice, darling, and they do look a bit shabby, don't you think?"

"Is that why you hid them away at the very end of my wardrobe, along with almost every other piece of clothing I've bought for myself over the years?" he said testily. "Because they look a bit shabby? Is there some reason why I should *always* be wearing only the clothing that you've bought for me?"

"I only put your clothing away because I love you and want you to look your best for other people. Let's be honest, your taste in clothing is rather drab and plain. And dark. Dark slacks, dark shirts, dark sweaters, dark jackets, even now in July when you should be wearing bright colours, like many of the things I've bought for you over the years. And plain, everything plain, not a pattern in sight. I'm sorry, darling, but you really are a rather dull dresser, and I simply wanted to liven up your wardrobe so others would appreciate you more, including me. And you have been wearing some of the things I've bought you, haven't you?"

"Only because that was practically all I could see. And remember this: I dress for myself, *not* for other people. Maybe I don't have your taste in clothing, but it's *my* taste and I like it. I'm not interested in what other people wear; I'm only interested in what they *are*."Amazed at how good it felt to actually be speaking his own mind, he pressed on. "And I don't want you buying me any more clothing unless you ask me first and get my approval. Do you understand?"

She smiled beautifully. "Yes, of course I do."

"I don't tell you what to wear, do I? Sometimes when I see you in one of your skimpy outfits I wonder how someone out there hasn't raped you. But even though I disapprove, I don't tell you to change, do I?" He paused, thinking, and finally said, "Tell me this: do you like this house?"

She looked bewildered. "I don't see what that—"

"Do you like this house and the way it's decorated?"

"Yes, of course I do, I did the decorating myself, but I don't understand—"

"If you asked an interior decorator to come into this house and give you a list of all the things she would do to redecorate this house, and that list showed dozens of areas she wanted changed, how would you react?"

"Well, I'd assess the changes and decide which ones I thought would improve the house, and have those done, and reject the rest."

"So you wouldn't allow changes to be made which you didn't agree with, would you?"

"No, of course not." Suddenly she saw where he had led her. "But—"

"But nothing. *You* don't want someone telling you to make changes you disagree with, and *I* don't want you trying to tell me to wear things I disagree with."

"All right, darling. But I was only thinking of your appearance because I wanted you to look your best."

He pressed on, determined to continue asserting himself, and reminded Claudia that earlier she had said she would tell him about some of his little foibles which sometimes annoyed her, but she was prepared with her answer. She spoke of how she picked his teeth with a toothpick after every meal, then sucked them to make certain that they were clean, always immediately after a meal with her sitting opposite him. She spoke of how, even after ten years of marriage, he still couldn't seem to find the way to the laundry hamper with his dirty laundry.

When she began to speak about a third foible, he raised his hand and said, "Okay, I get the picture. From now on, I'll try to do better on both counts. So, neither one of us is perfect."

"Of course we're not. I had no idea that my smacking my lips bothered you that much, but if it does all you have to do is not be in the bedroom while I'm doing it." She reached across the table and placed her soft, warm hand over his. "I don't think I've ever told you this, but I really don't like being watched while I'm putting on my face."

He said firmly, "Then maybe I'll just make certain that I'm not around."

"Fine." She drew her hand away and continued with her dinner. "Then it's settled."

So there it was. Submission on his part, but none on hers. Business as usual. If you don't want to hear her smacking her lips, stay out of the bedroom. Still, he was glad that he had mentioned it, glad that he had shown her by his firmness that from now on he intended to be a different, more assertive man, and that she could no longer expect him simply to fall into her way of thinking on every issue.

As far as she was concerned, he had to know definitely where she stood on the burning issue which now plagued his own life. He recalled what she had said that morning about his merely going through male menopause which would soon pass, but he knew that this feeling he had, which he couldn't shake, represented much more than that. And before he could move ahead with somehow

changing his life into something more meaningful, more rewarding, he had to know definitely whether she would be beside him,
supporting him, or would she simply insist on continuing to pursue her present hedonistic lifestyle.

That afternoon, while trying to find some direction for the
strange need which disturbed him, he remembered that several
years ago, disgusted with the bilge he churned out at Drummond,
he had decided to try to express his own true, personal feelings
by writing a novel. He had begun making notes in his laptop computer, occasionally adding a few lines to them, but as time went on
he added fewer and fewer notes and the periods between additions
grew longer and longer. Nothing he wrote excited him. Although
he believed that writing even a bad novel would be better than
writing no novel at all, he simply couldn't work up any enthusiasm
for his subject matter because the story he thought of telling seemed dull and pointless. He hadn't even looked at his notes for years.

While Claudia attended her open house, he became curious as to how he would view those notes today and went to his den
and opened the laptop computer. He had only to read a few paragraphs to confirm his worst suspicions. To write such pap would
probably be better than writing ads for pussy pads and asswipe,
but only marginally. He closed the laptop computer in disgust.
His gaze shifted to the books on the shelves; he read some of the
authors' names on books he had ignored for years: Thomas Merton, Emerson, Thoreau, Pascal, Thomas A Kempis, all books he
had started reading in his teens at his father's recommendation.
Still there. Still waiting, gathering dust. But they would wait even
longer—until his issues with God were resolved. The issues which
only seemed to surface after he married Claudia and became attached to his present comfortable but pointless life. But could he
allow Claudia's influence on him over the years to shoulder all the
blame, or had he at least some hand in compiling the list of griev-
ances against the church and against God which had grown appreciably over the years as he searched diligently for more and more
reasons, no matter how paltry, to rationalize his life with Claudia?

He noticed some yellow ruled sheets sticking out from between *The Waters of Siloe* and *The Imitation of Christ* and pulled them

out. For a few confused moments, he stared at the several folded handwritten pages which had apparently been torn from the stapled binding of a five-by-eight-inch notebook, wondering where they came from before recalling that he'd found them years earlier tucked inside a book in a box of donated books while working as manager for Peerless Books, a used bookstore in Northside Mall. He'd read the pages at the time and later brought them home and placed them in the bookcase, where they had languished unread ever since. Bewildered as to why he'd even brought the pages home, he began reading.

August 14, 1996

Today is the first day of the rest of my life. Today I start the Universal Energy journey, knowing and breathing and accepting the wonderful gifts of the Universe, that Great, Creative, Infinite God-Energy of the entire Universe. I am NOW receiving everything I desire with each and Every Breath I take.

From this second on, my breathing now works in threes, which means that if I breathe 460 times per minute [sic], with every First Breath I inhale perfect health and Healing Energy flows through my entire body, replacing every single molecule, muscle, cell, and tissue of my entire body and making every one of them perfect.

Every Second Breath brings with it the reshaping of my physical form. Yes, I am thankful to the Great Universe for all the extra weight It has given me, but that extra weight is now being MOVED, reshaping my plump body into a slender and healthy and young and shapely figure with a firm 36" bust, a firm torso with a 24" waist, a flat and firm belly, shapely round and firm buttocks, and shapely 36" hips. I know in my mind exactly the figure I desire, and I know that every Second Breath will bring it closer and closer to me.

Every Third Breath brings me the creativity to bring me loads and loads of money, all that I will ever want for everything I want, and even more. Each exhale will remove all my energy blocks and all my negative thoughts and I become a wide open channel for the Great Universal Energy.

Every breath is now a Rodham [sic] of flowing energy repeating again and again 1-2-3-1-2-3-1-2-3. I SEE, I FEEL, I

KNOW this to be true. My fears have gone and my body feels HAPPY, HEALTHY, FREE, now KNOWING all this to be absolutely TRUE.

Now I know My God, the Infinite Creative Energy of The Universe, The Universe I acknowledge. I thank The Universe for the flow of money , and the great abundance of monies that will flow easily and effortless to me. I receive it all in great joy, I use it wisely, release it joyfully, and it returns to me TENFOLD. My great wealth will be shared with others, to bring joy to them, and the knowledge of the Great Power of the Universe—LOVE.

My Budget. To be revised every two months.

I need a New, Larger House, New Furniture, Appliances, Pots and Pans, Dishes, Pillows, Lamps, Lawn Furniture, a Swimming Pool, a New Car, Garden, Fencing, Radio-Recorder, TV, Iron, Books, Lawn Mower, Snow Blower, Solar Energy, Central Air, New Clothes.

My New Budget. These things I need every month and I will upgrade every two months to the new flow.
Rent—$350.00
Hydro—$100.00
Insurance—$70.00
Cable—$40.00
Car Payment—$450.00
Car Insurance—$100.00
New Clothes—$300.00 (for one NEW outfit each month. My old ones are too small.)
Church—$50.00
Correspondence Course—$100.00
Shoes—$200.00
Gas—$140.00
Savings—$300.00
Gifts for others—$300.00
To pay off all Bills—$2,500.00 Needed each month.

I feel it. I have the flow of money coming into my life every single day. I WIN with every LOTTO ticket I buy until I reach 8.5 million dollars! Yes!

It's on its way to me NOW! TODAY! I FEEL IT!

I will have everything I desire and I will serve the Great Universe (God) and my fellow man. My Creative Thoughts will lead me to my new career, and the Great Universe will present it to me.

Rodger wondered what had prompted him to keep these silly, shallow pages. He pictured an overweight, naive young woman of perhaps eighteen to twenty-five who actually believed that sitting in some meditative pose doing breathing exercises and asking the "Great Power of the Universe" to bring her everything under the sun would eventually bring her all these things. Instead, why not try making an effort by trying to eat properly to lose weight. And why not try concentrating on improving her education so that she can qualify for a better-paying job and actually *earn* the money to buy what she wants, instead of clinging to the silly, childish notion that the "Great Power of the Universe" will supply her, at odds of millions-to-one, with winning LOTTO numbers. This sort of pipe dream thinking was tantamount to the group of young people in *The Celestine Prophecy* sitting around among a bunch of plants and expecting them to grow faster if they urged them to do so with the mere strength of their thoughts.

Again, he asked himself why years ago he had kept these shallow pages and never bothered rereading them. Until now. If he'd brought the pages home merely to gloat over this young woman's foolishness, wouldn't he have reread them a number of times? But he hadn't. Why? Why had he simply stuck the pages between books on a shelf and neglected them, as he neglected the books surrounding them? And what had urged him to suddenly *want* to reread them? Thinking, he realized that, at forty, with a ten-year marriage behind him which he now considered largely wasted, he saw himself as a much different man who recognized the pages as a warning to avoid frivolousness and somehow concentrate his energy on worthy achievements.

Now, as they sat at the dining room table, he asked suddenly, "Who are you, Claudia?"

She looked bewildered, then smiled indulgently, and he knew that she thought of his question as more of his mid-life crisis showing its face. "You mean you've been married to me for ten years and you don't even know."

"You're not the woman I married ten years ago. We believed in ideals then. I'm not sure I really know the current Claudia. Tell me. Refresh my memory."

"But I thought we went through all this this morning."

"Humour me. Refresh my memory. What do you believe is the purpose of life, and how do you fit into it?"

"Nothing—that's the purpose. We live, we try to enjoy life, and we eventually die."

"And that's it?"

"That's it. It just gives me a headache if I start thinking about other things."

"What other things?"

"Well, life after death and all that nonsense. I prefer to take the sure thing and enjoy it, and that's here and now. And when I die I'll die happy, knowing that I've gotten everything l could out of life."

He recalled how, when over ten years ago he and his parents had insisted that they get married in a Catholic church, and that they would be required to first take a marriage course with the parish priest, Gunderson had said, "Hell, take the course and get married in their church. Who cares? What difference does it make? You don't have to start going to church just because you get married in one." And Claudia had listened to Gunderson, on both counts. She became, not simply Claudia Blackwell but Claudia Hewitt-Blackwell, insisting on retaining her maiden name. Could this have been the clue which told him that she intended to be the dominant person in their marriage? As far as Rodger knew, she hadn't been to church since their wedding day. And his attendance record, which he blamed at least partly on Claudia, was barely any better.

"And that's all there is to it?" he said.

"That's all there is to it. I believe that the only purpose in life is to enjoy ourselves by getting the things we want because we're only here for a short time. And when you find something better than this, just let me know so that we can enjoy it together. And by enjoying ourselves I definitely *don't* mean being totally out of control by jumping into bed with the nearest person at hand merely because you get the sexual urge. But I do enjoy making love with my husband, who knows exactly what buttons to push to give me the greatest pleasure, so why should I ever look elsewhere? And I definitely *don't* mean boozing every night and getting foolishly drunk, or getting high on drugs. That isn't living; it's nothing more than a living death.

"I enjoy good things, and enjoy buying them for myself. I enjoy good clothes, and never seem to have enough good things to wear. I enjoy looking good, even sexy at times, so that people will admire me. I enjoy possessing good things, like this house and the things in it, but I want an even better house with larger rooms and a three-car garage. I don't want to be left behind.

"And, of course, I enjoy good food, both eating it and preparing it. I know you're basically a meat and potatoes man, but I do love preparing my fancy little dishes sometimes. You do think I'm a good cook, don't you, darling?"

"I think you're a fantastic cook. This roast beef practically melts in my mouth. But now that I'm forty I'm going to have to start watching this." He patted his belly. "You know what they say about middle-aged spread. And don't forget that in about three years you'll be forty. You have a wonderful figure now, but you may have to start cutting back on your 'fancy little dishes' if you want to keep it that way."

"I'll cross that bridge when I come to it," she said confidently. "I certainly have no intention of becoming fat. If I did, my husband would have the perfect excuse to begin exploring the field, wouldn't you, darling?"

Rodger quickly recognized her loaded question and made the appropriate response. "No, I wouldn't. I'd still love you just as much as I do now. Besides, at some point we may both be fat. Then we'd be on equal terms, wouldn't we?"

"You do say the nicest things." She sipped her coffee and sat back in silence.

"Are you finished?" he asked. "Is that all you want out of life?"

"Yes, it is. I'm a simple person with simple but demanding needs, and I'm trying to fulfill them."

"And that's all you care about?"

"That's all I care about. And you, of course. I've always cared about you, and I always will."

"You've changed, Claudia. You changed once you went into real estate and started working for Gunderson and started making good money. Early in our relationship, you had ideals. We talked about living a fuller life, about helping others, about becoming a part of something good, about making the world a better place, about leaving the world better than we found it. Now all we do is think about ourselves, our jobs, our possessions. Let's face it, we're about as selfish as you can get. What happened to us?"

"We grew up, that's what happened. It's so easy to be idealistic when you're in your twenties and you're filled with the vigour of youth, and you're so callow that you think you're going to be instrumental in curing all the ills of the world and make it a wonderful place for everybody to live in. But as you grow older, and approach middle age, you begin to see the world for what it actually is, filled with greed and corruption, and begin to see what a hope-lessly impossible task it all really is. So you give up, and you say to yourself, 'If *I* can have a good life, and *I* can be happy, that's all that really matters because the world is going to hell in a handbasket anyway.'" She reached out, placed her soft, warm hand over his, squeezed gently. "And we *are* happy, you and I, aren't we, darling? What more do we need but each other?"

"You may have given up, but I haven't. What more do we need? I'll tell you what more we need. We need to swim out of this fish bowl existence we're in and try to develop some kind of worthwhile life for ourselves."

"And how do you propose that we do this? Would you expect me to start by volunteering as a part-time candy striper at Head-waters?"

"Would you actually do that?"

She drew her hand away. "Of course not. I'd look absolutely silly in one of those childish uniforms that look like they were designed for teenagers. Besides, they probably wouldn't even allow me to wear makeup, or nails, or heels."

"Then why did you even bother mentioning it?"

"I was only joking. Can you honestly see me handing out little plastic cups of apple juice and packages of Peek Frans to patients? What if some of my business acquaintances saw me with *no* makeup on and wearing *flat* shoes?"

"They might think that you're actually helping someone without trying to make a buck. Is that all you care about—your *outward* appearance? What about your *inward* appearance? Don't you ever care about anything but *externals*?"

"Now you're being insulting again. That's the second time today. But then I've never seen you like this before today, have I? Tell me, darling, what would *you* do about *your* inward appearance?"

He rubbed a hand across his forehead. "I don't know," he admitted. "But at least I know that I have to do *something*. But I also need to know that you'll support me."

"Support you? How?"

"Just in case I decide to do something...well, strange. Something you might think is totally out of character for me."

"You're apparently going through your mid-life crisis, so I expect you to do strange things. Of course I'll support you, providing you don't embarrass me by doing something absolutely outlandish." She stared at him sternly. "And providing that it doesn't involve another woman. I don't know if I could ever forgive you for that."

"Why would I want to bother with other women," he blurted out. "when I've got a beautiful wife who loves me and who's the best lover in the world."

But immediately after he said this, he wondered if he'd spoken too strongly just to cover up his true feelings, for in the back of his mind he *had* been thinking about other women because he felt almost certain that in the end Claudia would refuse to change her lifestyle in any appreciable way, but he saw nothing in her face which indicated that she suspected anything. Claudia was a great lover, and they certainly loved each other, so that his thoughts of other women had nothing to do with sex or love. He simply wanted to venture out on his own and meet other women, something he hadn't done for over ten years. Even the women who worked at Drummond he only greeted with a few words and had never had personal relationships with any of them. Except for Claudia, and what he witnessed on television or heard on the news, he felt that he knew very little about the personal or even public habits of modern women.

Were they all like Claudia? Did they all have this frivolous urge to lavish attention on the external person while the internal person stagnated? Of course not. In passing, he had seen many women who still had that natural, well-scrubbed look, and who obviously hadn't resorted to facelifts, buttlifts, liposuction, or breast implants to augment the external person. These women appeared to be saying, "Here I am. This is me, just as God made me. Take me or leave me." But the question which needs to be answered is this: If this type of woman has had the courage to assert her originality by presenting her real *external* self to the public, has she also had the courage to develop her *internal* self.

Did such a perfect woman exist? Or would the internal self also be left completely alone to passively absorb the mercenary beliefs of North American society? Like Claudia. He had to find the answer, not because he didn't love Claudia any longer, but because he needed to investigate the internal side of such a woman to use as a guide for his own internal development. And how could he best achieve this? Well, he'd simply tell these women that he wasn't interested in sex; he was simply doing a survey. Yes, a survey for an upcoming book he intended to publish....

Rodger suddenly realized that Claudia had reached across the dinner table and was squeezing his hand. "My, you have been miles away, haven't you, darling?" she teased gently.

"Sorry."

"Were you thinking about me?"

"Well, yes, as a matter of fact I was."

"And what were you thinking about me?"

"I was thinking about how great you are in bed, and how sad it would be if something happened between us which made it impossible for us to continue enjoying each other."

"Nothing like that is ever going to happen between us. You're thinking about this male menopause thing again, aren't you? You're thinking that your whole life is going to change and that it's never going to pass. But it will. Remember, darling, it's only a momentary blip in your life which will soon be gone and you'll forget about all these strange ideas you've been having lately. Then we can get back to normal again."

He shook his head. "I don't think I'll ever be back to normal again."

Smiling, she rose and came around behind him, kissed the side of his neck, placed her arms around him and hugged him. "Yes, you will, my darling. Yes, you will, and soon."

3

Rodger had known Ray Foley for several years, primarily as a working partner at Drummond. Although he had never asked his age, he knew that Ray appeared to be in his fifties, had been in advertising for over twenty-five years, and that his fertile mind constantly overflowed with ideas for copy, some silly, but many quite inventive and original. Ray had divorced his first wife ten years ago after a two-year marriage, and his second wife five years ago after a three-year marriage. Both marriages had ended for the same two reasons: his excessive drinking, and his excessive womanizing. These two habits were also the two reasons why, although talented, he never rose into a management position in advertising. At times he became irresponsible, preferring to have another drink or two with some woman while staying up until the small hours and then sleeping it off until noon. He then phoned Drummond and apologized profusely. Only his unique value as a writer had kept him at Drummond for six years; other companies he'd worked for over the years had been far less patient. After his second divorce, Ray had decided that marriage had no place in his life. Although he still continued to play the field, he at least knew that his relationships were no longer hamstrung by that possibility.

Even the single women at Drummond's whom Ray found desirable (he never approached married women, wanting to avoid irate or violent husbands) became part of his sexual quest. In spite of his age, Ray approached nubile, naive young things in their twenties at coffee breaks, chatted with them for a few minutes to relax them, then asked them in his gentlest, kindliest voice to go out with him. The answer was usually no. But over the years there were also a few yesses, once even a torrid, three-month affair with a twenty-five-year-old blonde named Sally which ended only when she moved to Toronto after being dismissed by Drummond for poor production.

Careful, Ray never pressed the issue with these women. If they answered no, he left it at that and retreated graciously, making no future advances unless the woman began showing signs of interest. Aware of his already tenuous hold on his job because of his drinking and carousing, the last thing he needed was to be dismissed by Drummond because one of these women complained of sexual harassment.On Monday at lunch hour, as they had done for years, Rodger and Ray sat across from each other at a table at Tim Hortons on Broadway consuming their regular lunches of sandwiches on buns, soup, and coffee. As usual, Ray wore the standard garb of the young: T-shirt, jeans, and sneakers. The T-shirt always showed either a message or an illustration or both on its front, usually pertaining to sex or masculinity. Today's message read: "READY, WILLING, & ABLE."

Although Rodger disapproved of Ray's hedonistic lifestyle, he still liked him. He hadn't yet decided whether he liked Ray because of his generosity, for he seemed always willing to help others, or only because of the pity he felt for him. He gazed now at the six-foot-two man who sat across from him, noting the bulging belly, the hairy arms, the pudgy face with the graying beard and moustache to assert his masculinity and compensate for the receding hairline of the graying hair which fell to his shoulders. The pink sponginess of the nose and the gray pouches beneath the brown eyes were telltale evidence of the thousands of glasses of beer and the dozens and dozens of women he had consumed over his lifetime.

He found something sorrowful about a man well into middle age who still tried to behave like a young man, still tried to mingle with the younger crowd, still tried to find younger women to share his bed.

Although they had been lunching together for years, their conversation usually centred around work in progress, and although they were familiar with each other in broad terms, they knew little about the finer details of each other's private lives. Being a married man with a satisfactory sex life, Rodger never accompanied Ray on any of his bar-hopping jaunts in search of sexual partners, although Ray had once asked him. Rodger saw this asking as a mere courtesy. Perhaps Ray felt that Rodger's married sex life had grown stale, or had even become nonexistent, and needed a boost. But upon reflection Rodger believed that Ray had never asked him again to accompany him because he feared that Rodger, being over ten years younger than him, would probably end up with most of the women and relegate him to playing second fiddle. Vanity, Rodger knew, but his assumption sounded reasonable.

Now, as they sat eating their lunches in Tim Hortons, Rodger asked, "How old are you, Ray?"

"Fifty-three. Why?"

"So you must've already gone through your mid-life crisis. Do you recall how it affected your life?"

"Why do you ask?"

"Because I'm convinced that I've started to go through mine now. And I thought I could get your opinion on the kinds of things to expect."

"The way it affected me might not be anything like the way it's going to affect you. It affects men differently."

"Just tell me what happened. Maybe it'll help me. It's not too embarrassing, is it?"

Ray shrugged. "No, not really. As a matter of fact, for a while there I thought I was actually going to change my life. I was married to Myrtle then, my first wife, and running around as usual. Myrtle was never much in bed. She withheld sex until after we were married, and then I found out why. She just didn't have the goods in the bedroom. She'd just lie there like a slab of cold ham and let you do your business. No participation, no passion, no imagination, know what I mean? I felt cheated. Hell, I might as well've just masturbated for all the satisfaction I got from it. So I started running around, looking for something better, at least someone with a developed libido who could get excited about having sex with me. When Myrtle found out, she cut me off completely and said she wanted a divorce. That didn't worry me much because our marriage wasn't going anywhere anyway, so I just stalled her for the time being.

"But a few weeks later I must've entered my mid-life crisis period because I felt this sudden powerful urge to turn my life completely around, stop running around like I'd been doing all my adult life, and make a supreme effort to live a clean, moral life. With Myrtle. I'd try my damnedest to make our marriage work, and try my damnedest to convince Myrtle that good, passionate sex was a vital part of a happy marriage. I promised Myrtle that I wouldn't be chasing after other women any longer, and I did stop. I even started going to church, and eventually convinced Myrtle to join me. She loved it, and began feeling secure again, even stopped talking about divorce and let me have sex with her again, if you can even call it that. I tried like hell to get her going, to get her to move her ass a little, but nothing helped. And whenever I tried anything new or more daring, she balked and absolutely refused to have anything to do with it. I couldn't stray beyond that mouldy old missionary position, and because we were now also going to church, she was determined that I never would. Hell, Rodger, she must've been raised by puritans. Anyway, I eventually accepted everything as it was and it went on like that for about a year."

"But you divorced her."

"I divorced her. But that situation might've lasted a lot longer if something else hadn't happened. I was getting regular sex, such as it was, and we were going to church together every Sunday, and there was no more talk about divorce, and I felt that I was living a decent, moral life. But after about a year all that suddenly changed because my mid-life crisis ended and when that happened I quickly reverted back to the old Ray. And began to think like the old Ray again. Sure, I'd been living a clean, moral life, but it was so *damn boring.* And it never stopped irritating me that I couldn't bring Myrtle to orgasm, mainly because she wouldn't let me do the things I felt were necessary to make it happen. I didn't feel like a real man. I felt like some pathetic wimp who can't get himself a real woman and goes to whores just to get his rocks off."

"And you divorced her because of that?"

"Soon after. I stopped going to church and started running around again. And when Myrtle found out about the other women we both decided it was time to call it quits. Now she's married to some wimp named Cyril who looks like he doesn't even *have* a pair of nuts." He smiled sheepishly. "Hell, Rodger, I guess I'm just a bloody sexaholic. Getting off with women, especially the young ones, and making them scream or cry out with pleasure when they're coming, is the only thing that makes me feel like I'm actually *achieving something* with my life. Think about it, what else have I got? I'm a junior writer who writes advertising campaigns and trashy commercials, and I'll always be a junior writer because I'm a lecherous boozer who spends too many late nights in bars and bedrooms with women. I earn a decent salary, but I'll never be rich because Drummond is never going to move me up to head writer, or, God forbid, offer me a partnership in the company. You, maybe, me, never. So what've I actually got besides my reputation as an accomplished stud who knows how to give women sexual pleasure?"

"And I guess the motorcycle helps in your...in your endeavours."

"You'd be surprised. When women see a man on a bike wearing a black leather jacket they automatically think three things: he's into sex, he's into booze, and he's into drugs. For me it's only two things, sex and booze, and cigarettes are the only things I smoke. And I never touch the other crap, like coke and heroin. It's bad enough that I'm a boozer without getting hooked for life on drugs. And I'm a loner; I don't belong to any motorcycle clubs. That's a sure way to get hooked on drugs. I do my own thing, and that's it."

"But how do you actually feel about these women? Do you ever get attached to them?"

"I love them, that's how I feel. Every last one of them. But not the way, maybe, you love Claudia. I guess you'd say I love them physically. I'm drawn to their bodies like a bee to flowers. I just can't get enough of that nectar. The legs, the asses, the tits, the juicy lips—the incessant, infinite variety is endless...endless. It just drives me nuts. Every time I turn around I keep seeing new, different, wonderful things that I've never seen before and want to sample. And yes, sometimes I do get attached, but it's only a physical attachment which usually doesn't last longer than a few months, and right up front I tell every woman I meet that I'm definitely not interested in marriage, only a good time. If any of them even mention the word marriage, I'm gone like a shot. No commitment. If I'm having a relationship with one woman, and meet another woman whose body attracts me and who shows an interest in me, I jump ship. But I always tell the other woman that we're finished." He smiled wryly. "I guess I still have a few shreds of morality left because I refuse to bed down with two women at the same time. "And I avoid married women like the plague. I've got enough problems without having some irate husband after me."

Ray removed a cigarette from a du Maurier package and shoved it between his lips. "This damn non-smoking bylaw is a royal pain in the ass. Get me another coffee, will you? I'm going outside for a few drags."

"Sure. But don't you think it's time you gave those things up? I hear you coughing at the office all the time, and that cough doesn't sound healthy. You need to see about it."

"Yeah, maybe I've got bronchitis or something. I can't seem to shake the damn thing. I've got a doctor's appointment coming up—he's going to check into it."

"Good. You need to do that."

Rodger mentally compared his view of women with Ray's view. Where Ray's attraction appeared to be purely sexual, Rodger had never been able to either accept or reject a woman purely on sexual grounds. But he wasn't dead either; he had to admit that he viewed a woman's bodily attributes first, then considered the pleasantness of her voice (nasal voices were definitely out), but only made his final decision after learning something about the woman herself: her personality, her beliefs, her intelligence. And if he found her to be nothing more than a pretty face and a sexy body attached to an empty head, this would dampen his sexual desire even better than an icy shower.

When Rodger returned to the table with two coffees, he looked out the window just as Ray inhaled a mouthful of smoke which doubled him over in a severe and lengthy coughing seizure which violently shook his body.

He reviewed what Ray had told him about his relationships with women and realized that the types of women Ray associated with were hedonistic, a far cry from the type he was searching for. Still, since Rodger had been married and out of circulation for the past ten years, Ray's relationships with women over that time had been far more frequent than his own, and perhaps he could still learn something from his experiences.

When Ray returned, looking pale, Rodger said, "I saw you out there. When did you say that doctor's appointment was?"

"I didn't say. It's in a few weeks." Ray tried to placate him with a raised palm. "Don't worry, I'll be fine."

"Just remember to keep that appointment, that's all."

"Relax. All I need is a little medication."

Rodger reverted to their original subject. "I know that the type of relationship you were always looking for was mainly a quick sexual one, but you must've met plenty of other women who didn't fit into that category. What were some of them like?"

"Yeah, I've met plenty of other kinds, but most of them weren't for me. From what I've seen over the years, there are basically two types of women: the physical types, and the romantic types. The physical types are those who are out to have a good time. To have a few drinks, do some drugs if they're into that crap, maybe go dancing, and end the night by getting laid. Many of those are career women, and in some ways many of them are reflections of me. They're selfish. Their careers are first and foremost, and the only reason they go out to bars or dance halls is because even selfish people need some type of companionship sometime. Being in love with yourself and your own company can be very lonely. Even though you're obsessed with your career, and don't give a damn about anybody but yourself, occasionally you still feel compelled to descend from your ivory tower and mingle with the masses. To satisfy your starved libido. To hold a man in your arms. To listen to *someone else* tell you how wonderful you are. And then you can forget about men—until the next time. Or they might simply hire a gigolo for the evening and avoid most of the preliminaries. Maybe they figure that even phoney companionship is better than no companionship at all.

"They refuse to make any kind of firm commitment. They refuse to get married—that's me, but at least I gave it a shot, twice—because it means sharing your life with your husband, and you might even have to give up some of your hard-earned cash. They refuse to have children because it means sharing your life with them. They even refuse to shack up with a man because it will infringe upon their careers, and, horror of horrors, they might become so attracted to him that they might actually want to marry him! They're like me. They don't want marriage, they don't want romance, they just want to have a good time and get laid."

"And what about the romantic types?"

"Hell, this type wants the whole ball of wax. She wants love, marriage, children, and she might even live in a shack with you if you'll give her those things. She's in love with love, and in love with being in love. She's probably so convinced that sex must be an integral part of this love that she won't even go to bed with you until you're married. She's possessive, and jealous as hell. She's willing to give you every last crumb of her love, smothering you with it, and expects to get the same from you. And if she doesn't get it, she gets suspicious and afraid and starts wondering if you still love her. The main driving force in her life is this constant search for romantic love. And when she finds it, she wraps her arms around it and clings to it and does everything in her power to maintain it as long as possible. Love, and being in love, is the only vital necessity in her life. And if it's physically absent, she might resort to fantasy love lives, like the kind you find in books like Harlequin romances. And believe me, once she gets her hooks into you, she's tenacious. And treacherous. She'll stop at nothing to maintain her love life. No scruples. She'll lie, cheat, steal, you name it, anything to keep it going."

Rodger was taken aback by the intensity of Ray's description. "You sound as though you speak from personal experience."

"My second wife, Rebecca. Even the name should've sent me running for cover, but I asked myself, like Shakespeare did, 'What's in a name? A rose by any other name would smell as sweet.' Sure it would, but in this case the name meant plenty. In many cases this name is shortened to 'Becky,' but Rebecca refused to let anybody call her that. That should've warned me that she was either a snob who wasn't with it, or a romantic. Well, she wasn't a snob, but what a nauseating, idealistic, saccharine bore! And she sucked me into marriage by making me believe that she wasn't actually like that, that she was more like me, cool and easygoing, although before we got married all I ever got from her were a few goodnight kisses. It was only after we were married that she unveiled the complete range of her full-blown romanticism."

"How do you mean? How did these things play themselves out in your relationship with her?"

"Maybe the difference in our ages had something to do with it. She was only thirty-five, I was forty-four. Even so, I found it almost impossible to believe that any woman could have lived thirty-five years and still be almost as naive as a child. She lived in a total dream world and refused to acknowledge or accept any of the misery, deceit, and horror of the real world. And her father didn't help. He worked long hours building up a successful construction business, and she hardly knew him, so there was no masculine influence to give her a more balanced and more realistic view of life. He was killed in a construction accident when she was only eight, and she was raised by her mother who never remarried. I guess you could lay the blame for the way Rebecca turned out at her mother's feet. No, it all started before that. I'd have to lay most of the blame at her father's feet."

Ray paused, sipped his coffee, scratched his graying beard. Rodger knew that Ray scratched his beard often, but he saw this not as a nervous habit but merely as an attempt to relieve a persistent itch. Because of this nuisance, he felt that Ray would probably prefer to be rid of the beard but refused to shave it off so that he could preserve the bearded, masculine image he wanted to present to women.

Rodger asked, "Why do you say that? What was her father like?"

"Her father, his name was Eric, was a cowardly bastard. After he became a wealthy and successful builder, he lorded it over Penelope and Rebecca. He was the big shit and they were nothing. He drank, and he was a belligerent drunk. He beat Penelope, his wife, and abused her sexually, forcing her to do perverted acts she hated, and beating her into submission if she refused. Because of him, she became a nervous wreck, afraid of every man she saw."

"Did he ever abuse Rebecca?"

"She said he slapped her in the face a few times, but he never abused her sexually, at least that's what she said. More than anything, he affected her emotionally because she had to stand by while her mother was being abused. Anyway, after Rebecca's father was killed, Penelope became even more possessive and protective of Rebecca. She'd always been antisocial, rarely going anywhere with her husband, locked up in her own private, little pink world. But now she became paranoid. They lived in a large country home her husband had built on a large piece of land on Highway 10 just a few miles north of Orangeville. She was terrified that something horrible would happen to them as soon as they ventured into town. She taught Rebecca that the only way to be happy was to isolate yourself from the big, bad world outside and live in your own dream world. She took Rebecca out of school and hired a private tutor. She could afford it—her husband had left her plenty. Besides, after he was killed she knew that she could never run the company herself and sold it for big bucks. And she made sure that she hired a *female* tutor because her paranoia made her terrified that a male tutor, since they were isolated, would try to rob them, or sexually assault them, or even murder them. She trusted nobody and never even took her eyes off the female tutor for a second while she was there. For the rest, she herself taught Rebecca how to sew, knit, embroider, do rug-hooking and cross-stitching, you name it. They did paint-by-number art, they painted plastic sun-catchers, they did collages, they made junk out of popsicle sticks. Hell, I can't remember half of what they did. Penelope even bought a loom and a potter's wheel. They made their own throw rugs and flower vases and fruit bowls."

Short of breath, Ray rested for half a minute and sipped his coffee before continuing. "And, of course, they read books. Penelope screened everything. She started Rebecca on wholesome children's books which she'd kept since her own childhood. Over the years, she'd read hundreds of Harlequin romances that still filled several bookshelves, and later, when Rebecca was well into her teens, she began doling them out to her. But before giving her the first one, she warned her. She said, 'Remember, this is fiction. This isn't the way the world is, but this is the way it *should* be.' She was possessive and didn't want Rebecca to ever think that if she ever left the house she'd find a better world outside. She refused to join the library because that meant leaving the property and going into Orangeville to search for books. Instead, she joined mail order book clubs and made selections from their pamphlets. And if she found violence or sex in any of the books, she burned them in the fireplace.

"Although they had a large satellite dish on the grounds that could bring in hundreds of channels, they rarely watched television. Penelope's investigations had proven to her that almost everything being shown was trash. She hated sports, the news was all bad, the sitcoms were silly, and most of the other programs and movies were loaded with sex, violence, and foul language. Things she didn't want Rebecca's lily white eyes and ears to see and hear. She never let Rebecca watch anything without her approval. So, instead of watching television, they entertained themselves by listening to music, mostly classical stuff, either that or syrupy love songs.

"And they studied nature, mainly birds. They had several feeders outside the house in different shapes and sizes to attract specific birds. And they kept a log. Every time they saw a bird, or birds, they entered the name, date, time, and place. In case they couldn't identify a bird, they had several bird field guides to help them. As I said, their house was on a large piece of land, some of it still bush. When the weather was good, they'd sometimes take their binoculars and log and field guides and go out and explore, hoping to find and record a new species." Ray sipped his coffee, scratched his beard. "And this is how they lived. A daughter and a paranoid mother."

"But how could they keep up this type of isolation? What if one of them became sick? What if they needed groceries? Or gas for the car? Or repair of the car? Or money? Or even materials for the crafts they worked on? How could they possibly avoid going to Shelburne or Orangeville? It just doesn't make any sense."

"I didn't say Penelope *never* left the property, but she tried every way she could think of not to. She was obsessed with birdwatching, and they occasionally went for drives along the back roads, where there wasn't much chance of seeing anybody, searching for new species. And if she needed gas, which wasn't often, Rebecca told me that Penelope phoned a neighbour, a friendly young woman who she trusted named Alice, who she asked to drive the car to the Shell station up the highway for a fill up. Remember, Penelope was terrified of men, not women. She mistrusted women, but she wasn't terrified of them. And the same for the groceries and other supplies. She'd write out a list and hand Alice her car keys to go into Orangeville and pick up the stuff. And force her to accept ten or twenty bucks for her trouble. Hell, she could afford it."

"I don't get it," Rodger said. "Something must've happened in Rebecca's life to change her. Otherwise how could you possibly have met her hidden away there in that country house."

"Well, something *did* happen. And remember, I met her quite a few years later, when she was thirty-four." Ray ogled the young, shapely bleached blonde serving coffee and doughnuts behind the counter, something Rodger knew he had done at least a dozen times since they had arrived. Ray lowered his voice almost to a whisper. "Look at that lovely thing, will you. Even in that sexless uniform, standing there, her ass sticks out so far that it looks like you could use it as a shelf for a glass of beer and never spill a drop. And those tits are like cantaloupes, only softer and sweeter. They look like they're ready to pop the buttons on her uniform any minute. Believe me, that baby knows exactly what she's got."

"For God's sake, get a grip on yourself. She looks like she's only about nineteen, young enough to be your daughter. And her face is no hell to look at. It looks like she's got buckteeth."

"Oh, has she?—I hadn't noticed. The trouble with you is you're looking from the neck up; I'm looking from the neck down."

"You're always looking from the neck down," Rodger accused, surprised again by his newly dis-covered frankness yet determined to say his piece. "And as far as you're concerned, you're always thinking from the belt down."

Surprised, Ray drew back but smiled knowingly. "In all the years I've known you, this is the first time you've ever commented on my sex life. I know it's only your mid-life crisis talking. Hell, I was a bit snappish myself when I went through it. But I like the new Rodger and I hope he stays around for a while. He's got balls. And I'll tell you another thing: One of these days I'm going to wait for that delicious looking thing to get off work and ask her for a date."

"You're crazy, do you know that?"

"Yeah, crazy like a fox. Or should I say 'wolf.'"

"Do you honestly believe that a nineteen-year-old woman is going to go out with a fifty-three-year-old man?"

"Stranger things have happened. Thousands of times. Did you ever hear the joke about the guy who stands on a corner and asks every attractive woman who comes by if she'd like to go to bed with him?"

"No, I haven't, but I'm sure you're going to tell me."

"Well, every woman he asks slaps him in the face and walks away. Anyway, there's a guy watching and listening just about ten feet away and he comes over and says to the guy, 'Boy, you must get slapped in the face a lot.' And the guy replies, 'Yeah, but I also get a lot of tail.'" He smiled lasciviously. "Well, in a way that's me."

"Are you trying to tell me that you're simply going to ask that young blonde if she wants to go to bed with you?"

"Hey, wait a minute, how crass do you think I am? I know we get off work earlier than she does, so I'll just sit out front on my bike waiting for her to come out, and when she does I'll just ask her if she wants a lift. And when she sees this"—he stroked his graying beard lovingly—"and the black leather jacket, and the black helmet, and my bike gleaming with chrome, she'll climb aboard. Then I'll ask her if she wants to go for dinner and a few drinks. And if she says yes, we'll do dinner. And *then* I'll ask her if she wants to go to bed with me."

"And if she says no?"

"Then I'll be a good boy and drive her home. Tomorrow's another day. I'll keep on asking for a couple of weeks, meanwhile exploring other prospects, and if she still says no then I'll move on. Hell, it never hurts to try."

Rodger sighed heavily. "Well, now that you've teased your rampant libido with the little blonde, can we get back to the subject at hand? What happened to Rebecca to change her life?"

"Well, over the years her mother's condition kept getting worse, and she wouldn't go to her female doctor for medication because she was afraid her doctor would have her committed. She'd heard about some herbal medications and had Alice buy them for her in Orangeville, but they did no good. She began having hallucinations. She thought she saw ugly men coming after her to harm her, to rape her. At night, she thought she heard noises from the same men trying to break into her house to attack her and Rebecca, who is now in her twenties. At times, which were becoming more and more frequent, she became hysterical and Rebecca couldn't control her. Even so, Rebecca refused to desert her. But Alice next door could see the writing on the wall and called the authorities. In no time, Penelope was sent to the Penetanguishene Mental Health Centre."

"What happened to Rebecca then?"

"Years before, Penelope was afraid that she'd one day be committed and had made a living will leaving everything to Rebecca. Rebecca was rolling in it. With the investments her father had left, and buckets of cash in the bank, she wouldn't have to work a day for the rest of her life unless she wanted to. And she kept the house. In the back of her mind she always had this vision of her mother being released and returning home. And even though whenever she visited her mother and saw no hope, she still kept hoping for some kind of miracle. It never happened.

"What happened to make her change her life? Loneliness happened. She spent her days alone in that barn of a house. Alice no longer visited because Rebecca had told her never to come back after she had called the authorities on her mother. You have to understand that Rebecca wasn't like her mother. In the past, she'd only lived the isolated life she had because of her mother's demands. Except for being a hopeless romantic, she had the same desires and ambitions as any normal young woman, the main difference being that even in her late twenties she was still a virgin. She wasn't afraid of men, she was just…well, cautious. She still enjoyed doing her crafts, but her loneliness kept telling her that she had to become more self-sufficient so that she could meet other people.

"The car still sat in the yard, unused. The first thing she did was take driving lessons and get her licence so that she could become mobile. Then she started driving into Orangeville to do her own shop-ping for groceries, clothing, cosmetics, whatever. Rebecca is no raving beauty—she runs about one-forty but it looks good on her—but when she puts on her new clothes and puts on her new cosmetics she turns a few heads. And one of those heads was on a creep named Bert Crimps. She met him one day while shopping for groceries in A & P. He was about her age, tall, husky, good looking, with straight black hair that went to his shoulders. He asked her out and she accepted. He took her out for dinner three nights running and drove her home afterwards. Never touched her. On the fourth night, after he'd wined and dined her, he asked her to go up to his apartment and she accepted. That's when his true colours came out. When she tried to refuse to go to bed with him, he raped her, and before he let her go he warned her that if she ever told anybody he'd kill her. She was abhorred at the thought of her rape being made public and never pressed charges. And wouldn't have even if he hadn't threatened her. She never told me about the rape until after we were married. Luckily for Crimps, by this time he'd moved out of town, because if I'd ever caught the bastard I'd've strung him up by the nuts. One thing about me, I might have an active libido and spend a lot of time looking for women, but I've never ever forced any woman to have sex with me. And never will. Hell, I'm not ugly, and there are plenty of women around. I'd sooner take a willing second best than force myself on any woman. I like women too much for that."

Rodger said, "After learning that she was raped, I wonder how you ever managed to meet her, let alone get her to marry you. When women have a horrible experience like that they often become terrified of men. Isn't that how it affected her?"

"It was years later that I met her. By that time she had reached a point where she could at least talk to men, but remained very cautious and suspicious. We met in the Orangeville Mall parking lot one Wednesday morning, my usual shopping day, on a lousy winter day. It was cold and snowing. And blowing. I'd just put my groceries into the trunk of my car after coming out of A & P when I saw her. She had a cart filled with groceries and was struggling to unlock the trunk of her car. It seemed like she wasn't able to turn the key. I went over and asked if I could help. I wasn't thinking of sex; it was just the gentlemanly thing to do. But when I got a look at her face, she didn't look half bad. I wasn't wearing my riding gear because it was winter, but I could see right away that she was defensive because she backed up a little and said she'd been having a lot of trouble trying to open the trunk lately. I tried wiggling the key up and down and then turning it. Nothing. I pulled it out and saw that it was badly worn along the edges. I told her that she needed a new key, and volunteered to go into the mall to the shoemaker, who I knew cut keys, and have a new one made. 'You don't have to bother,' she kept saying, but I finally convinced her and removed the key from her ring. Her old car had different keys for the doors and the ignition and she got inside to keep warm.

"Well, the new key worked fine and I helped her load her groceries into the trunk. She thanked me warmly, even smiled a little, but insisted on paying me for the key, obviously not wanting to feel too obliged to me. I let her. Before I left, I asked, 'Is this your usual shopping day, and do you usually come at this time?' After a brief hesitation while she looked me over, she said it was. I had the information I wanted. I knew her car colour and licence plate number, but the next Wednesday she didn't show. She had a pile of groceries the previous week, so I thought maybe she only shopped every second week. And I was right. The following week I spotted her car and asked her if the key still worked properly. She said it did. I noticed that she didn't back away from me now, even smiled a little, so I asked her out to dinner. She played it cool and said no to Wednesday or Thursday, but she gave me directions to her place and we made a date for Friday evening.

"Friday evening the weather was miserable. I was right on time, and I swear that she was standing on the other side of the door when I knocked because she opened it immediately and already had her coat, gloves, toque, and scarf on. And she barely opened the door wide enough for her to slide through. She told me months later, when I finally did get to see inside the house, that she didn't want me to see the living room on our first date because she hardly knew me. She didn't want to lie to me, and felt that if I saw the crafts she'd have to explain about them and about her mother.

"When I finally did see that living room I was absolutely blown away. The walls were crammed with crafts of every category you could think of, and many you couldn't. There were dozens of paint-by-numbers, from small to large, mostly landscapes, flowers, or still lifes, some painted on boards, others on black velvet. There were collages, and string art, and bead art, and rock art, and sequin art, you name it. There were dozens of cross-stitches, and rug-hookings, some as large as murals that must've taken months to make. The big bay window probably held over fifty suncatchers, mainly of flowers, birds, and wildlife. The coffee table and end tables were cluttered with hand-painted pottery vases and bowls. Most of them were empty; a few contained flowers or candy. Along the arms, and across the tops of the backs of the two chesterfields and two La-Z-boys, were rows of doilies in different sizes, patterns, and colours. It was incredible, like a craft museum in there. And on the floor, under one of the end tables, were about half a dozen boxes of crafts which still hadn't been started.

"Anyway, that's how it all started. Like I said, it took me months just to get inside that house for a cup of coffee. We went out about three times a week, but it took me at least a month before I could even touch her without her stiffening up, so I backed off. It was about two months before she let me even kiss her goodnight, and even then I got nothing more than a peck before she turned her face away. Let's face it, even though I didn't know it then, she was still scared as hell after being raped and still didn't trust me. She eventually softened up enough to let me give her a little squeeze, but sex was absolutely out. Yet I knew she wanted to marry me. She kept saying that she wouldn't willingly have sex with anyone until she was married, the inference being that if I wanted to have sex with her I had to marry her. Anyway, maybe I loved her at the time and decided to take the plunge for the second time, without even knowing if we were sexually compatible.

"I'd known her for about nine months when we got married. I gave up my apartment and moved into her house. The first time we bedded down I found out that having sex with her was like walking on eggs. I couldn't use any strength at all or she'd start to panic It was like trying to have sex with a flower. That's when she told me she'd been raped, and kept saying, 'Please be gentle and patient with me, honey.' And I was, month after month. For the first six months of our marriage I must've heard her use that line at least a hundred times. I got sick of hearing it, but I still felt sorry for her. Oh, I got my rocks off okay, but no matter what I did she was always left high and dry, and I was severely limited because of her need for extreme tenderness. She did have some sexual feeling, but it was very low grade, and I was lucky if during a session I even got a faint moan from her. Later on, her moans grew a bit louder, but I'd been with enough women to know that she was just trying to fake it, trying to make me believe that she'd climaxed just to get it over with. When I confronted her with this, she even admitted it. It was completely unsatisfactory for me; I don't feel like much of a man when I can't give a woman the same kind of pleasure she's giving me. And I knew that Rebecca wasn't satisfied either. She wanted to enjoy sex more, but she just couldn't break down the mental wall that had been built the day she was raped."

Rodger asked, "Did you try to resolve the problem some other way? Get some kind of professional help?"

"Yeah, I did. I convinced her to start seeing a psychiatrist. His name was Dr. William Fenech. But after dozens of sessions and several thousand dollars virtually nothing had changed. I told her I thought it was a waste of money, that he was just bleeding her, but she insisted on continuing with the sessions. I think she actually enjoyed going to this guy and unburdening herself. She probably told him things she wouldn't even tell me. And I couldn't say no because she was paying the shot.

"Anyway, during this period her romantic nature was subdued and I hardly noticed it, but once she became convinced that her personal sex life was hopeless, it blossomed and began to take control of her life. Now she became clingy. Whenever we were together she'd be either holding my hand, or resting her head on my shoulder, or gently stroking my neck, or running her fingers through my hair or stroking my beard. Her hands were on me all the time. Sometimes she asked me to kiss her, gently, or kiss her hand like a knight in shining armour, or stroke her hair, or whisper sweet nothings. All these things only served to make me horny, but she was only thinking of romance in its purest sense, not sex. Once she even said, 'Wouldn't it be lovely if neither one of us had any genitals. Then we could go on like this forever.' I was getting irritated with the whole damn thing and wanted to bring her back to reality, so I replied, 'But we wouldn't want to kiss each other.' 'Oh?' she said. 'And why not?' 'Because,' I said, 'if we had no genitals we'd be pissing through our mouths.'" Ray laughed loudly.

Although Rodger cared little for toilet humour, he couldn't help joining in. "And how did she respond to that? I'll bet she wasn't very pleased."

"No, she sure wasn't. But it didn't deter her. And no matter how often I tried to jolt her back to reality by making crass remarks or constructively criticizing the *real* world, she absolutely refused to relinquish her grip on the syrupy, saccharine romantic fantasy world she insisted on living in. And I knew that if I couldn't get her to do that, there'd be no hope of our sex life ever improving. So eventually, after trying every way I knew to make her come around, I just gave in and played along...and hated every minute of it. She just wouldn't leave me alone. She was all hands. But the hands never touched me where I wanted to be touched. It was a stalemate. She wanted all romance and no sex; I wanted all sex and no romance. And if she *had* to indulge in sex, she wanted *it* to be as romantic and insipid as possible.

"One night, after she'd been mauling me for a couple of hours, and we'd hurled about a gross of sweet nothings at each other, I finally got her to go to bed. When I finally got her to surrender her clothes, and we were both lying naked on our backs, and I was just about to mount her, she hit me with a blockbuster. Very softly, she said, 'Honey, isn't this lovely, just lying here quietly like this? Why don't we just lie here, quietly, and each fantasize in our own minds how we'd like to be made love to.' I stared at her stupidly, my mouth hanging open a mile, and when I finally found my voice I groaned, 'You mean just lie here and not even touch each other?' 'Yes,' she said. 'Wouldn't that be just too sweet, honey?' Too sweet? Fantasizing? I'm lying there with a wang as stiff as a baseball bat and she's talking about not touching each other!

"If we went out together, she made nauseating comments about things as though she were seeing them for the first time in her life. If she saw some drooling infant, she said, 'Oh, isn't she the cutest, sweetest thing! I could just eat her up!' If she saw someone with a puppy or a kitten, she'd ask if she could hold it, then she'd pet it and talk baby talk to it, and weep with joy. She read buckets of Harlequin romances, and watched sloppy movies on the women's channel, weeping and wiping her eyes at the sentimental parts. If she looked at a beautiful sunset, she wept. If you gave her a bouquet of flowers, she wept. Every little piece of syrupy sentimentality brought tears to her eyes. I tried to play along with her, but after a few years I just couldn't take it any longer. She was driving me nuts, and I just couldn't go on living like that."

"So your sex life with her didn't improve."

"Not with her, no, but it did improve. I couldn't take the passive, sorry excuse for sex that Rebecca doled out to me. She rarely refused, but she never participated either. She never even bothered faking an orgasm any more. I felt like I was no longer a man. That she'd turned me into some kind of pathetic wimp. I needed a real woman, a passionate woman, one who knew how to move her ass, so I started making excuses and going out again. And I found what I needed. I tried to hide it from Rebecca, but I didn't really care if she found out. Her money meant nothing to me—I've always despised men who live off women. I had my job at Drummond and was self-sufficient. If our marriage broke up I'd simply move back into an apartment. As a matter of fact, I was almost hoping that she *would* find out so that I could get out of a life I'd grown to hate."

"And did she eventually find out? Was she the one who initiated the divorce proceedings?"

"Well, let's just say that she suspected, but her romantic nature wouldn't allow her to believe it. Here's what happened." Remembering, Ray laughed. "It must've been fate because it came right out of the blue. You hear about this kind of thing happening to other people, or see it in B movies, but you never expect it to happen to you. I told you that she had an appointment with this Dr. Fenech every week. Suddenly it became twice a week. And that's when I noticed that she wasn't pawing me all the time, wasn't clinging to me and whispering sweet nothings, wasn't even paying much attention to me any more. "Well, it didn't take me long to get the message. And Rebecca isn't the type of person who can live with a lie very long. She soon told me that she had fallen in love with Dr. Fenech, and out of love with me. He was about ten years older than her, but from what she said he apparently believed in all the same romantic nonsense she believed in. To her they were like two intertwined souls. He apparently shared every one of her feelings, apparently had exactly the same syrupy, fantasizing outlook on the world that she had. Apparently he had no interest in sex, only in romantic love.

"I say 'apparently' because this guy was just putting on a big show to gain his own ends. And his own ends meant getting his hands on some of her money, which he'd found out about through the history Rebecca had given of herself during their sessions. She found out, much later, that he liked to live high off the hog, but his meagre practice wouldn't allow him to do so. Evidently, I found out from reliable sources, Orangeville didn't think much of Fenech as a psychiatrist, and half the time his waiting room was empty. Anyway, he advised Rebecca as a professional psychiatrist. He wanted her to believe that they were kindred spirits, that they had so much in common that they couldn't possibly fail to make a perfect couple. And she bought it, hook, line, and sinker."

"So she asked you for a divorce so she could marry him."

"Right. I tried to talk her out of it. Not the divorce, I mean— I was just as happy to get out of our marriage as she was, and told her so. No, I tried to talk her out of getting hooked up with a guy like Fenech because I'd checked him out and knew what he was. But she was so smitten with this creep that she wouldn't listen. Before they were married, Fenech had a Prenuptial Agreement drawn up by his lawyer which entitled him to half her fortune if they ever divorced. All except the house. He also wanted half of that, but I managed to convince her to have that removed from the agreement. And she did, mainly because she still had this dream that someday her mother would return. Even so, Rebecca was on cloud nine and couldn't possibly believe that they would ever separate. She was so infatuated with Fenech that she signed the agreement without even showing it to her lawyer, even though I warned her to do exactly that.

"Well, you know what happened next. Once married, our boy Fenech began showing his true colours. And they certainly weren't what Rebecca expected. They never had sex, which suited Rebecca fine, and she told me that he treated her nicely for six months, and then he dropped a bombshell on her. He told her he was gay, and told her that he had no desire to kiss or fondle or have sex with any woman. He wasn't lying. He actually was gay, but this was all part of his plan to get out of the marriage and get his hands on half her money. He was a good boy for six months only because he felt that if the case ever went to court he could prove that he had at least *tried* to make the marriage work."

Rodger said, "She let her heart run away with her head, and now she had a real problem. Still, it is possible to live without sex. If Fenech's homosexuality was latent, they could've had a relationship on other levels."

Ray scratched his beard and laughed. "Latent, hell. To you or me, his homosexuality would've been as plain as the nose on Barbra Streisand's face. You or me would've probably spotted it in a minute. Shit, half the people in Orangeville knew he was gay. I'm not against gays; if that's your life, fine, but I have to believe that that was one of the main reasons why he had so few patients. But to Rebecca, poor, naive Rebecca, he was just, well, a bit effeminate, a bit gentle, a bit refined. Which she liked because it placed him on the same plane as herself.

"Anyway, she still thought they could make an acceptable life together, as long as Fenech avoided sexual relationships with other men and reserved his affection for her. But she was dreaming again. Fenech would have none of that. He knew that their Prenuptial Agreement mentioned nothing about restricting sexual preferences, so he could just go on his merry way and indulge in all the male-to-male sex he wanted. And he wanted to hurry things up so he could get out of the marriage. One night, the bastard became so blatant that he brought one of his lovers home and they began performing right in front of her right there in the living room. Naturally, she was abhorred and rushed into the bedroom and locked the door.

"But it kept happening. With different men. Rebecca knew that her sole right to the house was protected in the Prenuptial Agreement, and that she could order Fenech to leave, but she also knew that if he did leave he'd have grounds to start divorce proceedings against her. Which meant that, excluding the house, he'd be entitled to half of her fortune. She went to her lawyer, who first scolded her for not having first brought the Prenuptial Agreement to him to examine, then laid it on the line. He told her that he'd fight the case, and might even be able to reduce the payout, but doubted that they could ever win the case outright. In the end, the judge agreed that, since Fenech failed to tell Rebecca before their marriage that he was gay, and had no intention of fulfilling his sexual role, that Rebecca had some grounds for some compensation. On the other hand, she had willingly signed a Prenuptial Agreement, so the judge awarded Fenech half of half of her fortune. In any case, she's still pretty well off. If she doesn't want to, she probably won't have to work a day for the rest of her life."

Rodger asked, "And is she still living in the same house? Has she remarried?"

"Yeah, still there, still waiting for her mother to return. Which is never going to happen. Since her bad experience with Fenech, she's drawn back into herself. She's become extremely suspicious of men and rarely goes out, only when it's absolutely necessary. She just sits at home, all alone, and does her crafts and reads her Harlequin romances and watches syrupy movies on the

W channel. And watches the birds around the place. Living in her own little dream world. She's got two strikes against her, like me, and right now she's terrified of even picking up the bat again. But eventually I think loneliness and the need for companionship will force her out of the house again. What she needs is a friend."

Ray tried a sip of his cold coffee, made a face, put the cup down, suddenly broke into a heavy fit of coughing. When he finally gained control of himself, red faced, eyes watering, he said, "Damn cough—I can't seem to shake it."

"When was the last time you had a chest X-ray?"

Ray shrugged. "I don't know, I can't remember. Maybe ten years ago."

"Ten years! Make sure you get it done when you see the doctor."

"Yeah, don't worry, I'll take care of it. Getting back to what I was saying, as you can see, neither one of us, Rebecca or me, has been very lucky in picking spouses. I don't intend to go for the third strike either. But the difference between the two of us is that I'm still in the ball game, but now I'm only playing in the field. And you can't strike out if you're only doing that."

"Don't be too sure. If the right one comes along you may not have a choice."

"I'll take my chances."

Rodger thought about Rebecca, sitting alone in that big house, and suddenly found himself blurting out, "I want to meet her."

"What?"

"I want to meet Rebecca. Unless, of course, you still have some attachment toward her and don't want me to."

"There's no attachment. We're still friends, that's all. I visit her once in a while just to keep in touch, or phone her, and we talk, but there's nothing serious and never will be." Ray gazed at him suspiciously. "What the hell's this all about, Rodger? You just told me that you're happily married, and now you want to meet Rebecca. What's going on?"

"Nothing's going on, and I am happily married, but there's something missing in my life. Me wanting to meet Rebecca has nothing to do with sex. How could it when I've never even seen her. It's just that women have a different slant on life, and Rebecca strikes me as the type of person who might be able to put me on the right road."

"What's wrong with Claudia putting you 'on the right road.' After all, she's your wife."

"I've already tried with Claudia; she doesn't have the answers I'm looking for."

"And you think Rebecca does? Hell, Rebecca is just about the most neurotic, confused woman I've ever met. You won't find any gems of wisdom there. Or by talking to women about your life. When was the last time you ever heard of a woman philosopher? Like I said before, there are only two types of women, the physical and the romantic, and you won't find a philosopher in either one. If you want to look for an answer, read Spinosa or Plato or Kant, but you won't find any answer there either because there just isn't any. So why not just wait for your mid-life crisis to peter out and then get back to normal?"

"I just can't do that. And I don't think this thing is going to just 'peter out.' If I don't find an answer, I think it's going to plague me for the rest of my life."

Ray laughed. "You poor, dopey bastard. You've got a gorgeous wife, a beautiful home, a good sex life, a good-paying job, and you're still not satisfied. And the worst of it is that you don't even know what you really want."

"That's true, I don't, but that doesn't mean that I should stop looking. I just don't believe that having a wife, a home, and a good sex life is all there is to life. There's got to be something more important than all that. There's got to be something more important than material possessions and hedonism, and even love." Rodger reflected for a few moments, then said, "You're fifty-three now. Have you ever thought about what your life will be like when you're sixty-five?"

Ray laughed again, but sadly. "Hell, that's easy—I won't have any life because I'll be lying in my grave. I've been smoking for forty years, drinking for almost forty years, and indulging in sex since I was fifteen. How much longer do you think I'm going to live? How much longer do you think it'll be before throat or lung cancer, or cirrhosis of the liver, or AIDS gets me and wipes me out? Hell, I feel like I'm living on borrowed time already."

"But what about between now and then? Don't you feel that, instead of simply seeking your own pleasure all the time, you need to *contribute* something to the world before...before it's too late?"

"That phase of my life has passed. It passed when I finished with my mid-life crisis. My contribution days are over. Now it's just a matter of pressing on diligently until the end."

"But what if you can't do that? You're fifty-three now. What if your sexual prowess begins to fail and you can't perform any more?"

Ray smiled. "Haven't you heard? We've got Viagra and Cialis now. Unless I live long enough to become old and decrepit, there's no reason why I can't perform."

"You could contract prostate cancer, which could put you out of commission."

"Not entirely." Ray leered at him. "There's more than one way to skin a cat."

"But as you grow older, do you think you'll still be able to attract the young chicks? What happens when the women in their twenties won't bother with you any more?"

"Then I'll move on to the thirty-year-olds, and if necessary the forty-year-olds, and if I'm really desperate even the fifty-year-olds. Hell, beggars can't be choosers, can they? There are plenty of women out there. If the young ones won't bother with me any more, I'll be okay as long as I'm getting something that excites me on a regular basis."

"But isn't this exactly the time, when your powers are failing, that you should be thinking of trying to live your life on a higher plane?"

"Like what? Like joining Big Brothers, or Lions, or Kinsmen, or some church that puts on strawberry suppers or bake sales. Or maybe you want me to fill in at the Orangeville Food Bank and dole out macaroni and cheese and corn flakes to the needy, and the not so needy. Is that what you want me to do?"

"Yes, something like that. Today people are too inside themselves. They don't believe in anything worthwhile, and they don't care about others, so they end up only looking out for number one and to hell with everyone else."

"And why should they? Have you ever seen the world in a worse mess than it is today? What motive does the world give to anyone to do anything generous, especially if you don't believe that there's any-thing more once they put you in the ground?"

"Is that you, Ray?"

"Yeah, it's me. I've had my bout with mid-life crisis, had my fling with the church, read the philosophers and found them wanting, and now it's back to the old Ray, the Ray who intends to get all the sex he can, drink all the beer he can, and smoke all the cigarettes he can until they come and haul him away." He stared sternly at Rodger. "And don't you try telling me anything different."

Rodger smiled. "I wouldn't think of it, even though I think you're making a big mistake with your life."

"It's my life, not yours."

"Right. But I'd still like to meet Rebecca. Can you phone her for me and ask if I can come and meet her tomorrow night? Tell her I'm only interested in doing some research. Tell her…tell her that I'm writing a book about women. A comparative study. I'll take a notebook along and actually take some notes."

Ray shook his head. "I don't believe this. What's really going on here, Rodger?"

"What do you mean? Nothing's going on."

"C'mon, level with me. You say you've been married happily for ten years. That's a long time for a marriage to last these days. And now, suddenly, you're asking me to set you up with my former wife. Is that just the mid-life crisis talking, or is there trouble in wonderland? What kind of a relationship do you *really* have with Claudia?"

"Look," Rodger said angrily, "Claudia and I still have the best possible sexual relationship, but when it comes to changing our lives for the better she wants nothing to do with it. She's perfectly happy with the *status quo*, but I'm not. And that's the *only* reason I'm asking you to do this favour for me. I'm looking for answers, and maybe Rebecca has some. Now, will you help me or not?"

"Okay, okay," Ray said, raising his hands defensively, palms outward. "I'll phone her now—she should be home." He pulled a cell phone from his pocket, keyed in the number, made small talk for a few minutes, gave Rodger's name and explained that Rodger worked with him and wanted to meet her to just talk to her, then pushed the cell phone at Rodger. "Here, you tell her why you want to talk to her. She wants to know."

Caught off guard, Rodger took the cell phone and nervously introduced himself, then explained that he'd like to interview her for a book he hoped to have published on different types of women.

"What did he tell you about me?" she asked suspiciously.

"Well, not much," he lied. "But he did tell me that you two were once married, and from the little he told me you sound like a very interesting and sensitive person who might make a very good subject for a chapter in my book."

"A *chapter* in your book?" Now she sounded impressed.

Rodger was amazed at how easily the thoughts were coming. "Well, I do want to do a thorough job. I intend to devote an entire chapter to each woman I use in the book. Of course, some women won't qualify, but you sound like a good possibility, assuming that we can collect enough interesting information about you to fill a chapter."

"I've had some hard times," she admitted. "But I certainly don't want my life made public in a book. What will people think?"

"You needn't worry about that because they'll never know that I'm writing about you. I'll give you a fictitious name and address. And remember this: you'll be helping other women to cope with their lives because the book will offer solutions to the problems presented. And many of those solutions will be those of the women in the book, who have actually discovered the solutions themselves. Maybe you're even one of those women."

"Well…"

"May I drop by your place tomorrow evening, say, seven o'clock. And if at any time you find me becoming a nuisance, I'll leave, and respect your privacy. Is seven o'clock okay, or is it too early?"

"Well...actually seven-thirty would be better."

"Fine. I'll see you then, Rebecca."

"Wait. What will you be wearing?"

He told her.

"And what are you driving? What colour is it?"

He told her.

"Fine. When you come, park your car directly in front of the front door."

"Okay."

As Rodger handed the cell phone back, Ray had a smirk on his lips. "You bagger. You're determined to meet her, aren't you? Something's going on here. Are you sure you're not interested in bedding down with her?"

"No, I'm not. Look, I've already told you why I want to meet her, and that's the truth."

Ray kept nodding his head. "Sure, I know what you've *told* me, but I'm beginning to wonder if you haven't got some kind of a marriage problem." He scratched his graying beard several times." Tell me, in ten years of marriage have you ever bedded down with another woman?"

Rodger folded his arms defensively. "That's really none of your business, is it?"

Ray shrugged. "Maybe not, but you're certainly not being fair about sharing information, are you? Especially after all I've just told you about myself. By not answering, I guess the only thing I can assume is that you *have* bedded down with another woman." He eyed Rodger sharply. "Am I right?"

Rodger sighed heavily and unfolded his arms. "No, you're not. I've never been unfaithful to Claudia since the day I met her."

Ray's eyes widened. "Are you *serious*? Wow, that's heavy. I've never even *heard* of any married man being faithful for ten years. That's absolutely remarkable." He grinned. "Hell, you're...you're almost as extinct as the Neanderthal. Are you *sure* you're not putting me on?"

"I'm sure. I guess it's pretty hard for you to believe, given the type of life you lead. Too many people expect everyone in the world to be like themselves."

Ray grinned. "Touche , buddy, touche . And what about the other side of the marriage? What about Claudia?"

Rodger stretched his neck upward and raised his chin nobly. "She's never been unfaithful," he said firmly.

"Oh? How do you know for sure? Have you ever asked her?"

"Of course not. Why would I ask her when our love life has always been great and she hasn't given me even the slightest reason to suspect her?"

"Well, I look at it this way. I've seen Claudia a few times when she came to the office to talk to you, and she's a very attractive woman, and she meets a lot of men in her business. And the way she dresses sometimes would give plenty of men ideas. Hell, we're not made of wood. And...well...if you don't want me to pursue this, just let me know, but I think it's important that you know the truth."

"Where the hell are you going with this?" Rodger demanded, glancing at his watch. "It's late. We're already overdue at the office. We'd better be getting back."

"This'll just take a few minutes." Ray cleared his throat, studied Rodger for a few moments. "Tell me, what kind of a woman is Claudia? The physical type or the romantic type?"

Never having been asked these questions before, or thought about the answers, Rodger reflected for almost half a minute before replying. "I don't think you can place her neatly into either category. I don't believe your system of classifying women can possibly work for everybody. You're oversimplifying. Surely all women can't fall into only those two categories. Women are more complex than that. There must be others who are mature, intelligent, and know what life is all about."

"Well, I've never met any."

"Maybe you just haven't travelled in the right circles. As far as Claudia's concerned, I guess I'd have to say that she's both, leaning a little more to the romantic."

"Okay, so you'd say that she's *primarily* a romantic type."

"Yes, I guess so."

"And is she a very mercenary person? A very materialistic person?"

"Yes. Definitely."

"She wants the bigger house, the bigger car, plenty of new clothes. All the things that are part of the so-called Canadian Dream."

"Yes."

"And I guess she earns some pretty hefty commissions in real estate, doesn't she?"

"Yes." Now Rodger began to get the message. "You *bastard.* If you're going where I think you're going, you're crazy. Maybe you think every man and woman in the world should be as loose as you are, but they're not. Claudia may be mercenary, but she loves me and she wouldn't think of…of giving herself to another man just for the sake of closing a real estate deal. If she did that, it'd soon be all over Orangeville and her career would be down the drain. She's a smart woman, not an idiot. Which is what you seem to think she is."

"No, I don't. Okay, maybe that isn't what's going on. Maybe it's something else. But statistics show that marriages which have lasted ten years with *neither* of the couple ever having been unfaithful are almost as extinct as the Dodo bird. And you deserve to know if something's going on, don't you?"

"Nothing's going on," Rodger rasped through gritted teeth. *"Nothing!"*

"Ask her, that's all. Just ask her."

4

For the rest of the afternoon, Rodger found it impossible to concentrate on the advertising campaign that the creative department had been working on for an Orangeville restaurant. Ray had voiced the very question which he himself had worried over on Sunday morning as he lay in bed trying to recover from his Saturday night binge.

Suddenly, as he ruminated more and more on the question, it gained some validity. Is Claudia offering her body to potential buyers in exchange for closing real estate deals? Claudia is a clever woman. True, she loves making money too much to risk jeopardizing her career, but there are safeguards which she can implement. For example, what if she gives herself only to *married* men and limits herself only to deals which offer substantial rewards in commissions? Such men have a great deal to lose if they decide to brag about their conquests and the information reaches their wives. Claudia could be fairly certain that they would keep their mouths shut.

Ray had also said that it could be something else. And by "something else" he had obviously meant an affair with another man. What if Claudia had been having a secret affair for weeks, months, maybe even years without his knowledge? Rodger tried to shake off such thoughts. Was it this damn mid-life crisis that made him so suspicious, so negative about everyone and everything? In all the ten years of their marriage, although he vaguely recalled that years ago he had a suspicion which had never been fully resolved, he had never been able to find any convincing evidence that Claudia had ever been unfaithful to him. But how hard had he looked? Their marriage had been one of trust from the beginning, and their sex life had always been so fulfilling that the question, and his suspicion, had only arisen once.

Until now. Now Rodger knew that, even though he still believed in Claudia, he had to know the answer to the question. But to receive an answer to a direct question, you must first be able to ask the direct question, yet as Rodger sat across the dinner table from Claudia that evening he found that, even though since Sunday he had found himself more capable of being direct, he now found that the words refused to come. To ask the direct question would be accusatory. To ask the direct question would reveal his suspicion; otherwise why ask the direct question at all?

No, he'd have to try to use innuendo. Be more cagey. More devious. Try to get Claudia to commit herself without actually accusing her. As he chewed his smoked ham, he searched for a way in which he could approach the question indirectly, and finally came up with a possibility.

He said, "Over the past several years, ever since you've been selling real estate, you've dealt with plenty of male buyers. I know I've mentioned this to you before, but it's time I mentioned it again." He found that he couldn't keep the nervousness out of his voice. "It's the way you dress for them sometimes…with your mini-skirts and your low-cut blouses. I'm…I'm afraid for you, Claudia." He felt like he was walking on eggs—and breaking them. "I know if I was one of your clients and saw you like that…well, you look so sexy that I'd want to go to bed with you." The eggs were shattering beneath his feet, but he had to press on. "Maybe…maybe I'd even say to you, 'If you go to bed with me, just once, I'll sign on the dotted line.'" Suddenly, he found his voice and it became strong, assured, manly. "I want you to tell me if anybody ever tries anything like that, or if anybody ever tried anything like that in the past. Just tell me who it is and I'll find him and beat the shit out of him."

Claudia's pursed lips, stretched into a tight, grim line, told him that his comments had been as transparent as a pane of freshly cleaned glass. "Why do you insist on beating about the bush?" she accused coldly. "Why don't you just come out and say what you really want to say?"

"I don't know what you mean," he said weakly.

"Of course you do. Why would you even say such a thing? You're not a violent man. You and I both know that you'd never beat anybody up even if I was raped. You'd be furious, yes, but you wouldn't beat anybody up. You won't even watch violent movies on TV. What you'd do is call the police. So what you're trying to do in a roundabout way is ask me if I've ever been unfaithful to you. Isn't that what you *really* want to say?"

"Yes, I guess it is," he admitted sheepishly, then felt a sudden twinge of anger at having been found out. "Well, have you?" he demanded loudly.

Surprised, Claudia shrank back in her chair, then quickly gained her composure and blurted out, "Have *you*?"

"No, I haven't," he said easily, knowing it to be the truth. "I've never ever been unfaithful to you since the day I met you."

"Why?"

"Well…because I love you. And, because of that, I'm not interested in going to bed with other women."

"And don't you think I feel the same about you? In ten years of marriage, have I ever done anything to make you think otherwise? I may dress like a tease at times for certain male clients, but do you actually believe that I'd ever go to *bed* with them?"

"No, I just thought—"

"You just thought that you'd *ask* me. But why ask me unless you're *suspicious*? In ten years, you've never asked me…and now.. suddenly…" She picked up her napkin, dabbed at her eyes. "Suddenly you don't trust me any longer. You think I'm capable of cheating on you. Have I ever given you any reason to believe that I've ever gone to bed with another man? I've never cheated on you. *Never!* You're suspicious of everyone lately. Even me. You're down on the whole world. And I can only attribute it to this damn male menopause you're going through." She dabbed at her eyes again." If it wasn't for that, I'd have to believe that there's something wrong with our marriage. But I don't believe that, because of your…because of your condition. I know we still love each other, and we'll just have to both be strong…until this thing passes."

Rodger realized that this was the point when he should reach across the table and take Claudia's hand and soothe her, reassure her with comforting words. But he refused to do so. Instead, he forked a large piece of smoked ham into his mouth and used his chewing as an excuse to remain silent while he reflected. He had witnessed her tears many times over the past ten years, and almost always he had reacted exactly that way, but he also knew that most women could cry on cue and their tears were often nothing more than a ruse to get their own way. In the past, he had usually given in to her tears, even though he often disagreed with her, because in the end he had rarely found the issue important enough to fight over.

But what about now? Why the tears now? It seemed a strange time to inject them. After all, he had dropped the ball by accusing her, yet she had eventually softened her blow by eventually turning the conversation back to their love for each other. And yet... why the tears now? Could they be a smokescreen hiding something else? Hiding the truth? She was right, wasn't she, when she said she'd never given him any reason to believe that she'd gone to bed with another man? But wasn't that a strange way of putting it? Almost as though there actually *was* a reason but he simply couldn't find it.

As he chewed another piece of smoked ham, Rodger pored over the past, trying to unearth something, anything that would cast suspicion on Claudia's sexual conduct. *Had* she ever been unfaithful? No...no...except...and the memory which had caused his suspicion years ago began to come into focus. He recalled how, to amuse themselves on their seventh wedding anniversary, they had rent-ed the video of *The Seven-Year Itch* starring Marilyn Monroe and Tom Ewell from Blockbuster. As they shared a bottle of ice wine and watched it, they laughed and laughed. And when it ended, they both jokingly said that any day now they would both be going out to find new lovers for themselves. And they thought it was so ridiculous that they laughed some more.

But about two months later, *The Seven-Year Itch* no longer seemed funny. Claudia had phoned to say that she'd be late, and he'd told her not to rush because he'd prepare a simple dinner for himself. When she arrived at about eight o'clock, he sat watching a Blue Jays game on TV. She greeted him quickly, then hurried toward the stairs, saying over her shoulder that she just *had* to use the bathroom. He thought this strange at the time because at the end of each work day they always first greeted each other with a kiss, and what difference would another few seconds make. As she hurried toward the stairs, he wondered why she had avoided the main floor washroom and thought he saw a long run in her pantyhose down the back of her left calf. His suspicion intensified when he failed to hear the toilet flush. A few minutes later, he heard the bathroom shower come on, and shortly after she turned it off he heard the toilet flush. Had she used the toilet *before* the shower, and only remembered to flush it *after* the shower? Or had she never used the toilet at all?

She came down about twenty minutes later, smelling flowery and completely changed into beige slacks and a white tank top, and promptly gave him his kiss, a much longer kiss than usual. He smelled whiskey on her breath and she appeared to be still under its influence. When he asked her if she was all right, she laughed and said, "Of course." Normally, he would have accepted this, but he thought she sounded nervous, and wondered about the bathroom incident and the long run in her pantyhose. And why had she changed so quickly? And why would she be wearing slacks in the house on a hot day when she usually wore shorts?

Later that evening, when he had to relieve himself, he checked for the pantyhose in the laundry hamper in the ensuite bathroom but found nothing, then realized that she would have disposed of them if they had a run. He checked the wastebasket be-side the toilet, even dug down to the bottom thinking she might have wanted to hide them. Still nothing. Would she have flushed them down the toilet? No, Claudia was too bright for that. She knew that they could easily clog up the system, presenting even more problems.

Then where? He turned back to the laundry hamper and began digging down. He found two pairs of pantyhose, both without runs, then, near the bottom, he found a third pair rolled tightly and tied with a knot at the feet. Untying the knot, he unrolled the pantyhose and examined them. The long run was there, and along its edges several reddish stains which he took to be dried blood. After examining the crotch area for telltale stains and finding nothing, he carefully rerolled the pantyhose, retied the feet, and returned them to the bottom of the laundry hamper.

Still, the bloodstains made him fear that Claudia may have had some sexual encounter. She probably wouldn't have told him even if she had; he'd warned her often enough and her admission would have forced her to admit that he was right.

He felt like a detective attempting to find some evidence to convict a criminal. Yet he needed to know. He knew that Claudia always wore underwear beneath her pantyhose. If she had changed her clothing, she must also have changed her underwear, but as he studied the clothing at the top of the hamper he saw only the shirt he'd changed from when arriving home. As he dug down, he found underwear, but he had no idea if any were the ones she'd removed that day. And if they were, shouldn't they be at the *top* of the pile? Except early in their marriage, he'd never known Claudia to be so modest as to actually hide her used underwear...unless... unless they were stained? He felt himself becoming obsessive. He rationalized his behaviour by telling himself that the main purpose for his search was to discover whether or not Claudia had been raped so that he could convince her to lay charges, but he admitted that he also wanted to know if she'd been unfaithful to him. He examined her underwear one by one, but found nothing, until he reached the bottom. There, rolled up, he found a pair of pink underwear, almost as long as men's boxer shorts and with unusual white frills circling the hems, different from anything he'd ever seen Claudia wear. They were stainless, which, he realized, was perfectly normal. He knew that Claudia always wore a sanitary minipad to protect her underwear. He'd even often bought them for her when she ran short. Nor were they damaged. Then why had she separated the pink, frilly underwear from the rest by rolling them and placing them at the bottom of the laundry hamper? He had a strong suspicion that they were linked to the damaged pantyhose, and that she intended at a more convenient time to dispose of them both. And the only reason he could think of why they would be linked was because someone had removed them....

He felt perplexed, stymied. He had suspicions, but they were only suspicions and nothing more.

He returned everything to the laundry hamper, careful to put each item in its proper place, then checked the vanity drawer where she stored her underwear. He found nothing which even vaguely resembled the pink, frilly underwear. Claudia pre-erred bikini underwear, and even sometimes wore thongs, yet the pink underwear in the laundry ham-per were almost matronly. Still, she could have decided to try changing her image with something dif-ferent.

He went downstairs and found Claudia at the kitchen table drinking coffee.

"Are you *sure* you're all right?" he asked.

"Of course." She stared at him suspiciously. "Why wouldn't I be?"

"Well, it's just that you looked a little upset when you came in, that's all."

"Is it any wonder?" She gave a short laugh. "Wouldn't *you* be a little upset if your bladder was bursting and you felt that you were about to pee in your panties? I'm fine, really." She giggled. "As a matter of fact I'm better than just fine. I'm *exceptionally* fine, I'm *incredibly* fine. I have some *fantastic* news for you...but I can't tell you now. Wait till morning...I'm still too tipsy...wait till morning."

Soon she was in bed and deeply asleep. But even her prom-ise of "*fantastic* news" failed to allay his suspicions. He slept poorly that night, brooding about the long, blood-spotted run in her pantyhose, and the full-length satin pajamas she'd worn to bed instead of one of her usual short summer nightgowns.

Still tired, he rose at six-thirty with Claudia still asleep. Usu-ally, she was a restless sleeper, often moving about during the night, and also had the habit of sleeping with part of one leg outside the covers. He noticed that she'd removed the covers completely and her restlessness had bared her left leg almost to the knee, expos-ing two parallel scratches each about six inches long, almost as though they'd been made by the fingernails of someone's forefin-ger and middle finger. Now he knew why she'd worn full-length pajamas to bed. Dressed, he went downstairs, put on the coffee, made himself a simple breakfast of shredded wheat and orange juice. When Claudia entered about a half hour later, wearing her pink satin dressing gown and pink, fluffy slippers, she poured herself a cup of coffee and joined him at the table.

They exchanged good mornings.

Tired, miffed at having lost sleep over what he'd discovered the previous evening, Rodger tried again. "Are you absolutely sure you're all right?"

"Yes, of course I am. Why shouldn't I be?" she added testily. "Why must you keep asking?"

If nothing had happened, he wondered at her anger and defensiveness. "I'm just worried about you, that's all. Being protective. When you kissed me last night, you had liquor on your breath, and you looked like you'd had a few drinks too many. Did a client take you to dinner?"

"Are you spying on me now?" she demanded coldly.

"No, I'm just worried about you. I'm *concerned*. Can't a husband be concerned about his own wife?"

"But this certainly isn't the first time I've come home after having dinner and a few drinks with a client, is it? And you've never acted concerned be-fore. You've simply accepted it as part of my job. So why now?"

"It's just that you looked nervous, upset, and I thought maybe something...something might've happened."

He wanted her to confirm his suspicions, to admit that some type of sexual attack had occurred, to beg for his love and his help.

Instead, she said,"*Nothing* happened. Last night, for the fourth time, I showed my client an estate in Caledon East, which he'd liked right from the start. I've been telling you about him and this property for weeks. His name is Harry Danker. He's a millionaire who made most of his money in the commodity markets. He made an offer of $1,200,000.00, which I'll be presenting to the owner today, and which I'm fairly certain he'll accept. He then took me to dinner, to celebrate, he said, and we had a few drinks. That's all. After dinner I came *straight* home. So-o-o-o, my darling, everything is *perfectly* all right. Even *more* than perfectly all right. It's absolutely *stupendous!*" She hugged herself and laughed happily. "I didn't want to say anything last night because I was...well, a bit under the weather. I was afraid of messing it all up. And the only thing I was nervous about was this deal." She rose, came around behind him, hugged his chest and kissed his cheek. "Don't you understand what this means, darling? If this deal goes through, it will mean the *biggest* payday of my life! For just a few week's work, I could earn a commission of *$30,000.00!* Wouldn't *you* be excited? Wouldn't *you* be nervous?"

"I guess I would," he admitted, smiling broadly up at her, placing his arms over hers and hugging them. But, as he'd been hearing about this big real estate deal for weeks and felt confident that Claudia would finalize it, he found it difficult to become genuinely excited. He knew that her money would not change his life. On Claudia's urging, they'd each had separate savings and chequing bank accounts since their marriage and pooled their resources in another chequing account to pay regular monthly bills. Even their investments were in their own names. Only the deed to their home was registered jointly. "And I'm very happy for you," he continued enthusiastically, for her satisfaction. Rich people, with their lives often centred around the world of money, actually bored him, and he had never seen the mere accumulation of money as a worthy lifetime goal. "*Very* happy. When you get that com-mission, I'll expect you take *me* out to dinner."

She smiled her most beautiful smile. "That's a deal, darling."

And there it had ended. He had believed her. As he usually did, he gave in and began to rationalize her behaviour. After all, the run in her pantyhose and the scratches on her calf could have been caused by any number of other things. Some kind of minor accident. Scraping against something. Anything. Claudia had given him seven wonderful years of marriage; he had no decisive proof that that had ended.

The deal did go through, and when she received her commission she did take him out for dinner and they celebrated with the best bottle of champagne the house could offer. And as the incident receded into the past, from weeks to months, he thought about it less and less, until he only rarely thought about it at all. Even so, it remained securely fastened to a corner of his mind, and he asked himself the same question whenever he recalled it: Why had she hidden her damaged pantyhose and pink, frilly underwear? And why, when he searched her vanity drawer after the laundry had been done, had he not found or ever seen the underwear again?

Whenever this happened, and they were together, he still found himself gazing at Claudia and wondering...wondering...

And now, almost three years later, as he sat across the dinner table from her chewing a piece of smoked ham, forty years old and growing older each day, his life on that back side of the mountain and moving downward, he found himself wondering again. Only now he knew that he had to do something about it. Now he knew that he had to finish what had never been finished to his complete satisfaction. Only to Claudia's. He had to—

"Rodger?" she said loudly. "Are you listening to me?"

"I'm sorry. I was thinking about something else. What were you saying?"

"Never mind," she said coldly. "I'm more interested in learning what you were thinking about that was so important that you couldn't even bother listening to what I was saying."

"Well, I was thinking about an evening almost three years ago when you came home with a long run down the left calf of your pantyhose and smelling of whiskey."

Watching her, he could have sworn that she shrank back a little in her chair. He'd never mentioned the run in her pantyhose before.

"What run?" she asked. "What are you talking about?"

He knew that she knew exactly what he was talking about, but decided to humour her. "Don't you remember? It was about two months after we watched the video of *The Seven-Year Itch*. You came in and I was watching the Blue Jays game. You'd had quite a bit to drink and you said you couldn't stop for a kiss because you had to rush to the bathroom. I enjoy looking at your great legs, so I saw the run in your pantyhose as you hurried toward the stairs. Do you remember now?"

"Oh, *that!* But we've been all through this before, years ago, and I told you that everything was fine. Why are you bringing it up again now?"

"Because you only told me part of the story. You never even mentioned anything about the run in your pantyhose, or why you tried to hide it from me.

"I never tried to hide it from you. You just said you saw it as I walked toward the stairs."

"Yes, I saw it, but you didn't want me to see it. That's why you didn't kiss me when you came in and why you hurried toward the stairs."

"I *told* you, my bladder was bursting. I had to *go*."

"But you didn't go, did you?"

"What are you talking about? Of course I went."

"You did? I happen to know that you *always* flush the toilet immediately after using it, but you didn't that night because the first thing I heard was the shower coming on. And *then* I heard you flush the toilet, a few minutes *after* you came out of the shower."

When she realized that he'd kept secrets from her for years, she pursed her lips and gave him a sharp glance, then quickly shifted to her most al-luring smile and reached across the table and gently took his hand. "Darling, aren't you making far too much of nothing," she cooed. "What difference does it really make *when* I flushed the toilet? I'd had a little too much to drink and forgot, that's all, because I was in such a hurry to get under the shower so I could sober up a little."

He knew that her hand on his and her gentle words only signified her attempt to convince him to forget about the whole thing, which had succeeded so often in the past, but he pulled his hand away. "Or you lied because you were trying to hide something," he accused coldly.

"Hide something? Hide what? Darling, what on earth is the *matter* with you lately?"

"You tried to hide the fact that something happened to you that evening which you didn't tell me. Otherwise, why would you roll up and tie your dam-aged pantyhose, with blood on them, and hide them at the bottom of the laundry hamper? And why would you fold up the underwear you wore that evening and hide *them* in the same place?"

She jerked back in her chair and blurted out angrily, *"You've been spying on me!"*

"Only because I was concerned, and you refused to tell me the truth about the damaged pantyhose, or even mention them. Or mention the scratches on your leg. I had to find out about them the following morning, while you were still sleeping. I wondered why you'd worn long pajamas to bed."

"And what did you do?" she sneered. "Sneak around and gently pull the covers off my leg, then gently pull up my pajamas leg?"

"No, all I had to do was look. You know you al-ways sleep with your left leg outside the covers, and because you're so restless at night the satin pajamas leg had slid up almost to your thigh. Where did those scratches come from, Claudia? And the run in your pantyhose?"

When she hesitated with her reply, he quickly said, "Where did they *come* from, Claudia? Were they from some man? Were they from the client you saw that evening, the guy who took you to dinner and made the offer on that million-dollar estate in Caledon East? Did he make a play for you, Claudia?"

She laughed loudly. "You must be joking! Harry Danker? That *creep!* I wouldn't let him lay a finger on me. The only good thing about him was that he was a millionaire. But he was the most conceited, the most cocky, the most inconsiderate, the most rude and selfish person I'd ever met. He reminded me of John Gotta, that Mafia boss who eventually died of cancer in prison. The expensive suits, and that sickening smug expression always on his face. I *despised* him!"

"If he didn't touch you, then what happened?"

She laughed self-consciously. "It was the silliest thing, darling. As I was getting out of the car at the restaurant, the back of my leg scraped against the bottom corner of the door. It was rather embarrassing to walk in and out of the restaurant that way—I didn't have a spare pair of pantyhose in my purse—but I kept a little behind Danker and he didn't even notice." She spread her hands wide, palms upward. "And that's all there was to it."

"Not quite. Haven't you forgotten something? If that's all there was to it, why did you hide your underwear and pantyhose at the bottom of the laundry hamper?"

"I just didn't want you to see them," she replied glibly. "I knew you'd make a big issue of it, which is exactly what you did. Right from the start you thought the worst, didn't you?"

"Maybe I did, but I was just concerned about you, that's all. And that still doesn't explain the fancy underwear. Once you finished the wash, I never saw you wear them even once. They just disappeared. I didn't even know you'd bought them."

"They were brand new. I thought maybe I'd make a change from my usual bikinis and thongs. Make myself sexually more mysterious. For you. But I didn't like them, and I didn't think you would either. The long legs made me think of myself as an old woman, an old spinster. So I put them together with some old clothes I wanted to get rid of and donated them to the Salvation Army."

"But you couldn't possibly know that I wouldn't like them since I've never seen you in anything like that," he said lamely. "I might have—you should've let me see you in them."

"I'm sorry if I disappointed you, darling," she said, smiling. "If you like, I'll buy another pair and model them for you."

"Don't bother. It's too late now."

He realized that Claudia had all the important answers down pat. And why shouldn't she? After all, the incident happened almost three years ago and she'd had plenty of time to rehearse them. He felt convinced that even if he'd asked her these questions when she came home that evening that she would already have had prepared answers for them. Surely she must have suspected that he *might* see the long run in her pantyhose and question her about it. And when he failed to, she certainly had no intention of volunteering the information.

Yet he couldn't rid his mind of his suspicion.

5

On Tuesday morning, Rodger and Ray were informed that they would be required to work until seven on the Paragon Chinese Restaurant's radio campaign because of an impending deadline. At lunch, Ray asked Rodger if he'd asked Claudia if she'd ever been unfaithful to him, but Rodger remained noncommital, saying only that she had proclaimed her innocence and he had no definite proof one way or the other.

During their mid-afternoon coffee break, to prepare himself for his upcoming meeting with Rebecca, Rodger phoned Claudia and notified her that he'd be working late because of the impending deadline, without specifying how late, something he'd done on many previous occasions. He assuaged his conscience by telling himself that even though he hadn't told her the complete truth, at least he hadn't lied to her. Claudia agreed affably and promised to leave his dinner in the refrigerator before she left for her evening appointment.

Afraid of unnerving Rebecca, he arrived at her home at precisely seven-thirty, parking the car on the driveway directly in front of the front door as she'd instructed. Pulling his briefcase from the back seat, he left the car and gazed around, impressed by the spread: the colourful gazebo on the front lawn, the mature maples, the rock garden filled with shrubbery and colourful flowers surrounding the large, immaculate house, the huge, well-manicured lawn, and the dense bush in the distance.

He'd been of two minds as to whether to include a small digital recorder with the writing pad in the briefcase and had decided to do so, giving Rebecca the choice of either option. He knew that some people were cautious about allowing others to re-cord their voices.

Claudia had once questioned the combination lock on his briefcase, implying that he didn't trust her, but he'd laughed easily and assured her that it simply kept others at the office from snooping into his papers, and that he'd be glad to reveal the con-tents to her whenever she wished to see them. But she'd merely shrugged and said that she wasn't interested in seeing his boring old papers. This scene had happened years ago and she hadn't mentioned the briefcase since, so he felt quite secure. Unless the situation changed. Unless, of course, he gave her some reason to be suspicious. But Claudia usually kept rigid working hours; he usually knew when she'd be away from home. He'd have to be diligent in transcribing the information collected from his interviews to his laptop computer as quickly as possible, where he knew they'd be safe. In all the ten years of their marriage, Claudia had never once asked to use his computer, since she had her own.

Although still light outside, a bright spotlight beamed down from above the oak front door which had two deadbolts and three small panes of glass near the top covered with thick, powder blue drapery. Just below the glass, he noticed a peephole. When he knocked three times with the brass lions-head knocker, a muffled voice inside immediately asked, "Who's there?"

He knew that she'd been waiting on the other side of the door for him to arrive, and that she'd probably already observed him through the peephole. Even so, he still sensed that she need-ed to be reassured. "It's Rodger. Rodger Blackwell. I spoke to you on the phone yesterday. I'm here about interviewing you for the book I'm going to write."

"Please step aside. You're blocking the window."

For a moment, he couldn't understand her reasoning, then realized that if she'd been viewing him through the peephole she now wanted him to step aside so that she could see his car. When he did so, he saw the drapes part slightly and a sliver of face ap-pear. He heard the dead bolts sliding open. The door opened a few inches on a chain latch and a single eye viewed him up and down. Finally satisfied, she closed the door, slid the latch, and opened the door just wide enough for him to enter, then closed both dead-bolts and reset the chain latch be-fore turning to face him.

"You're very cautious, aren't you?" he observed.

"After what I've been through," she said flatly, "I've earned the right to be cautious."

He saw that she was about five-foot-four and dressed in a plain, loose-fitting dark gray pant suit which effectively hid the contours of her body. Still, Ray's estimate that she weighed about one-forty appeared close to the truth. The jacket, closed at the throat and long enough to cover her posterior, hung loosely over her modest breasts, effectively hiding their cleavage. She wore plain, low-heeled black leather slippers. He thought, if she wanted to appear sexless—and he had no reason to believe otherwise—she had succeeded admirably. Too small for her body, her little face with its pointed chin and clear, freshly-washed skin fell about halfway between plain and pretty, the brown eyes too small for the straight, slightly jutting nose and the wide, thin-lipped mouth. If he were to describe her face to someone, he'd have to fall back on that horrible, meaningless word by saying that she look-ed "nice." Her black hair, streaked sporadically with gray tendrils and tied into a neat ponytail with a piece of black, glossy ribbon, hung half-way down her back.

Rodger liked the practical and sensible hair style. He abhorred the loose styles of today which fifty to a hundred or more times a day caused women to either tuck stray hair behind their ears or shake their heads back to keep stray hair out of their eyes.

"I'm Rodger Blackwell," he said, smiling, extending his hand. "I'm very pleased to meet you."

She gazed at his hand, but refused to take it. "Come into the living room," she said flatly.

"Ray has told me what an incredible home you have here. Especially the living room with all its crafts and wall hangings."

"Oh? He always gave me the impression that he thought they were quite frivolous."

He tried to redeem himself. "I'm speaking from my own perspective. I've always admired people who can do things with their hands, especially fine things. Me, I do the odd jigsaw puzzle and that's about it. I understand that the amount and quality of the work you and your mother have done is incredible."

She smiled, obviously pleased with the compliment, and he thought he even detected a light blush coming into her cheeks. "I'll let you be the judge. See for yourself."

She led him into the spacious living room. When he glanced around at the walls, he was dumbfounded, unable to move, his mouth falling open involuntarily. He'd thought that Ray had surely exaggerated when he'd told him about the amount and variety of the crafts hanging from the walls, but now he realized that his description hadn't even done justice to what he now gazed at in wonder. Mahogany wainscotting about a yard high covered the bottoms of the walls, but above this he could find no space where anything but small pieces could possibly be added.

When he finally found his voice, he blurted, "This is unbelievable, fantastic!"

Her pleasure now obvious, she said, "Would you like me to show you around? I'll give you the grand tour."

"Sure, that'd be great. But first I need to ask you something." He indicated his briefcase. "I've got a digital recorder and a writing pad in here. Would you prefer that I take notes, or simply record our session?"

"I'd prefer that you take notes. I don't like the idea of my voice being recorded."

"May I make a suggestion? And remember, it's only a suggestion. I don't know shorthand, and I may make mistakes when you're talking, maybe even misquote you. I wouldn't want to do that. If I simply record our session, there won't be any possibility of my doing that. If you wish to listen to the recording when we're through, and make any corrections you wish, I can take notes. And when I get home I'll simply transcribe our session into my laptop computer, using another name for you. After that, I promise you that everything will be erased from the digital recorder."

She gave him a long, hard look, then asked, "Are you married?"

"Yes."

"Any children?"

"No."

"And does your wife know what you're doing? That you're seeing other women and planning to write a book about them?"

"No," he admitted,"she doesn't."

"And you don't want her to know, do you?"

"No. Not right now. I'll wait until I'm sure that the book is going to be published."

She nodded, a thin smile flickering across her lips and disappearing. "Then you don't want her to have access to the information you're putting into the computer, do you? Not right now, that is. I've never owned a computer, and I don't know much about them, but I do know that they can have something called a password, which keeps other people out of your computer. Does yours have one?"

"No. We each have our own computers. But I'll install a password in mine before I start transcribing our session."

"If I give you permission, I'd strongly suggest that you do exactly that, especially since you don't want her to know. At least, not right now."

Again he saw the thin, quickly disappearing smile and realized that she'd taken control of the conversation and that she still doubted his complete sincerity. Yet her effort at a smile convinced him that she'd relaxed enough to at least believe that he had no intention of harming her. "I *am* preparing a book, you know. And I do hope to get it published. And it will probably help others to find themselves and perhaps help themselves. But I must admit that I also have an ulterior motive for being here, and it has nothing to do with looking for a relationship with another woman. But it has everything to do with me, my life, and where it's going. Right now I'm dissatisfied with it. I feel that it's been wasted. I don't feel that I've done anything worthwhile, important with it, and I'm looking for some direction from the people I'm interviewing for the book."

"Then you're *not* having a problem with your wife?"

"No. Our sex life is great. But her view of life is a mercenary one and that doesn't give me the answer I'm looking for. Money isn't the answer. I'm looking for something deeper, something more worthwhile. Maybe what you tell me will help. Will you allow me to record our session?"

She gave him a long, sympathetic look. "Yes," she said finally. "As long as you promise to delete my voice after you've finished transcribing the information."

"I promise." He placed his briefcase on the living room coffee table, opened it, removed the digital recorder. "May I start recording now?" When she nodded, he started the recorder and slipped it into his shirt pocket.

"Now I'll give you that grand tour."

She spent the next twenty minutes escorting him around the room, pointing out crafts that had been done by her mother, by herself, and by both of them, explaining techniques and tricks, pointing out the many difficulties inherent in the making of many of their creations. Rodger had the strong feeling that this was a first, that no one before him had ever shown such interest in the crafts, and that she was finally venting her need to let someone know of a mother-daughter achievement, and of the thousands of hours spent to attain it. He felt that by her intense explanation she was trying to justify those thousands of hours by making them appear important and not simply time wasted.

Finished, she asked, "Would you like a cup of tea?"

Although he preferred coffee, he agreed, but added, "May I see the rest of the house first?"

"Well...I

He could see that she hadn't anticipated this request and quickly said, "It's just that I'd like to get a rounded-out view of your life for the book. Is something wrong?" He smiled. "I don't mind if your bed hasn't been made."

"Oh no, it's nothing like that," she insisted. "It's just that... well...all right then."

She started by showing him the dining room with its large crystal chandelier hanging above a gleaming oak table surrounded by six sturdy oak armchairs. A huge oak china cabinet, far wider than any Rodger had ever seen, filled with crystal, gold-edged tableware, and bone china tea sets, monopolized one wall.

The kitchen table, chairs, and cabinets were also solid oak. Ceramic tile covered the floor, the top of the large preparation island in the centre of the room, and the backsplash wall at the back of the long, wide counter top.

"Very impressive," he said honestly. "Has anything changed here since your father died and your mother left?"

"No. Father built this house many years ago. He loved oak. He felt that it was the only wood that could really stand up to years and years of wear. He had the china cabinet in the dining room built especially for the house."

At the back of the kitchen, sliding doors opened onto a large patio which covered the entire width of the house. Beyond it, the huge, manicured lawn led to the dense bush in the distance. "There's really nothing upstairs except the bathroom and three bedrooms," she said. "Nothing you'd find interesting. Would you like that cup of tea now?"

He detected her reticence and felt certain that she wanted to avoid his upstairs inspection. "Not yet. I'd like to see upstairs. That is, of course, if you don't mind."

"No…I don't mind," she said, but her voice sounded strained. "Just wait here a moment. I'll be right back."

She hurried upstairs, where he heard doors closing, and returned within a minute. When they reached the top of the stairs, he noticed that the bathroom door at the end of the hall stood open, but all three bedroom doors were closed.

"This is the guest bedroom," she said, opening the first door.

Decorated in brown tones, the room measured about twelve feet square . The bookshelf headboard of the double bed held dozens of paperback books standing neatly side by side. On closer examination, he found that they were mainly westerns novels, mostly by Louis L'amour.

"Not much reading variety here for your guests, is there. Especially if they were women."

"No, but we never had any overnight guests anyway. And I'm afraid father's taste in reading was very limited. He was more a man of action; the only time he ever read was in bed. I suppose Ray told you that he was killed in a construction accident."

"Yes, he did. I'm sorry. That must've been quite a blow for you and your mother."

She shrugged. "Perhaps I shouldn't say this, but I will anyway. He wasn't much of a father—I barely knew him—and even less of a husband. I can't honestly say that I miss him."

"He appears to have used this bedroom often. It still looks like he hasn't left."

"Mother wanted it left this way, just the way he left it. Like some type of memorial. I don't touch anything, just dust and vacuum now and then. When mother comes home, I want it to be just the way she left it. Strangely, she still loved him, even at the end, in spite of all he did to her." She sighed heavily. "Yes, he did use this room often. You see, he drank. And when he drank he became abusive, both physically and…and sexually. And when he was finished abusing mother, he wanted nothing more to do with her and came here to sleep. And he also came here whenever he had any kind of an argument with mother, which was often."

"What about you? Did he ever abuse you in any way?"

"He slapped me in the face a few times, that's all."

Her prompt answer made him believe that she had told the truth. "For what reason?"

"No reason. When father was drunk, he didn't need any reason." She turned away abruptly. "I'll show you the master bedroom now."

Much larger and also with solid oak furniture, the room measured about twelve by eighteen feet. An immaculate king-sized bed flanked by massive bedside tables holding huge lamps, again with a bookcase headboard filled with paperback books, dominated the room. Along opposite walls stood a bulky, nine-drawer vanity with a large mirror, a sturdy, hardbacked chair before it, and a six-drawer highboy with a dressing stand beside it. To Rodger, as a piece of furniture even the vanity appeared masculine. He noticed that the dark brown drapes at the wide window were closed. The vanity top held only a hairbrush, a comb, a few nail care instruments, and a few skin creams and other cosmetics. Some of the jars looked like they hadn't been opened for years. A pair of white satin slippers were before the bedside table, and a yellow nightgown lay across the bed. Idly, he wondered why, in light of the sexless clothing she wore, she'd left her filmy nightgown out for him to see when she decided to close the doors.

Rodger checked the books and saw that they were mainly Harlequin romances, some quite old.

"You enjoy reading these, do you?" he asked.

"Yes. The older ones. The newer ones aren't the same."

"How do you mean?"

"Well, Harlequin has surrendered and gone with the times. It's not like the old days."

"How have they changed the books?"

"They've...they've put sex into them. They never used to have sex in them. They were just good, clean, wholesome stories. Now they're not the same, so I only buy the old ones at the second-hand bookstore. Would you like that cup of tea now?"

"If I may, I'd like to first see the third bedroom. I do want to create a well-rounded picture of you and how you live. Is there something there you don't want me to see?"

"No, of course not," she blurted out. "It's just that...well, you might find it rather silly. Childish."

"Is that why you came up and closed the doors?"

"Yes," she admitted. "It's not important that you see the room."

"Will you let me be the judge of that?"

She shrugged helplessly, opened the door and led him inside. Like the first bedroom, the room measured about twelve feet square, and again the bookcase headboard was filled with dated Harlequin romances, but there the resemblance ended. A pink carpet covered the floor. The top half of the pink double bed with its pink bedspread was covered with dozens of stuffed teddy bears of various sizes, shapes, and colours, all neatly laid out row upon row upon row, and the walls, edged with pink wood trim, were covered with wallpaper crowded with scenes depicting Winnie the Pooh in his various adventures.

"I thought you lived alone," Rodger said. "Ray told me that you had no children. Do you have a young girl living with you?" And when he saw Rebecca blush crimson, he knew that he'd made a terrible mistake and knew exactly what she intended to say.

"This…this is my room," she almost whispered.

Rodger found himself stumbling stupidly for words. "Oh, I'm sorry…but I thought…the master bedroom…the yellow night-gown…the slippers…"

"How could you even think such a thing," she chided. "Those are mother's things. I *never* sleep in *her* bedroom. I'm just keeping it clean and ready for her when she comes home."

"Oh. Do you visit her often, at Penetanguishene?"

"I see that Ray has told you about mother," she said coldly.

"Well, he's told me a bit."

"If I know Ray, he's told you *more* than a bit."

"You can tell me your side when we go back downstairs. Do you visit her often?"

"About once a month."

"And do you see any progress?

She turned away. "I'd rather not talk about moth-er's condition."

"Tell me. I'd like to know."

She still refused to face him, but he felt a need within her to unburden herself to him. "She's in her own secret little world, somewhere off in space. Most of the time she doesn't even know me. I take her hand and hold it, but it's limp and lifeless. As though she were…"—she took a deep, shuddering breath—"as though she were already dead."

"And what do the doctors say? What's her prognosis?"

She whirled on him, fire in her moist eyes. "The doctors? What do they know? They say that she's schizophrenic and will never improve enough to return home. But I *know* that she will! Some day she'll snap out of it, and then she'll be back home again with me. I *know* she will, I just *know*. And until that day comes I'll keep everything ready for her."

"How long has it been?"

"It's been…a few years."

Knowing that her mother would probably never return, he decided to change the subject. "This room," he asked, waving an arm. "Was it decorated like this before your father died?"

She laughed bitterly. "Are you serious? Father would never allow anything like this in *his* house. This bedroom looked manly, just like the others. Mother gave me permission to have it redecorated, the way I wanted, but she refused to change the other bedrooms, out of respect for father. She did love him, you know, in spite of the beatings, the cruelty, the degradation. He was the only man she ever had in her life."

He picked up a large, brown, stuffed teddy bear from the bed, turned it idly, discovered a white cloth label meticulously stitched to the bottom of the left back leg which read "BRUNO."

"Did you do this?" he asked, indicating the label.

"Yes."

He picked up three others, all with their own masculine name labels. "You've given them *all* names?" he said, unable to keep the accusative tone from his voice.

"Yes."

"But why?"

"Because they're my friends. I don't suppose you'd understand, but each one of these teddies is my friend. And I say that because when someone is your friend he doesn't lie to you, or cheat you, or beat you, or rape you like you were some kind of animal. That's why these teddies are my friends—because they can be trusted never to do any of those horrible things to me."

The words slipped out before he could stifle them. "No, I guess not, especially since they're all stuffed."

"What's that supposed to mean? Do you think, after what I've been through, that I don't have the *right* to be suspicious of every man I meet?" She glared at him. "Including you?"

"I'm sorry. That was uncalled for. But let me simply ask you this: do you believe that this…"—he waved an arm to encompass the room—"this teddy bear menagerie is the only way to deal with your fear of men?"

"No, I don't. And I didn't say I was afraid of men. I said I was *suspicious* of them."

"But doesn't your suspicion cause you to be afraid of them?"

"No, but it makes me extremely cautious. I still do go out with men, occasionally, but I'm always on my guard, and I'm not looking for a relationship, just a friend for company, someone to talk to. My horrid past has given me that right."

"And that past is certainly what I'm interested in hearing about."

"Then we'll go downstairs and I'll make the tea."

As they left the bedroom, she closed the door gently and led him downstairs and into the living room where she invited him to make himself at home, and left for the kitchen.

While he waited, Rodger removed the large, ruled writing pad fastened to its clipboard from his brief-case and began scribbling notes on his impressions from the time he arrived in the driveway to the time he started recording.

When she returned and saw him still scribbling, she said, "I thought you weren't taking notes."

He had placed the activated digital recorder on the coffee table. "Oh, this. These are just some of my initial impressions before I came in. I wanted to make sure that I made a good description of this incredible living room while I was still here." He placed his notes casually on the coffee table. "Would you like to read them."

"No, I guess I trust you." She set a tray containing a bone china tea service and a plate of Oreo cookies on the coffee table and began emptying it. She poured two cups. "Milk? Sugar? Help yourself to cookies."

"Just milk, please." He liked Oreos and placed two on his plate, then began nibbling on one.

He expected her to have a sweet tooth, comfort food, and nodded inwardly when she added three teaspoons of sugar to her cup before seating herself on the sofa two feet from him. Daintily, she placed one Oreo on her plate, but left it there untouched.

Three teaspoons of sugar, Rodger thought, but only one Oreo. He realized that although she had to have plenty of sugar in her tea, she still wanted to convince him that she ate little, but her chunkiness spoke the truth. Having observed Claudia's eating habits for over ten years, he knew that the amount a woman ate in public could often be far less than she ate in private. In public, even heavy women wanted you to believe that their weight problem had more to do with a glandular condition than with the amount they ate.

At the end of the coffee table, he noticed a box of Tarot cards and three paperback books stacked neatly beside it "May I?" he asked, indicating the books.

"Yes, of course."

He reached for the books and read the titles: *Libra: 2006*, *The Art of Palmistry*, and *Teacup Reading Made Easy*.

He asked, "Do you read these books?"

"Yes. I read my Libra book every day before I venture out. And if it says there may be problems, I stay home."

"So you believe what the book says."

"Yes, of course. Don't you believe in astrology?"

"No, because it's not anywhere near an exact science. It's just a bunch of authors trying to make money by tossing around a bunch of generalities. You can read ten books by ten different authors and they'll all be saying something different, but only in general terms. So who do you believe, and why should you believe any of them?"

"I'm not interested in ten different authors," she replied testily. "I'm only interested in David's books."

"You mean David Steadman, the author of your book."

"Yes. I like what he writes. It's usually gentle...and kind, but not always. Some days he makes me stay home. But I have to believe in *someone*, don't I?"

"So you usually find him comforting, and that's the main reason why you read him as opposed to other authors."

"Yes, but I also feel that he's very sincere and is always trying to help me." She reflected a few moments, then continued. "I guess that means that...that my self-esteem isn't very high, but how can it be after what's happened to me." She shook her head, as though to shake out her negative thoughts. "But I still do believe in astrology. Many of the things David has told me have actually happened. Many of them." She looked him up and down, then said, "You say you don't believe in astrology, but let's see if it's accurate. What's your sign?"

"I'm a Pisces."

"Ah, yes. And tell me, are you moody?

"Sometimes. Sometimes I just want to be left alone."

"And are you a perfectionist? Do things need to be exactly right for you? If you see something out of place, must you put it where it belongs? If you see a picture on a wall just a wee bit crooked, must you straighten it. When you put on a tie, must the knot be perfectly symmetrical before you're satisfied?"

"Yes, I suppose those things apply to me, but that doesn't necessarily give credence to astrology. If you ask a hundred men, who equally represent all the astrological signs, the same questions, you'd probably find that about the same number of men under each sign would be moody perfectionists."

She shook her head. "No, I don't believe that. I believe that most of the men would be Pisces."

"But even if you're right, 'most of the men' still doesn't make it an exact science, does it?"

She smiled thinly. "Yes, you certainly are a Pisces, aren't you? You certainly are the perfectionist. But, outside of your exact science, nothing in this world is either pure black or pure white, is it?"

He decided to change the subject. "What about the palmistry and the teacup reading? Have you dabbled in that as well?"

"Yes, I've read my palm and know what it says. Only what it says is indecisive, just as my life is indecisive. Do you want me to read your palm?"

"No, thanks. I don't believe in that either. What about the teacup reading? Do you also use that to try to predict what to expect for the day?"

"Yes, of course. I have a package of loose tea and read my tea leaves every morning before I decide what I'm going to do."

"And the Tarot cards?"

"The same. I shuffle them and lay them out every morning."

"But don't you see, there's nothing proven or scientific about any of these procedures. Horoscopes are nothing more than hit and miss generalities, teacup reading is totally dependent on the way the leaves come to rest in your cup, and the way Tarot cards are laid out is totally dependent on the way you shuffled them. How can you let such totally random procedures define your day?"

"I didn't say the results are written in stone. I just use them as a sort of general guide. I like it when they tell me something good. It gives me...well, it gives me confidence to go out into the world when they tell me something I already believe."

"But these random procedures must consistently give you mixed messages. What do you do when they contradict each other?"

"Then I go with the majority. That's why I have three different procedures."

"But what if there *is* no majority? What if all three results contradict each other?"

"In that case, because the results are conflicting, I stay home, because if I go out my day will probably also be in conflict and I may get into trouble."

"And you actually believe that?"

"Yes, I do. I've seen things happen too often not to believe it."

"What things?" he asked. "What kind of 'trouble' are you talking about?"

"Sometimes I'm accosted by men I want nothing to do with. Men who look like they only want me for one thing—I can see it in their eyes. Once I was in a minor car accident. Another time I fell and broke a finger. Another time my grocery bag broke and my groceries spilled all over the mall parking lot. And they were all days when I was told to stay home. I learned my lesson; now I listen."

"But do you not think that these things would've happened anyway, regardless of what the Tarot cards or the tea leaves or your horoscope said?"

"Yes, I do. But I was forewarned, wasn't I, and I didn't listen."

"But what about the times you weren't fore-warned and something bad still happened?"

"Do you always reason things out like this?" she said evasively. "How boring for you."

"Not at all. I simply need to satisfy myself of the validity of things, that's all. Take, for example, dream books. Books that purport to tell you what your dreams mean. There are dozens of them on the market, and many people actually believe what they claim. But have you ever actually considered who the authors are?

What credentials do they actually have to tell anyone what their dreams actually mean? Maybe they've done nothing more than read Freud's *Interpretation of Dreams*, if that, and merely faked the rest of it, or simply copied the same erroneous answers from other dream books. So how do we know that such dream books are not basically works of fiction masking as fact? But you still haven't answered my question. What about the times you *weren't* forewarned and something bad *still* happened?"

She thought for a few moments before replying. "Yes, I suppose that happened sometimes, too. The predictions aren't *always* right." She turned her face away, embarrassed. "I suppose you think I'm just another silly woman, believing in silly things instead of having the courage to face life squarely. Well, maybe I am, but maybe if you were a woman who'd gone through what I have you'd be acting exactly the same way."

"Maybe I would," he admitted. "And that's exactly why I'm here. I want you to tell me what brought you to this point in your life. First, I'd like to hear about your marriage to Ray."

She turned and faced him again. "How much has he told you? About our marriage and…and about other things."

"He told me bits and pieces, but I need you to fill in the gaps. I wouldn't want to publish anything about you, even under a different name, until I'd heard your side of the story. Tell me about the marriage."

And she did, cautiously and hesitantly at first, but the longer she spoke the more fluently the words came until they flowed freely and fast, a catharsis purging her of a dismal past. He was pleasantly surprised. He had thought that her rendition of the episode would be far different from Ray's because he believed that Ray had probably padded his part by making himself appear more considerate than he actually was, but as he listened to Rebecca's passionate voice, now ringing clear and true, he could plainly see that Ray hadn't exaggerated at all. Repeatedly, she skirted the rape issue by calling it her "bad experience with a man" and blamed it entirely for her present sexual abhorrence and her failed marriage to Ray.

When she finally wound down, purged, she closed her eyes and sagged back against the cushions, limp and exhausted, red-faced and breathing heavily, as though she'd just thrown a huge weight from her shoulders.

Rodger felt that the last time she had unburdened herself by telling the story of her married life with Ray was when she had told it to Fenech, the psychiatrist.

When she finally calmed down, her breathing returning to normal and the redness gradually leaving her face, she opened her eyes and stared at him for a moment before turning away sheepishly. "I can't believe I said all that," she said, speaking to the wall. "You must think I'm a despicable excuse for a woman."

"No, I don't. I believe you had good reason to behave the way you did. Tell me about your relationship with Fenech, after Ray left."

"I don't want to talk about *him*," she snapped, staring at him again. "I don't know how I could have been so blind, so stupid, so naive as to fall in love with such a man and actually *marry* him. I'm ashamed every time I think about it."

"But I can understand that, too, because you were naive, weren't you? You'd spent most of your life here in this…"—he waved an arm to encompass the living room—"…this kind of Shangri-La with your mother, and then met two men who treated you badly, so when Fenech came along, who treated you well at first, you needed someone and actually believed him. And because of your naivete, you probably didn't even realize that he was gay. Tell me about Fenech. What happened after Ray left? I need to know that from you, not Ray, because I need to be honest with my readers."

She sighed heavily. "I don't want everyone in Orangeville to learn about this. Promise me that when you write about it you won't mention my name, or Fenech's name, or this place. I don't want anyone to know that I was foolish enough to fall in love with a homosexual."

"I promise. I'll even change the locale. Now, tell me about your relationship with Fenech."

Again, he expected that Ray had exaggerated the story, making Fenech's actions toward Rebecca appear even more reprehensible than they actually were because of Ray's pity for her, but as she spoke, hesitating often, struggling to find applicable words to describe Fenech's betrayal and her own misery, she embellished Ray's rendition even more, painting Fenech as a despicable beast.

When she finally finished, red-faced, breathing heavily, close to tears, and again sagged back into the cushions with eyes clamped tightly shut as though to close out repulsive visions, Rodger wondered which rendition to believe. He leaned toward Rebecca's, reasoning that she probably only told Ray part of the story. Still, at times he felt that she had exaggerated out of anger and hatred and debasement, and that the actual truth lay somewhere in between. But he couldn't deny that, one way or another, she had gone through a horrendous experience.

Her eyes opened and she gazed around for a few moments like someone who had just awakened. For an instant, her gaze met his, then flicked away and she stared at the wall. "Are you satisfied now?" she asked accusingly, but before he could answer she reached out and snapped up the single Oreo cookie on her plate and pushed it into her mouth and chewed viciously, following it down her throat with a large gulp of cold tea.

Comfort food, Rodger thought. Yes, Rebecca had eaten and needed plenty of comfort food in the past.

She stared at him coldly. "Well, *are* you?" Now her accusation included blaming him for causing her to wolf down the Oreo cookie.

"I'm sorry if I made you divulge something that you didn't want to, but it is necessary for the book to be honest. And you do feel better, don't you? Just getting it all out?"

She remained stubbornly silent, which to him meant that she agreed.

"There's just one more...one more unpleasant episode in your life I need to know about. You've touched on it here and there, and Ray has mentioned it, but I still don't have the full story." He paused, watching as she bit her lower lip and twisted her hands in her lap. "You know who I'm talking about, don't you?"

"Yes, Cripps, but I don't see why you need all the details of—"

"I don't need *all* the details. Only the details you want to tell me. You be the judge."

She nodded, but she required at least two minutes to decide where to begin and how much to tell. Yet when she finally began, Rodger soon saw that, regardless of how abhorrent she found the episode with Cripps, she also found it impossible to hold back and had every intention of treating it in the same cathartic way she had treated the others, her faltering, breaking voice delving into each dark corner of the episode and bringing it into the light, even supplying graphic details of exactly how she had been raped, horrible, crystal-clear visions which Ray had not provided and obviously still haunted her life.

Finally finished, she put more space between them by moving to the end of the sofa where she sagged back limply against the cushions and breathed a long, heavy, shuddering sigh. But now she refused to close her eyes. She stared suspiciously at Rodger, as though she suspected all men and that even he had come, not to interview her for a book, but to do her harm.

"I think you should go now," she said hoarsely.

"Not yet, but soon. Listen to me, Rebecca. You have absolutely nothing to fear from me. I came here to learn about you, for the book, and maybe to find something in your life that would help me in my own. That's all."

She laughed bitterly. "Help *you* with *your* life? Have you heard or seen anything here tonight that could possibly do that? Can't you see that *I'm* the one who needs help?"

"Yes, I can. And I want to help you, right now. And I think I know exactly what you need. Right now what you need is a comforting hug."

"No...I...I don't..."

He moved closer to her, and even closer when she failed to retreat. "Listen to me, Rebecca. I'm *not* talking about sex. I'm talking about a comforting *hug*. I'm talking about putting my arms around you and simply *holding* you. Do you understand?" When she merely stared at him dumbly, he moved even closer, their knees now only inches apart.

"Please," she begged faintly. "Please...hold me..."

When he took her in his arms, she initially remained limp, her arms outside his at her sides, her head lolling against his shoulder. Then he heard the sounds of her soft, stifled weeping, and as they grew louder he felt her arms circling him, clutching him desperately while her cheek rose and pressed tightly against his own. As her weeping grew louder, her body heaving against him, long, gasping, mournful wails broke again and again from her gaping mouth.

He held her tighter as she mourned the loss of her virginity to a rapist, and wondered if she had ever before, even during her life with Ray or her sessions with Fenech, wept and wailed for loss as she did now. In one loud, tearful reaction, she appeared to be attempting to purge her body, mind, and heart, once and for all, of every vestige of a horrible experience which had haunted her for years.

He continued to hold her, refusing to release her until she quietened down, and even after her wailing stopped and her weeping became progressively softer until it diminished into stifled sniffles, he still held her.

"I'm all right now," she said finally, lowering her arms.

Releasing her, he reached for a box of Kleenex on the coffee table and held it out to her. Nodding her thanks, she pulled out a few tissues and dabbed at her cheeks and eyes.

"I'm sorry," she said, turning away. "I'm such a fool. I must have sounded like some wounded animal."

"No need to apologize. You needed that. You needed it very badly. God knows what would've happened to you if you hadn't finally let it all out." To view her better, he moved about a foot away. "But I'm assuming that you've never reacted this way before. Did you never open up to Ray? Or Fenech?"

She remained turned away. "I just couldn't. I...I was too ashamed. I told Ray, of course, but only the bare facts. I couldn't bring myself to describe it in detail. And when I went for my first session with Fenech, I had every intention of telling him everything, but I just couldn't do it. All I told him was what I'd already told Ray, and even though he pestered me, saying that I had to relive the entire experience in detail before I could ever be whole again, I persistently refused. And, of course, he never bothered asking me about it after we were married because he knew what he intended to do and didn't care." Sheepishly, she turned toward him. "So I never *really* told anyone. Until today. And I don't even honestly know why I told you, except maybe some women will somehow be helped when they read about me in your book."

"I'll make sure that I write it in such a way that they are helped. But don't you feel better now? Now that you've confided in someone and forced this horrible experience out of yourself and into the open?"

She thought for a moment, as though examining her feelings, then said, "Yes. Yes, I *do* feel better. I feel as though something which has been festering inside me for years has suddenly left me. Like when you have an upset stomach, and then you feel nauseous, and then you know you're going to be sick, and then you bring up, and then you suddenly feel better. I feel something like that. As though something which has been poisoning me and making me sick all these years has suddenly left me." She shook her head, but her eyes flashed with excitement and anticipation. "Oh, I know that sounds foolish. And I'm certainly not silly enough to believe that I'm out of the woods by any means. But maybe if I... well, maybe if I start attending sessions again, with a decent psychiatrist, maybe some day I will be completely healed."

He nodded. "I think that's exactly what you should do. We're almost finished our session now. There's just one more thing I want to bring up before I go. It's about the bigger picture."

She looked bewildered. "The bigger picture?"

"Yes. I'd like to pick your brain, for my own sake. Let me ask you this, Rebecca: Why do you think we're here?"

"Here? Well, because you phoned me and we agreed to meet and—"

He cut her off with a laugh. "I'm sorry. I guess I didn't make myself perfectly clear. What I actually mean is this: Why do you think we're here, you and I and everybody else, whirling through space on this huge ball we call earth? What does it all mean? What does life mean to you?"

Rodger could see by her befuddled expression that she had probably never been asked the question before, and as the silent seconds ticked away, he felt that she probably could give no sensible answer. Still, as the silence lengthened and her eyes took on a faraway look, he could feel her wandering through the corridors of her mind searching for an answer.

Finally, she said, "I'm just an ordinary person, not highly intelligent. As you've seen, my main reading consists of romance novels. And I don't bother with programs on television that discuss things like what life is all about. My father never talked about things like that either, but I knew that he was an atheist because he constantly sneered at religion and the church. And I could tell what his attitude toward life was by the way he lived. Being an atheist, with no belief in any afterlife, he believed in things like money and power, and he believed that his money bought him the power to treat people like dirt. Which is why his employees kept quitting on him; they just couldn't stand the oral abuse any longer. He believed in drinking his fill whenever he pleased, which was often, and when he became drunk he became a horrid and frightful tyrant. And he was the same with sexual gratification—he wanted it whenever he pleased. And if mother resisted because he was horribly drunk, he beat her until she gave in. And he never missed a chance to go to bed with another woman. He cared nothing for anyone but himself and had only one main goal in life: to constantly feed his own hedonism. Mother was different. She rarely read anything but romances, but she once bought a book called *The Truth About Reincarnation* and read it. It was about karma and the Hindu and Buddhist religions. She found the subject attractive because it gave her a second chance at life, a better chance. Whenever father gave her another beating, she took it because she believed that in the end she'd have something to look forward to. Another life."

"And what do you believe, Rebecca?"

"I...I guess I believe the same as mother."

"So you believe in reincarnation and karma. Tell me, how are you working through your karma in this life. What are you doing in this life that you can use as a stepping stone toward a better next life?"

She reflected for almost half a minute before replying. "Well, I've never been cruel or intention-ally hurt anyone, like others have hurt me," she offered doubtfully. "I've tried to be a decent person."

A pertinent statement he'd once read, but couldn't remember where, floated into his mind and he said, "It isn't enough to simply avoid evil in your life and merely maintain the status quo. You have to actually do some *good*." Years ago, I knew a man named Melvyn who was about thirty-five years older than me and retired with a pension after spending over thirty years working for the Post Office as a letter carrier. He had a wife named Louise who hadn't worked for many years, and a grown, unmarried son named David who still lived with them. By living frugally, Melvyn saved many thousands of dollars over his working life. His house on Pacific Avenue had long since been paid for and he had no outstanding debts. He didn't even own a credit card. He was so cheap that he wore the same poppy year after year around Remembrance Day so he wouldn't have to buy a new one each year, until it finally fell apart. He collected a Post Office pension, began collecting his Canada Pension, and a few years later, when he reached sixty-five, began collecting his Old Age Pension. His three pensions alone easily paid his weekly and monthly bills and still left him plenty every month to add to his savings. But even this didn't satisfy him. Many years earlier, Melvyn had developed a simple system for playing the horses and had been using it ever since. His standard bet was $300.00 to show, which meant that he'd collect if his horse finished third or better. Because he was cheap, he was extremely cautious and pored over the *Racing Form* before each race and refused to make a wager unless every possible contingency had been considered and eliminated. Actually, he was trying to pick the *winner* of the race and felt that betting to show supplied him with his margin for error. Which meant that almost any horse he bet on was usually considered a 'sure thing' by the public. Even so, in most races he failed to find a play. On a very good day, he found two plays on a ten- or twelve-race card, but usually found only one. And found none about thirty percent of the time. And the payoffs were usually small because Melvyn rarely played anything but hot favourites. For a profit over the long term, the system depended on many winners and very few losers. If he had two winners in a row that each paid $2.60, he'd be ahead $360.00. But if he then had only one loser, his profit would drop to only $60.00. And if he ever had two losers in a row, he'd probably need several winners in a row just to get back to even. Whenever I asked him how things were going at the track, his favourite line was, 'There's no money to be made out there.' And he gave me a sad, defeated look. So I had to assume that even with his extreme cautiousness he still found it difficult to make a buck at the track.

"Melvyn and Louise's cheapness was almost be-yond belief. They had prominent signs saying 'NO PEDLARS OR SALESMEN' on both their front and side doors, which were always locked in case some nervy pedlar or salesman or anyone else tried to barge in anyway. Whenever the phone rang, they picked up but said nothing, and when the person on the line finally spoke and identified himself or herself as a salesperson or a telephone solicitor, they hung up. They never went to church, possibly because they'd refuse to put even a loonie or a toonie into the collection basket and be recognized by parishioners as the penny-pinching skinflints they actually were. From what he told me, they'd never donated even one cent to any charity in their lives. No, I guess I'd better qualify that statement. Louise went to bingos with David practically every night of the week, which meant that she indirectly contributed a portion of the money she spent to the service clubs who ran the bingos. But she never looked at it that way because she always expected to win. Which, according to her, she did often. And if she won, she knew that she was contributing nothing to the clubs. And even when she lost she made sure that she took something away with her. She always brought a large handbag with her and actually bragged to me that she never left without stuffing it with a few rolls of toilet paper and a bunch of folded paper towels. If you looked into her closet, you'd see a couple of dozen old, garish dresses that were decades out of fashion which she'd bought for a dollar or two at the local Goodwill store. She shopped there often. She did all her Christmas shopping there, filling a few plastic shopping bags for a few dollars with outdated comic book figures and small, worn toy cars. And small, stuffed animals. Which were to be distributed among her nieces and nephews by someone at the family Christmas gathering, which she or Melvyn hadn't attended for years because of their health. She also bought her adult family gifts at Goodwill. All used. Things like artificial flowers, fruit bowls, sets of glasses, bedspreads, or towels. There she also bought a few rolls of discontinued wallpaper to wrap the gifts in and used masking tape to seal the parcels, and taped on scraps of paper in place of printed gift tags.

"They never went out to eat together in restaurants because it cost too much. Neither of them had ever learned how to drive and so had never owned a car. It cost too much. In all the many years of their marriage, they had never once taken a holiday. It cost too much. Before they stopped attending Christmas gatherings, Melvyn wore the same navy blue slacks, gray sport jacket, white shirt, and plain blue tie every year. Even his tie clip, coloured gold, with a small, working doorknocker in its centre, never changed.

"And now it's too late for either of them to do anything worthwhile with their lives. Melvyn is now about seventy-five and in the Avalon suffering from Alzheimer's, and his sight is failing because of his diabetes. And Louise—except when she manages to make it to a bingo—is basically housebound, taking nerve pills all the time, losing her sight because of her diabetes, and barely able to walk because of advanced arthritis in her knees. For which she takes cortisone shots. On the rare occasions when she manages to visit Melvyn, they usually have nothing to say to each other, mainly because most of the time he doesn't even know who she is.

"The productive years of their lives are already over, and they've done absolutely nothing worthwhile with them. Over the years, they've hoarded their money and have piles of it in the bank and in various investments, but they've never even enjoyed the pleasure of spending it, either on themselves or on others. And the money still keeps rolling in, month after month. Uselessly. Because money can only buy possessions; it can't buy a person. Only you can buy a person.

"Unless you consider her petty thefts from the bingo halls, neither of them ever committed a crime. Neither of them ever physically hurt anyone. Some might even say that they were upright citizens. But neither did they ever become a positive part of the world around them. They lived inside their own little clam-shell, holding the rest of the world at bay while they pursued their own personal, money-grubbing interests. They hurt no one but themselves. They maintained the status quo. But that isn't enough. If everyone simply maintained the status quo, humanity would have stagnated and died thousands of years ago. Because you can't merely do something with your life; you have to do something *good*."

He breathed a heavy sigh and gazed at her. As he'd delivered his speech about Melvyn and Louise, he'd watched the expression on her face change from intent listening to discomfort to anger. But he had to follow through. "Tell me, Rebecca, what's your opinion of this couple?"

"I think that their lives have been completely wasted." she said coldly, barely able to control her anger. "But you knew I'd say that, didn't you?"

"How would I know that?"

She pinned him with an icy stare. "Because you've been baiting me, haven't you?"

He played dumb. "Baiting you? How?"

"Do you think I don't know why you told me that story? You told me because you wanted me to apply it to my own life. To look at all this"—she encompassed the room with a wave of her arm—"and ask myself, 'What's the purpose of all these crafts that mother and I have spent thousands of hours doing? Have they really done anyone any good but ourselves? Are they actually nothing more than a self-serving monument built by two women because they are afraid to venture outside and face real life?' Do you think I haven't asked myself these questions a hundred times? But in the end it doesn't help much. I guess that's why mother adopted the Eastern religions. So we could just go on doing nothing...and being nothing."

She reached for an Oreo cookie, pushed it into her mouth, chewed savagely and swallowed, then fol-lowed it down her throat with the last of her cold tea.

"Don't get me wrong," he said. "I think this craft...this craft museum is a marvellous achievement. You and your mother have very talented hands. Not like me—I doubt if I could've made any of these. But in the larger scheme of things your achievement is meaningless and carries little weight because it's hidden away here where only a lucky few, like myself, are allowed to see them. In a way, you're like Melvyn and Louise, only instead of hoarding money you're hoarding crafts."

"And what about you?" she retaliated harshly. "Are you so high and mighty? You came here tonight saying that you needed to write this book not just to try to help other people, but also to help yourself. You obviously don't believe in karma. What's so terrible about your life that you need *others* to help you?"

"My life?" He laughed coldly. "My life probably needs as much help as yours. That's one reason why I'm here: to listen to your input. My father told me many years ago that you should never work at a job you hate, regardless of how much money you're paid, because it will rot your soul. Why would any man in his right mind, he told me, spend forty hours or more a week doing something he hated? Because in the end you only learn to hate yourself. But that's what I've been doing for over ten years, starting with a job as a real estate salesman with my father-in-law's company. And now my job entails writing commercials that try to say something fresh and new about products as dull as sanitary napkins, toilet paper, and toothpaste. In other words, something that will make plenty of money for our accounts. I feel that my life is slipping away while I'm shackled to a meaningless job which I hate and am only doing for the money, and I don't know what to do about it. But I do know one thing—I just haven't acted on it. I know that it's not the *quantity* of what you do that's important. It's the *quality.* You're right, I don't believe in karma. I'm a Christian, if you can still call me that, and as such I believe that you only get one kick at the cat, not two or five or ten. You only have one chance to get it right. I believe that a belief in reincarnation can be used as a convenient excuse to do little or nothing with your present life. Why bother? Why not just relax and sit this one out? After all, there'll be another one coming along after this. I can see, with what you and your mother have gone through, why you were both so attracted to the idea. But for me it just doesn't cut it. For me the only important thing is doing something with my life here and now." He stared at her pointedly. "*Here* and *now*."

She smiled thinly. "Are you trying to convert me?"

"Only if you want to be converted."

"I'll think about what you said." But her limp words told him that she believed that she actually had nothing to think about. "In the end, time will tell which one of us is right, won't it?"

"How do you mean?"

"Well, one day, when we're both gone, we'll both know the true answer, won't we?"

He nodded. "Yes, I suppose we will."

"Unless, of course, the answer is total darkness, and then we'll know absolutely nothing."

"I can't buy that one. I've never believed that nothing is the answer. There's something after this life. I don't know what it is, nobody does, but there's *something*."

"Perhaps." She leaned back comfortably.

He compared her now to the cautious, suspicious, frightened woman he'd met earlier when she opened her door to him. Now she felt that she knew him, and trusted him, and could therefore relax in his presence knowing that he also had problems and felt insecure. This made him feel that he had achieved something worthwhile.

"Tell me one thing," she said finally. "You say you hate your job and are only doing it for the money. If that's the case, then *why* haven't you done something about it? *Why* haven't you quit your job and found something more rewarding?"

"Mainly because I've been a coward," he blurted out, his throat suddenly gorged with feelings straining to escape. "Until now. I've seen the money keep coming in steadily year after year. I've seen all our bills being paid on time every month. I've seen extra money going into savings and reliable investments. In short, I'd seen myself *getting ahead* and had fallen into a convenient rut. And even though I knew that getting ahead in a mercenary North American society meant getting a bigger house, getting a bigger car, getting a bigger TV, getting a bigger computer, whenever a tiny, persistent voice whispered in my ear and told me that life should mean more to a human being, I stifled it and pushed it into the background. And rationalized my behaviour by telling myself again and again that the pleasure given me by all the possessions I kept gaining was worth more than all the misery my lousy job gave me. Until now. Now that tiny, persistent voice has become a big, demanding voice that refuses to let me rest. Because now I see clearly what a load of crap it all is. Now I'm forty, and I see myself standing at the top of a hill looking down at the other side, and the other side of that hill represents the second half of my life. And, I don't know how yet, but *somehow* I've got to make it better than the first half."

As he'd spoken, a warm, knowing smile had curled Rebecca's lips and remained there, the first time he'd actually seen her smile with affection. While growing up, blundering into adulthood, he'd often seen his mother smile at him like this, and although he knew that Rebecca had no children and wasn't even old enough to be his mother, he felt her exercising her motherly instinct now.

"You must do what you must. And if you do, I'm sure you'll find your answer."

"I'd better. Because if I don't I think I might go crazy."

"Nonsense. Would you like another cup of tea?" she asked languidly. "I can easily brew another pot."

He glanced at his watch. "No, thanks. It's almost nine o'clock. I'd better be heading for home."

"As you wish." They rose and she extended her hand. "I didn't think I would, but I've enjoyed meeting you...Rodger."

He squeezed the warm softness of her hand gently. "My pleasure."

"And you will remember to let me see a copy of our interview before you publish it, won't you?"

"Yes, of course."

Driving home, he reflected on the interview. Although it provided material for the book, and he'd probably helped Rebecca by forcing her to bring the horror of her rape into the open, he recalled nothing in the interview which would benefit him in his search for his own identity. She'd suggested quitting his job, something he'd thought about many times over the years but had never had the courage to do. For he knew that in itself simply moving on to another job wouldn't solve his problem. If he merely found another job which he hated, what had he achieved? No, it had to go further than that. Finding another job which he enjoyed would at least be a beginning, but he needed to restructure his entire life to bring new meaning into it.

He pulled the car to the side of the Highway 10 and stopped to reflect, realizing now that he'd only been chasing shadows when he'd asked Ray to arrange a meeting with Rebecca for him. Ray's description of his life with Rebecca should have warned him that nothing pertaining to his own search would be gained by interviewing her. Cautious, rigid Rebecca, afraid of taking hold of life, wanted little more than to work with her crafts, tell her own fortune, cuddle her teddy bears, read her romances, listen to her music, observe nature, and enjoy her Oreo cookies. And hope for some self-fulfilment in a future life.

Rigidity, that's the problem. Yes, rigidity. The inability to be flexible and make worthwhile changes in our lives. We become creatures of habit and remain so even long after those habits have outlived their usefulness and have long since ceased to contribute anything meaningful to our lives, still clinging to obsolete ideas or actions simply because they had worked in the past, and we are too old, too stubborn, too lazy, or simply too deeply rutted in our ways to change them and thereby move our lives onto higher planes.

In an attempt to further explore these thoughts, he searched his mind for experiences with people he had met in the past and found himself recalling how several years ago, between his job at Supreme Real Estate and Drummond, he had taken a manager's job in an Orangeville mall at Peerless Books, a used bookstore, simply because he loved books and enjoyed being around them. Seeing himself as a prospective writer from his early teens, he enjoyed observing the human condition, forming opinions, and attaching labels to actions. As a result, in his capacity as the bookstore manager, he soon learned the idiosyncrasies of his customers, putting faces to them and understanding their shopping habits, distinguishing among the browsers, the one-book five-dollar customers, and those who spent twenty-five dollars or more. He also soon learned the various comments and actions that potential customers made, which quickly became repetitious, and determined from these whether they represented buyers or nonbuyers and categorized them into various types.

The Complimenter. Sometimes a first-time visitor said something like, "My, you certainly have a lot of books here!" Initially, he believed that this statement probably meant a sale, but soon learned that such a preliminary compliment was actually meant to make him feel good about the store and to soften the blow when the person left empty-handed. Usually no sale.

The Hurrier. "I'll have to come back when I have more time," a favourite exit line, also meant that the person rarely seemed to find the "more time" necessary. Rarely a future sale.

The Vanisher. This timid type would browse for a half hour, making no selections, apparently afraid to leave without a purchase because they felt that you were watching them, but if you became distracted by a phone call or another customer and looked for them later, you suddenly found that they had silently and surreptitiously vanished. No sale.

The One-booker. This type entered looking for a specific book, and after you informed them that you didn't have it and offered to place the information on the store's want list and phone if the book arrived, they either accepted or rejected the offer, then said that they'd browse for awhile. But their browse proved to be only a superficial, token one and they left a few minutes later. No sale.

The Read-it. This type said that they were looking for books by certain authors, but never divulged the specific titles, and whenever you showed them something they always said, "Read it,"the perfect, indisputable reason for not buying. No sale, unless you can find something, *anything*, that they haven't already read.

The Dissatisfied. This type, usually arriving alone, asked for several specific titles by several specific authors, which you sometimes supplied, but kept rejecting them for various reasons—the book was too long, too short, too sexy, too gory, too badly written, etc., etc.,—and whose primary purpose for coming to the store seemed to be to assert themselves by having you obey their orders. Or perhaps giving themselves some badly needed attention. No sale.

The No-cashers. This type entered with bags or boxes of books to trade and, anticipating a certain credit amount, selected four or five books, but when they approached the counter found that their credit would only purchase two books. They then selected the two they most wanted, returned the others to the shelves, and placed their remaining credit on file. Some No-cashers were simply strap-ped for cash, but others lived by the philosophy that you must never ever give cash to a used book dealer.

The Resister. Rodger enjoyed observing the type who walked around the store with their hands either clasped behind their backs, thrust deeply and firmly into their pockets, or with their arms folded tightly across their chests. Sometimes they even bent forward and read titles in these positions. He had the impression that they were telling themselves, "As long as my hands stay where they are, I can't pick up a book, and if I can't pick up a book, I can't buy a book." But once this type spied something truly interesting, the hands often did free themselves and the person actually did pick up a book and study it. The chances of selling anything to this type of customer were about fifty-fifty.

The Tagalong. This type entered as half of a couple—either boyfriend/girlfriend or husband/wife—one a reader, the other a nonreader, with the tagalong being quickly revealed as the nonreader. Bored, the tagalong wandered aimlessly around the store, opening a coffee table book here and there and flipping idly through a few pages, the illustrations worth nothing more than cursory glances, impatient to be elsewhere. Others, even more impatient, followed closely behind their mates, making them uncomfortable while urging them to hurry up, often forcing them (especially women) to leave prematurely. Rodger would have liked to approach the tagalong and say gently, "Why not go to the mall restaurant and have a coffee and a doughnut while the lady finishes shopping." But of course you just didn't do that in business, and if the tagalong reported him to the store owner he'd probably be fired.

The Jumped-off-the-shelfer. This type represented one of Rodger's favourites. They sometimes spent as much as a half hour browsing before approaching the counter and saying something like, "Well, I guess I'll have to come back another time. Nothing jumped off the shelf for me today."

One morning, as Rodger opened the store, he noticed a pocketbook lying on the floor and immediately said to himself, "That book actually *did* jump off the shelf," but soon had to retract the thought. After all, how could a book, with no legs, jump anywhere? And even if it had succeeded in wiggling itself off the shelf to escape the ignominy of having every one of its pages fingered again by another reader, where could it possibly go? With no legs, how could it run? With no arms, how could it even drag itself away? And with no head, how could it possibly see where it was going? Still, Rodger felt a mischievous idea blossoming in his mind. He knew the faces of a few Jumped-off-the-shelfers and one afternoon one of them named Jack appeared, a short, rotund, bald man with a cheerful disposition who walked directly to the thriller department at the back of the store. Quickly, Rodger moved to the thriller department in the new arrivals section at the front of the store, removed a Robert Ludlum novel from the shelf and placed it front cover down on the floor. When Jack inevitably said, "Well, I guess I'll need to come back another time. Nothing jumped off the shelf for me today," and started edging toward the front door, Rodger said, "Just a minute, Jack. I think something *did* jump off the shelf for you today," and pointed toward the book on the floor. "Take a look."

When Jack looked, he said, "Well, I'll be damned," and went and picked up the book, studied the cover for a few seconds, then brought it to the counter.

For a few moments, Rodger couldn't breathe. Was it possible? Could this possibly be his very *first* Jumped-off-the-shelfer sale?

But Jack simply patted the book and said, "I'll let you put it back in its proper place. Sorry, I've already read it."

The Group. These were usually a male-female carload of four to six, of which about half were nonreaders. They were generally a garrulous, cheerful bunch, but most of their conversation dwelt on subjects other than books and their main purpose for entering the store appeared to be simply to stretch their legs after a long drive. Sales averaged about one book per group and sales of several books were rare.

The Talker. Although this type sometimes bought books, they were generally more interested in carrying on conversations with Rodger. They talked about their reading tastes, their jobs, their ambitions, their health or the health of others, their families, their political opinions, their pets, and a variety of other subjects, making Rodger feel like the proverbial bartender who gave a sympathetic ear to the woes of his customers who believed that anything they divulged would go no further. Rodger treated his customers the same, respecting their privacy, and on the few occasions when he did mention a customer it was always anonymously. He found the conversation of many of his customers intelligent, interesting, and stimulating, and at times had to force himself to end them and return to his work. Others he found boring because they were locked in on their favourite subject—them-selves—and couldn't stand back far enough to dim their egotism and see a broader spectrum. These he gave little time to, knowing that nothing more could be expected from them. Oddly enough, the elderly, those he expected to complain the most about health problems like diabetes, arthritis, heart conditions, hypertension, hip or knee replacements, back problems, cancer, and other ailments common to aging bodies, appeared to complain the least, and on the rare occasion when one did, he listened intently and sympathetically.

Now, as he searched his mind for a role model, he remembered other customers, particularly a thin, hollow-cheeked woman in her sixties with a collapsed left temple who took the opportunity to unburden herself as she paid for a few paperbacks. As though she had recently lost weight but hadn't bother having it altered, her black, high-necked dress hung loosely on her stick-thin body.

"See this," she said proudly, pointing to her collapsed left temple. "This is because of a brain aneurysm they found two years ago. They had to operate. But before they did I promised God that if I survived I'd dedicate the rest of my life to doing His work. And

I've done exactly that. *Exactly* that. I help out at the Avalon. I help out at Headwaters. I help out at my church. I'm *always* helping out, doing God's work. But it's not easy, because nobody else wants to help out Nobody's interested. I make fifty phone calls asking for help and get one volunteer. *One volunteer!* I get so tired, because nobody wants to help out and I have to do everything myself. But I don't mind. I'm doing it all for God because I made a promise. And I'll keep my promise. But nobody wants to help. Nobody."

After she had left, Rodger sympathized with her, but now he felt differently and asked himself this question: What charitable works had *she* done before her operation? Apparently she had given no more of herself to others than forty-nine of the fifty people she had phoned to volunteer. And now, after she had changed, and only under the threat of death, she resented others who hadn't changed *because their lives hadn't yet reached a crisis.* Although these forty-nine now presented her with a carbon copy of her former self, she failed to see or concede the connection.

Bragging about your charity cheapened and degraded it. Would it not have been better if this woman had remained silent instead of openly displaying her pride? Ah, how eloquent that silence would have been! When we complain about others (and we only complain about others when we *are different from them*), we show our own lack of charity toward them. Would it not have been far better if this woman had remained silent instead of openly displaying her rancour toward others? Ah, how eloquent *that* silence would have been! Charitable acts should be done for charity's own sake, not to aggrandize the giver. If the only reason people perform charitable acts is to brag about them to anyone who will listen, perhaps the only reason for their charity is to feed their own pride when they are complimented by others.

Rodger felt a self-disparaging laugh rising in his throat as he shone the charity spotlight upon him-self. How can I possibly be so pompous when I can't even remember the last time I performed a completely selfless charitable act? The only two people who benefit from my so-called charity are Claudia and myself, with every act tainted by my own selfishness. I give to myself only to please myself; I give to Claudia, even though I love her, with the expectation of gaining something in return. As for supporting registered charities, both of us want to preserve our money and regularly relegate mailed charity requests to the paper shredder.

He recalled with pleasure one incident at Peerless Books which actually made him feel that, in spite of his habitual selfishness, he still had some hope of some day becoming a moral human being. Estelle, a fellow merchant, owned a children's clothing store in the mall. One Monday morning, while on his way to the mall washroom to draw water for his coffee, he noticed a handwritten notice taped to her locked door during business hours, which he found himself reading. It stated that she would be closed for the day because of a doctor's appointment. Knowing that doctors' appointments didn't take all day and that Estelle was known to enjoy her Sunday liquor, even sometimes sneaking a few drinks on the job, Rodger immediately assumed that she had stayed home to nurse a severe hangover. Was it simple curiosity, or because he wanted to have a reason to condemn her for being closed during business hours? He had to admit that even as he started walking toward the notice he was already thinking, "Well, what's her flimsy excuse *this* time?" and his discovering what the sign read was only meant to feed this critical attitude. He had no proof, and simply fastened on the worst scenario instead of believing the notice. Afterwards, he chided himself for his arrogance and lack of humility

When the same situation developed a few weeks later, he felt tempted to read the notice to discover the reason for her closing and started toward it, then stopped and asked himself *why* he wanted to read the notice. And when the answer came back that he wanted nothing more than to feed his own arrogance, he walked past. By refusing to read the notice, he could no longer honestly believe that Estelle had a poor excuse for closing her store because he had no idea what the notice read, which left him with no honest reason to criticize her. Not knowing the notice's contents, he became able to believe that she had a perfectly acceptable reason for being absent.

Although this incident represented one of the few times when he managed to control his negative reactions to other people's foibles, it did provide him with some encouragement regarding his self-improvement. But that encouragement soon died in the womb when he reverted to his old, negative attitude. Now, however, as he sat in his car at the side of Highway 10, he realized the moral fallacy behind doing things merely because we felt like doing them, or because they made us feel better by propping up our own egos. Instead, we had to continually keep asking ourselves *why* we are doing what we do, and *how* these actions are improving ourselves as human beings. When we have a choice between filling our minds with negative thoughts about a fellow human being, or maintaining our respect for that human being, the correct choice is crystal clear. He realized that many of our negative opinions of others stemmed from our superficial judgment of them. He recalled a novelist who occasionally came into the bookstore always searching for hardcover novels in mint condition. This search had become so obsessive that even a tiny tear in a dust jacket was enough to deter him from buying. At times Rodger felt a strong, mischievous urge to pass him a magnifying glass to aid him in his inspections. Although none of the books he inspected was valuable, this novelist appeared far more interested in the superficial *appearance* of a book rather than in the literary quality of what it actually *contained*. Rodger realized that many of us mistakenly looked at people in the same way. We made decisions and judgments about them from such trivialities as the length of their hair, whether or not they wore beards, their facial handsomeness or beauty, the clothing they wore, instead of talking to them to discover the true, interior person.

From a need to feel superior, he had often weakened and done the same, even though he knew in the depths of his being that no amount of expensive clothing, expensive jewellery, or expensive perfume can mask the stench of a rancourous heart, and no amount of cheap clothing, cheap jewellery, or cheap perfume can mask the fragrance of a generous heart.

He had seen this superficiality acted out repeatedly by some of those who entered the bookstore. When the used clothing store next door was going out of business and had placed a large sign reading "CLOSING SALE" in their front window, over the next few weeks about thirty people entered the bookstore and asked,

"Are you going out of business?" Yet each of the two stores had its own store sign above its front window clearly indicating its own identity. Several times over the months he managed the store, he had seen customers examine shelf after shelf of books containing personalized white price stickers which clearly read "PEERLESS BOOKS," yet approached the counter and asked, "Are these your prices?" Had they not read the store's name on the white price stickers?

Before the plaza was converted into a mall, the double-door entrance into the plaza opened into a hallway which housed a single-door entrance into the bookstore. When the plaza became a mall, a mall entrance was built further along the front of the main building and the old plaza entrance opened directly into the bookstore. Large red letters over a foot high spelling out "MALL ENTRANCE" were fastened to the masonry above the entrance. Yet years later, when Rodger managed the store, people still mistook the bookstore entrance for the mall entrance several times a week because they failed to read the mall entrance sign.

Rodger realized that this same superficiality also extended into other aspects of our lives. Our eyes are open, but in our haste to move on with our everyday activities we fail to see beyond the surface of the life or objects which surround us, just as he for ten years had been content with his marriage, accepting it superficially without ever bothering to delve beneath its surface to unearth its problems. Until recently.

While employed at Peerless Books, one incident happened which he knew he'd remember for the rest of his life. Even if he lived to be a hundred, and suffered from advanced Alzheimer's disease, he knew that this incident would still cling tenaciously to his memory, rearing its ugly head again and again in total detail. One evening, Claudia had prepared a feast of her famous chili con carne for dinner, complete with about seven varieties of beans which included generous amounts of infamous garbanzo beans. On the following day at the bookstore, he felt increasing cramps in his belly as the chili con carne produced a growing flatulence which bloated his intestines with their malodorous gases. Occasionally, he'd look up from his book to see if any customers were present, and seeing no one would rise and gently squeeze out a tiny fart which exited his anus with a gentle *phhht!*, then waved his hand frantically at the seat of his slacks to disperse the swampish odour before another customer arrived only to be driven away in disgust. But by afternoon he could stand it no longer. The cramps were becoming severe, agonizing, and when he ran his hand over his belly it felt like a watermelon, as though he were about six month's pregnant, and the occasional *phhht!* did little to ease his agony as this gigantic fart grew rampantly inside him.

As his belly pain deepened, an elderly woman with a hooked nose approached the counter to pay for a few paperbacks. Almost dancing in pain, he bagged her books and made change hurriedly, but she began to chatter about her health problems, her arthritis, her lumbago, and finally he had to say, as though he'd just remembered, "Sorry, I've got to leave. I've got an emergency." No lie there—he had to rid himself of this horrendous flatulence before his belly exploded.

After she left, he glanced around the store and saw no one, grabbed a can of Air Wick, rushed to the front door and stared out across the parking lot to see if any customers were approaching. None. He placed the Air Wick on a handy shelf and locked the door to be safe, reasoning that if someone did approach while he relieved himself he could stall them long enough to drench the area in lavender Air Wick before allowing anyone to enter.

Awed, he gazed down at his voluminous belly which seemed to be growing larger by the minute and realized solemnly that this monstrosity which was about to erupt from his rectum would be no ordinary, miniscule blip on the fart metre. Oh no, this fart would be the fart of all farts. The Vapour of Viciousness. The Prince of Putridity. The Supreme Sketcher. The Rump Router. The Posterior Punisher. The Rectum Ravager. The Seam Splitter. The Anus Anaesthetizer. The Blue Ribbon Special. The Absolute Assifier. The Reek of the Century. The *Guinness Book of World Records* Fart. History would be made here today. This would become a day to remember in fart infamy. He could see it all now: King Fart Day would be declared, with a Farting Contest as the main event. The evening before, contestants would be allowed to eat as much of Claudia's chili con carne as they could hold, and as each felt the urge at the contest, the performance would be timed for length and recorded on a meter for decibels. And the award to the champion?—a plump, golden ass trophy.

But now he had to ease his own agony. Are you ready to rumble! Give me a drum roll! To remove any fleshy resistance, he spread his buttocks and drove his entire energy toward his rectum. Here it comes!

B-R-R-R-R-R-R-R-R-R-R-R-R-R-R-R-R-R-R-R-R-UP-UP-UP-UP-UP-UP-UP! Bring on the br-ass band! What an incredible stench! His face paled from the noxious, dizzying vapours as his fingers groped for his nose, finally found it, and hung on tightly. Good God, where was he? Had he stumbled into the Okeefenokee Swamp? Was that Pogo over there lying under a tree? Staggering, barely able to see through his watering eyes, he clawed blindly for the Air Wick, finally found it and sprayed wildly, staring out anxiously at the parking lot for incoming customers, saturating the area as he reeled to the door and unlocked it, stepping, he thought, into the pure air sanctuary of the small foyer, but his merely opening the door had sucked some of the swampish odour into the foyer. He sprayed again, wildly, turning back toward the inside of the store, and suddenly he stopped spraying and stood frozen to the spot, his arm raised like the Statue of Liberty holding a can of Air Wick, for inside the store only ten feet away he saw a balding man, who had apparently been there all along, crouching with an open book in his hands and staring at him, eyes wide, his thick lips still gaping open in astonishment. Rodger felt an urge to leave but knew that he had to go back inside. After all, somebody had to run the store. Entering, he placed the Air Wick on a shelf and, making the motion of dusting off his hands, said the first foolish words that came into his mind: "Well, that takes care of *that*."

But as he drew closer and stood over the balding man, Rodger saw him actually *cringing*, not, he suddenly realized, from the power of Rodger's mere presence but from the absolute stenching power of the enormous fart he could deliver. He'd heard of Gray Power, Women Power, Manpower, even Horsepower, but he possessed the ultimate weapon—FART POWER—and the balding man cringing beside him must have feared that another swampish explosion was about to be delivered.

Still shocked into silence, the balding man merely gave a short, fearful nod.

Rodger demanded, "What are you doing here?"

The balding man finally closed his mouth and fumbled awkwardly with the book in his trembling hands, finally dropping it before returning it clumsily to the shelf. "I…I was just looking for a gardening book."

"You're too short," Rodger accused. "I couldn't see your head above the display. I thought the store was empty."

"I was down here, that's why." The balding man rose to prove that he actually was taller than the display.

"Well, you should've been standing, that's all," Rodger said, adding proudly, "Do you see the trouble you got yourself into?" He picked up the Air Wick, gave a flamboyant wave, and said, "Okay, carry on," and returned to the counter.

As Rodger watched, the head disappeared again and never reappeared until he heard the back door click shut and momentarily saw the balding man on the other side of it, staring fearfully inside for a moment before scurrying away. Never to return.

He soon met Gretchen Corbett, an elderly British widow who owned and operated a collectibles store called The Past Is Present in the mall which dealt mainly in used collectibles and antiques. Since she no longer drove, and her latest driver had recently quit her job in the mall, she approached him to ask if he could become her new driver. When he found that she lived right in Orangeville, he agreed, and wanted no payment, but she insisted on keeping the drives on a businesslike basis and they finally agreed on five dollars for each round trip.

Although from listening to her stories from the past he estimated that she had to be at least in her early eighties, she clung tenaciously to projecting at least a semblance of still being youthful, vigorous, and healthy. Vain about her appearance and concerned about how her advanced age affected it, she tried to belie her actual age by wearing heavy makeup in an attempt to fill in the cracks and wrinkles of her face and neck; all year round, she wore nothing but slacks and long-sleeved blouses, ostensibly to cover the unsightliness of aging arms and legs. Yet in other ways her appearance presented a paradox by maintaining old fashioned ideas. Rain or shine, she always carried an umbrella, and never ventured out bareheaded, wearing various wide-brimmed sun hats during the warmer months, cloches during the fall and winter.

This vanity also revealed itself when she told Rodger about going to vote at the advanced poll on the second floor of a building on Zina Street, complaining that the stairs were very steep, yet when asked if she preferred to use the chairlift she replied stoutly, "I'm not 102, and I certainly don't need a chairlift! I'm quite capable of using the stairs, thank you very much!" And when asked again when coming down, she snapped, "I'd rather fall than use that chairlift!"

Gretchen's vanity, combined with her belief that elderly people had to be right about everything simply because of their longevity, sometimes forced her to cling stubbornly to even the most foolish statements. One morning, after a heavy overnight rain, as he parked at the Orangeville Mall to mail a few books at the post office, she complained about the puddles in the parking lot, saying that the mall should have sewers to drain away the water and prevent people from getting their feet wet. People like herself. For Rodger had noted when she entered the car that she wore only canvas summer shoes, and now, instead of graciously admitting that she'd made a mistake, she tried to turn defence into attack by blaming the mall and making a silly statement. When he mentioned that it would be a horrendous, unnecessary expense to install a sewer system in a large parking lot, and asked her if she knew of any such parking lots in Orangeville, she staunchly replied, "Certainly. They're all over Orangeville. All over the world. Don't you know that?"

"No, I don't, because I've never seen one. Can you tell me which parking lot in Orangeville has sewers, because I'd like to have a look at it."

"Oh, I can't remember right now, but they're there. All over the place." And she added stubbornly, "I guess there's no sense in trying to tell *you* anything because you obviously know it all."

That ended that discussion, because although Rodger and Gretchen both knew that she had only been trying to rationalize her own mistakes, Rodger also knew the absolute futility of trying to break down her stone wall of vanity and force her to admit the truth.

Over time, such incidents multiplied. One morning, when an A&P cashier informed her that she could get "cash back" if she paid for her groceries with a bank card and wouldn't be charged a bank machine fee, she returned excitedly to the car to tell him the news, but on reflection added, "I'll have to think on that." He'd heard her use that statement before and it had always meant that she'd do nothing differently.

"I always pay cash for everything," she once said proudly.

"Everything?"

"Yes, of course. Young people today don't know what that means. They think nothing of buying everything on credit, and before they know it they're in debt above their heads."

"Do you mean to tell me that if you went into Wal-Mart to buy a hundred-dollar microwave oven you'd pay for it in cash instead of using your bank card?"

"Yes, of course."

"But your bank card is the same as cash."

"No, it isn't. I need the cash in my hand. I've always done it that way."

Rodger had the feeling that he was cautiously leading her toward a corner. "And do you mean to tell me that if you went into Zellers to buy a new TV for five hundred dollars you'd still pay cash."

"Yes." She began to sound doubtful. "Yes, I would."

"And let's say you were going to a car dealer to buy a car for five thousand dollars, would you still pay cash?"

"I've no intention of buying a car," she hedged. "I don't drive any more."

"But if you did, would you still pay cash?"

"Yes," she said loudly. "I certainly would."

Even backed into a corner, she still refused to relent, still stubbornly attempted to save face regardless of how ridiculous she appeared.

"Do you mean to tell me," he said, "that you'd go to the Royal Bank, withdraw five thousand dollars, walk along Broadway with all that cash, and take a chance that someone who's followed you out of the bank won't snatch your purse?"

"Of course I would," she insisted. "You're just being silly. No one is going to steal my purse. This is Orangeville, not Toronto."

"There are desperate people everywhere, not just in Toronto. And women your age are perfect targets for purse snatchers. You'd be taking a chance of losing your money."

"No, I wouldn't. I'd be perfectly safe. Besides, I'd never be carrying that kind of money anyway because I no longer drive and I'd never be buying a new car."

And that ended *that* discussion.

Once, when she was a bit late for her drive home after they had closed their stores, she said, "That man delayed me because I had to wait for him to bring my dolly back."

"What man?"

"The man in the dollar store."

"His name is George."

"I knew that," she snapped.

"But you called him 'that man.'"

She reflected for a few seconds, then said, "I just thought you might not know who I was talking about."

Yet she constantly referred to other merchants or workers in the mall by their first names, leading him to believe that she actually didn't know George's name and only pretended that she did to save face.

During their drives together, he soon learned that Gretchen's stiff-necked, old-fashioned opinions also extended to her customers, where she practised a "my way or the highway" philosophy. She had operated for many years in local flea markets and had only decided to move her operation into a mall when these flea markets closed down because sales dropped off drastically when competition from Sunday shopping and dollar stores became too great.

He also learned that Gretchen had persisted for a few years with her own weekend flea market at the back of the mall until the mall owner informed her that she'd have to open at least five days a week because it hurt the mall's image for a business to be closed on weekdays. She then decided to end her relationships with the flea marketers she was renting space to and move into a vacant store at the front of the mall, which she opened weekly from Tuesday to Saturday.

Her crowded store offered a wide variety of collectibles including glassware, chinaware, silverware, kitchenware, small appliances, paintings, lamps, books, drapery, and furniture, with some stock on consignment. The items were tastefully displayed, and each morning several were placed in the mall hallway outside her door to attract customers.

Under normal conditions, Gretchen could have done a fair business, at least enough to pay the bills and have a little left over for herself. Unfortunately, when she moved from flea market to store, she brought the flea market mentality with her and failed to modernize her method of doing business with the public.

In connection with her business, she suffered from tunnel vision. Old herself, she always thought in terms of old people, and spoke as though old people were the only ones left on earth. It never seemed to occur to her that there were any other age groups in the world—infants, children, teenagers, adolescents, young people, middle-aged people—and that some of these groups could be potential customers for her store if she only made the proper concessions to attract them. She repeatedly spoke about the few "little old ladies" who were her remaining customers as though she, at over eighty, was a distinct breed from them, and complained regularly that her little old ladies were being inconvenienced, discriminated against, and alienated because of various changes in the mall, when actually she was simply looking for scapegoats for her own lack of business expertise.

Rigidity.

She had always operated a certain way, and continued to attempt to do so. She had no phone in her store, again the flea market mentality, which precluded potential customers from contacting her by this method. Although she gave out her unlisted home phone number to a select few, this did precious little to expand her business because it depended on those few telling a few others. Although North Americans were rapidly becoming a cashless society, many carrying little more than coffee money, Gretchen still accepted no credit or debit cards, only cash, or cheques from a few of her known customers. As a result, most of her customers were old fashioned and elderly, like herself. When younger people came to her door with purses or wallets containing little more than credit or debit cards, perhaps thinking that they might find something interesting inside, and saw no Visa or Mastercard or American Express or Interac decals on window display, they simply passed her by. And would continue to do so because, instead of recognizing and serving the public's needs, she was dictating to them by telling them *how* they should spend their money.

She had no store hours displayed. Her flea market sign had read "OPEN SATURDAYS AND SUNDAYS"; now, her doors simply read "CLOSED SUNDAYS AND MONDAYS." This meant that any new person coming to her store on a closed day would know the closed hours but not the opened hours, and with no phone number in sight they couldn't even contact the store on one of the opened days. When Rodger mentioned her lack of store hour signs, and even offered to print a few to her specifications, she simply said, "I'll have to think about that," which, he knew from past experience, meant that she intended to do nothing.

In short, she was doing almost everything possible to *repel* customers and nothing to *attract* them.

She clutched at the flimsiest excuses to rationalize her business failure, blaming other mall stores for stealing her customers by selling similar merchandise. When angered, she could be hypocritical. Until Rodger told her that he no longer wanted to hear her complaints, she badmouthed Christine, her major competitor, an elderly woman who owned a mall store which specialized in antiques, mainly jewellery, glassware, china, and collectors' plates, and whom she hadn't spoken to for years because of a bitter argument they'd once had. Yet when she discovered that Christine would be going out of business to retire, she suddenly befriended her again and spoke to her in the sweetest tones imaginable. Once she even complained that two blank signs above her front window, from a previously closed store, were making people believe that she had gone out of business, while her own store sign remained displayed directly above her front door, and when she later moved to a smaller store with its entrance inside the mall, she blamed her poor business on her lack of a parking lot entrance. Another time, when he mentioned that the only difference between her business now and when she ran a flea market was that now she opened five days a week instead of two, and suggested that if she would modernize her business by installing a phone and setting up credit and debit card accounts with banks, she would broaden her customer base and thereby improve her business, she lamely replied, "Yes, I guess I should do that." Not "will," but "guess" and "should." To Rodger, this meant that she intended to do nothing and he never mentioned it again.

Rigidity.

How many once high-flying companies who refused to see and act upon changes in merchandising had been forced to close their doors or sell out when Wal-Mart came along? Gretchen had become one of these: a retailing dinosaur.

When Rodger looked into other aspects of her life, he began to realize that Gretchen's rigid attitude toward business was merely a logical projection of her actual inveterate self. She carried an umbrella in her bag every day, even when the sun shone brightly in a clear blue sky and The Weather Network reported a zero percent chance of precipitation, even carrying it with her when she went into A&P to shop or into her doctor's office for an appointment. In the beginning, he propounded theories to explain why she carried her umbrella every day. He thought perhaps, since she used facial cosmetics heavily in an attempt to hide her age, that she might be trying to protect her makeup from the rain. Then why bring the umbrella on a sunny day? He next thought that she might be bringing the umbrella to protect her face from the sun. Yet she never actually used the umbrella on a sunny day. In the end, he had to admit that she carried the umbrella *every* day for only one reason: it had simply become an ingrained, illogical habit.

Rigidity.

On Tuesday and Thursday mornings, before driving to their stores, he stopped at the Orangeville Mall so that he could mail books to Internet customers and also allow Gretchen to shop at A&P and, if needed, extract some cash from their money machine. Over time, he soon noticed that she rarely bought any food other than fresh fruit, potato chips, and the odd loaf of bread, and the beverages consisted mainly of cartons of Minute Maid orange juice and huge jugs of bottled water, since she refused to drink tap water. Other than that, her main purchases consisted of paper goods: Kleenex, paper towels, and toilet tissue. Two boxes of Kleenex and a two-roll package of paper towels were purchased virtually every Tuesday and Thursday.

Rodger knew that some people, especially old people, sometimes stockpiled consumable items as a kind of security blanket against leaner days, hoarding them far beyond reason, and although he had never been inside Gretchen's home, he was convinced that somewhere, in a closet, pantry, linen cupboard, or spare room, or even all four, boxes of Kleenex and packages of paper towels and toilet tissue were piled high. And her rigidity, not common sense, forced her to continue hoarding these items.

He realized that these suspicions were only assumptions on his part, but where else could all these paper goods have gone? He also knew that we lived in a suspicious world, and that even he sometimes became ensnared by that suspicion. He recalled having once mailed a $150.00 book which the bookstore had sold on the Alibris website to a New York state customer. When future Alibris statements failed to show that the book had been delivered, he became suspicious. Shipped as a traceable Expedited Parcel, the $150.00 book value had been clearly stated on the label fastened to the parcel. Could the young, underpaid clerk at the sub post office, realizing this, have stolen the book with a view to selling it on E-bay? During further visits to the sub post office to mail other books, he searched her face while she dealt with him for some nervous movement that would convince him of her guilt, but saw nothing. After he had decided to question her on his next trip to the sub post office, the bookstore's next cheque arrived from Alibris and the statement showed that part of the payment was for the $150.00 book. Then he felt guilty, and heard again the words his mother had spoken so often: "You need to trust people more."

Gretchen also expressed her rigidity in her clothing. Rodger kept track and observed that she wore exactly the same outfit for six weeks running: tan slacks, a multicoloured, threadbare tunic of brown, orange, and black stripes, brown hat, brown purse. She then changed to her blue outfit, which she wore for the next six weeks: light blue slacks, a multicoloured, threadbare tunic of blue, red, and black stripes, blue hat, blue purse. The cycle was then repeated. He assumed that she laundered her outfits weekly on her days off, and that she changed her underwear regularly for he never detected any body odour, but because of her rigid clothing habits, combined with all her other rigid personal habits, he could clearly see how this overall rigidity had overflowed into her business habits and thereby insured her business failure.Like many elderly people, Gretchen never grew tired of talking about "the old days" and expounding on how much better they were than today. After all, when we see the road before us growing very short, it's more pleasant to reflect on times when that road still stretched out far before us. To dwell on the present brings death far too close for comfort.

After Halloween, she complained that her store window, among others of the mall, had again been pelted with eggs which had dried and become difficult to remove. She said that she would now turn her front window lights off every night, claiming that this would avoid any future attacks. Poor logic, Rodger thought, since the mall was located in a fairly isolated area just west of Orangeville and her dark window might invite break-ins. Her comment about the eggs quickly became a negative complaint about how in the old days women baked all sorts of goodies for the children on Halloween, but today you couldn't do that because the children's parents threw them out for fear that they contained razor blades or sewing needles or poison because there were so many evil people around today. "Not like the old days."

One day in the mall parking lot, she pointed out a van and said, "Oh, there's George's car." When he explained that it was a van, not a car, she snapped, "I know the difference between a van and a car. I call anything with four wheels a car." He assumed then that she'd call a wagon or a carriage or a truck a car, but said nothing. Not like the old days, when there were no vans around.

One evening, while driving Gretchen home on Highway 10, he saw a pickup ahead of them pulling a box trailer with the same name on it (Peerless) as the mall bookstore he managed but belonging to a car dealer, and mentioned it to her. Instead of commenting on the coincidence, she immediately asked for the location of the trailer licence plate.

"It's at the top of the box on the left side," he told her.

"But you can't read it because it's all muddy," she complained. "And there should be a light above it—where's the light?"

He noticed the light socket just above the licence plate. Apparently the bulb had burnt out, but he said nothing, knowing that to disagree with Gretchen was a total waste of breath.

"The plate should be at the bottom of the trailer," she insisted. "There's no reason for it to be way up there. In the old days, this wouldn't be allowed to happen, but today nobody cares about anything."

He became so *sick* of hearing about "the old days."

Instead of allowing others to simply be themselves, her tunnel vision forced her to want them to conform to her own image. When we discussed a new merchant recently moving in, she commented that he should have pretty, flowery drapes covering his windows while setting up his business which he could later open to display his merchandise, instead of the bed sheets he presently used. She lived in a world within herself, trapped inside the Gretchen box, expecting a *man* to put up pretty drapes just as she had done with her own store, ostensibly to make it look more like a home than a store, when in a few days or weeks he intended to exercise his own manly desire by pulling down the bed sheets and maintaining bare windows.

From his late teens, Rodger had affirmed that the most ignorant and stagnant people in the world were those who believed that
they already knew everything, and thus felt that they had nothing
more to learn. And if people believed that they had nothing more
to learn, and lived that belief, they remained ignorant and their
lives stagnated. Likewise, the sixteen-year-old son who gleans his
"knowledge" of life from buddies his own age soon begins to believe that this erroneous, immature information actually contains
all the important elements of life. He knows it all, and his parents,
poor fools, know nothing and can therefore teach him nothing. It
is only when he leaves the nest and strikes out on his own that he
begins to realize how pathetically inadequate his knowledge actually is. Similarly, elderly people often return to this stage, believing that their longevity alone automatically makes them wiser and
more knowledgeable than anyone younger than themselves. After
all, reasoned Gretchen, if she were in her eighties and you were
only in your thirties, she certainly had to know more than you on
the mere strength of having lived about fifty years longer than you,
and had to try to prove it at every opportunity, even when it meant
something as trivial as simply knowing a person's name. But Rodger knew that this was not necessarily true. Merely growing old
doesn't mean that wisdom will automatically accrue to a person
and drop into that person's lap. People who spend their lives living
in repetitious, trivial, senseless ruts will not become wise even if
they live to be a hundred. Wisdom and increasing knowledge over
the years can only come to those who continue to grow by actively
seeking that wisdom and knowledge. Therefore, elderly people
who have frittered away their lives in pointless frivolity are in many
respects no wiser than the sixteen-year-old, regardless of how stiff-
necked and insistent their opinions are.

Rodger thought, is this what growing old actually means?
Living in the past and having a stiff-necked, opinionated attitude
toward everything and everybody? Seeing life slipping away while
still clinging to early beliefs no matter how erroneous or silly they
now are? And eventually, perhaps, caving in and losing everything
when Alzheimer's appears and you can no longer remember who
you are, or where you are, or what day it is, or who your visitors are?

Providing I live long enough, is that all *I* have to look forward to? Losing everything? And if that's the case, doesn't that make it even more critical that I do something worthwhile with my life? *Now!*

And, worst of all, until my present awakening hadn't I become like Gretchen in some respects, for what have I actually achieved of any lasting importance through ten years of marriage?

He knew that there were three kinds of habits. There were good habits, like acquiring a decent education, like maintaining a job to support yourself and your family, like being punctual and reliable, like maintaining a healthy body by exercise and proper diet; there were bad habits, like drinking, smoking, gossiping, overeating, over-sexing, adultery, cruelty, rigidity, and violent behaviour.

And poor habits we seem totally unaware of. One morning, when he dropped into McDonald's for a coffee, he glanced around and saw a fat mother eating at a table with her three children: two boys aged about ten and twelve, and a girl aged about eight, all of which were already becoming paunchy. All were having breakfasts of Big Macs, fries, and cokes. He looked at the three children and saw that they were all chewing with their mouths wide open and wondered where they had all acquired this bad eating habit. Then he looked at the mother and saw her biting off large chunks of her Big Mac and chewing in the same way, quickly sending one load after another into her stomach. Were the children simply copying the mother, or were they all blindly copying the absent father? How long had this been going on? For how many generations, with no one apparently even realizing that they had a poor eating habit which many people found distasteful.

Many of us fail to, or refuse to, see the humps on our own backs. One morning, while buying a TV component in an electronics store in the Orangeville Mall, Rodger heard a salesgirl, while attending to a customer, loudly ridiculing an acquaintance who was apparently obsessed with playing a certain video game. Yet this same salesgirl blithely overlooked her own obsession, clearly eating, for she appeared to be at least fifty pounds overweight. And then there were the seemingly innocuous habits, like watching television, playing games, carrying an unnecessary umbrella, talking idly on the phone, and reading trashy novels.

On the surface, these innocuous habits seemed harmless enough, and they were when indulged in moderately, but when such habits began to absorb large portions of our leisure time they also began to diminish the amount of time that remained for serious, inner thought and productive action. How much time remained for building the ethical human being? So many people believed that merely staying out of trouble, regardless of how we lived, was all we had to do in this world. Something Thomas Merton wrote in *Seeds of Contemplation,* which he read many years ago, came into his mind: "To avoid sin and practise virtue is not to be a saint, it is only to be a man, a human being."

In all his ten years of marriage, how much time had he actually spent examining and critiquing his own way of life, his own rigidity? Precious little. His pathetic attempt at writing a meaningful novel had required only a minuscule amount of time. For the rest, he had merely pissed it away writing infantile, inane commercials for twelve-year-old mentalities, or lounging before the TV watching baseball or basketball games, or being the passive yes man for Claudia's materialistic ideas. Even the sex, which continued to be superb, had produced nothing lasting. No children, by Claudia's request. Her chronic habit of taking birth control pills insured that.

But now, at forty, looking downward from the far side of the mountain, he had begun to dismantle his rigidity and, hopefully, would be able to reassemble it into something meaningful and worthwhile.

6

By Friday, Rodger began to feel anxious and restless again. He had transcribed Rebecca's interview into his laptop computer, made a printout, and presented it to her directly after work on Wednesday for her approval. While reading it, she requested only a few minor changes. That phase of his search now over, he felt an urgent desire to continue, to look elsewhere, still convinced that the answer lay in the minds of women, and that his need to search them out had nothing to do with sex and everything to do with finding a profound purpose for his life.

To this end, he decided that a logical place to continue his search would be at a bar. But not in Orangeville. He knew that it would be far less time consuming to go to The Mad Hatter Pub on First Street or The Winchester Arms on Broadway, but quickly dismissed the idea. Too many people in Orangeville knew Claudia and himself, and the news that he'd been approaching women in bars would quickly reach Claudia. And he also knew how unpleasant the repercussions of that would be, regardless of how hard he tried to plead his noble purpose.

No, he'd drive south to Brampton and find a bar there, where it would be highly unlikely that anyone would recognize him. He'd told himself that he'd only continue his search one night a week, but felt that he could wait no longer, especially since Fridays were probably the busiest nights in bars and should provide him with numerous opportunities to make connections. He paved the way for his evening out by phoning Claudia on Friday afternoon and informing her that he'd be late for dinner, hoping to soften his lateness by adding that they expected to wind up the Paragon Chinese Restaurant campaign that evening. Not expecting the question and momentarily taken aback when she asked him how late he'd be, he finally said that they'd be working until at least nine o'clock.

"I'll have something nice for you when you come home," she promised. "Something *very* nice."

From past experience, these words meant that when he arrived home he could expect a vigorous and thoroughly satisfying sexual experience.

Driving south toward Brampton on Highway 10, he reflected on how he would approach a woman in a bar. Even before his marriage ten years earlier, he'd never been a barfly, preferring to be introduced to women by either friends or acquaintances, and his marriage hadn't changed that. Claudia, with her incessant visions of moving up in the world, usually avoided bars and taverns and chose to eat in fancy restaurants.

He decided that his approach would be no different than the one used on Rebecca. He'd ask permission to record conversations on the digital recorder now in his briefcase on the back seat. If refused, he'd either try to recall the main points of the conversation and make notes, or simply move on.

Hungry, he arrived in Brampton just after six o'clock and turned east along Queen Street looking for a restaurant and eventually spotted one called Majestic. On a hunch, he slipped the digital recorder into his shirt pocket before leaving the car. Inside, tables filled the centre of the room and booths lined both sides, all appearing as though they'd been in use for many years. Yet the restaurant was so jammed with a dinner crowd, indicating good food, that he had to search before finally finding a small table for two in a back corner, occupied by a young woman.

He approached her. "The restaurant is crowded. May I sit here?"

She looked around anxiously for another empty seat, saw none, turned back and looked down into her plate. "I suppose so."

"Thanks. My name is Rodger."

She said nothing.

"My name is Rodger," he repeated more loudly. "And you are?"

Her head remained lowered; she picked at her mashed potatoes. "My name isn't important."

"Everybody's name is important. You wouldn't want me to call you 'hey you,' would you?"

A cautious grin tugged at the corners of her mouth, but her head remained lowered. "It's…it's Katherine."

"Is that with a C or a K?"

"With a K."

"Katherine. May I call you Kathy?"

"No!" Suddenly her head jerked upward and her brown eyes pierced his. "My name is *not* Kathy, it's *Katherine!*"

He noticed an unpleasant, heavy nasality in her voice, and wondered if she'd ever thought of having her adenoids removed. "Okay, Katherine then."

The waitress arrived and he ordered a coffee and a hot chicken sandwich with french fries.

He said, "You look like an interesting subject for my book. It's a comparison among different types of women. I'm hoping that what women tell me will help other women find some worthwhile meaning in their lives. What can you tell me about yourself?"

"I don't see any notebook," she said suspiciously. "Aren't you going to write anything down?"

"I don't need a notebook because I have this recorder," he said, patting his shirt pocket. I'll transcribe what you tell me into my computer when I get home tonight. And don't worry, you'll remain anonymous. You'll notice that I didn't ask you your last name. May I turn on the recorder?"

She shrugged disdainfully. "I couldn't care less. Why should I tell you anything about myself anyway. You're a complete stranger."

He clicked on the recorder. "I just want to know what makes you tick. What turns you on. What your views on life are."

"No."

"Would you like to get to know me a little first?"

"No. I'm not interested in men and I don't go out with them."

This overpowering urge to speak his mind and blurt out whatever came into it struck him again, making him wonder if these urges were akin to the tearful outbursts of women during menopause. Before he could control himself, the words were out. "Oh?" He lowered his voice. "Are you a virgin?"

She swung away from him, looking wildly for an empty seat, found none and swung back, glaring. "I don't intend to answer that question! I have...other interests."

"And men are not among them."

"No, they are definitely not," she said smugly. "I prefer to be involved with my church. That's where all my love goes."

"And how young were you when you decided that men were not to be one your interests?"

"Eighteen."

"And what age are you now?" He decided to try flattering her to get the information. "You look about twenty-five."

"I'm just...just a bit older. " She studied his face, as though trying to determine *his* age. He knew that on a good day he could pass as thirty-five. "Actually, I'm twenty-six."

It never ceased to amaze him how women loved to lie about their ages, even when they claimed not to be interested in men. To him, she definitely appeared to be in her early thirties.

"I see," he said cryptically. "Tell me, Katherine, at the age of twenty-six do you ever have doubts about your role in life?" But she hadn't heard him. He saw her staring at his hands and realized that he still wore his wedding ring. He had to think quickly, had to try to establish some common ground that would allow her to open up to him. "I don't mind telling you things about myself."

"Oh?" She continued to stare at his hands. "Like what?"

"What would you like to know?"

She raised her eyes and stared into his, a victorious smirk spreading across her heavy lips. "I'd like to know how long you've been married."Ten years. We celebrated our tenth wedding anniversary just a few days ago with a big party." It was so much easier simply telling the truth, and it came out so much more convincingly. He watched as the smirk disappeared and her lips opened in surprise. She had probably thought that he had forgotten that he still wore his wedding ring and expected him to lie through his teeth, perhaps insisting that it wasn't really a wedding ring at all, or that he and Claudia had separated. Something. Anything but the truth. Did she actually believe that his asking to sit with her meant an attempt at a pickup?

"I see," she said, still doubtful. "So you're trying to tell me that you're happily married."

"That's right." He had to press his advantage. "But I have to qualify that. Sexually, my marriage is very happy. My wife is an excellent lover, the best, but in other areas, the more important areas, we don't see eye to eye. That's why I'm writing this book, so I can find out what's wrong and help myself and others as well."

"What 'other areas' are you speaking about?"

"I'll answer that question by repeating the questions I asked you just a few minutes ago. What makes you tick? What turns you on? What are your views on life? Aren't these the really important things?"

As she was about to speak, the waitress brought Rodger's coffee and hot chicken sandwich, then left. Rodger dug into his meal. Katherine tried to pour more tea into her cup from the pot, but only a dribble came out. Now cold, she stirred her tea and took a sip, but remained silent.

"Let me try to help you out," he offered. "Here's the impression I get from you. You dress simply, but protectively, your clothing usually covering most of your body. You wear slacks most of the time so no one can see your legs, or tell whether they're good or bad. You wear clothing which deliberately obscures your figure rather than accentuating it. You probably never go to the beach because you wouldn't be caught dead in a bikini. You never wear low cut blouses or tight sweaters, and you never go out without wearing a brassiere because you don't want your breasts to bounce around or your nipples to show through." He watched her face redden and her teeth, slightly bucked, clamp down over her lower lip. She seemed about to speak, but he raised his hand. "Please, let me finish. It gets better. You're not married because you wear no wedding ring. As a matter of fact, your hands are bare and you wear no jewellery of any kind. You don't appear to wear any makeup either, not even a bit of lipstick, and your skin tells me that you don't really need it, and your black hair appears to be its natural colour. You haven't even bothered to try to hide the mole beside your nose. All these things put together give me the impression of a woman who is far more concerned with what's *inside herself* than what's outside. Now, how did I do?"

"I'm a moral person," she bragged, her chin rising.

"In what respect? There are many different types of morality. Some people think they're being moral simply because they don't smoke."

"I mean moral in the only *important* way. In my relationship with God. I'm a Roman Catholic and go to church every Sunday and on every holy day of obligation. I donate a percentage of my wages to the church. I donate clothing and food to the poor. I never eat meat on Friday, and fast during Lent. I'm a lector at church, and help out around the church whenever I'm asked. I visit the sick at the Brampton hospital and help out at their Tuck Shop." Her chest expanded. "And I love every single minute of it."

"My God!" he quipped. "You should've been a nun!"

But the quip went over her head and she took his comment seriously. "When I was younger, I thought I *would* be a nun, but then I realized that I could do far more of God's work if I had more freedom."

"And have you found peace?"

"Yes, of course I have. I'm extremely happy doing what I do."

She turned her attention to her food. He studied her hands as they worked her knife and fork, slicing through her salmon fillet, and wondered how much peace she actually had. Would a person at peace with herself have ugly fingernails which had been chewed down to the quick as hers were? Nailbiting was a nervous habit, and nervous people were rarely at peace. He pictured her running around frantically doing God's work, never relaxing, never resting long enough to meditate on her own actual relationship with God. All hustle and bustle. Never at peace. But loving it? Well, perhaps she did. Some people, children mostly, even enjoyed running around in circles.

"Do you ever have doubts?" he asked. "Do you ever wonder whether or not you're doing the right thing?"

She laughed gently, as though she wanted only Rodger to hear. "Doubts? That's silly. Why would I ever have doubts when I'm doing God's work for the Roman Catholic church and I know that the Roman Catholic faith is the only really true faith in the world?"

"The *only* true faith? Then, if you go there, who do you expect to meet in heaven?"

"Why, Roman Catholics, of course."

"*Only* Roman Catholics?"

"Of course. Do you think I want to spend eternity with a bunch of Anglicans or Presbyterians or Baptists, or, God forbid, Uniteds?"

"Are you serious? Do you honestly believe that the only souls you'll ever meet in heaven are those that practised the Catholic faith?"

"Of course. Since it's the only true faith, all other souls would be kept out."

"But wouldn't that be intolerable? Nothing but billions of souls spending eternity praising God while they nitpicked through the archives of Roman Catholicism. How boring. I would've thought that God had a more stimulating plan for the souls in heaven than that. Can you honestly believe that God would exclude all non-Catholic souls from heaven, even other Christians? And why would he exclude all pre-Christian souls, those who through no fault of their own had no Christ to follow? Certainly, there are Catholic souls I'd love to meet in heaven, like Mother Theresa, Thomas Merton, C. S. Lewis, Chesterton, Pascal, Albert Schweitzer, Graham Greene, and T. S. Eliot, among others, but what kind of one-sided heaven would it be without great souls like Socrates, Plato, Aristotle, Gandhi, Marcus Aurelius, Thoreau, and Emerson, among others. Where would the stimulation in heaven come from without souls like these?

Ignoring his remarks, she waved an arm at the crowd surrounding them. "I'm not like them. Drinking, taking drugs, fornicating, committing adultery, consumed with jealousy and hate, consumed by materialism, consumed by hedonism. I'm not like *them*."

"And does that include people like me?"

"I didn't say that. I don't know you, so I can't say."

"Then what about all the people around us here? You don't actually know them either, do you?"

"No, but I do know the way most people in our society act today." Her disdainful gaze roamed around the room. "I wonder how many of them have ever even *seen* the inside of a church."

"Does that really matter? There are millions of good people in this world who've never seen the inside of a church."

She tilted her head back, her nose pointed toward the ceiling, and sniffed. "They are deluded."

"Deluded? Because they are good people who practise the golden rule?"

"*They are deluded!*" she cried, forking cold green beans into her mouth and chewing viciously. "Thank *God* I'm not like *them!*"

The story of Christ and the Pharisees suddenly came into his mind, a story he hadn't thought about for years. He said, "Since you go to the Catholic church regularly, I suppose you're familiar with the Bible, especially the New Testament."

"Of course I am," she said smugly. "I *live* by the words in the New Testament."

"Oh, *do* you?" He had no desire to have sex with this woman and saw no reason to cater to her by holding back what he intended to say. At forty, he had already catered to Claudia for ten wasted years. Now those days were over. "I haven't read the Bible in years, but I remember a story from the New Testament that my father used to read to me regularly when I was a child. It was about Christ and the Pharisees. You do know who the Pharisees were, don't you?"

"Of course I do." Her chin rose and her neck stretched upward. "That story is part of our liturgy once every year. The Pharisees practised their religion to the letter. They fasted, they gave alms. But Christ criticized them because they were hypocrites because they kept saying...because they kept saying..."

"Yes, Katherine. Because they kept saying, 'Thank *God* I'm not like *them.*'"

She stared at him malevolently. "You mean you think that I...that I..."

"That you're a hypocrite? Yes, I do. Don't you?"

"I don't have to sit here and listen to you. I go to church *every* Sunday. You…you said you haven't read the Bible for years, so when…when did *you* last go to church regularly?"

The smug words rolled effortlessly from his lips, as though he'd said them a hundred times before. "I have issues with God. He hasn't measured up to my expectations."

She laughed derisively. "*You* have issues with *God!* Can't you even see how *ridiculous* you sound? You still haven't answered my question: When did you last go to church regularly?"

Over ten years ago, he thought. Not since the day Claudia and he were married. Although they were both born and raised as Catholics, Claudia hadn't seen the inside of a church, except for their marriage, in fifteen years, when her parents separated and eventually had their marriage annulled. Claudia and her parents, and Roger's parents, had all agreed with Rodger that there should be a church wedding at St. Timothy Roman Catholic Church in Orangeville, while Gunderson, Claudia's stepfather, Rodger recalled again, merely shrugged and told her, "You don't have to start going to church just because you get married in one." And so it was. Claudia never returned to the church after their marriage, and he, who had attended occasionally before their marriage, saw his own attendance dwindle to practically nothing. Now, his Catholicism dangled by a thread.

"Well?" Katherine demanded, jerking him back to the present, her lips twisted into a malicious smile. "Answer me!"

"I go to the Catholic church three times a year: Good Friday, Easter Sunday, and Christmas."

"And *you're* criticizing *me*? You've got a nerve. You're nothing but a C and E Catholic."

"A C and E Catholic?"

"Yes, a Christmas and Easter Catholic. The church fills up with people like you at Christmas and Easter, and then you disappear for the rest of the year. You're not a true Catholic. You're nothing but a pathetic excuse for a Catholic." She rose, snapped up her purse and check, and said, "I'm getting away from you before you *contaminate* me," then marched quickly and proudly away toward the cashier.

As he sat there reflecting on the encounter, Rodger became convinced of one inescapable fact: He had learned nothing from Katherine's personality which would aid him in his personal search. Rather, he recognized only warning signs. He saw in her nothing but a woman who enjoyed vainly parading her "goodness" before others and placing herself on a haughty pedestal from where she could look down on them. She also obviously enjoyed all her busy spiritual activity, but did she not enjoy it mainly because it kept feeding her ego so that she could raise herself to an even higher pedestal? And if you actually *enjoy* doing something for your own selfish reasons, where is the sacrifice? For isn't sacrifice really what loving God is all about? Fluttering around and loving every minute of it so that you can feel superior to others hardly qualifies. He would use the episode in his book, but as a warning and certainly not as a recommendation on how to live a worthwhile life.

After leaving the restaurant, he continued to drive east along Queen Street until he saw a tavern called The Kosy Korner which had probably gotten its name because it sat on a corner at the end of a strip plaza. Fairly large, the building well maintained, Rodger saw it as a tavern where the drinks might be expensive but which would probably of-fer him a better opportunity to locate the type of woman he wanted to meet.

He parked the car in front of the tavern, noticing that there were already several cars parked there. He glanced at his watch. Six-fifty. Because it was Friday night, he expected that in another hour the tavern would be full.

Inside the dimly lit tavern, he could still discern the faces of the customers. Several people, mainly alone, sat at the long, polished bar on tall, high-backed swivel chairs of black faux leather and a few of the tables were occupied by small groups. His inspection of the female bar customers produced a possible prospect in a woman wearing a beige sweater, brown slacks, and sandals. As he drew closer, he saw that she was full breasted, small waisted, and appeared to be in her late thirties. No breasts or legs were invitingly exposed. Possibly just a conservative woman looking for a little company.

Before making his pitch, he took a final look around the room and saw several pairs of eyes, both male and female, staring fearfully at him, as though he were about to jump into the flames of hell, making him wonder what it all meant.

Shrugging, he placed his hands on the back of the chair to her left and gazed over her shoulder at her pale, slender hands resting languidly on the bar, naked except for a cameo on her left ring finger.

"Is this seat taken?"

She turned and surveyed him up and down, up and down, as though trying to determine whether or not she deemed him worthy to sit beside her. Although he detected a hint of approval in her lavender eyes, she said, "There are plenty of other empty seats."

He said, "But then I wouldn't be sitting beside you, would I?" and immediately berated himself for using such a pathetically corny line.

"Look," she said coldly. "I didn't come here to be accosted by married men."

He'd forgotten to remove his wedding ring and she'd obviously spotted it while looking him over. He thought fast. "Oh, this," he said, holding out his hand. "This doesn't mean anything. You see, I don't mind you knowing that I'm married because I'm not trying to make out with you. I'm actually a happily married man, at least sexually." He placed the digital recorder on the bar." The thing is, I'm doing research for a book and just want to ask you a few questions about yourself. May I record our conversation?"

"I've heard that book line before," she said disdainfully, gazing at the recorder. "You're just more thorough, that's all, bringing a recorder along. But you're still after the same thing you're all after."

"You're free to think what you like, but it's true. May I sit down and prove it to you?"

She shrugged. "It's a free country—you can sit where you like. You might as well because nobody else will be sitting here."

"Why not?"

"Because the others are all regulars, and they know I'm waiting for my date."

"And when does your date arrive?"

She glanced at her watch. "In about half an hour."

"Then I'd better get started." He sat down. "May I record?"

She nodded. "Just don't expect me to bare my soul. Because I don't have any."

Now, at close range, he noted her face, fine featured and passably good looking. Her thin lips, beneath a small, straight nose, were set in a small mouth covered with a thin coat of pink lipstick. Over her makeup, her cheeks were tinged with a faint hint of blush. Even so, he detected the beginnings of crow's feet at the outer edges of her lightly-mascaraed eyelashes. Her straight, light brown hair fell to her shoulders, its odd shade making him believe that she had coloured it. Examining this meticulous remaking of her appearance, and wondering if a woman who spent so much time on her external image could have any serious internal life, he began to doubt whether she could provide him with any useful information.

"Well, do I pass?" she demanded.

"Pardon?" He realized suddenly that he'd been staring at her.

"Do I pass your intense inspection?"

He laughed self-consciously. "I'm sorry. Of course you do. With flying colours." He saw the paunchy, bearded bartender approaching and glanced at her almost empty glass. "May I buy your next drink?"

"Yes. As long as you don't think that it's buying you something else."

"Of course."

She drew on her straw and drained her glass. "It's a rum collins."

He ordered a refill for her, a screwdriver for himself, and extended his hand. "My name's Rodger."

"Mary," she said, ignoring his hand. "Take my advice, Rodger. Women don't like playing second fiddle. You'll do far better if you remove that ring, but not with me. You must spend most of your time inside because you're almost as white as milk. Maybe when you take the ring off it won't show."

"Thanks." He removed the ring and dropped it into his hip pocket. "Listen, I certainly meant it when I said I wasn't trying to make out with you, and I'm not saying you're not attractive either. But there's no problem with my sex life with my wife. It's great."

"Then why come here? Why do you think most men and women come here?"

"Maybe you're right, but I just couldn't think of anywhere else to go. My problem is something else, something deeper, and all I really wanted was to talk to a few women to find out what made them tick, and maybe find out what they thought were the important things in life."

She laughed. "Tell me another one. You mean to tell me that you came *here* looking for *that*. Who do you think you're talking to? We both know that you'd be miles ahead if you just went to a church somewhere and talked to a minister."

The bartender arrived with their drinks; Rodger paid him, adding a tip. Mary immediately took a few sips through her straw.

Rodger said, "Are you trying to tell me that no one in this room has any worthwhile purpose in life? I find that hard to believe."

"Believe it, Mister, believe it. Right know I know almost everyone in this place. Most of them are here practically every Friday night. They hate me—every one of them. That's why you'll never see any of them sitting with me at the bar. We talk about freedom in Canada. We talk about nondiscrimination, treating everyone as equals. But if you're part of a minority group, there is no equality. People might pay lip service to equality, but once they get within ten feet of a minority person, they avoid that person as though they were terrified of being contaminated."

"But why you?" He paused a few moments, reflecting, then lowered his voice. "You're not a hooker, are you?"

"No, of course not," she snapped, insulted. "Do I *look* like a hooker?"

"Actually, I've never been with one so I don't really know what they look like. I just thought—"

"Then don't talk so stupid."

"Sorry. Okay, so you're not a hooker. But I know that some bars have a nice looking woman who just sits at the bar waiting for a guy to approach her. Then she gets the guy to buy her a bunch of drinks over the evening. He goes home drunk, she gets paid and makes money for the bar because her drinks are always watered down."

"They don't do that here. The management won't allow it." She laughed disdainfully. "They want to try to keep the place *respectable*." She held out her glass. "Here, try my drink and tell me if it's watered down."

"There's rum in it, isn't there?"

"Of course."

"Then I can't touch it. I got sick on rum quite a few years ago, and now if I try to drink it I bring up. But it's okay, I believe you."

"Are you afraid I'm going to contaminate you if you drink out of the same straw, is that it?" she blurted out angrily. "Just like everyone else in this room thinks I'm going to contaminate them?"

"No, I just told you the truth, that's all. I just can't drink rum. And why should you contaminate me? Do you have some kind of infectious disease?"

"No, it's not infectious, and it's not a disease. It's just that the people in this room think it is, so they avoid me."

"Why?"

"Never mind. You'll know soon enough, and then you can avoid me, too."

"Fine. Then I'd like to get back to the purpose of why I came here. So I'm asking you again. Not a minister or a priest, I'm asking *you* what *you* believe is the most important thing in life."

"For me that's easy." Her voice began to break. "Easy to say... but very hard to do."

"What's very hard to do, Mary?"

"To just be yourself," she said hoarsely, tears glistening in her eyes. "To just be yourself...and have people accept you for what you are...without trying to change you...without trying to tell you how you should live your life."

"That's very interesting. Have you ever read Shakespeare?"

"We took him in school, but I found him boring. The old English—it was hard to understand so I guess I just kind of gave up on it. Why?"

"Well, maybe you gave up on him, but maybe you also remembered something he once wrote. It goes something like this: 'This above all else, to thine own self be true. And it shall follow as the night the day that thou canned not then be false to any man.' Isn't that what you're telling me you believe?"

"Yes, I guess it is. And maybe that's where I got it from, I don't know. Maybe it's just stuck in my mind all these years. But believing and doing are two very different things. Believing something is right can be easy—all you have to do is think that it's right. But actually *doing* and actually *living* what you believe can often be very, very hard."

"But you do believe that you must live it, don't you? Regardless of how hard it is?"

"Yes. Yes, I do. But for some of us it's much easier than others."

He nodded. "I agree. But the problem for some of us is this: Before you can *be* yourself, you need to discover *who* yourself is. That's my problem. I feel alien. I feel like I'm inside someone else's skin and I want to shed that skin, like a snake, and discover the real me beneath it. But I haven't been able to do that. Yet. And I'm the same as millions of others who haven't discovered what their true role in life is, and hate the life they're living. You're very lucky because you're being yourself and you know it."

She laughed harshly, bitterly. "Be careful what you wish for. What you find may not be very pleasant, or even what you wanted." She turned to her left and stared malevolently past him down the bar. "There's a perfect example. Look at her—that's Vicky. She's twenty years old and so naive that she actually believes that she's being herself, that this is it, that she's doing exactly what she should be doing with her life. The bitch. She hasn't a clue what life is all about."

Rodger turned and saw an attractive blonde with bleached shoulder-length hair several chairs away. Surprised, he suddenly realized that her steady, interested gaze pointed directly at him.

"Why is she looking at me?" he asked. "I've never seen her before in my life."

"You'll see. Just keep looking at her. She's hungry. Looking for more meat."

The blonde, leaving her half-filled glass on the bar, said something to the bartender before sliding off her chair and starting slowly toward Rodger, her shapely hips swaying, and in the ten or fifteen seconds it took her to reach him his eyes swept over the bare, excellent legs with most of their well-rounded thighs exposed below a red miniskirt, the pink peasant blouse with its widely scooped neckline exposing her plump, bouncing breasts almost to their nipples. He'd always believed that women tried to attract men by accentuating their best features and hiding their worst. Bow-legged women probably preferred wearing slacks. Women who worked in sex shops were asked by management to dress scantily to insure that customers kept their minds on the business at hand, like selecting sexual attire or pornographic videos. The way women dressed was meant to send men a message, and to Rodger peasant blouses and miniskirts relayed only one message: "I'm easy. Come and get me."

When she stopped at his chair, he realized that as she'd approached he'd unconsciously swung around to meet her. His eyes couldn't resist exploring the tight cleavage and the generous nakedness of her bulging breasts, and when he raised them to her face they were stunned by a pair of large, almost round, pale blue eyes and a dazzling smile from wide, thick, pouting bright red lips which enclosed straight, sparkling, very white teeth. A small red purse hung from her shoulder. Finally lowering his gaze, he noticed that she carried a package of du Maurier cigarettes and a Bic lighter.

"New here, aren't you?" she purred, her voice deep and suggestive.

Before he could answer, Mary swung around and hissed, "Get lost, bitch!"

Still smiling, the blonde walked slowly away to-ward the door, her shapely buttocks shifting seductively.

Slowly, Rodger turned back to the bar. "I guess she's going outside for a smoke," he said inanely.

"You've got that right," Mary said, turning back. "Vicky smokes like a chimney. I've just taken a look around and I think I know every man here. They're all regulars. So you ought to consider yourself honoured."

"Honoured? Why?"

"Because you're probably the only guy here who hasn't had his balls between her legs."

"C'mon. You must be joking. I can't believe that any woman can be that promiscuous."

"Believe it. She must be a nympho. The only men I've ever seen her not bother with in this place are the old ones, and you don't see many old men coming into this place." She smirked. "Maybe she doesn't bother with them because she just can't stand old men—I've seen how she blows them off whenever they try to get near her. And maybe she thinks they just can't get it up any more. That'd be the worst case scenario for her: a man who didn't love that brick shithouse body of hers enough to even get an erection. That'd send her to her psychiatrist for help, the neurotic little bitch."

"Is she a hooker then?"

"No. Not a hooker. I already told you—they don't allow hookers in here. Sometimes you see a few of them hanging around outside, catching the singles as they leave. No, she's worse than a hooker. Hookers are at least trying to earn a living; they at least get *paid* for what they do. But *she* does it for nothing, just *gives* it away to any stud who comes along. How despicable is that?"

"So I take it then that you believe that the only worthwhile relationship is a monogamous one."

"Of course. How can you possibly ever be true to yourself if you can't be true to another person?"

"And you believe that you have that kind of a relationship?"

"Yes, I do. My friend should be arriving soon."

"You seem to dislike Vicky intensely," he accused. "Have you had a run-in with her? Is that the reason?"

"Nonsense. How could I have had a run-in with her when I don't even talk to her?"

But he could see that she'd taken a defensive attitude and felt that he'd touched on the truth. "Maybe that's the reason you don't talk to her," he suggested.

"Nonsense. I don't talk to her because of what she represents. The men around here have even given her a nickname. Do you know what they call her?"

"No, of course not."

She sneered, "They call her 'Vicky Loves Dicky.'"

"Behind her back, of course."

"Hell, no! Right to her face. They come right up to her and say, 'Hi, Vicky Loves Dicky, any chance tonight?' And she's so stupid that she loves every minute of it, gloats over the attention, even lords it over the other women. She's so eager to be the centre of attention that sometimes I think she must've been neglected as a child, and I guess you know what neglected children are like. They eventually reach a point where they crave any kind of attention, even bad attention, rather than being ignored. So they begin to do things that they know their parents will definitely disapprove of and will certainly find out about. And when they do, the child is punished, perhaps even beaten. But at least the child has received some *attention*, and even though it's negative attention, it's still better than *no attention at all.*" She paused, breathing heavily, her face red, and when her breathing subsided she reached for her drink and took a long sip. "And...and that's Vicky. Always craving attention. Even when it's the kind of negative attention she gets around here."

Rodger realized that even though she'd purportedly been talking about Vicky, her emotional outburst told him that Mary had also been talking about herself. "And what about you? Do you still crave attention?"

"Me? Don't be ridiculous," she snapped. "Why would I need attention when I have a firm, trusting relationship?" She saw Vicky returning and quickly changed the subject. "Here comes Vicky Loves Dicky. Try to keep your eyeballs in your head this time."

As Vicky passed them, she turned her head, stared into Rodger's eyes and ran her pink tongue across her upper lip as she continued toward her chair, hips swaying.

"Do you need any more of an invitation?" Mary said, disgusted.

"I need to interview her."

Mary laughed. "*Interview* her. You'll end up doing a lot more than that." She glanced at her watch. "You'd better go. My friend will be here in a few minutes."

"Good talking to you," he said as he picked up his digital recorder and walked casually toward Vicky, who sat next to the wall in the last bar chair. When she met his gaze, he delivered one of the most threadbare cliches in existence. "Mind if I buy you a drink?"

Her smile, almost a victorious sneer, said, 'I knew you'd come,' but she only said, "It's your nickel, honey."

My God, he thought. His line was mouldy enough, but hers sounded like something out of a Bacall-Bogart movie. As he seated himself in the chair on her right, he caught the strange scent of some exotic perfume emanating from her shapely body. Had she applied it when she left for her cigarette? As though detached from his mind, his eyes stared down at her prominent breasts squeezed together and bulging over the top of her blouse, and he felt an almost overpowering urge to nuzzle his nose down into the warm slit of her cleavage.

What the hell am I doing? he suddenly asked himself. I've got a beautiful wife at home, great in bed, ready to give me all the sex I'll ever need, so why am I thinking sexually about this...this *child*?

But his libido quickly settled down when his eyes finally made their way to her face. Apparently, while he'd been admiring her breasts she'd shoved a stick of Juicy Fruit gum into her mouth and had begun chewing happily. Delicately, she tucked stray wisps of blonde hair behind her ears. He tried to rationalize her gum chewing by telling himself that she probably used the gum only to sweeten her smoker's breath for his benefit, but her constant bovine ruminating still annoyed him and he hoped that she'd dispose of the gum in a few minutes.

He'd always thought of gum chewing as a habit of empty-headed people seeking to fill that void with some inane, repetitious activity. He found that women were more apt to be gum chewers than men, and that cashiers appeared to be at the head of the class. Several months earlier, after using the same gum-chewing Wal-Mart cashier many times, the only one in service shortly after the store opened, he filled out a complaint card suggesting that cashiers would present a far better public image if they refrained from this habit. To his surprise, a Wal-Mart representative phoned him about a week later and spoke to him about his concern, saying that he would speak to the store manager but that he couldn't promise anything, largely because they could only request, not demand, that employees stop chewing gum. They must be careful, mainly because the low wages they paid didn't exactly attract the cream of the crop when it came to employees. So the gum chewing continued. He wanted to tell the cashier that she looked like an old cow chewing its cud, but refrained from doing so. In the end he felt that he should be thankful that at least the younger cashiers weren't wearing body- piercing jewellery in their lips, tongues, noses, or eyebrows. The problem eventually resolved itself when Wal-Mart installed several express checkouts, providing him with a possible cashier choice.

Vicky ordered another Singapore Sling, Rodger another screwdriver.

"My name's Rodger," he said, extending his hand. "That's spelled with a 'd.'"

"That's 'Dodger,' isn't it?"

"No, I mean the 'd' is between the 'o' and the 'g.'"

"Oh. Well, I'm Vicky."

"I know." He felt her soft, warm hand slide into his and gently return his grip before pulling away.

The bartender dropped their drinks and left when Rodger handed him a bill and told him to keep the change.

"Sure you know," she said. "Bigmouth Mary's always telling everybody about me. But I can't waste my time talking about her." She ran a hand lovingly across her lap. "Like my new miniskirt? Don't you think it's cool?"

Looking down, he saw that her right leg was crossed over her left, the bright red miniskirt so high that even part of her buttock lay exposed, making him think that she might be wearing a thong. Or nothing, God help him. As he stared, her right leg began swinging rhythmically, her shapely thigh flexing and relaxing, flexing and relaxing.

He was suddenly reminded of a Havelock Ellis sex manual he'd once read—was it *The Psychology of Sex?*—where Ellis sat waiting in a bus station when he noticed a young woman seated opposite him rhythmically swinging her crossed leg, and knew that women could secretly stimulate their clitorises by doing this and tensing their pelvic muscles, thus masturbating themselves. He believed that Vicky might be doing exactly that when he saw the vacant look on her face. Rodger knew that Havelock Ellis was right—women could do this. Claudia had even admitted it. Could Vicky now be doing the same thing?

Nervous, he quickly placed the digital recorder on the bar between them and blurted out, "I'm writing a book. Do you mind if I record our conversation?"

Delicately, she tucked stray wisps of blonde hair behind her ears. "You're making a book? How totally awesome! No, I don't mind." She shrugged, thrust out her plump chest. "Am I going to be in it?"

"That depends on you."

Her leg swinging slowed and stopped. He eyed her and realized with relief that it had been nothing more than a nervous habit.

"On me? How?"

"On whether or not you tell me something worth writing about, without lying."

"That's a plan. What do you want to know?" She stared steadily into his eyes. "But before, tell me, what do you think of my eyes?"

He gazed in wonder into her pale blue orbs, so large that their whites actually showed both above and below their pupils, and he found himself thinking about Little Orphan Annie, except, of course, Little Orphan Annie had no pupils. "I think your eyes are incredible, fantastic," he said truthfully. "I've never seen anything like them."

"All the guys say that. They are really awesome, aren't they?" She placed her hands on her hips and thrust out her plump chest. "And what about the rest of me?"

"That's incredible, too," he agreed. He'd never been so blatantly propositioned, and had to force himself back to his real purpose. "Look, Vicky, you're a great looking girl, but I'm a happily married man with a great sex life. And I don't play around."

Her laugh was high pitched, almost like a little girl's. "*Everybody* plays around."

"Not me," he insisted. "Can we get back to the book now? You asked me what I wanted to know about you. What I want to know is—"

"If you want to know more about Mary, take a look. Jo just came in."

Rodger turned, expecting to see a man. Instead he saw a tall, husky, broad-shouldered woman wearing low-heeled shoes and a dark gray suit complete with white shirt and black tie. Her short hair, almost resembling a black skullcap, crowned a large, masculine head, scrubbed clean, with a prominent nose, thick lips, and a jutting chin.

The two women greeted each other by clasping hands, then embracing. As they embraced, Mary looked sadly toward Rodger, and her look said that this was her true self, and she had to be her true self even though she disliked it because she just couldn't help herself. He knew now why the others ignored her, scorned her, talked about her behind her back, for even though notable gays in North American society were constantly coming out of the closet, even though gay pride parades were regular events, even though gays were prominently represented in movies and on television, even though gays were apparently accepted, the stigma still remained and the public still heard of them being beaten and even murdered because of their sexual preferences. Rodger simply nodded and Mary turned away.

"She didn't tell you, did she," Vicky said.

"Tell me what?"

"That she's gay." Delicately, she tucked stray wisps of blonde hair behind her ears. "She's a real winner, Mary is. She never tells anybody, never yaps about it, thinks it's her own private business. I found out about her several months ago, like long before Jo started coming around, because she came on strong to me, like tried to get me to go back to her pad with her. I think she's just disgusting!"

"So you're a gay basher, are you? Do you believe that all gays should just be penned away from all heterosexual society, like animals?"

"No, I...I...."

"Then exactly what do you believe? Do you even know? Have you even given the subject any serious thought?"

"I...I just think she's *disgusting*, that's all," she said angrily. "She makes me absolutely *sick*."

"Do you believe that every woman in the world should behave exactly the same? Like you, for example?"

"No, but—"

"Have you ever read a book on human physiology?"

"Huh?"

"Have you studied the differences in human beings, and learned *why* they're different?"

"No, I don't read, but I know what I feel." She took an angry sip of her drink, then frowned as a knowing look came into her face. "You're gay, aren't you?" she accused triumphantly. "That's what this is all about, isn't it? Why you're defending them."

"No, I'm not gay. I've already told you that I'm happily married and have a good sex life with my wife. I won't lie and say that the image of two women or two men having sex together doesn't disgust me, because it does. But I'm trying to deal with that disgust because I know where many gays are coming from." He felt himself warming to his subject now, wanting to convince Vicky to change her attitude—and to further convince himself. "Human beings are as different as the grains of sand on a beach. To the naked eye, many may appear identical, but when closely inspected each becomes unique. Each person's total makeup is different. Without going into bisexuals and hermaphrodites—"

"Huh?"

"Never mind. Let me try to explain in the simplest terms possible. You look the way you do be-cause your makeup is predominantly female; I look the way I do because my makeup is predominantly male. Sexually, you seek men, and I seek women. That's normal. But there are many women in the world whose external appearance is more or less female, but whose *internal* makeup is more male than female, which makes them desire women in stead of men. And there are many men in the world whose external appearance is more or less male, but whose *internal* makeup is more female than male, which makes them desire men instead of women. Now do you understand?"

Her blank stare told him that she had understood next to nothing. Instead of inquiring further on the subject, which seemed to bore her, she referred to one of his earlier statements when she asked, "What would be so ditzy about everybody behaving like me?"

"Ditzy?"

"Like, silly."

He felt an almost overpowering urge to laugh in her face, but managed to restrain himself. "I've been told that you've been to bed with practically every man here. Is that true?"

"And you've only yapped with Bigmouth Mary, so I guess she's the one who blabbed."

"You haven't answered my question."

She looked around the bar, now beginning to fill up with the Friday night crowd. "Not all of them. There's a few here I haven't tried yet. Like, I do have standards, y'know. And some of them just don't cut it. Older men. Just to try something different, I went with an old geezer once, thought I'd give him a mega-awesome thrill, y'know, but I learned my lesson. I'll never do that again. Pathetic, he was. Poor old fart just couldn't get it up." Delicately, she tucked stray wisps of blonde hair behind her ears. She thrust out her chest, her plump breasts overflowing her blouse. "Can you imagine any man not being able to get it up with me? Like, he must've been im*po*tent is all I can say."

"How...how old was he?"

"I haven't got a clue, but he looked absolutely *ancient.*" She studied his face. "By the way, how old are *you?*"

"Forty."

"Forty?" Concerned, she looked him up and down, up and down, as though this could somehow assess his sexual prowess. "And you can still do it?"

He laughed. "Yes, I can *still* do it. But you needn't worry, I'm not here for that. I'm here to find out about you, what makes you tick, what your views on life are." He could barely believe that he'd actually said those last several words. What could he possibly learn about life from this...this bimbo, whose sole goal in life appeared to be going to bed with as many young studs as she could? But wouldn't that be the wrong attitude? Wouldn't the book be incomplete if he failed to show the other side of the coin by also mentioning ways *not* to live and delineating their pitfalls? "A few minutes ago you asked what would be so wrong if everybody behaved like you. Well, just how do you behave? And what do you think is so exemplary about it?"

"Exem...?"

"Exemplary. Worthy of imitation. What is it about your life that makes it worthy enough that other people, even me, might want to imitate it?"

"Well, like, I have lots of fun because I get to be with some really hot guys, don't I? Isn't that worth trying to imitate?"

"But what about the *worthy* part? How is what you do worthy of admiration or respect? From what Mary says, none of the women here admire you or respect you because they think you're nothing but an easy lay. And the men think the same thing and are just trying to take advantage of it. So where's the worthy part?"

"It's a bummer, y'know—most of the women around here are just ditzes and don't understand me, that's all. And they're jealous, green with envy. And the guys..." Rodger stared as she slowly, deliberately uncrossed her shapely legs and recrossed them the opposite way, and when he raised his eyes to her face they were met by her triumphant smile. "Well, they're just being guys, y'know, aren't they?" She took a slow sip of her drink. "I'll tell you where the worthy part is. I'm giving pleasure and love to every guy I go with. And I'm good at it. Very good. They tell me all the time how awesome I am. How they never knew anyone who put so much energy into it." Her wide, round, pale blue eyes stared into his. "Y'see, like, when I'm in bed with a guy I just lose control and I can't help myself. Can you honestly tell me that loving guys isn't a good thing?"

"But you're not loving them. You're just having sex with them. There's a vast difference. When you really love someone, you make a commitment to that person by becoming faithful. You can't say you love someone and then go bouncing from bed to bed with a bunch of other men. That's not love, it's only sex."

She gazed at him, her jaws working the gum, as though she were thinking, and as the seconds lengthened out he had the feeling that she wanted to say something but wasn't sure whether she should. Delicately, she tucked stray wisps of blonde hair behind her ears. God, Rodger, thought, how often did she do that with her hair in a day? A hundred times?

Finally, she said simply, "Maybe I've got a reason."

"What kind of reason? You don't take money from them, do you?"

"No, of course not. I'm *not* a whore. Sometimes they offer me money, but I've never taken a cent. *Never.* So some of them, like, give me little gifts. Clothes, joolery, things like that."

"Joolery?"

"Yes, bracelets, earrings, necklaces, things like that."

"Oh, jewellery."

"Yes, joolery. But I won't take a cent of cash from any of them."

"So, is that why you're doing it? Just for the gifts?"

"No."

"Then why?"

"Why?" she said evasively.

"Yes, why?"

"Like I said, maybe I've got a reason."

"Okay, fine, we know it's not the money, and it's not the gifts, so what is it?"

She looked past him at the two empty chairs on his right. Still, she lowered her voice, even though the burgeoning noise in the bar made it difficult for him to hear. "I just love sex." she admitted. "I love it…too much. And I…I just haven't found the right man, y'know, that's all." She removed the straw and the pineapple slice from her drink, picked up the glass and drained it. "I'd like another drink, please."

He had no idea how many drinks she'd had before he arrived at The Kosy Korner; he could detect a faint glassiness in her large, round eyes, but said, "Sure," called the bartender, ordered Vicky's drink, decided to nurse his own, and while he waited for her drink to arrive he reflected on how her words had suddenly become cautious and unsure. Earlier she'd been proud of her rampant sexuality, but now it seemed that he'd backed her into an unpleasant or embarrassing corner of her life that she wanted to avoid. And didn't even want to think about. Perhaps another drink would loosen her tongue enough to bring out the truth.

When the bartender left, Rodger tried to press his advantage. "Look, you don't have to tell me anything if it's something you're ashamed of. But—"

"I'm not ashamed of anything," she snapped. "Why should I be?"

"Well, maybe because of the way you've been acting. You're avoiding my questions. But just let me tell you this: Whatever you tell me won't go any further. If I put you into my book I won't even use your own name or even describe the way you actually look. You don't have to—"

"Wait." She reached out suddenly and gripped his wrist for silence as a tall, thin man with a prominent Adam's apple and a hooked nose slid onto the chair on Rodger's right.

"Hey, Vicky," the man said, leaning forward and ignoring Rodger.

"Hey, Larry."

"You here for the night?"

"That depends." She gripped Rodger's hand meaningfully. "Right now we're leaving, aren't we, Rodger?"

"Yes, we are," Rodger replied, quickly draining his glass, sweeping up the digital recorder and slipping it into his shirt pocket as he rose.

"Not leaving that drink, are you, Vicky?" Larry said. "It's almost full."

Joining Rodger and taking his arm, Vicky reached out and gently tapped Larry's shoulder. "You just watch my drink for me. I might be back...soon."

This brought a snaggle-toothed smile from Larry. "Sure, Vicky, sure."

Mary merely nodded and shrugged as they left the bar.

Outside, she asked, "You've got a car, haven't you?"

"Sure. Don't you?"

"Not here. I leave mine at home when I come here, in case I get trashed. My pad's only a few blocks from here; I can always take a cab home. Let's go and sit in your car. We can talk private there."

Rodger now began to feel that she intended to tell him the truth about herself. It hadn't yet grown dark, the sky clear as they walked through a warm breeze toward his car, Vicky clutching his arm and leaning heavily against him for support.

The car had become quite warm. Rather than starting the engine and turning on the air conditioner, he opened both front windows and allowed the breeze to flow through. He placed the digital recorder on the dashboard and said, "So you know Larry."

"Yes, I know Larry. Like I know most of the Friday nighters at The Kosy Korner."

He felt that her "know" probably meant sexually, yet he couldn't determine whether she was bragging, complaining, or simply feeling sorry for herself. "How well do you know him?"

"Well enough. Like, a few months ago I let him have me. Poor Larry, the geek with that long, skinny neck and that huge Adam's apple, and that big nose, and those awful teeth. He wanted me—guess he wanted any girl who'd have him—so I let him. I gave him the privilege of going to bed with me, y'know, a hot girl he could only dream of going to bed with, and something he'd remember for the rest of his life. Like, I felt *sorry* for him."

"You went to bed with a man because you felt *sorry* for him?"

"Sure, why not? Because I'm not really interested in what a man looks like—I'm only interested in how they…like, how they *perform*."

"And do they usually perform to your satisfaction? Did Larry?"

"Poor Larry. No, he didn't do too well. He told me after that he was a virgin. That made him too anxious and he got off way too quick. He was finished before I barely got started. But he was very grateful after, couldn't stop kissing me and thanking me. And he knew I wouldn't take any money from him, like, so when he came into The Kosy Korner the next Friday he handed me a big box of chocolates. I thought that was really sweet of him. Awesome, like."

"And since?"

"Well, it's over, isn't it. I gave him something he'd remember for the rest of his life, and that's it. He hangs around, and I don't mind, but it's over. I've moved on."

"To other men?

"To other men."

"And how have all these other men performed? Any better?"

She hesitated, as though trying to decide whether to answer or not. The breeze had messed her hair, causing it to partially cover her eyes, but instead of again carefully tucking the stray wisps behind her ears as she'd done incessantly while inside the bar, she simply tilted her head back and shook them away. As he saw this, Rodger thought how too much to drink caused people to become careless with their appearance and the impression they created.

She said, "Do you *really* want to know? Do you *really* care?"

Now he knew that she felt sorry for herself, and that what she might tell him would be a sorrowful story. "Certainly I care. That's exactly why I'm writing this book. To help women with problems."

"I didn't say I had a problem," she snapped.

"Then why did you ask me to come out here? Wasn't it because you wanted to tell me something that you didn't want other people to hear?"

She had no answer for that, simply gazed at him glassily, and finally said, "I…I just need to straighten something out, that's all, then everything'll be fine."

"Then, as I just asked you, what about all these other men? How have they performed? Is there a problem there?"

"A couple of years ago, there wasn't a problem. I was nineteen." She spoke as though her being nineteen had been decades ago. "I came here one night and met Kirk. I never seen him in The Kosy Korner before. He was twenty-one, but he acted millions of years older, y'know. Like, he knew a lot about a lot of things. Things I never even heard of. I couldn't believe he knew all that and was only twenty-one. He was truly hot, and he made me feel... he made me feel like I was the only girl in the world...and that nothing bogus could ever happen to me as long as he was around. I felt safe with him, because he knew everything, knew all the answers to everything, not like most of the clueless geeks I meet. Like, y'know, I just felt like I never wanted him to go out of my life.

"Anyways, he bought me some drinks and he talked and talked. He told me he was some kind of computer guy who travelled around to big businesses and repaired their machines. That's why he was staying in a motel here and would be on the road again next day. And I guess we got a little high. And the more he talked the more I wanted him to keep on talking, even though he talked a lot about his work and I didn't understand much, because I just loved to listen to the sound of his voice. Then he goes, 'Why don't we go to my motel room where it's more private,' and I go, 'That's a plan,' even though I knew exactly what to expect and it seemed like the most natural thing in the world to do because I really *wanted* him, *wanted* him to make passionate love to me. Because even though I'd been having sex since I was fifteen, I *still* didn't know what it felt like to get off. But Kirk changed all that. With him I got off for the first time in my life and it was so fantastic that I thought I was going to explode. Anyway, I stayed with him all night and we got off again in the morning and it was just as fantastic as the first time. And when he dropped me off next morning at home, he said he'd be back Friday and meet me at The Kosy Korner." Bewildered, her round, pale blue eyes stared at him. "But he never came back! That was over two years ago and I haven't seen him since. And I still can't understand it. We had an awesome time together, and, like, he knew I was crazy about him, so *why* didn't he come back?"

As Rodger returned her stare, he recognized her question as almost a demand, as though a man twice her age, especially one intelligent enough to be writing a book, surely *had* to know the answer to a question which had apparently been plaguing her for years. He simply said, "Maybe he met other Vicky along the way. Maybe they gave him all he wanted."

"No!" she cried angrily. "I'm the only Vicky, nobody does it better than me. I *loved* him. Why didn't he come back?"

He tried again. "Do you not think that he would have come back if he'd reciprocated?"

"Recip...?"

"Sorry. If he'd also loved you."

"Maybe not. Like, he drives a lot. I keep thinking maybe he got in an accident, maybe got killed, and that's why he never came back."

"Tell me, before he left you the following morning, did he take down your name, address, and phone number?"

"Yes, he did. He wrote everything in a little book."

"Well, don't you think that book would've been found if he'd been killed in an accident and that you'd have been notified about the funeral?"

"Maybe they never found it. Or maybe the car caught on fire." She shuddered. "Maybe everything got burned up."

Rodger could sense her determination to continue believing her fantasy and decided to change the subject. "What about the men who came after Kirk? How did they measure up sexually?"

"They just didn't. Not one of them. Nobody else does it like Kirk, and I haven't been able to get off once since the day he left." She smiled suddenly, reached out and began gently stroking his thigh. "But maybe you're different. Like, maybe you and me could make it together."

"That's the greatest offer I've had in a long time," he said truthfully, moving her hand away. "But I can't. As I told you earlier, I'm a happily married man and I don't believe in cheating." He tried to soften his words by adding, "But I may know why you're having so many sexual problems."

Miffed, she turned away. "Oh? And what does the great, super smart *writer* have to tell me?" she demanded coldly.

"Simply this. Maybe you're still looking for Kirk."

"No, Kirk's gone, I know that, and he's never coming back."

"What I meant was, maybe you're still looking for *another* Kirk. Just a minute ago you thought that even I might be another Kirk. You're always looking for a replacement, someone else who can make you feel like he did, someone else who can make you climax like he did. And that's why you keep offering yourself to almost every man you meet."

Irate, she turned on him, her glassy eyes wandering as she tried to focus. "And what's wrong with that? What's wrong with *me* getting some pleasure out of sex instead of just giving it to men all the time? Men aren't the only ones who are supposed to get off—I know plenty of women who do it all the time." She pounded her fists against her thighs. "But it never happens to me. No matter how much I try, *it never happens to me!*" Her eyes glistening with tears, she sagged helplessly against the door.

"Look," he said. "May I offer you a bit of friendly advice which may help? You need to try to forget about Kirk completely and start looking at each man individually, each for his own merits, instead of looking at them all as merely sexual partners for your own sexual pleasure. Before you can expect to climax with a man, I think you first have to like him and even admire him. So you have to start being *selective* instead of desperate, which is what you are now. If you do—"

"Yes," she snapped, suddenly pushing away from the door and jerking toward him, her face only inches from his. "I guess I'd have to be *damn* desperate to want to go to bed with *you*, wouldn't I? I'd have to be *really* desperate to do that."

She jerked away, slouched against the door again as she stared vacantly out the window, apparently ignoring him, leaving behind in his nostrils the mingled odours of liquor and tobacco. The Juicy Fruit gum, which she'd disposed of earlier, had failed to do it's job. He could see that she spoke purely from anger at having been rejected by him, and calling her "desperate" had only added fuel to the fire. He felt that he had lost her by saying the unthinkable. It was fine for Vicky to *show* herself as being desperate, but no one was actually allowed to *say* it. But he still felt that he might be able to salvage something and pressed on. "If you do that. If you look at each man's merits first, and then decide what to do, I think you still have a good chance of finding the man you're looking for."

"And if I don't?" she challenged, facing him again.

"Well, if you don't maybe it's because you actually don't want a man. Any man."

She glared at him. "What are you saying?"

"I'm saying that deep down you may prefer women to men. That your desperate search for the right man may be merely your way of running away from the truth, which may be that you prefer women. You said that a while back Mary approached you looking for a relationship. What were your true feelings for her at that time?"

"*What!*" She laughed derisively. "You're crazy! Absolutely *crazy*. I already told you that she absolutely disgusted me."

"But were you telling me the truth?"

Her large round eyes seemed even larger as they gazed into his. "Sure I was. Why would I lie about a thing like that when lesbians are coming out of the closet all over the place?"

"Not all of them. Plenty of them are still keeping it a secret because deep down they're still ashamed of their feelings for other women. Could that be you?"

"*No!*" she shouted. "I've already told you that they disgust me. I *hate* them. Why don't you believe me?"

"I do believe you…now. Remember, I'm only trying to help. So let's move on to something else. Deep down, do you ever suffer from feelings of low self-esteem? Do you ever criticize yourself for going to bed with almost every man you meet? Do you ever feel guilty about it, and tell yourself that you don't like yourself because of what you do? Do you ever tell yourself that you must stop and try to make a better life for yourself? Do you feel inferior to other women who are more…well, more normal?"

"No, I don't feel guilty or ashamed, and I don't feel inferior either. Like, I'm giving pleasure to men, and I'm good at it—so what's wrong with that?" She paused, thinking, then admitted,

"But instead of a lot of men, I'd love to have just one man who loved me for me, Vicky, instead of just for my body."

"Tell me, do you live at home?"

"*No!* Are you kidding? I left home about three years ago and was never so glad to get out of a place in my life. Like, I got sick and tired of listening to their lectures on sex year after year after year. They'd go, 'It's wicked, and you must never enjoy it completely. And if you get married, make your husband finish in a hurry so that you don't have time to enjoy it.' They kept saying that over and over and over. I doubt if they ever had sex again after I was born. I had to get away from them, y'know, because they were driving me crazy!"

"Ah, I see. So you started acting out."

"Acting out?"

"Yes. Do your parents know about the kind of life you're leading now?"

"Are you going to tell them?" she challenged. "Do you want their phone number? Because I'll be glad to give it to you."

"No, thanks. But it sounds to me like they already know."

She laughed contemptuously. "Oh, they know all right. I made sure of that. Like, some of the old biddies who come in here, who couldn't get a man if their life depended on it, keep coming up to me and threatening to tell my parents. They're jealous as hell. So I give them my parents phone number and tell them to go ahead. Just go ahead, see if I give a damn. And I know they do squeal because the next time they see me they can't wait to tell me all about it. Y'know, would you believe it, even a few of the *men* here have phoned my parents. And I make sure they know when I'm going home with a man because I parade right by them as we leave and I'm holding onto his arm. Oh, they know all right. *Believe* me they know."

"So, as I said, you're acting out."

"Speak English. What's that supposed to mean?"

"It means that you're trying to punish your parents by doing exactly what you know they don't want you to do. And isn't that really what this is all about, Vicky?"

"Sure that's what it's all about, and why shouldn't it be? After the hell they put me through with all their stupid restrictions year after year. They had me, but that's all. Neither one of them knows what sex or passion is all about. So how do you expect me to feel? I hate them. I *hate* them both, and I'm never going to stop punishing them."

"Never?"

"*Never!* I'm going to go on punishing them *forever!*"

A gentle smile spread across his lips.

"What's so funny?" she demanded angrily. "Is this some kind of joke to you?"

"No. No joke. I was just thinking of a famous German saying, which goes like this: 'Vee grow too soon oldt, and too late schmart.'

"What's that supposed to mean?"

"Never mind," he said, shaking his head. Try this. Have you heard about the eighteen-year-old daughter who left home because she couldn't stand her parents?"

"And?"

"When she returned home at twenty-five, she was amazed at how much her parents had learned."

"I don't understand. Do parents *ever* learn *anything*?"

He saw now the pointlessness of trying to make her understand any statement which contained even a crumb of intimation, especially when meant to criticize her own conduct. Only bald-faced bluntness would penetrate Vicky's callow mind.

"See," he explained, "it was actually the twenty-five-year old daughter who had finally learned what the parents had known all along."

She glared at him. "Are you trying to tell me that I'm stupid just because I don't believe what my parents believe? That I'm supposed to spend the rest of my life believing that sex is bad, that it's evil?"

"No, I don't think you're stupid. But I do think that you're still very young, and still clinging to very young ideas and beliefs. You still believe that today is forever, that your attitudes toward your parents and your life will never change. But we do mature, and we do change, and when we compare our earlier life with our life today we see that change." Tentatively, he reached down and gently gripped her hand. She didn't pull away, but neither did she return his grip. "Vicky, I want you to do me a favour. Not tonight, or next month, or even next year. I want you to do me a favour on your twenty-fifth birthday. On your twenty-fifth birthday, I want you to sit down and remember tonight and honestly ask yourself how you feel about life and about your parents."

"I won't feel any different. Why should I?"

"Because if we don't grow, we stagnate, and if we stagnate we can never mature and move on to more productive lives. I'm going through that right now with my own life, and eventually I'll be making changes, even though I still don't know what those changes will be. Will you promise me that you'll do what I asked on your twenty-fifth birthday?"

She shrugged. "Sure. Okay. What difference does it make."

He could see that she was still taking his suggestion lightly, that she expected nothing to come of it, and decided to give her something serious to think about. "See, Vicky, you still think you hate your parents, but subconsciously you actually don't."

She jerked her hand away. "I'm tired of this conversation. You don't know what you're talking about." She unlatched the door. "I'm going back inside."

"Wait. Don't you even want to know why?"

She sighed heavily, but left the door unlatched. "All right, Mr. Know-it-all, tell me why. Tell me how I can possibly not hate them when I'm doing everything they told me not to do for years and years."

"Not everything, Vicky."

"What do you mean? I told you that I'm going to be with men all the time and making sure they know all about it. Isn't that everything?"

"No, it isn't. Oh, I'm sure your behaviour is hurting them, as I'm sure such behaviour would hurt any decent parents. But subconsciously you must be still listening to them because you're *not* doing the other thing they told you not to do. You're not *climaxing.*"

Her wide, round eyes became even rounder as the truth of what he'd just said dawned on her. The door latched gently. Her mouth opened and closed, opened and closed, soundlessly, until finally she managed to squeeze out, "But...but..." And then, succumbing, her head fell back against the headrest, her slender neck arching as her mouth opened wide in a harsh, bitter, self-deprecating laugh.

Her laughter went on and on, but Rodger waited until, exhausted, she sagged limply into silence, her eyes tightly closed. She remained still for so long that he thought she may have passed out from the liquor, but finally she roused herself and gazed at him with what he saw as a new respect. Now he could clearly see the desperation in her eyes as she chewed nervously on her lower lip.

"Like, what am I supposed to do now?" she pleaded.

"Well, for a start, stop acting out and trying to punish your parents all the time. That's immature. I believe what you really want to do, even though you refuse to admit it, is to gain your parents' respect, get them to like you, even love you, something you've apparently never been able to do in the past. And that I suppose is because of the way you've acted."

"How do you expect me to act," she cried, "when the only kind of daughter they'd appreciate is one who went and lived in a convent and became a nun."

"I don't believe that. I believe that you were on the right track with Kirk. The only problem was you were on a one-way street. You loved him, but to him you were just another one-night stand, just another sexual conquest in another motel as he travelled around Ontario. No commitment. And he proved that when he never came back, even though he must've known how you felt about him and that a serious, permanent relationship was possible. No, Vicky, you definitely *don't* want another Kirk, someone who's only interested in you for your great body. Stop using him as an example and try to wipe him completely out of your mind, because when you do that you will allow yourself to pursue a serious relationship. Because that's what you *do* want: someone who's looking for a serious relationship. Someone who loves you for yourself, for the person you are, and not just for your body. A lasting relationship has to go far deeper than just two bodies connecting. And when you find such a man, and you feel the same about him, nothing can stop you from being successful, both personally and sexually. Not Kirk. Not even your parents."

She continued to gaze at him, thinking. Finally, she asked, "And what about you? Are you *really* happily married?"

"Yes, I am. Claudia and I have been happily married for ten years." But even as he voiced the words he wondered how much longer their happiness would last. Since his fortieth birthday, their previously calm marriage waters had become choppy and muddied. Where would this search, this exploration, eventually lead him? "And speaking of marriage," he said, glancing at his watch. "It's eight-thirty and I want to be home by about nine."

"But..." She sounded anxious. "But I still have this urge. Like, *all* the time. What am I going to do about it? Now?"

"Channel it. Channel it toward someone you're interested in as a *person*. For your part, you could start by changing the way you dress. The way you look now you're nothing but an open invitation to any man on the make. Dress more conservatively. Then men will approach you as a person instead of a sex symbol." He glanced at his watch again. "Now I've really got to get going. May I drive you home?"

"No, it's too early to go home yet. I'm going back inside for a while."

He didn't know exactly how many drinks she'd had before meeting him, but two would mean that she'd now had a total of four. And it still showed. "Haven't you had enough to drink? Wouldn't it be wise to go home now?"

"No." She opened the door. "Don't worry, I know when I've had enough. I'll let Larry buy me a few drinks. That always helps. A girl don't make much as a cashier at Zellers. Then he can drive me home. Unless, of course, someone more promising shows up. Someone like you said, y'know. Will you be here next Friday? I'm only here on Fridays; I'll bring you up to date."

"I'll be here," he said, his curiosity piqued, although he still hadn't planned that far ahead. "And you'll remember what I told you?"

"Sure." She swung her shapely legs out of the car and stood. "Later, Rodger."

"Yes. Later."

He watched her as she moved toward The Kosy Korner, hips swaying less than earlier, her walk reasonably steady. At the door, she turned and waved, smiled radiantly, and disappeared inside.

On the drive north on Highway 10 to Orangeville, he left the digital recorder on and wedged it securely into one of the coffee cup holders in the caddy and recorded his reflections of the evening. What had he actually learned that evening at The Kosy Korner which would help him on his quest to bring some purposeful meaning into his own life? Apparently nothing. Mary had told him that the most important thing in life was to be yourself, but he already knew that. And he also knew the sad truth that you couldn't possibly *be* yourself unless you knew who you actually *were*. Vicky, of course, still groped around in the angry adolescent stage, and her only hope lay in learning and advancing toward maturity. He had tried to help her and, hopefully, the shock of discovering that in one way she still observed her parents' will might help her to change her life. Although he wondered why he had even bothered speaking to Vicky after Mary had already described her character (perhaps he believed that Mary's hatred toward Vicky had caused her to lie), and Vicky's clothing certainly failed to fit the conservative bill, he still felt glad that he'd spoken to her and tried to advise her. But did he sincerely *want* to help her? Or had he merely exhibited the ageless male attraction for a sexy female, regardless of her mental capacity.

As for himself, other than having had an interesting evening with three very different women, he felt that nothing important had been achieved. It seemed that instead of learning how to live from these three women, he had only learned how *not* to live.

7

One truth that Rodger had learned from being married to Claudia for ten years was that women were impetuous and unpredictable. He once came home from his day's work at Drummond to find Claudia dressed in a smart beige pantsuit and ready to go out. She told him to eat his dinner quickly, then shower and dress because they were going to the Orangeville Opera House to see Rod Beattie in *Wingfield*. She had caught him completely by surprise. Knowing that he enjoyed *Wingfield,* she had bought the tickets weeks earlier and had deliberately failed to tell him. This typified only one of many incidents over their married life when she suddenly, at least to him, decided to do things which he knew nothing about until she actually brought them forward. Not for his consideration, but for his acquiescence, which he seldom refused. He began to expect these impulses, although he rarely knew their content, and attributed her need for them as a contrivance to continually rejuvenate her own mysteriousness and thereby maintain his interest in her. And they did. Rodger knew that only foolish women played all their cards early in their relationships; wise women doled them out one at a time over the years from a very large deck.

And Claudia certainly proved this again when he arrived home from The Kosy Korner and entered the living room where the only light glowed from the blue television screen, and he knew that Claudia had tuned in one of the commercial-free music channels. He listened, his mouth falling open in surprise as he heard a soft, gentle piano rendition of *No Other Love,* one of their favourite compositions, almost as though she had contrived, through some form of witchcraft, to have it played just as he entered the living room. A dark shadow, Claudia sat lounged on the living room sofa, a wine glass raised in her hand. As he watched, she took a sip and placed the glass on the coffee table.

"Ah, you're home at last," she said, coolly, he thought.

"Yes." The smell of fried onions floated in from the kitchen. As he approached for their habitual greeting kiss, he noticed that her bare feet were up, her shapely legs outstretched with ankles crossed. As he reached out and gripped her shoulder, he felt the distinct, scant silkiness of her long-sleeved black negligee, which ran from neck to knees, and knew from past experience that she lay naked beneath it. Occasionally in the past, Rodger had been treated to the scanty, ultimately sheer black negligee, whose few seams provided the only miniscule shielding for her nakedness, and now, fearing that even his touch would damage it, he softened his grip.

As he bent to kiss her, he thought he might have heard her sniff. If so, had she sniffed for perfume? Or a womanly body odour? Or perhaps simply because she needed to blow her nose. In any case, her kiss, cool and quick, unnerved him. Was she already suspicious? Did she already suspect, or actually know, that he hadn't worked that evening? Still, here she lay, naked beneath her flimsy black negligee and emanating that musky perfume she knew he enjoyed so much, ready to take him to bed. And even if she did know, what had he to fear? He'd done nothing more than innocently speak to a few women and try to help them. And he'd already warned her that, because of his mid-life crisis, he might be doing some strange things, hadn't he?   "You've been drinking," she accused.

"Yes," he admitted, having forgotten that she'd smell the liquor on his breath, but instead of confessing the truth he found himself clinging to it possessively and saying, "Ray and I had a couple after work. To relax."

"I see." She smiled radiantly, but he had no idea what her smile meant. She sat up and placed her bare feet into her slippers. "Do you know what I want you to do, darling?"

"What."

"I want you to go upstairs now and take a good shower. Then I want you to just put on your pajamas and come back downstairs. I've prepared a lovely dinner for us. One of your favourites—steak and fried onions. Hurry! I'm simply starving!"

"You prepared dinner? This late?"

"Yes. Just for you, darling. You *are* hungry, aren't you?"

"Of course I am. Famished." The last thing he wanted her to know was that he'd already had dinner in Brampton, but that had been over three hours ago and he knew that he could do justice to her excellent steak and fried onions. "What's the occasion?"

Laughing softy, she took his hands and placed them against the warm mounds of her breasts. "This is the occasion. I've been thinking about you for hours. Now, hurry!"

He gave her breasts a gentle squeeze, then headed for the stairs. "I'll be right back."

Later, when he walked into the dining room, bare-armed and bare-legged in summer pajamas, Claudia, with her back to him and bent over the table with its white linen tablecloth, had just lit the first of two tall, red candles. He saw that she had bent over too far, having to reach up to light the candle, and realized that she had deliberately done this for his benefit when she heard him coming, giving him and excellent view of her incredible posterior. He stared as she repeated the motion on the second candle, pretending to be oblivious to his presence, and wondered why any sane man would ever leave a woman with a body like this for sex with another woman.

She straightened and turned, smiling. "My, don't you look sexy in your shortie pajamas."

He knew when a return compliment was required, and made it gladly. "Not half as sexy as you in that black negligee."

Rodger laughed as Claudia, her almost empty glass carried high, flounced into the kitchen, hips swinging wildly, and returned a few minutes later with two steaming platters.

White wine had already been poured, and salads served. He noted that his platter also contained two of his favourite vegetables: baby carrots and green peas. They dug in eagerly, taking intermittent sips of their white wine as they ate, saying little and frequently gazing possessively at each other, enjoying their dinner but enjoying the anticipation of what would follow even more.

Rodger suddenly recalled the doubtful, round-eyed look Vicky had given him when he admitted that he was forty, as though his days of performing sexually were already over, and now, although he felt absolutely raunchy, he began to question his ability to perform when the moment of truth arrived. *Could* he perform? Or had he already begun to descend that slippery slope which bottomed out at impotence? Would he soon be a likely candidate for Viagra? Although still hungry, he found himself cutting his steak into smaller pieces and chewing them longer, going to the wine glass more often, attempting to push the inevitable bedroom scene further away.

"Is something wrong?" Claudia asked suspiciously. "Aren't you hungry?—you're eating like a bird."

"Yes. Yes, I am." Now he had to eat faster. "I'm sorry…I was daydreaming."

"About what?"

"About you. About how beautiful you look in that black negligee. And how much more beautiful you'll look after I've taken it off."

She smiled, pleased. "Then eat up, and soon you'll be able to find out."

He ate faster, drained his second glass of wine, asked for a third while telling himself to slow down on the drinking because he wasn't used to it, yet wanting to drink a little more to calm himself.

Claudia finished ahead of him and rose. Bending over, she reached across the table and patted his hand several times, giving him a tempting view of her full, pendulous breasts. "I'm going up now, darling. *Please* don't be long."

"I'll be there in a few minutes," he promised.

He gazed at the provocative shift of her buttocks as she walked away, then returned to his dinner, now forcing the food into him until he had emptied the platter. He reached for his wine glass and brought it to his lips, intending to drain its contents, then stopped and returned it to the table. Drinking more would probably relax him, but it could also weaken his ability to perform. He drank some water instead.

When he reached the bedroom, he found the bedclothes removed and Claudia lying invitingly on the bed, still wearing the black negligee, smiling, with eyes closed. When she heard him approach, she opened her eyes and extended her arms.

"Come, darling."

He slid in beside her and gathered her into his arms and kissed her passionately until he felt the heat rising dangerously between their bodies, leaving them gasping for each other as her muskiness invaded his nostrils, then pulled the black negligee over her head and hurriedly undressed himself before reaching for her again.

"I want you to love me like you never have before," she said softly, almost whispering. "I want you to make me come like I've never come before. I want you to make me see a million stars exploding in the dark. I...I want you to make me...to make me scream with pleasure. I...want...you...to...to...to...

And he did. Magnificently.

Later, as they lay side by side, his arm cradling her as she relaxed with her head on his chest, eyes closed, each of them still luxuriating in the afterglow of their lovemaking, he mentally tapped himself on the back for his sterling performance. He'd never been better, and had worried for nothing. Even so, the doubts began to creep back in. Sure, he was fine now, but what about next month, next year, five years from now? Ten? Twenty? Whatever it took to reach the bottom of that slippery slope where he would no longer be able to perform at all. What then? What would replace the sexual experience when even Viagra or Cialis would no longer work? Or when his prostate had been removed? What would be the substitute then? Booze? Gambling? Fishing or hunting? Collecting stamps or coins? Doing wild, stupid, dangerous things like bungee jumping, skydiving, or car racing? Yes, any of these pursuits would certainly relieve the boredom, but would any of them bring any *meaning* into his life? Would any of them—?

"Rodger?"

"Yes?" He stiffened involuntarily, knowing from past experience that what followed after her "darling" turned to "Rodger" usually brought a problem with it.

She pulled away, raised herself on one elbow, stared demandingly into his eyes. "Rodger, where *were* you tonight?"

Now he knew absolutely that she knew he hadn't worked late, and he also knew that it would be pointless to lie. After all, why should he when he had done nothing more than have a few drinks and speak to a few women.

"How did you find out I wasn't working?"

"When I arrived home I found that we needed milk and phoned your office to ask you to pick some up at Mac's on the way home, but there was no answer. Everyone had gone, including you. Where *were* you?" I went to Brampton. I've started work on a new book and went to a restaurant and a bar to interview a few women, try to find out if they had something to tell me that would help me in my own search. You've already told me that you like your life the way it is and have no intention of changing it. And I've already told you that I need to change mine, find some worthwhile purpose for it. I didn't do anything wrong with these women, just talked to them, asked them questions about themselves. The same kind of thing you do practically every day with your male clients." He paused, thinking, then added, "Only I didn't wear a miniskirt."

Claudia ignored the innuendo. "And tell me, what did you learn from these three women?"

"Nothing worthwhile," he admitted. "The one in the restaurant was a homely Catholic hypocrite, the first one in the bar was a lesbian, and the second one in the bar sounded like a nymphomaniac. The only thing I learned from all three was how *not* to live, and that's how I'll put them into the book, as negative examples." He paused, expecting a response. When nothing came, he asked, "Aren't you interested in the nymphomaniac? I thought you'd want to know everything about her, about what happened."

"Oh, I know nothing happened. I'm absolutely certain of that."

"You are? How?" Her reaction disappointed him. Where was the jealousy?

She smiled confidently. "Don't you know yet? You're a rifle, Rodger, not a six-shooter. You just made love to me, didn't you?" She reached down and slid two fingers under his flaccid penis as it lay on his thigh. "This thing," she said, flipping his penis to the other thigh, "is finished for at least twenty-four hours, probably more. So I have absolutely no fear whatsoever that you had sex with your little nymphomaniac just a few hours ago." She lowered her head to his chest and placed her arm across his body. "I do trust you, darling. I do. And I'm trying very hard to understand what you're going through, and I do sympathize with you, but I do wish you'd give up this silliness as soon as possible." She hugged him possessively and planted a few kisses on his chest. "Isn't this enough for us? What we had tonight? And all the other wonderful things we have? Why can't you be satisfied?"

"Well, for one thing, I don't like what I'm doing being referred to as 'silliness.' For another, I'm going to continue with my search until I find what I want." He reached down and gripped her shoulders firmly, until she raised her head and looked at him. "Claudia, where are we going?" he said desperately. "Where the *hell* are we going?"

On Saturday evening, as Rodger and Claudia sat in the living room watching television and sipping red wine after a good dinner, Claudia had another surprise for him.

Clicking the remote control mute button, she said casually, "Mom and dad will be coming for dinner tomorrow."

"Oh? Why wasn't I informed earlier?" He couldn't keep the irritation from his voice. "Why didn't we discuss this before *you* made the decision? We're married, aren't we? Aren't married people supposed to agree on things before they're done?"

"Aren't you being just a tiny bit petulant, darling? I've invited my parents for Sunday dinner dozens of times over the years and you've never said anything, and now, suddenly, you're upset. Why now?"

"I'm not the same person I was years ago. I'm not even the same person I was last week."

"Oh, we're back to that again, are we? You and your mid-life crisis. Am I not supposed to be able to make any decisions now without consulting you first?"

"I didn't say that. I just feel that this is one of the things that *should* be discussed, that's all. Is that asking too much?"

She stared at him long and hard, finally said, "I know you don't like my father. I know—"

"He's not your father. He's you *step*father. It's not the same thing."

"All right then. I know you don't like my *step*-father. I know you don't like his principles, and that's why you stopped working for him."

"You're right, I don't like him. I never have. But that isn't the only reason why I don't like the way you've kept me in the dark about this."

"Then what is it?"

"I just don't like the timing, that's all."

"The timing? What timing? What are you talking about?"

"I go out last night and meet a few young women, and two days later Gunderson is coming over for dinner. Did you phone him and tell him what's been going on? And invite him over so that he could browbeat me?"

"Of course not!" she blurted out. "I may have mentioned it to mother…and maybe she told him…but they're just coming over for dinner and a few drinks, and to play some cards."

"Sure, tell me another one. If you told your mother, she certainly told Gunderson, which you knew she would. And if Gunderson knows, he'll be coming over here with both guns blazing. You made sure of that, didn't you?"

She reached out and placed her soft hand gently over his. "I know you're going through a difficult time, darling. But you need someone to talk to, and I don't seem to be that person. He's been through it—maybe he can help."

"Help?" He drew his hand away. "Hell, Gunderson only helps when there's money to be made, and there's no money to be made out of me. No, he's coming here for one reason only: to try to tell me how to run my life. And I don't intend to listen to him. As a matter of fact, for the first time in my life I'm going to tell him exactly what I think of him. I'm going to—"

"No!" She gripped his forearm so tightly that he felt her fingernails digging in. "You can't do that, you just *can't*."

"You just wait and see. Remember, I'm not the same person I was a week ago."

8

On Sunday afternoon, Gregory and Sally Gunderson arrived at four o'clock, an hour before dinner, and joined Rodger and Claudia in the living room where soft, relaxing music played on one of the television music channels.

As Rodger knew he would, Gunderson carried a purple Crown Royal string bag which he dropped to the coffee table with a heavy thud and said, "For later. Nothing like a little poker game to spice things up."

Rodger stifled a heavy sigh. The same old story. The Crown Royal bag containing several rolls of pennies and nickels, the penny-to-a-nickel dealer's choice poker game after dinner which no one liked except Gunderson. The women would have much preferred bridge, and Rodger cribbage, but Gunderson sneered at bridge as being "a fag's game" and cribbage as being "just plain stupid." How he arrived at these appraisals, Rodger never learned. So they had always played dealer's choice penny-to-a-nickel poker, as Gunderson demanded, and Rodger suspected that he knew Gunderson's motive: Gunderson knew that he played bridge or cribbage ineptly, but also knew that he played poker well, rarely losing, especially when competing against three players who were bored with the game. Only winning mattered to Gunderson—even when those winnings were only pennies or nickels.

While Sally gave Claudia and Rodger gentle hugs, Gunderson boomed, "Get any of my beer in, Claudia? Labatt's Blue?" More than anything, his loud baritone voice made his question a demand.

"Yes, dad, I'll get you one."

Gunderson glanced suspiciously at the two mugs of coffee on the coffee table. "Nobody else drinking? I'm not drinking alone," he warned.

"We're having wine with dinner," Claudia said. "We thought we'd wait."

"Wait, shmait. What's wrong with you people?"

"We just didn't want to spoil our dinner," Rodger said firmly. "Is there anything wrong with that?"

Gunderson turned toward Rodger, his brow wrinkling as a confused look came into his beady brown eyes. Rarely had he ever been contradicted by Rodger, and as he searched for a reply, Sally said softly, "I'll join you, dear. Claudia, may I have a glass of white wine?"

"Of course." Claudia left for the kitchen.

Gunderson gave Rodger a long stare, grunted, plodded to a sofa and sat down heavily. Five-eight and weighing over two hundred pounds, at fifty-seven Gunderson still thought of himself as manly, but Rodger found him to be a comic figure, dressed as always in his cowboy costume: expensive brown cowboy boots, expensive jeans with a wide belt sporting a large, brass lion's head buckle, expensive pale blue western style shirt with snap metal buttons, fancy, colourful embroidery, two curved, arrow-ended pockets, and a black string tie with a brass ram's head clip. Today, he wore a black stetson—he had them in many colours—which Rodger knew he wouldn't remove unless he began to sweat profusely, mainly because the stetson covered a balding head where wisps of hair had been allowed to grow long and been pasted across his scalp in a feeble attempt to cover the baldness. He had no neck, his fat, round, red, double-chinned, clean-shaven face, with its pudgy lips and slightly hooked nose, sitting squarely on his shoulders.

On the surface, Gunderson appeared to be nothing more than just another jolly, carefree fat man, exactly the image he tried to foist on his clients, jauntily backslapping the men, obsequiously flattering the women, and pandering to the children with chocolate bars or suckers. Rodger knew better. It was all nothing more than a memorable image Gunderson had deliberately created to make himself stand out from other real estate salesmen so that he could get more business and fatten his own bank account, while lying to his clients whenever required to close a sale. Beyond that, he had little use for home buyers.

Now, as Rodger gazed at Gunderson slouched smugly on the sofa, huge beer belly overhanging his belt, knees spread vulgarly apart, he sensed the pompous disdain emanating from the man. Whenever he met with clients, he always wore his belt up on his belly and supported it with a pair of wide, usually red, suspenders. Nor would he ever dare to sit with his knees sprawled vulgarly apart. After all, he had an image to maintain. No, he reserved his disdain for the three of them: Sally, Claudia, and Rodger. And why not? Why put on a show here? Was there any money to be made?

Claudia returned and handed out the drinks, giving Gunderson his Labatt's Blue in the bottle because she knew he never drank beer from a glass, and seated herself beside Rodger. Gunderson guzzled down half the bottle without stopping, then placed it on the side table, ignoring the coaster there.

"Would you mind putting the bottle on the coaster," Rodger said firmly. "We don't want rings on the table."

"What the hell's the difference?" Gunderson laughed loudly, insolently. "Is it a Chippendale or something?"

"Greg...please..." Sally murmured.

Rodger felt Claudia's hand gripping his tightly, and recognized this as her warning for him to stop, but he had listened to this kind of thing from Gunderson for too many years, ever since he had quit working for him, and refused to comply.

"No, it's not a Chippendale," he said. "But I still don't want to see it marked with water rings. There's a coaster right there. Use it, please."

Gunderson stared at him long and hard, his face reddening even more than normal; Rodger stared back, refusing to look away, bolstered by the thought that at that moment he could read Gunderson's mind, which told Gunderson that Rodger Blackwell was suddenly no longer his passive lapdog.

"All right!" Gunderson roared, his eyes shifting to the bottle. "I'll use your goddamn coaster!" Grabbing the bottle, he slammed it down so hard against the coaster that beer and foam flowed out onto the table.

"Greg...*please!*" Sally pleaded.

Claudia snatched a box of Kleenex from the coffee table and rushed to wipe up the spill. Satisfied, she returned to Rodger, giving him a warning glance as she sat down, reinforcing the glance by gripping his hand tightly.

Rodger gazed at Sally Gunderson, whose history he knew well, learning most of it over the years from Claudia. Sally had refused to retain the Hewitt name because she had wanted to distance herself as far as possible from Charles, her first husband, who had been quiet, passive, elementary school educated, and ambitionless, perfectly content to take any menial, low-paying job that came along. Rodger spoke to him occasionally when he went to pick up the odd article at Wal-Mart, where Charles worked happily as a greeter. But, with Rodger usually in a hurry, their brief conversations had never developed beyond the small talk stage. Now, as Sally's image reminded him of the forgotten Charles, he felt a desire to visit the man, perhaps where he lived, to discover how a person can work at a job which probably paid him barely minimum wage and genuinely enjoy it, while he, Rodger, who had a lovely home with all the trimmings, a lovely wife, and a well-paying job, apparently all the requirements necessary for happiness, felt miserable and trapped inside an alien's body.

Petite Sally once admitted to him that she had loved Charles in the beginning, but this love was contingent upon achieving something which many wives thought they could achieve: a transformation of the man she married into the type of husband she actually wanted. But this never happened. When they met, she was eighteen, he twenty-two, and when they started a sexual relationship without using protection she quickly became pregnant, and her parents, being Roman Catholics, ordered her to marry Charles and have the baby. She obeyed, largely because at that early stage of their relation-ship she loved Charles and felt certain that she wanted to spend the rest of her life with him.

Before marrying passive Charles, she thought that she'd be perfectly happy being the boss of the household and telling her husband what to do, and in the beginning, busy raising Claudia, she was, but as their years together became five, ten, fifteen, twenty, she had long since realized that no amount of womanly wiles, or

pleading, or tears would ever convince Charles to become the kind
of ambitious, driving, extroverted person required to give her the
financial and social life she had always craved. She wanted both
layers of a chocolate cake, which she loved, but had been given
a cake with both chocolate and white layers: his passivity toward
her chocolate, his lack of ambition toward the rest of the world
white, and the filling separating the two layers like concrete. This
perpetual incompatibility forced them to live in a small, cramped
apartment, and forced Sally to take waitressing or cleaning jobs to
help them survive.

Finally, absolutely certain that their marriage held little
fulfilment or happiness for her, she informed Charles that she
wanted to end it, and Charles, who by now had grown tired of her
incessant nagging, agreed passively. Since they were both Roman
Catholics at the time, and had been married in St. Mary's Catholic
Church, they agreed that they should proceed properly by having
the marriage annulled. This they did, the process taking years to
finalize, Sally citing mental and emotional cruelty. As neither of
them desired to fend for themselves, they also agreed to live together platonically until their annulment finalized.

It was toward the end of this waiting period while waitressing at the Dufferin Restaurant on Broadway that Sally met loud,
flamboyant Gregory Gunderson, dressed in full, colourful cowboy
gear, who came in early one evening to wine and dine a real estate
client. His appearance and manner immediately enthralled her.
Here was a real man, a man with ambition, a man who knew where
he was going, a man who wouldn't take "no" for an answer from
anyone. As for Gunderson's part, he became infatuated with her
on successive visits to the restaurant and they soon began dating,
but she adamantly refused all sexual contact, not even allowing
him to kiss her, informing him of her pending annulment and
promising to be more lovable in the future.

Months later, when she finally found herself free, they began
a sexual relationship which soon became a marriage proposal. Her
first disappointment came when Gunderson laughed and flatly refused when she mentioned being married in a Catholic church.
Unthinking, she had assumed that he attended church regularly,

but soon discovered that he had once belonged to the Anglican church but hadn't attended services there for many years, and had no intention of setting a foot inside *any* church. For weeks, she agonized over breaking with her church to marry him, but finally relented as day after day he kept pouring on the many material and hedonistic benefits of being married to Gregory Gunderson.

But Sally still ended up with only half the cake—the opposite half. Where with Charles she'd had a meek and passive husband and no spare money, she now had a generous allowance with which to buy herself a large, impressive wardrobe and multifarious accessories and jewellery, vacationed in places like Aruba, Miami Beach, Mexico, and Paris, became part of the local country club set, belonged to euchre and bridge clubs, attended parties, and regularly ate out at Orangeville's finest restaurants, but had a husband who ruled the roost, browbeating, criticizing, and nagging her until *she* became the meek and passive partner.

Still, Rodger knew that she preferred this marriage over her marriage to Charles, accepting its drawbacks philosophically, believing that she had been too selfish by expecting to possess the entire cake, her main regret being that she'd had to leave the church.

Now, as he gazed at Sally sitting quietly on the sofa, taking occasional nips from her white wine, so tiny, he couldn't help pitying her, yet wondered, although her superficial, hedonistic life probably made her a poor subject, if he still might learn something from her which would aid him with his own predicament. As he continued to wonder, he caught a movement out of the corner of his left eye and turned to see Gunderson moistening a now glossy cigar between his fat lips.

"What do you think you're doing?" Rodger demanded.

"What does it look like I'm doing?" Gunderson said, reaching into a pocket and removing a lighter. "I'm having a cigar."

"Not in here you're not." He felt Claudia's fingernails digging into his forearm, but continued firmly. "Every time you leave here it takes about three days to get rid of the cigar stink."

"You never objected before. What's so different about today?"

"I'm a different person today, that's what's different, and I'm saying that you can't smoke in here. This is *my* house."

"*Our* house, darling," Claudia corrected gently.

With the glossy cigar in a corner of his mouth, a smirk spread across Gunderson's fat lips. "So, Blackwell, what part of the house are we in now? Yours or Claudia's?"

Rodger turned to Claudia and met her eyes. "I'll let my wife answer that."

After a few moments, she said, "You're in *our* part of the house."

Gunderson scowled, his face reddening, but refused to remove the cigar or put the lighter away. Looking for support elsewhere, he turned to Sally and asked, "What do you think of this shit, Sal?"

"Greg…*please!* That kind of language isn't necessary."

"Just tell me what you think!"

"Well, I think that this could all be settled very easily and very amicably." She waved toward the sunny bay window. "It's a lovely, warm day. We could all go out onto the patio and you could smoke your cigar there."

Rodger could see by Gunderson's scowl that he again felt betrayed but was still determined to exact his pound of flesh. "Not you, Sal," he commanded. "You stay here." He pointed at Rodger. "And you, too." He guzzled the remainder of his beer and lumbered to his feet. "Claudia, get me another beer; I want to talk to you on the patio."

"Yes, dad."

When Rodger heard the patio door at the back of the kitchen slide closed behind them, he thought he knew what they'd be saying to each other. Gunderson would demand an explanation, and Claudia would blame everything on Rodger's mid-life crisis and beg him to be patient, promising that Rodger would soon be back to his normal, passive self.

But Rodger had no intention of reverting to his normal, passive self. Ever again.

He gazed at Sally Gunderson sitting primly a few feet away, dressed in sky blue Bermuda shorts, a matching halter easily supporting her petite breasts, the demurely crossed nut-brown legs of her nut-brown body still smooth and shapely . At fifty-six (Claudia had confided her age to him), and five-foot-two, he felt certain that she weighed under a hundred pounds and had often thought that he could pick her up and carry her under one arm. Claudia told him that she'd once been a lovely woman, and he believed her, but even when he met Sally ten years earlier he could see that loveliness beginning to fade and become, as it was today, a pleasing but conventional prettiness. Her hair, once black, glistening, vibrant, still caressed her naked shoulders, but had become a dry, dull blonde, the gray roots meticulously touched up almost daily. Although the light brown eyes, boldly outlined with mascara and brown eye shadow, still sparkled, and the sensual lips were painted as red as ever, even her makeup could no longer hide the creases running from her small nose to her mouth, or the crow's feet fanning out at the edges of her eyes. She wanted to look young, feel young, be young forever, but he knew that her face, when stripped nightly of its protective covering, would look much older than her fifty-six years.

He realized that over the years he'd never actually carried on any lengthy, personal, one-on-one conversation with Sally, mainly because Gunderson, who invariably seemed to monopolize the conversation, had usually been around. Either that or she and Claudia would be indulging in girl talk. Also, Rodger had previously felt no need or desire to speak personally with Sally. But now, with Gunderson on the patio with Claudia, he had an opportunity.

"I'm sorry," Sally said. "Greg can be such a boor at times. But he can also be very gentle and loving."

He detected a tiny smile as she spoke, as though she were congratulating him for finally standing up to Gunderson. "Oh? I guess I haven't been lucky enough to see that side of him yet."

Although detecting the dig, her smile remained. "I know he can be difficult at times, but try not to be too hard on him. He's simply one of those people who must feel that he's always in control of every situation, and when he loses that control he finds it very difficult to accept. Once you realize that that's the way he is, you can usually determine how he's going to act in most situations—and try to accept him."

"And do *you* accept him? Entirely?"

"Well, not entirely, that would be foolish. But I do try very hard never to make waves. After all, there are certain compensations."

"Are you happy, then? With these compensations?"

She reflected for a few moments before answering. "Yes, I think I am. I now get to do many of the things I wanted to do when I was married to Ducky, but never could."

He noticed that she still called Charles "Ducky," the pet name she had for him during their marriage. "Have you ever considered your life a waste?"

"A waste?" She appeared surprised by his question. "Why would I ever think that?"

"Well, what I mean is do you ever feel that life is passing you by, that you're not actually doing any-thing important with it?"

"But I am doing something important with my life. I've just told you that."

"You mean because now you can do many of the things you want, and are given the money to buy yourself many of the things you want."

She frowned, affronted. "You talk as though I'm nothing more than a common kept woman. Believe me, to live with a man like Greg is no picnic. I earn every penny he gives me, and more."

"I didn't mean it that way—I know what he's like. I've been the butt of his insults for years. What I meant was, you believe you're happy because of the things money allows you to do, and to buy, and to have."

"Of course. I've spent too many years with Ducky, scrimping by and always watching every penny, and I know how awful that is. So why shouldn't I be happy now?"

It never ceased to amaze Rodger how North Americans almost always equated happiness with the possession of plenty of money, and it never occurred to them that there were other roads to happiness. "Has it never occurred to you, now that you're reasonably happy, and reasonably content, and have access to money, that you could expand your horizons? That you could move outside the box?"

"Outside the box?"

"Yes. Move outside yourself and do something for others less fortunate than yourself. Like volunteering. Or donating to worthwhile charities. Have you ever considered anything like that?"

"Why should I?" she said angrily. "Did anyone help Ducky and I when we were struggling to sur-vive for all those years? We couldn't even collect welfare because our earnings were too high. So why should I help anyone else? Let them struggle and try to make a better life for themselves, as I did. Besides, if Greg ever found out that I was using my credit cards to make donations to charities, he'd take them away. He absolutely *hates* charities, thinks they're all a bunch of crooks lining their own pockets." She reflected for a few moments, then continued. "Of course, I could make a few donations to the food bank; Greg would simply think I was buying groceries for ourselves." She nodded. "Yes, I might just do that. And maybe I could even offer to volunteer there now and then."

Rodger had learned many years ago that "could" or "might" or "maybe" didn't mean "would" or "will," and strongly suspected that she would do nothing. He had his answer and decided not to pursue the subject any further. "So why do you think we're all here then, on this tiny planet floating around in space? Do you think there's any real point to life?"

He had changed subjects so quickly that her mouth dropped open in surprise. Finally, she said, "I used to think, when I was still going to church, that all that mattered was to be a good, generous, loving person and in the end, when I died, I'd be rewarded." She laughed. "But I don't believe that nonsense any more. Not after what Ducky and I went through. Even when Greg absolutely refused to marry in the Catholic church, or any church, I wasn't devastated, just disappointed in him. Yes, it took me months of soul searching to make my final decision. But in the end I felt only a tiny pang of guilt at leaving the church, and a little disappointment because I still sometimes felt that maybe, just maybe, the church still had something to offer." She laughed again. "But not any more—that's all behind me now. I realize now that you can't have everything you want out of life, but I've got *most* of the important things I want, and that makes me happy. And that's *all* that matters."

"Is it? Is it really?"

"Yes, it is," she said firmly.

He detected nothing in her voice which told him that she believed otherwise. Still, he had doubts. "So, if I were to ask you what you thought life was all about, you'd say it was all about having plenty of money to buy the things you want, travelling to exotic places, eating in fancy restaurants, belonging to the local bridge club and the local country club, going to parties, and owning a fancy car and a fancy house. Is that about what you'd say?"

"You're teasing me, aren't you," she said, smiling gently. "Oh, I can see by your face that you're disappointed in me, that you were expecting something more from me, perhaps something inspirational, something filled with high ideals, and that you must think my life is nothing more than a great deal of pointless, foolish nonsense. A great deal of utter selfishness. Well, maybe I am selfish, but I've become this way because of my empty, destitute, miserable past. And now that I've got something I want, I'm going to cling to it with every ounce of my strength."

Rodger could now clearly see Sally's influence on Claudia's way of life. And combined with Gunderon's insatiable greed, the two had made a potent alliance which had convinced Claudia to become a materialistic replica of themselves.

At dinner, Gunderson said very little, merely grunting at the mundane conversation made by the others. As usual, Rodger thought. In many ways, he found Gunderson predictable, habitual. Put a large plate of food in front of him and he becomes entranced, shutting out the world, digging in viciously to stretch his gut to the limit as rapidly as possible. Which usually required two large plates of food and two, even three, desserts. The only difference Rodger noticed was that periodically, while chewing hungrily on his roast beef, Gunderson would stare malevolently at him, as though to say, "Who the hell do you think you are, telling *me* what to do," and he knew that they weren't through with each other yet, that regardless of what Claudia had said to him on the patio, dinner was only a reprieve. The pattern had never changed. Gunderson's egomania prevented him from giving in, and Rodger knew that the next round would begin after dinner.

Later, after the women had cleared off the dining room table except for the wine and they sat two on each side, the women to the right of the men, Gunderson emptied twenty dollars in rolls of pennies and nickels from the purple Crown Royal bag onto the table and sold each of them five dollars worth, two rolls of pennies and two rolls of nickels, the stipulation being that once you lost your five dollars you were out of the game. They played five-cent ante dealer's choice poker, with betting from a penny to a nickel and no limit on the number of raises allowed.

As usual, Rodger thought. The same game they had played for years every time the Gundersons visited. And it would play out the same way it always did.

And it did. The women, who had been bored with the game for years, played lackadaisically, foolishly, pretending to be trying while actually deliberately losing as they countered Gunderson's onslaught of raises with raises of their own on poor hands, their only motive being to leave the game to the men and retire to the living room for girl talk. Gunderson laughed derisively at their ineptitude as he raked in pot after pot, his blind egomania still forcing him to believe, even after all these years, that they were actually trying their best.

After the women left, Gunderson gave Rodger a steely stare and growled, "Now we'll see what you're made of, Blackwell."

At this point, Rodger had about eight of the twenty dollars. In the past, although he had tried to play his best, the final outcome of the game had no vital importance to him. He saw it as merely a game, an entertainment, and the loss of five dollars meant nothing to him. But he knew that Gunderson felt differently. Although the loss of five dollars meant nothing to him as well, he had this burning desire, this almost maniacal obsession to win at any cost, just as intense in a penny ante poker game as in the sale of a half-million-dollar property. And now, although he'd never beaten Gunderson, the new Rodger Blackwell had an intense urge to do exactly that, to wipe that smug smirk off his fat face by winning every cent in front of him. And at one point, when his stake had risen to almost fourteen dollars and the smugness of Gunderson's smirk began to weaken, he felt that he might do exactly that, but Gunderson rallied, winning the final hand of jacks or better by beating Rodger's pair of aces with two small pairs: fours and deuces.

When Rodger heard Gunderson's taunting, victorious roar of laughter, he felt an almost overpowering urge to punch his fat face as hard as he could. Instead, trying to keep his voice calm, he said, "Let's join the ladies, shall we?" But he knew his face had reddened and the words came out tight and strained.

Gunderson started shoving coins and rollers into the purple Crown Royal bag. "I want to talk to you."

"We can talk in the living room." Rodger picked up his wine glass, still a third full, and drained it, knowing that the next round was coming, that Gunderson intended to say his piece, and that he, Rodger, would be prepared for him. "I'm sure the ladies will also be interested in what you have to say, don't you?"

"Damn right they will. They'll be *damn* interested in what I've got to say."

The two women sat together facing each other at one end of the sofa. Whatever conversation they were having stopped suddenly when Rodger entered alone.

"So Greg won," Sally said, casually moving to the vacant end of the sofa. "We couldn't help hearing his laugh. Probably half of Orangeville heard it."

"Yes, he won," Rodger admitted, seating himself between them. "He says he wants to talk to me. So be prepared for the onslaught."

Concerned, Claudia squeezed his hand. "Darling, please don't antagonize him. You know how he gets when people disagree with him."

"I wouldn't know. Because I've never really dis-agreed with him. Believe me, that bit earlier about the beer and the cigar is only the tip of the iceberg, and the iceberg is about to rise."

She squeezed his hand harder, her nails digging in. "Darling, please...*please*—"

She stopped abruptly as Gunderson entered, looked at them suspiciously, dropped the bag of coins onto the coffee table with a heavy thud, flopped onto the sofa with legs spread wide, picked up his empty beer bottle and held it out toward Sally, saying, "I want another beer."

"Yes, dear." Sally rose immediately, took the empty bottle and retreated to the kitchen, returning shortly.

Easily twisting off the bottle cap, Gunderson dropped it carelessly onto the end table, then guzzled down half the bottle before placing it carefully on the coaster and meticulously fussing with it for several seconds to make certain that it was perfectly centred. "Is that okay with you now, Blackwell?" he asked sarcastically.

But Rodger merely nodded, disgusted with Gunderson whose pettiness and vanity were so great that even a simple, sensible request rankled him.

"I want to talk to you, Blackwell. I want to know what's going on here. I want to know why my daughter—"

"Your *step*daughter," Rodger corrected.

Gunderson glowered at him. "I want to know why Claudia tells me that you've gone off the deep end. Talking crazy. Acting crazy. Going out and talking to strange women in bars, as though you were looking for some action, and telling Claudia that it's all some stupidity called mid-life crisis. Well, I'll tell you something, Blackwell—*I* never had any mid-life crisis and I think it's nothing but a huge load of crap—"

"Greg...please."

"—that you're just using as an excuse to start stepping out on your wife. Isn't that the *real* truth, Blackwell? Isn't that what you're *really* doing? Cheating on Claudia?"

"No. It's just that I'm forty years old and think it's time to reassess my life, that's all. I'm simply *talking* to these women, trying to find out if they can give me some direction because I haven't been able to do it myself. And Claudia hasn't been able to help me with my problem either."

"*What* problem?" Gunderson shouted. "You've got a beautiful, faithful wife, an impressive home, two new cars in the driveway, probably a fat bank account, and investments. You're living off the fat of the land. What the hell do you want, for Christ's sake?"

"Greg...*please!*"

"Be quiet, Sally."

Rodger said, "What I want is to do something *productive* with my life. To achieve something *worthwhile*. There are four of us in this room, and none of us has ever achieved anything worthwhile."

"You're crazy," Gunderson said. "Absolutely nuts. I can buy and sell you any day of the week. I can—"

"In the name of God, I'm not talking about *money*." He tried to raise his hands to express himself more strongly and suddenly realized that both Claudia and Sally held his hands down and were squeezing tightly, but he had to continue. "Can't you get it through that fat, empty head of yours that there actually *are* more important things in life than money?"

"You lousy creep!" His face reddening, Gunderson began to rise, as though to rush at Rodger with fists swinging, then sank back onto the sofa as Rodger knew he would. Gunderson was so grossly out of shape that even that would have made him breathe heavily. And one solid punch to that flabby belly would send him gasping and moaning to the floor. "If it wasn't for me you'd still be working for peanuts selling those lousy air cleaners. If it wasn't for me you wouldn't have a damn thing. And if you'd stayed with me you'd have a hell of a lot more than you've got now." He laughed sarcastically. "You say it's not about money, but if it isn't about money why are you still writing those stupid, inane commercials for pussy pads and asswipe? Those stupid, inane commercials that wouldn't be believed by a ten-year-old. You are still writing them, aren't you, Blackwell?" he sneered.

"Yes, I am," Rodger admitted. "But I might not be writing them much longer."

He felt Claudia's hand suddenly leave his as her body jerked toward him. "What do you mean?" she demanded.

"I mean I may be creating a whole new life in the future. I don't know yet."

"We'll discuss this later," she said softly through clenched teeth.

Rodger faced Gunderson again. "Yes, I'm still writing pap for the masses, and for all these years you've been on my case and never forgiven me for that, have you? You've never forgiven me for leav-ing you and going to Drummond. Because your fat, swollen head won't ever allow you to forgive anyone who tells you that you're second best, who tells you that you're amoral and that they don't want to work for you any more. Yes, I'm still at Drummond writing commercials for pussy pads and asswipe, and you're still selling houses to people, especially older people, who actually don't want them. Still browbeating them into buying large homes, for prestige, you say, when small homes are what they actually need. Still lying to people who don't bother investigating about the quality of homes, who are naive, who trust you and don't both-er getting a lawyer or reading the fine print, selling them shoddy goods which you know will require expensive repairs, just to get your lousy commission." Now he felt Sally's hand leave his, as he knew it would. She couldn't possibly go on holding his hand while he insulted her husband. "You used to think that the people of Orangeville were stupid, didn't you, Gunderson? Just a bunch of country yokels who weren't really smart enough to know what they were doing when it came to business. You used to think that all you had to do was go on playing the jolly fat man in the cowboy suit and the big red suspenders, disarming your clients by slapping your big, fat belly and laughing at yourself, making them laugh by saying that you couldn't ride a horse any more because horses ran away as soon as they saw you coming. But things are different now, aren't they, Gunderson? Business isn't what it used to be, is it? Sales have dropped off, haven't they? Why? Because the word has gotten around, and many people in Orangeville now know that the jolly fat man isn't really so jolly after all. Underneath, the jolly fat man is dead serious, especially when it comes to money."

Rodger rose and advanced on Gunderson. "Do you know what's going to happen to you, Gunderson?"

"Don't hit him!" Sally cried.

Laughing, Rodger turned and smiled at her. "Don't worry, Sally, I have no intention of hitting him. I wouldn't want to get grease on my fist." He stopped directly in front of Gunderson, so close that he lacked enough room to rise. As he stared into red-faced Gunderson's brown, piggy eyes, all the years of listening passively to countless demeaning insults from the man, allowing them to seethe and fester inside him, now flooded his mind demanding retribution. He had never hated anyone, and believed that hating anyone meant a certain failure as a human being, but he hated this man, and that hatred, bubbling up and burning like acid in his throat, made him fear that he would choke unless it found release. "What I meant, Gunderson, was this: Do you know what's going to happen to you in the future?"

Gunderson sneered, "No, but I'm damn sure you're going to tell me, even if I think it's a load of crap."

"In less than a year you'll be leaving Orangeville. You'll be leaving because hardly anyone looking for a home in this town will trust you any more because your name will have been smeared all over town and almost everybody will know who you are, and what you are. Your income will become almost totally dependent on new people thinking of settling here, and that won't be much, believe me. Certainly not enough for a person as greedy as you.

People are on to you, Gunderson. I know for a fact that your business has been dropping off for years. That jolly fat man bullshit doesn't work any more, does it? You may be fairly well off now, but pretty soon, maybe even already, you'll be digging into your capital to support Sally and you in the lavish style you've become accustomed to." Gunderson's piggy eyes shifted away quickly, just for a moment, but long enough to betray what Rodger had suspected all along. "And you won't like that, will you? You just can't stand the thought of eating into your capital, of getting *poorer* instead of *richer*. So what'll you do then? Chop several hundred dollars a month off Sally's allowance? Cancel your—"

"You can't do that, Greg!" Sally cried. "I *need* my allowance!"

"Be quiet, Sally," Gunderson growled. "I'll do what I damn well please with my money."

"Cancel your membership in the country club? Cut back on your trips abroad? Stop eating out? Stop putting on lavish parties? Those parties which at-tract only a bunch of freeloaders because you have no real friends?" Rodger shook his head. "No, Gunderson, you won't do that for very long. You'll get out of town. You'll—"

"I don't want to leave Orangeville, Greg." Sally whined. "I absolutely *refuse* to leave Orangeville."

"Be quiet, woman. We're no going anywhere. He doesn't know that the hell he's talking about."

"Oh, don't I? Like I said, you'll get out of town, head for the hills as you cowboys say. You'll move to another town, because that's what people like you have to do eventually, after you've alienated the people in the town you've been living in so much that no one trusts you any more or believes a word you say. So you'll set up shop in another town and do a pile of advertising and start the whole process all over again." He stared piercingly into Gunderson's piggy eyes. "And do you know why you must continue to do what you do?"

"I know that you don't know your ass from a hole in the ground."

"You must continue to do what you do because the sad truth is that you're so pompous, so blind that you can't even see the scaly, festering hump on your own back and actually still believe, because of your money, that you're better than other people. You must continue to do what you do because you're a greedy, self-centred, insensitive, egomaniacal slob who hasn't even got the morals of a cockroach."

Satisfied, a calmness spreading through him, feeling as though a ragged, open wound inside him had suddenly healed, he turned his back on Gunderson and returned to his seat between Sally and Claudia, where he was met by Claudia's frigid stare, her mouth still open in shocked surprise.

Sally rose immediately, dabbing Kleenex at her eyes, apparently about to begin weeping, and went to Gunderson's side and placed a gentle hand on his shoulder. "Greg, he didn't mean it," she soothed. "He's...he's just been drinking, that's all, and—"

"Shut up, Sally!" he roared, jerking his shoulder away from her hand, his face almost beet red. He pointed a stubby forefinger at Rodger and shook it. "You thankless bastard. If it wasn't for me you wouldn't have a pot to piss in today. If it wasn't for me you wouldn't have Claudia, or this house, or even the car you're driving because without her you haven't got two cents worth of ambition. You're a pathetic loser, Blackwell, who hasn't got the guts to dig in and grind it out with the rest of us and be somebody. Understand, Blackwell? A pathetic *loser*!" Grabbing the half-filled beer bottle, he raised it and slammed it down, beer spilling and frothing onto the table. "And I don't associate with losers." With this, he lumbered to his feet, picked up the Royal Crown bag of coins by the neck and slammed it down against the coffee table, splitting it open, causing several dozen coins to spill out onto the table and the carpet, then raised the bag high as a river of coins flooded loudly to the table top, hundreds bouncing off onto the carpet. Dropping the empty bag to the table, he marched toward the door while Sally rushed to retrieve her purse and follow him.

"Dad, wait!" Claudia pleaded, but moments later the front door slammed, and shortly after tires screeched as Gunderson backed out of the driveway, and screeched again as he drove away.

"How could you, Rodger?" Claudia demanded, staring icily at him. "How *could* you? You *insulted* him!"

"Yes, I did, didn't I? And hasn't it been a long, long time in coming. He's insulted me and walked all over me for years, ever since I left Supreme, practically every time he spoke to me. So why shouldn't I? And tell me this: How often did you defend me in the past when he insulted me? How often, as a wife, did you stand up for your husband? How often, Claudia?"

"How often did *you* stand up for yourself? Never. You just let him go on saying anything he wanted to you whenever he wanted to, and he knew it and took advantage of it. Did it ever occur to you that I've been waiting for you to stand up to him and defend yourself all these years? Did *that* ever occur to you?"

"No, it never did. I always thought that you were on his side, that you revelled in his insults, that you enjoyed listening to him degrade and humiliate me."

"That's not true! I was always hoping and praying that you'd eventually defend yourself."

Rodger smiled, for he realized that Claudia's words had backed her into a corner. "Then why aren't you perfectly happy now?" he said calmly. "Because I've just done exactly that."

But she refused to back off. "No, I'm not happy. You went too far—now you've *alienated* them. Do you think they'll ever invite us to their parties again? Or to their cottage? Or to the country club as their guests? Or on holidays with them? Do you?"

He shrugged. "That's fine with me. It just gives him fewer opportunities to insult me, that's all, and he'll be even more determined to do that after today, won't he.. As far as his parties are concerned, because he doesn't have any real friends they're nothing but an abysmally boring gathering of a bunch of freeloaders getting together to talk about money and hunt for new sexual partners. As for the cottage, when we go there all he ever does is brag about the place and insinuate that we're a couple of peasants because we don't own one. The country club? Why would I ever miss that? Most of the members are nothing but a bunch of arrogant, stiff-necked creeps who think that they're shit doesn't stink because they've amassed a bit of money. And that's all they talk about—money. As for going on holidays with them, it's nothing but the severest penance to spend two weeks with an arrogant ego-maniac like your stepfather, and a woman as frivolous as your mother."

"She may be frivolous," Claudia said firmly, "but she's my mother and I enjoy her company. And I enjoy Greg's company, too, maybe because he doesn't treat me the same way he treats you. And I enjoy doing the other things with them, too. I enjoy being with successful, wealthy people. But now I won't be able to because you've ruined everything for us. Now practically all I'll be able to do is phone mom to have lunch with her, or go shopping, or perhaps play bridge, and all because Greg probably won't have anything to do with us any more."

"Well, you won't have to worry about that much longer. How much longer do you think they're going to be around? What I said about his business is true and you know it. I wasn't just speaking from anger to get revenge. You've told me often enough that you're not nearly as busy as you used to be, and I know for a fact that Gunderson isn't either. He's just about had it in Orangeville; I give him maybe another year tops, and then he'll be looking for greener pastures. And those greener pastures could be a long way away, especially if he wants to make certain that his reputation hasn't followed him. So what do you intend to do then?"

"I...I don't know. I haven't thought much about it. Do you *really* think he'll leave?

"Of course he will. He's greedy, and eventually he won't be able to stand seeing his so-called empire crumbling." He thought a few moments, then said, "I'll tell you what you *could* do."

"What's that?"

"Get your real estate broker's licence. You could start up your own brokerage. It may take a little time to live down the stigma Gunderson left you with, but I'm sure that in a little time, when enough people see that pretty face of yours in your ads and they begin to build trust in you, you should soon be quite successful."

"Maybe I could, but I'd first have to wait and see if Greg leaves Orangeville."

"You're afraid of him, aren't you?"

"Yes," she admitted. "Yes, maybe I am. Like you've been for the past ten years. Until now. I just don't want to give him any reason to treat me like he's treated you. Maybe you don't, but I need mom and Greg."

"But you do want to be successful, don't you? You certainly don't want to go down the drain with him, do you?"

"Maybe I still don't truly believe that he actually *is* going down the drain. Maybe I still persist in believing that he'll find some way to recover the lost ground."

"That's nothing but a pipe dream and you know it. If I were you I'd start making plans right now to set up your own brokerage."

"Do you mean while Greg is still here? And be-come his competition? I just *couldn't* do that. I'd never hear the end of it. He'd disown me, just as he apparently has with you. Then where would I be?"

"Suit yourself, but just think of the kind of money you could be making with your own brokerage. A hell of a lot more than you're making now. If you opened your own office you could hire a few hotshot salespeople and collect a commission on every sale they made, and a full commission on every sale you made. Just think of how quickly that would add up."

She remained silent for several seconds, then said, "I am thinking, and you're right. And don't think I haven't thought about doing this before. If I'd been my own broker when I made that million-dollar sale in Caledon East, I'd have made $60,000.00 instead of just $30,000.00." She shook her head. "No, it certainly would be nice, but I just can't do it. Greg would disown me, I just know he would."

Yet he now detected a softening of her position, far less conviction in her words. His entire motive for this real estate discussion suddenly became clear to him. He wanted Claudia to do something that *would* cause Gunderson to disown her because he wanted Gunderson out of *both* of their lives so that he'd never have to look at his fat, ugly face again. For a few moments, he felt a twinge of guilt at his own selfishness, but quickly and easily pushed it aside and out of his mind.

"Then wait," he said finally. "Wait until he's gone. And think of all the opportunities you've missed, and all the money you've lost while waiting for him to leave."

And as the silent seconds multiplied, he could see that she was thinking exactly that, and coming to the only conclusion he knew her capable of. He felt amazed at how speedily her anger with him over his insults to Gunderson had dissipated and quickly vanished once the subject of money came up, and been rapidly replaced by greed.

Yes, Claudia, you certainly are your stepfather's stepdaughter.

"I'll think about it," Claudia promised.

And he knew she would. Seriously.

9

On Wednesday, Rodger had just returned home from work when the phone rang.

"May I speak to Rodger Blackwell," a voice said.

"Speaking." The voice sounded vaguely familiar, but he couldn't place the caller's name.

Then he heard, as though the caller had cupped his hands over the phone to create a tunnel effect, "This is a voice from the past."

But he still failed to make the connection. "I'm sorry, I—"

"Toronto…fifteen years ago…the Greek guy," the voice, now normal, hinted.

"Good God! Andreas? Andreas Savakis?"

"The same."

"But how did you find me?"

"Easy. Remember sending me a Christmas card several years ago? I eventually threw it out, and never replied, but remembered that the address was somewhere in Orangeville. There are only two R. Blackwells in the Orangeville phone book, and you're my second call, so it had to be you unless you had an unlisted number."

"I tried sending you a card the following year, but it came back marked 'address unknown.' I guess you moved without leaving a forwarding address. And your phone number was out of service."

"Yeah, I moved. I move…well, regularly. There's nothing to keep me in one place any more, now that Oksana's gone and no children to worry about. And I don't bother with Bell any more. I just use a cell because I'm on the road a lot."

Suddenly suspicious, Rodger wondered about the "regular" moving. People who moved regularly, and who no longer had phone numbers listed in the book, quite often were running from their creditors, sometimes even their previous landlords.

"But what are you doing here in Orangeville?"

"Well, I'd like to say that I came here just to see you, but that wouldn't be exactly true. Don't get me wrong, I'll be happy to see you, but I'm also here on business, making some confirmed calls in the area. I'll be leaving Orangeville tomorrow morning."

"So you're in sales?"

"Right. You know me, Rodger. I've been in sales of one kind or another all my life."

Yes, Rodger thought, he did know Andreas. He knew that many of the sales gimmicks he became involved with when he knew him in Toronto were worked at the very edge of the law. "So who are you with right now?"

"Britannica. I'm just here in a supervisory capacity. Showing one of our salespeople the ropes. I demonstrate and he observes, then he tries it on his own and I observe. We've had a good day... several sales. But it's just a fill-in position for me, something I'm just doing until my next big real estate deal comes along, which will probably be next week. I'm in with a few partners and we're investing in a high-rise apartment building in Toronto."

But Rodger knew better. The more things changed, the more they remained the same. And he could already see that, although they hadn't spoken to each other in fifteen years, Andrea's blather hadn't changed a bit. Jokingly, the guys used to call him "The Big Wheel," the guy who consistently dreamed up all kinds of wild, often ludicrous, often borderline legal, sometimes blatantly illegal schemes that were only ever realized in the privacy of his own fertile mind. And when the guys grew tired of listening to one of his schemes, he moved on by creating another. The Big Wheel. All thought, no action, dreaming impossible dreams, mainly because his minuscule resources usually prevented him from doing otherwise, and his financial backers never seemed to materialize. Just as the backers for his high-rise apartment building deal would never materialize. The Big Wheel was actually a very small wheel fastened to a very small car that just seemed to be putt-putt-putting along.

Rodger played the game. "So you'll be giving up your job with Britannica next week then."

"Yeah, probably. Hell, I can't be bothered with this penny ante stuff. I've got too many hot irons in the fire. By the way, have you had dinner yet?"

"No, I just got home, and my wife isn't here yet."

"Then why don't we do dinner. We can reminisce. Can you recommend a good restaurant in town?"

"Do you like Italian?"

"Am I a white man?"

Rodger laughed, expecting Andreas to join in, but heard nothing. "Well, I don't know about that. With that Greek blood in you, you can look pretty swarthy."

Still no laughter. Nothing. Where had the sense of humour gone?

"So where is this place?" Andreas asked.

"It's called Rudolf's. No reservations required, and it's on Broadway, just a few doors east of the Royal Bank. Do you know where that is?"

"Yeah. How about six o'clock?"

"Fine."

The mould, Rodger thought. How did the old saying go? "After they made you, they broke the mould." But isn't that true for everyone? Isn't everyone congenitally cast from a different mould? And how many of us destroy our own congenital moulds, replacing them with impenetrable, indestructible brass moulds of our own choosing and thereby becoming human beings which we were never meant to be. And if, whenever we look into a mirror, we can only see that impenetrable, indestructible bronze mould, we are eventually duped into believing that this is actually the real person, the congenital mould.

Over the ages, innumerable people had done exactly that. Andreas certainly had. Since they met in Toronto during their teen years, nothing had changed. Rodger could see that Andreas remained exactly the same Big Wheel, the same hopeless dreamer he had always been.

And what about himself? Was he any better? Hadn't he also strayed far from his own congenital mould? Was this the actual person he truly wanted to be? Of course not. Which is why he kept saying to himself again and again, "I am not me!"

Before leaving for Rudolf's, he phoned Claudia's cell number and informed her that he'd be having dinner with an old, male Toronto friend. When she sounded suspicious and asked where, he told her, wondering if she intended to phone the restaurant later to verify his presence.

As Rodger waited at a table at Rudolf's for Andreas to arrive, late as usual, he thought about Andreas' wife, the former Oksana Korolenko. In Toronto, when he was nineteen and she just a sweet, gentle, lovely eighteen, Rodger had had a terrible crush on her, spending as much time as he could, when Andreas wasn't around, visiting with her in the apartment above a store on Spadina Avenue where she lived with her mother, and trying desperately to ingratiate himself in Oksana's eyes. Although she liked him, and always treated him kindly, her friendship for him remained platonic because he knew that she loved Andreas. And a few years later they were married. And five years later, while they holidayed in Greece, Oksana became so ill that they had to cut their holiday short and return to Toronto, where tests and a thorough physical examination revealed that she had spreading breast cancer. About a year later, after a mastectomy, the removal of cancerous lymph nodes, radiation, and months of futile chemotherapy, she died at twenty-seven.

At the memorial service at the Unitarian Hall, what angered Rodger was the crudity of the minister, who, after the memorial service, said presumptuously, "Now let's all have a big party and get good and drunk because that's what Oksana would have wanted." But was it actually what Oksana would have wanted? A bunch of sloppy drunks celebrating her death? It seemed to Rodger, knowing Oksana, that she would have much preferred that they respected her memory by proposing a simple toast to her life and preserving the solemn occasion, which is what Rodger did, silently, before leaving in disgust.

Even worse, when Rodger saw Andreas a few days later and again offered his commiseration, he heard the coldest words he had ever heard when Andreas said, "Better her than me." How many of us would actually *say* that? Instead, you heard expressions like "Better me than her," or "Better me than him," or "I'd give my life for her," or "I'd give my life for him." But how many of us actually believe what we say? Most of us are simply paying lip service to a generous sentiment. But not Andreas. He said what almost every one of us is thinking when we lose a loved one: Better her (or him) than me. Yes, we may think it, but we never say it. And when Andreas actually said it, it shocked Rodger because he'd never heard anyone say it before. Some words are meant to be said, even when they are lies. Others, never. And that cruel statement, that vocal denial of his love for Oksana, lowered Andreas in Rodger's eyes. Even now, many years later, the memory of those few short, callous words still lingered resolutely in his mind, making him realize that he had never forgiven Andreas, and probably never would.

When Andreas finally arrived, twenty minutes late, Rodger recognized him immediately. Still a relatively slender six-foot-three, still darkly handsome, clean shaven, his glossy black hair brushed neatly back, still exuding confidence as he recognized Rodger and walked toward the table.

"You look good," Andreas said, as Rodger rose and they shook hands firmly before giving each other a gentle hug. "Great to finally see you again. Sorry I'm a bit late. We were on our last call, and it took a bit longer than I thought. Anyway, the main thing is we got the sale. It's been another pretty good day."

"Glad to hear it," Rodger said, looking Andreas up and down, noticing the pouches starting beneath his brown eyes, the slightly downward turn to his lips when at rest, something acquired since their last meeting. The black dress shoes were highly polished but slightly down at the heels, the obviously ready made navy blue polyester suit too shiny, as though it had been hand ironed too often without using a protective cloth. His light blue dress shirt had begun to fray at the collar, from which hung, ten years out of date, a very wide maroon tie with a large knot.

Rodger recalled how in the old days Andreas had his own tailor (was his name Pifko?) and wouldn't be caught dead in a ready made suit, and wore French-cuffed shirts with gem-stoned cuff links. But that had all gone. Now, when you could buy a Chinese or Bangladesh made dress shirt at Wal-Mart for about ten dollars, he'd been reduced to wearing a shirt with a frayed collar. Yes, The Big Wheel had become a Very Small Wheel, brought crashing down to earth with the vengeance of time.

Andreas ordered meat lasagna, Rodger spaghetti with meatballs, and they agreed on a carafe of red house wine.

Rodger decided to probe a little. "I thought you preferred the hard stuff. The top of the list. Like Crown Royal, or Chivas Regal, or...what was the other one?"

"Canadian Club," Andreas answered softly.

"Aren't you drinking them any more?"

"Sure. Still do. But I prefer wine with dinner. Besides, I've already had a couple of Chivas today. So what have you been up to all these years?"

Rodger had smelled no liquor on Andreas' breath and doubted that he'd been drinking earlier. Although he remembered him as a steady drinker, he questioned that even Andreas would be foolish enough to visit clients with liquor on his breath. Had he been forced by circumstances to change his drinking habits completely? Or did the frayed collar mean that, even now, he'd prefer to spend his money on liquor rather than on clothing?

Rodger filled him in on the main points of his life since they last met: his job selling air purifiers, his job with Supreme, his marriage, and his current job with Drummond. He kept the details sketchy, not even mentioning his present mid-life situation, and made the details even more sketchy when he realized that Andreas appeared distracted, barely listening. Frustrated, Rodger asked, "And what about you? Have you remarried?"

"Hell, no."

"Why not? Oksana has been gone for about fifteen years. You've had plenty of time to find another wife."

"Are you kidding? And go through all *that* again."

Rodger dug into his memories of the Unitarian memorial service again, hazily recalling Andreas' odd, passive behaviour, which he had labelled as grief at the time but now saw in an entirely new light. "Do you mean the Unitarian service for Oksana?"

Andreas looked at him sharply, as though he had been found out. "Why do you say that?" he demanded.

"Because you were acting very strangely. Totally out of character."

"How did you expect me to act? Like my usual, jovial self? I was in mourning, for Christ's sake."

Andreas' anger convinced Rodger that he was on the right track. He still tasted the bitter bile of Andreas' shabby treatment of Oksana, the lovely, gentle woman whom he, Rodger, had once loved and who spent her entire married life nibbling on the crumbs of Andreas' 'love,' knowing the truth but loving him resolutely even while he indulged in his numerous extramarital affairs. And now, angry himself, Rodger felt an urgent need to speak for the dead Oksana and somehow punish Andreas for his past debauchery.

"No, it wasn't that," Rodger said firmly. "It was something entirely different. You were actually *ashamed.* Maybe a little ashamed for the rotten way you had treated Oksana, but mainly ashamed because you felt that her death actually *reflected on you*, made you look bad, made you look weak and helpless in the eyes of your friends, made your friends pity you. And you couldn't stand that, could you? Couldn't stand anyone thinking of you as anything but The Big Wheel. But you just couldn't play the part of The Big Wheel that day, could you, Andreas, because Oksana's death brought you down, brought you down to the level of all those ordinary people around you. That's why you were ashamed, and wanted to get out of there as quickly as possible."

"Get off the pot. You don't know what you're talking about." But Andreas had turned away, his voice subdued. "When I said I didn't want to go through *that* again, I meant Oksana's death. What the hell do you know anyway. Do you know what it's like to live with a woman whose had a double mastectomy, had the lymph nodes under her arms removed, had months of chemotherapy, and watching her withering away, begging you to help her die, until there isn't an ounce of flesh left on her body, until finally, *finally* they take her away to the hospital and she falls into a coma, and you weep with relief because you know that your agony, and hers, will soon be over. Do you know what *that's* like?"

"No," Rodger admitted. "But I do know what it's like to lose a good friend to cancer, and to watch him wasting away. Claudia and I met a couple, Denny and Margaret Richardson, shortly after we were married ten years ago, when we lived in an old rented house on Church Street. They were our neighbours. They were just ordinary, good people about twenty years older than we were and with no higher education, he working as a service station attendant at Esso, and she as a cashier at K-Mart, now Zellers. They liked to move around. A couple of years later, they moved to Guelph, and then to Barrie, where over the next several years they lived in three different apartment buildings. But we always remained friends and kept in touch and visited them regularly.

"About four years ago, Denny started having health problems. First he developed a heart condition, then he suffered a stroke, then some mini strokes, then he discovered he had prostate cancer and was fitted with a perpetual catheter, and finally lung cancer. Inoperable. He'd always been a heavy smoker, and probably drank at least ten cups of coffee a day. When he could no longer work, he spent most of his time just sitting at the table or in front of the TV with another cup of coffee and another cigarette. Even the lung cancer didn't stop his smoking, just slowed it down when the horrible coughing fits racked his body. And when the coughing finally stopped, and he had trouble breathing, he took his puffer and sprayed it down his throat to open his lungs.

"As the months went by, and we continued to visit regularly, we watched him gradually wasting away, a little thinner each time. Now he smoked only sporadically because almost every drag brought on another heart-wrenching coughing fit, after which he'd say, "Die, you old bastard, die." Even the coffee had deserted him, making him vomit whenever he tried to drink it, forcing him to drink cans of Pepsi instead. Eventually, we often found him in bed when we arrived, and he only emerged, now in a wheelchair, for brief visits of maybe half an hour before returning to his bed.

"The last time we saw him was about a year ago. It was a hot August day. They had a main floor apartment at the front of the building, and Margaret had wheeled him out onto the small patio shaded by the balcony above. He was almost senseless by this time, groggy and barely aware of his surroundings. We heard bells ring as the Good Humour truck pulled into the parking lot and children ran to meet it. Margaret bought us all chocolate covered cones. Denny handled his carelessly, like a child. He took awkward bites of the chocolate and as it cracked some pieces fell onto his shirt but he didn't even notice. When I saw that Margaret was about to comment, I caught her eye and put a finger to my lips and she kept quiet. This was a dying man enjoying an ice cream cone, maybe his last; what the hell did it matter that he had pieces of chocolate on his shirt or that the ice cream was running down his chin?

"I may not have lived with Denny, watching him die day after day, week after week, month after month, and he wasn't my wife, but I do know what it feels like to lose a very good friend to cancer. And I haven't told myself that I'll never have another very good friend just because Denny died. Because we've all got to try to go on living no matter what happens." Rodger paused, thought for a few moments, then continued. "Not just existing. But I don't think you've ever actually faced up to life since the day Oksana died. She's been gone for about fifteen years and you still haven't found the nerve to remarry." His voice became vindictive. "And I know damn well that it has nothing whatsoever to do with holding Oksana's memory sacred in your heart. The truth is you're running scared, aren't you, Andreas?"

"Maybe I am," he admitted. "But that doesn't mean that I'm not enjoying myself. I don't need to live with a woman, or marry her, to enjoy her. And I'm still handsome enough," he added smugly, "that I don't have to look very far to find myself another piece of meat. There's plenty of it around. I just go to the nearest bar and the women are there just waiting for me. Then it's a few drinks, to bed, and it's all over. And don't ask me for any commitments because you won't be getting any. Because you see, Rodger, that's exactly what women are to me: just pieces of meat. Sometimes delectable pieces, and sometimes necessary pieces, but still just pieces of meat. I don't expect them to supply me with any kind of mental or psychological stimulation. Only physical."

"And Oksana? Is that all she was to you as well?"

Andreas hesitated, choosing his words. "Until she became sick, Oksana was a very delectable, very necessary part of my life. But let's face it, she wasn't exactly a bundle of brains, was she? Most of her conversation revolved around feminine subjects which I found extremely boring, and when she tried to cater to me by changing to masculine subjects I could see that *she* was extremely bored. About the only two things we had in common were sex, which was great, and cooking. I'm a pretty good cook, you know. I even worked as a chef in a Greek restaurant for a few months. Anyway, we both enjoyed preparing our native dishes and serving them to each other, she the Ukrainian dishes like cabbage rolls and perogies and borscht, and me the Greek dishes like souvlaki and kakavia soup and leftedes. And that was about it."

"You still haven't directly answered my question," Rodger said vindictively. "Without the cooking aspect, was Oksana nothing more than a delectable, necessary piece of meat to you?"

Andreas smiled sheepishly, and shrugged, which answered Rodger's question eloquently.

"Look, " Andreas said, "I thought we came here to reminisce. Remember when we were about nineteen, the night we walked along Richmond Street, half drunk, singing our fool heads off at one o'clock in the morning? We were in the industrial area somewhere between Spadina and Bathurst, nobody around, and we sang the old Johnny Mathis songs like *Chances Are*, and *Stranger in Paradise*, and *It's Not for Me to Say*. Remember that?"

"Yes. Yes, I do now that you remind me. We were nuts then, weren't we? Two young bucks with raging libidos and no women around, singing our stupid heads off. And as I recall we harmonized well and sounded pretty good. At least we thought so at the time. Hell, we thought a recording contract was just around the corner."

"Yeah, some recording contract. If we heard that performance on tape today we'd probably think it was pretty damn rotten, don't you think?"

"Probably. But what did we know then. We both thought we'd someday tear the world apart and become *huge* successes."

"Yeah, huge successes." Andreas reflected for a few moments, then added glumly, running a finger subconsciously along the inside of his frayed collar. "But it wasn't that easy, was it?"

"No, it wasn't." Rodger saw Andreas' glum words and the finger to his collar as further evidence that the mask had momentarily slipped, that Andreas remained the same fraud he had been since the day they met over twenty years ago. "And most of us end up with far less than we expected."

Ignoring the insinuation, Andreas forked a mouthful of lasagna into his mouth and began chewing.

Rodger dropped the subject. "Do you remember—I guess we were about twelve years old—how ignorant we were about sex? I got this information from somebody that Oriental women went the other way. Instead of their pussies being vertical, they were horizontal. We couldn't figure out how this could possibly work. If her pussy was horizontal, how would you ever get in? When she spread her legs to take you, she'd close up as tight as a bear trap."

"Hell, you'd need a damn Roto-Rooter to get in," Andreas offered. "We were as green as grass in those days, weren't we?"

"We certainly were." Rodger recalled how, when they were in their late teens, he went into a drug-store to buy some condoms because they had a date with two girls and they expected to get lucky. First, he sized up the situation. If he saw a female clerk at the counter, he'd leave, too embarrassed to deal with a woman. Seeing a male clerk, he selected two pack-ages, medium and large, and took his purchases to the counter, smiling smugly as he said, "The medium ones are for a friend," although he knew perfectly well that they were for himself and that the large condoms were for Andreas. The clerk smiled wanly, making Rodger suspect that he doubted him and knew the truth.

Rodger said, "Do you remember the night we had a couple of girls in your dad's panel truck, the one he used for his linen service, and you parked in a wooded area near the Humber River? I was with a girl named Janet, and you were with…?"

"I'm not sure. I think her name was Darlene."

"Anyway, it was pitch black, and we had a case of beer, and we kept drinking, and tried to keep the girls drinking because we were trying to make out with them. But the beer got to us first and we had to go out for leaks. Like I said, we couldn't see a damn thing so we just walked about ten steps away and relieved ourselves. I remember you saying, 'Rodger, we've really got it made tonight. We might as well not even bother putting our dicks back in our pants.'" Rodger laughed, expecting the same from Andreas, but received only a wan smile. Where had the man's sense of humour gone? Had the frayed collar and the shiny suit and the worn heels also taken that away?"

"Yeah," Andreas said. "But we didn't get any, did we? And it wasn't very funny next morning, was it?"

"No, we didn't get any, but one of us could have if he'd been alone. I don't know about Darlene, but I knew Janet was hot to trot when I put my hand between her legs and felt her flaming pussy."

"Darlene, too."

"But it wasn't to be, was it? We were so horny that we would've done it right there in the panel truck, but they wouldn't come across because they had no privacy. They just didn't think it was *ladylike* to have sex while your girlfriend was having it just a few feet away. Anyway, we eventually all either passed out from the beer or just fell asleep."

"Yeah, and when we woke up next morning and saw where we were we almost shit ourselves."

"Only about twenty feet from the edge of a cliff that dropped about fifty feet straight down to the Humber River, that's where we were. If we'd taken a few more steps when we went for our leaks we'd've both ended up as dead as doornails."

"Yeah, still clutching our dicks."

Rodger laughed, but his laughter earned only a feeble smile from Andreas.

"We had a room on Pearson Avenue then," Andreas said. Remember the Saturday night we got in a case of beer and brought Darlene and Janet back? We turned off the lights and started mauling each other in the dark and drinking our beer, trying to keep quiet because we knew the landlady lived upstairs and didn't allow visitors, especially *female* visitors. When the beer got to me and I had to go to the can, I didn't want to go to the bathroom upstairs because I thought the landlady was sleeping and I didn't want to wake her, so I—"

"You crazy bugger," Rodger accused, the memory flooding back. "In the dark, you went to a corner of the room and took a leak into one of the empty beer bottles and put the cap back on. And then, when Darlene asked for another beer, you gave her the bottle filled with your piss."

Now Andreas laughed. Brutally. "Yeah, she mentioned that the bottle felt warm, but I told her it was just because we had no refrigerator. Hell, she was so drunk by this time that she would've believed anything."

"But once she took a sip, she wasn't drunk enough or stupid enough to believe that she was just drinking a warm beer."

"It was just a joke, that's all."

"Sure, just a joke," Rodger said angrily. "Just a malicious joke. Just a cruel joke. And it ruined any chance we might've had to make out with them that night because shortly after that they were gone. And why wouldn't they be. And that's why they wouldn't go out with us again. Nobody likes being treated like a piece of crap."

Andreas shrugged. "Relax, Rodger. Think of it this way: They were just two pieces of meat, that's all. On display in the butcher shop. And there are plenty of pieces of meat in the butcher shop."

"Maybe I'm just not much of a butcher," Rodger said through clenched teeth.

They lapsed into silence, both forking pasta into their mouths. Involuntarily, Rodger recalled the first time he actually did have sex with a woman, for it turned out to be far different from the idealistic image he'd carried in his mind since puberty and regularly embellished. He was nineteen. Walking along Grange Avenue, heading home to his father's house on Huron Street after eleven o'clock one rainy summer night after leaving Andreas' apartment above a store on Toronto's Spadina venue, he was approached by a tall, plump woman of about thirty who asked, "Do you want to come home with me?"

She caught him completely off guard; he felt his stomach reaching for his throat and couldn't believe that any woman except a prostitute could possibly make such a blatant sexual offer. Still, she hadn't asked for any money and he didn't want to insult her by asking her price. Maybe she simply wanted him for himself. He decided to play it cool, pretend that he slept with women regularly, and said casually, "Sure. Why not," trying to keep the quaver out of his voice but only half succeeding.

As he followed her up Larch Street, she turned and said, "Don't walk behind me. I don't want you getting up my ass."

Her last remark concerned him for now she did sound like a prostitute, making him wonder if she'd ask for money after they had finished and be satisfied with his last ten dollars, but his concern did nothing to quell his burgeoning sexual desire. He decided to make no offer of payment unless she asked.

At a building at the corner of Larch and Dundas, she unlocked a side door and they entered a small bachelor apartment. She turned on a dim lamp.

"Do you have any rubbers?" she asked.

He knew that she meant condoms. "No," he admitted. "I forgot to buy some. I didn't think—"

"Never mind—we'll do it this way." She pulled off her panties and tossed them aside, raised her skirt to her hips and stretched out on the shabby davenport. Spreading her legs, she reached for a box of Kleenex, drew out a few tissues and stuffed them up her vagina, then began massaging her crotch. "Let's do it, honey."

He stared at her widely spread legs, her genitalia. This squalidness—the dim, dingy, cramped apartment with its faded floral wallpaper, threadbare carpet, shabby davenport, a small, scarred table with two rickety chairs, the air suffused with the mingled odours of fried hamburger and cheap perfume—was far different from the romantic, idealistic initial sexual experience he'd so often en-visioned. Yet, almost hypnotized, he kept staring at her naked flesh as he pulled off his slacks and underwear and went to her, for all the squalidness in the world, regardless of who or what she was, could not prevent his penis from reacting to that sight.

He expected her to be dry because there had been no preliminary petting or kissing, and felt that she expected none, but he need not have worried. When in his anxiousness he fumbled with trembling fingers to find his way inside her, she grasped his penis and guided it gently and easily into her. She actually clung to him, making him wonder again if she sincerely felt something for him. Embarrassed by his inability to enter her without help, he tried to assert his manhood, to let her know that he'd done this many times before.

"Wrap your legs," he ordered.

And she did, crossing her ankles tightly over his back. He wanted some reaction from her, like moaning or groaning, for he wanted to make her climax, but his excitement at finally having sex was so great that, before she barely had a chance to get started, his ejaculation came. His first sexual union had lasted barely two minutes.

After pulling on his underwear and slacks, he turned back to her and saw that she had closed her legs and lowered her skirt but still lay on the davenport, staring at him. He realized suddenly that they didn't even know each other's names, but somehow that no longer seemed important. They had been nothing more than two strangers clinging together for a few minutes to give each other comfort.

"That was great. Thanks," he said foolishly, unable to think of anything else to say.

She merely nodded and made no move to rise, disappointment clearly evident in her brown eyes. He understood that look. She had expected so much more from him, apparently believing him to be some kind of stud with limitless stamina who could bring her to a wild climax, but he had failed miserably. That look also said that she probably knew the truth about him, that he couldn't control his ejaculation because sexually he was as green as grass. Believing this, his failure made him want to get away as quickly as possible. As he pulling on his jacket, he wondered if she intended to ask him for money; he had no intention of possibly insulting her by offering any because he felt that she had sincerely wanted him, wanted him to give her pleasure.

He started for the door, half expecting her to say something. When he reached it, he turned back to her. She still lay there, staring at him with that knowing look of disappointment.

"Sorry," he murmured, then opened the door and left.

In spite of the squalidness and embarrassing failure of his first sexual union with a woman, he felt elated as he walked home through the drizzling rain. He could barely restrain himself from shouting out his achievement. Instead, he pounded his chest and shouted it out in his mind. "I got laid, I got laid, *I got laid!*"

Although he walked home using the same route many times after that, he never saw the woman again.

Now, as they sat across from each other at the restaurant table, Andreas spread his hands and extended them, palms upward. "Look, I didn't come here to argue. I know you don't condone my way of life, so let's just leave it at that. We came here to reminisce, talk about old times, so let's just do that."

"Okay, let's just do that. We were about nineteen and I had a job at Slumbermaster, the mattress company. Remember that?"

Andreas reflected for a few moments before replying. "No, I don't."

"Sure you do. You know damn well you do."

"What the hell are you bringing that up for?"

"Because I got you a job there and you let me down. You weren't there more than a few weeks when they went looking for you one day and found you sleeping behind a pile of rolls of felt. And they fired you."

"So what. We stayed up late those days and I was tired, that's all. So I wanted to sleep and they caught me. So what. I didn't care because it was a lousy job anyway and I was glad to get out of it. Most of the time I was nothing more than a gopher. 'Go get this, go get that, go get some coffee, bring those over here,' that's all I ever heard. And half the time there was nothing to do, so why wouldn't I go to sleep. Besides, I had bigger fish to fry than to work in a crummy joint like that."

"And is that what you're doing now? Frying bigger fish?"

"Yeah, that's exactly what I'm doing. And you're in the picture, too. We'll talk about it later."

Now Rodger saw the real reason Andreas had come to Orangeville to look him up. Fifteen years had changed nothing. The Big Wheel wanted something from him, probably money to put into another one of his half-baked schemes.

"You remember what it was like," Andreas continued. "We used to hang around Spading Bowl, and sometimes we worked as pin chasers, and sometimes we bowled sweeps, trying to win each other's money. But you and I usually lost; we weren't quite good enough. Billy Reilly usually went home with our money. Remember Larry, the big guy who used to hang around? Never bowled, just hung around looking for boys."

"That's the gay guy you got involved with, isn't it? Weren't you going with Oksana then?"

"Yeah, but she wasn't giving me any. I was so horny I would've had sex with a skunk."

"Bull. You were in her apartment almost every time her mother went out, and sometimes even when she was home, trying to make a good impression. If you weren't having sex, what were you doing?"

"Trying, man, *trying.* We necked, but that's as far as I got. They were religious, you know, and she promised her mother that she wouldn't have sex with any man until after she got married. I've never told anyone, but that's the way it turned out."

"Let me get this straight. Are you trying to tell me that Oksana was a virgin when you married her?"

"I'm telling you exactly that. Why do you think I was so horny all the time while I was going out with her? Hell, I'm not gay, but I had to do *something,* didn't I? I just used Larry to get my rocks off, that's all. What's wrong with that?"

Half smiling, Rodger still gazed at him suspiciously, still unable to believe that Andreas, The Great Lover, who had constantly bragged about his sexual conquests to anyone who would listen, had not been able to conquer lovely, petite Oksana until after they were married. Still, Andreas' admission had a certain convoluted logic.

Thinking not only of Andreas' relationship with Larry, but of all the many times Andreas had cheated on Oksana during their marriage, Rodger said vindictively, "So, Oksana was faithful to you, waiting, but you weren't faithful to her."

"You must be crazy. What's going with a gay guy got to do with being faithful to a woman? Is a woman going to be jealous just because you went with a *homosexual*?"

"Did you tell Oksana about Larry?"

"No. Why should I?"

"You were afraid to tell her, is that it?"

"No. I just didn't see the point, that's all."

"Well, I believe that you *were* afraid to tell her. And I also believe that she would've been very jealous, and very disgusted with you. So much so that she probably never would've married you. And that's why you were afraid to tell her."

"Crap. All I was doing was getting some relief. Did you expect me to just go home and pull myself off every time Oksana got me hot and bothered?"

"That would've been better. Much better. How did you ever get involved with Larry anyway?"

"It was during the summer, and hot as hell. I went to Harrison's Baths for a swim to cool off. You know what it's like there, all men and everybody swims naked. It's a great place for gays to look for lovers. They can actually see the merchandise before they decide to make an offer. Anyway, Larry probably spotted me then because a few minutes after I went to the showers he walked into my stall—you know what it's like there, no doors—and asked me to wash his back. Without even thinking, I followed him back to his stall and he handed me a cake of soap. I barely got started when he started backing me toward a corner where nobody passing by could see us. He kept rubbing soap in the crack of his ass and saying, 'Knock me up, baby, knock me up.' But I wanted nothing to do with that and told him so, but I was horny, because of Oksana. Anyway, he took my hand and wrapped it around his dick, then reached back and grabbed hold of mine and began jerking it, and said, 'Pull me off, baby, pull me off. C'mon, pull me off.' Christ, he was hung like a horse. His dick must've been eight inches long and as round as a piece of kolbassa.

"Anyway, we gave each other hand jobs, then he asked me where I hung out and I told him Spadina Bowl, and I knew he'd be around. Hell, I wasn't gay. I just didn't know if Oksana was ever going to come across until after we were married, and I needed a backup, that's all. When he started coming around Spadina Bowl, we used to go upstairs into the stall in the men's washroom. He'd sit on the toilet while I stood in front of him and use his mouth on me while he pulled himself off, because I wouldn't touch him again. This went on a few nights a week for about a month, then he just disappeared. I even went to Harrison's Baths a few times looking for him, but he wasn't around so I didn't go back. I guess Larry found somebody who was brave enough to handle that kolbassa of his."

"Then what happened?" Rodger asked, knowing perfectly well what the answer would be but wanting to hear Andreas admit it. "How did you satisfy yourself after that?"

"You were around. You know damn well what happened. I started playing the field. I found some nice pieces of necessary meat who were more than willing to put out the fire that Oksana had started." He smirked. "More than willing. If I hadn't done that, I probably would've ended up raping Oksana just to get into her pants. Do you think *that* would've been better?"

Rodger saw clearly the moral and ethical smallness of the tall, handsome man who sat across from him and who he had lionized during his teen years. The hedonistic enslavement to his sex organs, regardless of who he hurt. The cruel treatment of Oksana. The total lack of consideration for anyone but himself, resulting in a cold disinterest in other people. Unless, of course, he wanted something from them. And even though Rodger knew that Andreas did want something from him, Andreas hadn't even bothered listening attentively or asking questions when Rodger had spoken of his own past. Like asking him about Claudia's appearance, her age, her work, the length of their marriage, children, the common questions an interested person would ask of a person he hadn't seen for fifteen years.

Instead of directly answering Andreas' question, Rodger decided to try a circuitous route. "I'd like to tell you a little story. May I?"

Andreas shrugged. "Go ahead."

"A few months ago, on a Tuesday morning, I went into our ensuite bathroom and saw a large black spider in the bathtub. My first inclination was to immediately turn on the tub water and flush it down the drain, but I hesitated and decided instead to observe it. It kept trying to escape by scaling the tub's smooth wall, but only managed a few steps before sliding to the bottom again. I told Claudia about the spider, and what I was doing, and asked her if she'd take her shower in the other bathroom. She wanted the spider dead, right then, but when I told her that the spider couldn't possibly escape the bathtub, she finally gave in. But she told me that she'd be sleeping in one of the spare bedrooms until the spider was gone.

"On Wednesday morning, the spider was still at the bottom of the tub, only now I had to crouch to see it in a corner under the bathtub seat. I watched it for five minutes and it never moved. I started asking myself some questions. Does it already realize that it can't possibly escape? That it's doomed? Has it ever come into contact with a human being before? Does it see, through its poor eyes, my large form as a menace? Does it feel fear? Does it know that I know it's a living spider? Or does it believe that if it remains perfectly still I'll think that it's merely a spot on the tub and leave it alone?

"On Thursday, I can't see the spider anywhere in the tub and think that it may have crawled down the drain. Or it may be on the black Rubbermaid mat at the bottom of the tub, which offers perfect camouflage. When I return after breakfast to brush my teeth, it has reappeared and is crawling along the bottom of the tub, as though it doesn't know what else to do, but stops and remains perfectly still when I enter and turn on the light.

"On Friday morning, a millipede has joined the spider, neither of them able to escape, the spider, hungry as it must be, but webless and unable to trap its prey. Later, the millipede has disappeared, ap-parently down the drain, and each time I enter later in the day, the spider is either crawling along the bottom of the tub or trying to hide in a corner.

"On Saturday morning, I take a shower. End of story."

Andreas looked bewildered. "What the hell was *that* all about?" he demanded.

"Have you not tried to relate the spider to *human* life?"

"No. Why should I when you're talking about a spider?"

"Because if we, like the spider, have given up and become resigned to the bottom of the tub, we can expect nothing better from life. I've become resigned, and so have you, but neither one of us can really enjoy life until we succeed in overcoming its obstacles by persevering until we find out who we really are. I don't know who I am—do you? Do you know why we're here on this ball called earth floating through space? Do you know what life is all about?"

"Probably I don't. Who does? But I know what *my* impression of life is. And I've had the same impression for quite a few years, and over those years I haven't seen much or heard much to change that impression. Do you remember the actor George Sanders?"

"Sure. He played The Saint in the late thirties and early forties, then played The Falcon." "Right. I never told you this, but when I was growing up he was my idol. Tall, slim, handsome, soft-spoken, debonair, usually well-off, and a ladies' man—in his movies he was all the things I wanted to be. I've collected every video of every movie of his I could get my hands on. When he died in 1972, he left behind a message that told me what life was all about, and I've lived by it every since I was a teenager."

"He killed himself, didn't he, after his film offers dried up. In the end he became so type-cast that all he could get were cameo roles as a stuffy, upper-class gentleman. I believe his last movie was a stinker called *Psychomania*. Apparently he hated it so much that he didn't even want to be around when it was released. So what did the note say?"

"I memorized that note a long time ago, and here's exactly what it said: 'Dear world: I am leaving because I am bored. I feel I have lived long enough. I am leaving you with your worries in this sweet cesspool. Good luck.' I don't know what he meant by 'sweet cesspool' because a cesspool can't be sweet. It just stinks like hell, and that's what I think life is all about—just one huge, foul, stinking cesspool driven by greed, crime, and sex, and you and I are just another couple of schmucks being victimized by it."

"Are you trying to tell me that you think that there's no hope for mankind?"

"Hope?" Andreas laughed derisively. "Are you kidding? Listen to the news. Read the papers. Hope went out to lunch a long, long time ago and never came back to work. Yeah, the sign once read 'OUT TO LUNCH,' but now it's so old and worn and neglected that you can't even read it any more. And the same goes for his brother and sister, Faith and Charity."

"I disagree. I still believe that there are hundreds of millions of good people in the world, even though in my recent search I still haven't been able to find one I can look up to as an example. But that doesn't mean that I intend to stop trying. In the past I've read many books by authors I respected and would've loved to meet. One of the problems is that most of what we see or hear on the news or read in the papers is negative, mainly because the media believe that negative news is far more exciting to report than positive news. So they may tack on some cute little human interest story at the end of the newscast, and that's it. Watching these newscasts, one would wrongly believe that ninety percent of the world's population are criminals or terrorists. Actually, the opposite is probably more true. Most of us are just leading ordinary, humdrum lives, or, as Thoreau said, 'lives of quiet desperation.' We work, play, eat, drink, sleep, copulate, get married, have children, buy the house, the cars, the giant LCD TV, the computers, the cell phones, wanting all the creature comforts we can lay our hands on, then struggle like hell to maintain the payments on all the bills we've created. We embrace the message of the media, wrap ourselves up in it, and when we get older and begin seeing the end of the trail we begin asking ourselves what the hell we've actually *done* with our lives. What worthwhile, lasting accomplishment have we actually *achieved*?

"We seek pleasure in many different places. We may have copulated hundreds, even thousands of times, eaten tens of thousands of meals, drank tens of thousands of litres of liquids, taken drugs for years, slept ten thousand hours, accumulated wealth and worldly possessions, but all these pleasures are only transitory. When we copulate, our true goal is ejaculation, which lasts only a few seconds while we empty our testicles, and is gone. When we enjoy a delicious meal, and we feel full and satisfied, the satisfaction lasts only until we feel hungry again. When we drink a beverage to quench our thirst, the satisfaction lasts only until we feel thirsty again. When we drink liquor, we may feel a warm glow for a time, but that warm glow soon vanishes and we are soon faced with the real world again when we stop drinking. And if we try too hard to prolong this warm glow, we may get very drunk and remember nothing, or pass out, or stagger home, and probably wake up the next morning with a horrendous hangover. Because the pleasure from drinking is only meant to be transitory. The dependence on drugs is a major problem in North American society, and much of the world. But taking drugs solves nothing because the high of pot or heroin or whatever is only transitory and soon wears off, and then you're left with facing the real world again. And if you try to prolong the high by taking more, you may take too much and end up dead.

"Most of us will sleep away about one third of our lives, but even though we may be having sweet dreams we must get up every day after about eight hours and face the real world. We may amass ma-terial possessions: money, big fancy houses, big fancy cottages, big fancy cars, big fancy TVs, and big fancy computers, but we soon discover that we've only succeeded in placing ourselves on a senseless treadmill because the satisfaction from all these possessions is only transitory. And when we realize that, all we can think of to do is to accumulate more money, buy bigger houses, bigger cars, bigger TVs, and bigger computers, but soon even these fail to satisfy because nothing ever does when you're marching to a senseless treadmill's tune.

"Years ago, when I managed an Orangeville bookstore, one of our customers, who collected antique books, was a tiler named Gino who had worked in many expensive homes. He told me of a Burlington woman he sometimes worked for who lived in a two-million-dollar home with her wealthy husband. Gino told me that about every three months she would have an area of the house completely remodelled. Once she did the living room, which she'd done only six months earlier, redecorating the walls, changing all the furnishings, even removing and replacing a fireplace worth thousands of dollars, and having the tradesmen haul everything away without costing them a cent. Her inane reasoning? She had simply grown tired of the decor. And besides, she was giving a house party in a few weeks. Another time, simply to change the colour and design of her kitchen, she had every cupboard, every appliance, ever light fixture, and every piece of tile removed and replaced. Another time, she tackled the grounds by having every plant, flower, and shrub removed and replaced from a rock garden which stretched across the front of the house.

"This silly, selfish, shallow woman, chained to a senseless treadmill, had nothing better to do with her life than to constantly keep changing the appearance of her house, both for her inane self and to impress her wealthy friends. How much better if she had taken the many thousands of dollars she spent so easily on her house and donated that money to some worthy cause, like helping the millions with AIDS in Africa."

Andreas shook his head. "Man, you sound like you've got an angry bee up your ass. You've changed, Rodger. When we were in our teens and hung out together in T.O., you were passive as hell. I could ask you to do anything, go anywhere, and you'd go along with it. But now...now you're full of piss and vinegar and sound like you're trying to redeem the world."

"No, not the world. Only myself."

"Why? What happened?"

"I turned forty."

Andreas shrugged. "So what? We're both forty, and I'm not talking like you. So what's that got to do with anything?"

"Claudia believes that I'm suffering from mid-life crisis, and I believe she's right. I feel that I've now started on the second half of my life, and when I look back over the first half I see nothing but a great emptiness, a great waste, and I can't think of even one thing I've achieved which has any lasting value. We don't even have any children."

"So what's your solution then? I've heard about this mid-life crisis stuff. Guys do crazy things. What are you going to do, start preaching to the unwashed masses from the rooftops?"

Rodger smiled. "No, nothing as crazy as that. The fact is, I don't know yet exactly what I'm going to do. But I do know that I have to change my life. Tell me, have you ever read Emerson?"

"Emerson who?"

"Ralph Waldo Emerson. He was a very wise man."

"Never heard of him. You know I never read much."

"I thought maybe you'd changed over the years."

"No. Over the years I've read most of The Saint books, and some Erle Stanley Gardner and Ellery Queen, and a few Mickey Spillane, but that's about it. What about this guy Emerson?"

"Well, many years ago, back in the nineteenth century, he wrote an essay titled 'Self-Reliance.' My father first read it to me when I was in my early teens and I was so impressed that I memorized one paragraph, which I believe should be the proper direction of any man's life. And I still believe that, even though I haven't practised what it says. I still remember the words, and think of them regularly, running them through my mind, knowing that this is the only proper way to live and telling myself that some day I've got to try to do the same. The paragraph goes like this: 'There is a time in every man's education when he arrives at the conviction that envy is ignorance; that imitation is suicide; that he must take himself for better or worse as his portion; that though the wide universe is full of good, no kernel of nourishing corn can come to him but through his toil bestowed on that plot of ground which is given to him to till. The power which resides in him is new in nature, and none but he knows what that is which he can do, nor does he know until he has tried.'"

Andreas stared at him incredulously. "Are you trying to tell me that you want to be a *farmer*?"

Roger laughed. "No, Andreas, Emerson is writing figuratively. He's writing about the conduct of life, not about farming. He's saying something about life which I've believed for a long time but have been just too weak and gutless to act upon. He's saying that each one of us has a certain role to play in life, and unless we search diligently and find that role we'll never be lastingly contented or happy. Our contentment, our happiness, will always be merely transitory. I firmly believe this. I firmly believe that each on of us has only one road to happiness. Can you imagine the late great Vladimir Horowitz being anything other than a classical pianist? Or Beethoven being anything other than a composer? Or Tolstoy being anything other than a writer? Or Pavarotti being anything other than a tenor? Or Olivier being anything other than an actor? They did what they loved and what they were meant to do and did it supremely well. But that isn't Rodger Blackwell. Rodger Blackwell is living inside someone else's skin, and instead of trying to find himself he's writing pap for the masses, commercials for pussy pads and asswipe."

Rodger took a long, hard look at Andreas, then asked, "Have you never felt that you were out of your element, that you're not really living the life you should be living?"

Andreas replied immediately. "No. Never. You've known me for about twenty-five years. Do *you* think I've changed?"

"Well, I haven't actually known you for the past fifteen, but no, from what I've seen of you here tonight I don't think you've changed." Except, Rodger thought, that The Big Wheel image, once arrayed in Mr. Pifko's fancy, expensive suits, now reduced to shiny polyester, and fancy shirts now reduced to frayed collars, and fancy shoes now reduced to rounded heels, had become somewhat tarnished. "So you have no regrets. You're happy with the way your life is going."

"Sure," Andreas blustered. "Why shouldn't I be? I still get plenty of women, and I've still got plenty of irons in the fire, this big apartment building deal in T.O. next week for just one. And speaking of deals, I've got one for you. Of course, the real reason I came up here was to see you and renew our friendship, and since were old buddies I thought I'd be remiss if I didn't give you a chance to get in on the ground floor as a partner in a business that will probably make you a pile of money."

No, Andreas, the *real* reason you came up here was to try to get some money out of me for another one of your hair-brained schemes

"This job of yours," Andreas continued. "Writing ads. Have you been with the company long?"

"Several years."

"So you've moved up the ladder, have you?"

"Yes. Drummond recently hinted that I may be offered a partnership in the near future."

"So you're making pretty good money, are you?"

"Yes."

"And I guess you've managed to save a few grand over the years, have you?"

"Yes. I save and invest regularly."

"Good. Now here's what I've got in mind. I'm telling you, Rodger, it's the chance of a lifetime, and you won't even have to leave Orangeville to cash in. Listen, you're going to love this. In Scarborough, in a plaza at Kingston Road and Birchmount, there's a billiard hall for sale. It's in a basement next door to a bowling alley that does a thriving business during the bowling season, and the bowlers pass right by the billiard hall's door. But right now the place looks pretty crumby and is attracting too many lowlifes and bums. The owners have let the place run down and they want out. They've got eight six-by-twelves and two Boston tables, but most of them need recovering. Most of the cues are warped, the floor needs to be retiled, and the place needs a good paint job. Because of all this, they're letting the place go cheap. My idea is this: We buy the place and convert it into a gentlemen's billiard club. We could even call it that: Gentlemen's Billiard Club. And it'd be for members only, and no women allowed. Each member would pay an annual fee, say three hundred bucks, and the membership fees would just keep rolling in because we'd be getting new members all the time. And every member would have to show his current membership card every time he entered.

"We could get a liquor licence and convert the lunch counter that's there now into a bar. And we'd also serve food—there's plenty of room at the front to put in several tables and plenty of chairs. And if members wanted to play pool, they'd pay. And if they wanted to gamble, they could. I tell you, Rodger, this is a great opportunity for you to make some easy cash, right here from Orangeville. And you wouldn't have to lift a finger."

"Rodger asked, "How much do the owners want for this business?"

"Fifty grand."

"And what about the renovations?"

"Another twenty."

"And how much would you be putting up?"

Looking sheepish, Andreas spread his hands above the table, palms upward. "That's just it, Rodger. Right now I've got everything tied up in this apartment building deal, but we'd be equal partners, every dollar of profit split right down the middle, and you wouldn't have to do a damn thing. I'd take care of the sale, handle all the renovations, and manage the place."

"And all you want from me is seventy grand."

"Well…yes, but it's a terrific investment for you. You could keep your job and still have all this extra money rolling in."

Rodger gave him a long, hard look. "Andreas, do you actually think I'm still the teenager you knew back in Toronto? Do you honestly believe that I'm still so naive that I'd just hand over seventy grand without even seeing this place, without even having something on paper? How gullible do you think I am?"

"Hold on, buddy." Andreas raised his hand, like a traffic cop making a stop sign. "I know you're not gullible. If you want to see the place, fine, I'll be glad to show it to you. I just thought you might not want to bother driving all the way down to T.O., that's all. And as for the paper,"—he tapped his breast pocket—"I've got it right here. All perfectly legal. I want you and your lawyer to read it."

Rodger stared at him, astounded, not certain whether to believe him or not. "Do you mean to tell me that you're so presumptuous that you've actually had a paper already drawn up?"

"Sure, why not?" Andreas replied promptly. "I wasn't sure if you had the money or not, but I didn't want to waste any time because this deal isn't going to last. It's just a simple partnership agreement: you supply the money, I supply the labour, and we split the profits equally, taking regular draws from the company." He pulled several stapled sheets from his inside pocket and extended them toward Rodger. "Here, take a look."

"I don't need to take a look. I know I can't do it."

Still, Andreas placed the sheets beside Rodger's plate. "Why? You don't have the money, is that it? I thought you said you had a well-paying job."

"I do. And I do have the money. But I don't have seventy grand just lying around in some savings account just waiting for you to come along and ask me for it."

"I wasn't expecting that. So you've got investments. So cash something in. You'd be foolish to pass this up. This investment is going to make you a hell of a lot more than some GIC paying you a few per-cent a year."

"No, I don't intend to cash anything in. Because I don't intend to invest in this." He gave Andreas a long, hard look. "I've changed, Andreas. You mentioned it earlier. I'm not the passive guy anymore who used to idolize you and hang onto your shirttails and follow you around, agreeing with everything you said and just trying to be your buddy. I'm my own man now, doing what *I* want to do, and I'm definitely *not* interested in putting my money into a deal that I can't even keep an eye on because it's about a hundred kilometres away from here."

"So you don't trust me, is that it? Just because you're not around, you think I'll doctor the books and skim off the cream. Sure, maybe I would've done that to some guys in the past, and maybe I'd even do it today to some guys, but not to you, Rodger. Never to you. We grew up together, we were buddies, we were like family. I'd never cheat you, Rodger."

But to Rodger that said it all, only confirming his suspicion that Andreas hadn't changed. Although Andreas tried to exclude Rodger when he admitted that he'd still cheat "some guys," Rodger knew that he was *not* excluded. Fifteen years of complete separation no longer qualified them as "buddies" or "family" and Rodger saw himself as just another potential sucker.

Rodger pushed the sheets back to Andreas' side of the table. "As I've already said, I'm not interested, and that's *final.*" By this time they were halfway through a second carafe of red house wine and their glasses were almost empty. Rodger refilled their glasses, draining the carafe. "But that doesn't prevent us from enjoying our last glass of wine together, does it?"

The inference was clear: the investment discussion had ended, they'd finish their wine and each be on his way.

"Okay," Andreas said grudgingly, picking up the sheets and waving them before Rodger's face. "But you're going to be sorry that you missed out on this sweet deal. Don't worry, I'll get somebody else to come in with me. And when I phone you a few months from now and tell you how great things are going, and how much money I'm making, you're going to be sorry as hell that you passed this up. Yeah, sorry as hell, but it'll be too damn late. To damn late because you missed the boat on this one." Angrily, Andreas thrust the sheets back into his inside jacket pocket.

But Rodger knew that Andreas' words were mere bluster. There would be no phone call, no bragging about a hugely successful billiard club, and no censuring of Rodger for missing out on it because Andreas' plan would eventually become just another big idea by the Big Wheel which had turned sour.

Rodger said, "I've never been a greedy man, never had any aspirations of becoming a millionaire because I've always felt that more money simply produces more headaches. Right now I'm comfortable financially and I'm not looking to become rich. Right now the most important goal in my life is trying to discover who I actually am." Feeling a need to placate Andreas, he raised his glass. "But I wish you every success in your new venture. I hope it brings you everything you want, and more. As a matter of fact, let's drink a toast to that, shall we?"

"Sure, why not," Andreas agreed, but his voice sounded lifeless, and the listless clinking of his glass against Rodger's told him that Andreas now held out little hope for the project.

They remained silent for a few minutes, each breaking up the silence by taking regular sips from his wine, Rodger aware that now that he had adamantly refused Andreas offer, Andreas apparently had nothing further to say. There would be no further reminiscences to soften up Rodger to extract money from him. That gambit had failed, and now, as Rodger gazed across the table at Andreas sipping his wine, apparently bored, Andreas' protracted silence spoke reams about his true purpose in Orangeville and laid bare his innate selfishness.

Rodger waited, and Andreas finally broke the silence. "How about a Britannica, Rodger? Every home needs a Britannica."

Rodger could barely keep from laughing. When you can't catch a marlin, try to land a salmon. "No, thanks, I've already got a *Britannica*. Have had one for years. And before you ask me, I've also got a set of *Great Books Of The Western World*. I wouldn't be without them."

"Do you know anyone who might be interested in either? We could call on them before we leave tomorrow."

"Not offhand. I can talk to a few people and let you know it there's any interest."

Andreas reached into his breast pocket and removed a business card. "Here. Let me know if you get any leads."

"Sure." But Rodger wondered what Andreas needed with leads when he'd be leaving Britannica in a few days. Apparently The Big Wheel had momentarily forgotten about the big apartment building deal.

They drained their glasses and Rodger reached for the check.

"I'll get that, " Andreas said weakly, a token offer which clearly stated that he preferred that Rodger paid.

"No, this one's on me. You can get it next time."

"Sure, thanks. When I come back a few months from now and tell you how great the billiard club is doing. We'll celebrate." Andreas' weak smile barely curved his lips. "I might even rub it in about how you missed out on a terrific deal."

Rodger smiled back but said nothing, almost certain that he'd never see Andreas again because The Big Wheel had nothing to gain by returning.

As the two men rose and shook hands, Andreas glanced at his watch and said, "I've got to run—my partner's expecting me. Good seeing you again, Rodger. Take care."

In a few seconds, Andreas had disappeared out the door, leaving Rodger to wonder at his haste. He walked to the window and looked out in time to see Andreas, in his shiny suit, frayed shirt, old-fashioned tie, and round-heeled shoes, hurry across the parking lot.

Then the still defiantly proud Big Wheel climbed into his car—which Rodger recognized as a 1995 Plymouth Acclaim because he had once owned one—and quickly drove by the window, the large bare patch where the paint had peeled covering half the car's hood.

10

When Rodger arrived home just before eight o'clock, Claudia, unable to keep the suspicion from her voice, greeted him with, "Well, did you enjoy your dinner with your *male* friend?"

"Yes, I did." He sat down at the opposite end of the living room sofa and faced her. "Do you honestly believe that I met a woman and took her to a motel and had sex with her, then came home, all in less than two hours? If you want, I can prove to you right now that I didn't have sex with anybody. Remember what you said: I'm a rifle, not a six-shooter."

She gave him a long look, sighed, then relaxed back against the cushions. "No, I don't need any proof. I believe you. It's just that I love you so much, darling, that I don't want another woman even touching you. What did your friend want?"

"First, we talked about old times in Toronto. We grew up together there. Then he let me know what he really wanted."

"What was that?"

"Money. He wanted me to become a partner with him in a billiard club in Scarborough. I'd put up the capital and he'd run it and we'd split the profits. He wanted me to put up seventy thousand dollars."

"Seventy thousand!" she shrieked, suddenly bolt upright. "You didn't...I mean you wouldn't...you couldn't..."

He raised a hand to placate her. "No, of course not. I won't be giving him a cent. I haven't seen him in about fifteen years and he hasn't changed a bit. I thought maybe he had, that I might even be able to get some direction for my own life from him, but he's always been a hustler, not reliable, not trustworthy, only out for what he can get out of other people, and all I could learn from him was how *not* to live. But that doesn't mean that I've stopped looking."

"But why *don't* you stop looking? Darling, don't you think you're becoming obsessed with this...this quest of yours? I'm afraid that you might become *so* obsessed with whatever you're looking for that you might develop some kind of…well, some kind of mental *disease*. I realize what you must be going through, but I'm afraid for you. Don't you think it's time that you started trying to get this obsession under control?"

He recognized her fear tactics for what they were, and said,"I don't intend to try to get anything under control until I've found what I'm looking for. And once I've found that, I'll be fully in control of my own life. As a matter of fact, I'd like to visit your father this weekend. Would you like to come along?"

"My *father*? Are you mad? When he left here last Sunday he—"

"I don't mean Greg. I mean your *real* father. Have you forgotten that you have a real father?"

"Sometimes I wish I *could* forget. Why on earth would you even *think* of visiting *him*? What do you expect to learn from a sixty-year-old man whose done absolutely nothing with his life and spends most of his time alone at home just playing with his toys?"

"I don't know, but I'd like to see him anyway. I haven't seem him for a long time; neither have you. Would you like to come along?"

"No. I've too much work to do this weekend. Besides, I've absolutely no desire to see Charles, this weekend or any weekend. He's no longer a part of my life."

"Too bad. I'm sure he'd be glad to see you." But actually Rodger felt relieved that Claudia had declined; he still felt obliged to ask even though almost certain of her answer. He much preferred to speak to Charles alone, without the distraction of the negative side comments that Claudia would surely make.

On Sunday at three p.m., the time that they had agreed upon, Rodger arrived at the small, old, two-storey frame house on Bythia Street where Charles lived as a tenant. Covered with chipping, pale gray asphalt siding, chipped white woodwork cracked and blistered, the shabby house still used old-fashioned wooden storm windows which were apparently no longer removed during the summer. A rusting TV antenna with several of its aluminum rods bent stood slightly tilted on the roof. The thirsting brown grass of the tiny front lawn was rife with flourishing dandelions turning to seed.

Feeling a mild twinge of guilt because he'd never visited the house, Rodger mounted the worn wood- en staircase fastened to the renovated side of the house and knocked on Charles' apart- ment door.

The door opened a few seconds later revealing Charles, barely over five feet, still slender at sixty, wearing brown, horn-rimmed bifocals and dressed in a dark gray T-shirt and navy blue shorts, with sandals on his naked feet. His once blonde hair, now mainly gray and receding, topped a thin, green-eyed, small-nosed, small-mouthed face, the pale, clean-shaven cheeks dotted here and there with several liver spots.

"Come in, come in," he said as they shook hands briefly, quickly closing the door as Rodger entered, as though to keep out the summer heat.

But as Rodger tried to acclimatize himself to the stifling liv- ing room, where a large, oscillating pedestal fan, with its front screen removed for more air circulation, droned bravely on, he began to wonder if anything short of air conditioning could pos- sibly help.

Before leaving the car, Rodger had slipped the digital re- corder into his shirt pocket. Now, he re-moved it and showed it to Charles and explained about the book and its purpose.

Charles shrugged. "Doubt that you'll record anything here worth putting into a book, but go ahead. Just don't use my name if you do."

"No, I won't."

"Fine."

Rodger started the digital recorder and slipped it back into his shirt pocket. Gazing at Charles' profile, he observed again the small hump on his back which forced his slender neck with its prominent Adam's apple to push forward and curve upward, causing his head to sit slightly in front of his shoulders. Sally had always called Charles "Ducky," and Rodger had believed that she meant it as a term of endearment, but now he wondered if she had actually meant it more as a comment on the ducklike appearance of his curved neck.

Grinning, Charles said, "Have a look around. Shouldn't take you more than a minute. Like a cold glass of lemonade?"

"Sure."

As Charles left for the kitchen, Rodger wandered around the small, cramped living room, barely able to find walking space. Thick brown drapes, tightly closed, covered the single window; against one wall, a bulky, old-fashioned maroon chesterfield dominated the room. Before it, on a shabby, four-by-eight foot imitation Oriental rug, rested a scarred coffee table with several cigarette burns dotting its wooden top, a cheap bouquet of assorted artificial flowers in a plastic vase serving as its centrepiece. A nineteen-inch TV in a cracked case and mounted on a stand stood in a corner, its brown antenna wire leading to the nearby window. In another corner, a hardbacked wooden chair stood in the recess of an old wooden pedestal desk with several thick albums stacked on each side of it, each cover displaying a title label. The first Rodger opened held a collection of book matches, hundreds of them in row upon row and mainly representing local area businesses, each neatly inserted into its clear plastic pocket. As smokers became fewer and fewer, Rodger thought, new ones would become increasingly difficult to find. Other albums contained collections of postage stamps, business cards, store discount coupons, hockey cards, baseball cards, and basketball cards. But the one album one would expect to see in any home was conspicuously absent: a photo album. As Rodger glanced around the room, nowhere could he see a single photo, as though Charles wanted to remove every vestige of painful past relationships: a failed marriage, and a daughter who ignored him.

While he examined the hockey cards album, Charles returned with two tall glasses of cold lemonade and handed him one.

"Like my collection?"

After taking a few grateful gulps, Rodger nodded. "Some of these hockey cards are incredible. These old Leafs cards. Max and Doug Bentley, Syl Apps, George Armstrong, Red Kelly, Bobby

Baun. And a lot of others. Bobby Orr, Bobby Hull, Gordie Howe. Not to even mention the baseball and basketball cards. How long have you been collecting these?"

"Actually, the sports card collections belonged to my father. Haven't had the money to add much to them for a long time. I started the other collections—they're a lot cheaper to maintain. He started collecting the cards when I was a kid, and left them to me when he died. He told me a long time ago that they might be valuable some day."

"And he was right. They're probably worth quite a bit of money. Have you had these sports card collections appraised?"

"No, but I own a price guide. I've got a pretty good idea."

"Then why don't you sell them?" Rodger waved an arm, encompassing the living room. "Think of it, you could modernize this place, buy yourself a new sofa, maybe even a La-Z-boy, a new coffee table, a better TV, an air conditioner."

"Not necessary. Things are fine the way they are. Promised my father I'd never sell the collection."

Rodger shrugged. "Suit yourself. May I look at the rest of the place?"

"Sure."

Placing his lemonade on the coffee table, Rodger walked into the tiny kitchen, passing under a crucifix mounted above the doorway, Charles following close behind. A few cupboards were above the only counter space, barely two feet wide, to one side of the white-enamelled sink which still contained breakfast dishes, cutlery, and a greasy frying pan. The rest of the room held only a small refrigerator, a small gas stove, and a small wooden table and chair in a corner. The table held the remnants of Charles' lunch: a few bites of a drying cheese sandwich and a half empty mug of cold instant coffee. Plain dark brown linoleum, worn bare in several spots, covered the floor. The pale yellow walls, apparently an attempt at cheerfulness, were bare except for a picture of Pope Benedict XVI on the wall above the table.

A mingled odour of stale sweat and soiled socks emanating from a mound of dirty laundry in a corner met them as they entered the small bedroom.

By way of suggestion, Rodger asked, "Do you take your laundry out?"

"Naw. Tom and Barb have a washer and dryer in the basement they let me use."

"Oh?" Rodger stared pointedly at the laundry. "Is the washer broken?"

Charles laughed self-consciously, his right hand suddenly gripping his right hip. "Naw. But the old back isn't too good these days. I'll try to do it later on today…if I can."

The only pieces of furniture were a single, un-made bed against one wall, a cheap, striped mat on the wooden floor beside it, and a narrow four-drawer dresser with one drawer left slightly open because it contained no handle. Rodger saw the handle lying on the dresser and wondered at Charles' laziness. Not only had he not bothered refastening the drawer handle, an easy two-minute job, but he hadn't even bothered tidying up the apartment when expecting company.

Besides a small oscillating fan and a layer of dust, the only other item on the dresser was a well-used copy of *The Book of Psalms*, but on a small shelf above the dresser Rodger saw something which appeared entirely out of place: an excellent model of the sailing ship *Bluenose* on a stand and encased in a bottle.

Given the neglected condition of the apartment, and his apparent laziness, Rodger doubted that Charles had built it, but asked anyway. "Naw," Charles replied. "Bought it at a flea market a few years ago. Guy was desperate for a sale. Gave it to me for ten dollars."

"You're kidding! Are you sure it's the real thing? Is the bottle made of glass?"

"Oh, it's glass all right."

"I've heard that some of these are made by cutting the top off the bottle and glueing it back on once the ship is inside."

"I guess some of them are done that way, but not this one. Look all you want, you won't see a seam. This one's the real thing. I asked the guy who sold it to me and he told me how they did it."

"And how's that?"

Charles grinned impishly. "I don't know if I should tell you the secret."

"C'mon, you know you want to."

"Okay, then, I will." Charles shrugged. "I guess plenty of people know already anyway. They build the ship outside the bottle with the masts folded down, making sure that the hull fits through the neck,, then slide it into place. Once it's in place, they use special tools to raise the masts again."

"So that's how they do it. Tell me, Charles, have you ever thought of building one of these?"

"Naw, too much work. And too picky. Can't be bothered spending hours and hours on something like that."

"Then how do you like to spend your free time? You only work a few days a week as a greeter at Wal-Mart."

"Usually three, occasionally four."

"So what do you do for the other three or four days a week?"

"Not much really. Of course I help out around here. Tom and Barb, the landlords, can't do much. They're both in their seventies. Tom has arthritis in his knees and hands, and Barb can barely walk be-cause she's as fat as a barrel from sitting around all day watching TV and stuffing herself with Vachon cakes. They gave me a real good deal on the rent when I moved in here for taking care of the odd jobs around the place."

Moving to the window, Charles pulled back the dark brown drapes and gazed down at the tall grass of the weed-choked backyard. "Like mowing the lawn?"

Charles shrugged. "Not to worry. It'll get done eventually. Right now it's just too darn hot." His right hand went to his right hip. "Besides, my back's been acting up lately. Can't do much. Barely able to take care of myself these days. And when I get home from Wal-Mart, after a long day standing on my feet, I can barely walk. But it'll get done…eventually."

Rodger smiled inwardly. He knew a malingerer when he heard one and felt no sympathy for Charles' tales of woe. Turning away from the window, he returned to the dresser. He found the soiled laundry odour offensive and suggested that they return to the living room.

When they had seated themselves at the maroon chester-field, Rodger gulped down the rest of his lemonade. He could feel sweat trickling down his armpits, and the droning fan took too long to swing back to him. "By the way, you don't have a car any more, do you?"

"Naw, can't afford it. Got rid of that a long time ago."

"So how do you get to work and back. Walk?"

Charles laughed. "Not likely. I couldn't make it even if I tried. And even if I could, how could I then stand there all day long with my poor old back killing me all the time? And then walking all the way back home? Heck, I'd have to spend several dollars taking a cab."

"So do you have a friend drive you then?"

"Naw. I've got a bike downstairs in the back shed. It's got a basket on the front for groceries. That gets me where I want to go." As though suddenly remembering, his right hand went to his right hip again. "But even pedalling that old bike's pretty hard on this poor old aching back of mine."

Ignoring the plea for sympathy, Rodger said pointedly, "So, when you're not attending to your *duties* around here, what do you do with your free time?"

"Just try to take it as easy as possible, and be as careful as possible. The back, you know. Spend time sorting and rearranging the collections, especially the store coupons and book matches. New book matches are getting harder to find, maybe because most people aren't smoking any more, but the flyers in the weekend *Banner* usually have some new store coupons for the collection."

"Do you just collect these coupons, or do you actually *use* them in the stores to save money?"

"Sure, they're used, when possible, but only a few. You probably noticed that the book is arranged in categories. It's really a collection which keeps getting bigger all the time. Besides, most of the coupons keep expiring and you can only use them for a certain length of time anyway."

"Well, what else do you do?"

"Watch a fair bit of TV evenings when I get home from work, mostly sports, or listen to music on the radio, mostly classical. Sunday it's church—I'm an usher there. On days off during the week, I usually bike up to the Orangeville Mall around eight o'clock for a coffee and muffin breakfast and join the guys at the tables outside A&P until noon. Then it's back to the apartment for the rest of the day, and to bed at nine."

Rodger found it difficult to keep the agitation from his voice. "Do you mean to tell me that you spend about *four hours* each morning on your day off sitting around Orangeville Mall drinking coffee? What the hell do you do for all that time?"

Charles shrugged. "Not much, really. We're mostly just killing time." His voice became disdainful. "First we solve all the major problems of the world. War, crime, starvation, AIDS, politics, you name it—we've got solutions for them all. And when we're finished with those, we start in on the minor problems of the world, and as you know there are hundreds, even thousands of those. And when we get tired of that, we start in on our favourite subject: complaining. Complaining about our government, our corrupt politicians, our paltry pensions, our foul-mouthed young people. And the complaining never ends because you can complain about anything under the sun, can't you, if your discontented enough or unhappy enough. Even something as silly as the colour of a person's hair."

"You sound as though you don't participate much in these discussions."

"Naw. I get bored after about ten minutes. Every morning it's the same old thing, like a broken record—the same old men with the same old complaints, or the same old solutions to the same old problems, and the ones with the most solutions and the most complaints are usually those with the most money: savings, investments, and pensions rolling in every month. But they're discontented with everything, even though they've got a loaf of bread under each arm and two between their legs. But there's no use complaining; we all make our own lives. We're the way we are because of what we did or didn't put into our lives. Nothing to get excited about. That's why, after the coffee and muffin are gone, I get away from them and take a walk, usually up to Zellers where I look at all the things I don't have, and don't need or want." He looked away sheepishly. "But I come back. I always come back... eventually."

"But why? Why spend hours and hours with men who bore you, who go on and on with their litanies of complaints which you're not interested in?"

"I have my reasons."

"What reasons?"

"Well, I..."

"What possible reasons could you have for wasting time with people you're not interested in?"

Charles still refused to look at him. "Don't you understand? It's the company, just the company. It's just being with other people instead of being alone."

"But I thought you were a loner. I thought you *enjoyed* being alone."

"Sure, I do. But not for three whole days a week."

"I don't understand this. Couldn't you make friends with *other* people? People you'd be interested in talking with? What about Tom and Barb? Have you ever visited them, tried to make friends?"

Charles stared at him and laughed. "You must be joking! Tried that. Even stayed for dinner once, and ended up leaving with a headache. These two can't talk about anything but themselves, and complain, complain, complain, mainly about their health. Barb complains about her weight, that she can't seem to lose even a pound, while she stuffs her face with Vachon cakes. And Tom complains about his arthritis, that he can't seem to do anything to help himself, but all he does is lounge around all day, not even moving most of the time, and does nothing whatsoever to cope with his condition." He shook his head emphatically. "Naw, I can't go back there again—I'd rather go to the Orangeville Mall."

"Then what about *female* companionship? Wouldn't you like to meet a nice woman about your own age? Maybe someone from your church. Someone you could talk to. Someone who could come in here now and then and cook you a decent meal." He swept the room with an arm. Someone who could come in here and tidy up this place, keep it clean, maybe even do your laundry."

Rodger stopped talking because as he spoke he could see Charles' mouth widening in shocked surprise, his eyes bulging dangerously, as though they were about to pop out of his head.

"After *Sally?*" Charles cried. "You expect me to go out and look for another woman after what I went through with *her?* You must be mad." He shook his head vigorously. "Been there, done that, don't intend to ever do it again, thank you very much."

"Then what about different *male* companionship? You said you were an usher at church; surely you know some of the men there."

"Sure, I talk to a few of them now and then, but the younger ones are too immature. Don't have anything in common with them. And the older ones, well, most of them are married and attached to there wives. If I tried to develop a relationship without a wife of my own on hand I'd feel out of place, like I was intruding, like a third wheel." Staring steadily at Rodger, he gripped his left hip and emitted a low moan. "Surely you can understand that."

No, Rodger thought, he didn't understand that for a moment. Further, he noticed that Charles had gripped his left hip instead of the right, yet common knowledge said that back pain almost always af-fected either one side of the back or the other, not both. In his eagerness to present himself as a decrepit old man living daily in pain, and anxious to elicit Rodger's sympathy, he had slipped up. Malingerer, Rodger thought. Nothing but an inveterate malingerer trying to blame his laziness on an imaginary illness. He wondered how often Charles used the same evasive tactics while greeting customers at Wal-Mart, seeking out those who would commiserate with him, even if it also meant commiserating with them. Like a neglected child, aware that any attention was better than no attention at all, sought attention by being disobedient and deliberately lying to his parents, so Charles sought the brief attention of a few of the hundreds of shoppers who rushed by him mutely each working day, gripping his hip and lying to them about his aching back in the hope of gaining a few minutes of their sym-pathetic attention.

But Rodger felt no sympathy for him. Instead, he felt a growing anger at Charles' attempt to dupe him. He gazed distastefully around the neglected living room, eying the dusty drapes, the old TV in its cracked case, the shabby imitation Oriental rug, the dusty old maroon chesterfield, the burn-scarred coffee table, the droning pedestal fan, all contriving to fill his nostrils with the dusty odour of a room that had apparently never seen a vacuum cleaner. He recalled the kitchen with the stale cheese sandwich and cold coffee still left on the table, the bedroom with the unmade bed and mound of dirty laundry. All these, combined with the faked aching back and the manifold excuses, told the true story of the man. A man whose consummate laziness prevented him from regularly performing even the most mundane and simple chores. But what irked him even more was Charles' assumption that he, Rodger, was so naive that he actually *believed* the phoney aching back routine and would sympathize.

"Tell me, Charles, have you ever suffered from mid-life crisis? Sometimes it's called male menopause."

Charles shook his head. "New, can't recall that I ever have. Always thought only women have menopause. Apparently comes on soon after they've stopped their monthlies."

"No, some men have a version of it, too. Usually around middle age. I'm going through it now. You look back on your life and wonder what you've done with it, what you've achieved, and what you intend to do with the rest of it to make it better. Have you never felt that way, maybe in your forties?"

"Naw, can't say that I ever have. Nothing ever changes with me—I just keep plodding along."

Plodding along indeed, Rodger thought. Why had he even bothered asking such a stupid question of a man who possessed absolutely no ambition. What had brought Charles to this end? Had he been totally influenced by the superficial image he presented to himself and to the public? Had he stared into a full length mirror one morning, perhaps while dressing, and actually *seen* that image with all its imperfections? The curved duck's neck, the sharp, protruding Adam's apple which appeared ready to slice through his skin at any moment as it rode up and down as he spoke, the humped back, the badly sloping shoulders, with the shortness completing the negative picture, at least superficially, of a man who had nothing going for him. And had he then simply shrugged and sighed heavily and said to himself, "What's the use. How can anyone be expected to achieve anything looking like this?" and used this as his rationalization for giving up? He looked like a nonentity, Rodger knew, but he didn't have to *be* a nonentity. Damn it, *he didn't have to be a nonentity!*

Unable to hold back his anger and indignation any longer, Rodger gave Charles a stony stare and demanded harshly, "What the *hell* are you doing here? Living like this. Can't you spend a little time cleaning up this damn hellhole, vacuuming, washing dishes, doing your damn, stinking laundry? What's the *matter* with you?"

Surprised by Rodger's outburst, Charles stared at him for a moment, then shrugged passively. "Not important. It'll get done... eventually." He groped for his hip. "Besides, my back—"

"*Piss* on your back! You and I both know that there isn't a damn thing wrong with it, so stop using it as an excuse. Let's face it, Charles, you're just bone lazy. So bone lazy that you can't even be bothered keeping a little apartment clean. So bone lazy that you can't even be bothered mowing a lawn or changing storm windows for your landlords. You're only sixty, but you're acting like you're seventy or even eighty. When are you going to start *doing* something with your life?"

Abruptly, Rodger stopped talking, suddenly realizing that he had not only been making this last demand on Charles but also on himself, that his angry comments were also prompted by his frustration with himself in trying to discover his own identity. Had he and Claudia done *anything* with their lives over the past ten years besides embellishing the money tree? This obviously satisfied her, but not him. And now never would.

When am *I* going to do something with *my* life? When am *I* going to escape *my* alien body? When am *I* going to discover *my* true purpose in life?

Charles said, "I know it isn't much, but I do what I can."

"Like what?" Rodger snapped, unable to resist the sarcasm. "Like looking after your collection of store coupons?"

"Naw, didn't mean that. I go to church every Sunday and usher. I've never hurt anyone, never been in a fight, never been arrested, never given anyone any trouble. I'm a polite, peaceable man. Doesn't that count for something?"

"Yes, it does count for something. What it counts for is this: if everyone was like you we'd still be living in the stone age, or the human race would have died out completely because no one is lifting a finger to advance it. Tell me, why do you think you're here, on this earth? What do you think your purpose is here? What do you feel you should honestly be doing with your life?"

Charles shrugged passively. "Nothing more than I'm doing now. Because that's the way the mop flops, isn't it? Even if I wanted a better job, who's going to hire a man with no special training? And who's going to hire a man of sixty? Wal-Mart, that's who, or maybe Zellers, or maybe some restaurant that needs a dishwasher. Those are the options, and they all pay about the same: very little. So why spend the rest of my life worrying about it—that's not going to change anything. Like I said, that's just the way the mop flops. I made my life the way it is, and that's fine, I accept that. No complaints. No recriminations. Wouldn't have it any other way."

"I'm not necessarily talking about your job. You're sixty, Charles. *Sixty!* And your years are beginning to wind down. Don't you feel some sense of urgency? Haven't you ever examined your life and asked yourself why you're here? What your *purpose* is here?"

"Used to think about things like that when I was young. Even read some theology and philosophy once, but never came to any conclusions of my own. So I just accepted the teachings of the Church."

"Fine. And what does your church teach you?"

"It's pretty simple, really. If you're good you go to heaven, if you're mediocre you go to purgatory for a while, and if you're bad you go straight to hell."

"And where do you think you fit into the picture?"

Embarrassed, Charles said, "Well, I'm not bad."

"No, Charles, you're not bad. You're just sitting on the fence stagnating. Like me. We've both been sitting on the fence stagnating for many years, balancing there like mugwumps, telling ourselves that we won't jump down to one side or the other, the good or the bad, because maybe, just maybe, there might be something to this heaven and hell business. So we sit there, balancing and stagnating, doing our tiny bit as human beings and salving our consciences by telling ourselves that we're not bad people. We've never murdered anybody, never raped any women, never robbed banks, never beaten our wives or mistresses, never stolen from others, never gone to jail. But is merely obeying the laws of the land actually being *good?* No, of course not. That's simply *not being bad.* That's simply *being human.* And being human in this way may simply be prompted by a fear of being prosecuted. But actually being good is something entirely different."

"Oh? What is it then?"

Rodger's mind raced as he groped for the right words. "Being good is…being good is…being good is doing something in this world which makes a positive difference. You've heard it said, when a certain person dies, that he or she 'made a difference.' Which means that this person left some lasting good behind, improved the world in some way and made it a better or safer place to live in, even to the point of making great sacrifices to do so. And not prompted by money or fame, but driven to accomplish things *simply because they were the right things to do.* One of the most moth-eaten cliches you hear or read about when a wealthy public person dies is that he or she 'will be sorely missed.' Unless that person has used some of his wealth to benefit mankind, instead of hoarding it for his own personal self-aggrandizement, can any intelligent person honestly believe that this person will be sorely missed by anyone other than those people close to him who have benefited from his handouts? No, the person who will be truly sorely missed isn't the man who left behind five mansions, fifteen cars, and ten yachts. The person who will be truly sorely missed is the person who spent his entire adult life helping others and left this world a better place to live in."

"Idealistic ideas," Charles said. "But not mine. I gave up on the world a long time ago, after years and years of listening to practically nothing but stories about how amoral it actually is. Terrorism is running rampant; innocent people are being tortured and slaughtered right and left; wars continue to kill thousands and thousands; millions of Africans are dying of AIDS, and their children will probably be born with it; adultery, promiscuousness, and

254 LESLIE G. SABO

divorce have become as common as dirt; homosexuality is widely accepted, with same-sex marriages permitted in most parts of the world; our prisons are filled to overflowing with criminals; our cities are homes for countless alcoholics and drug addicts. Our population consists of more and more fat people. It's getting so people don't even care what they look like any more. And if you ask someone why they steal or lie or cheat on their spouses they just say, 'Well, everybody does it, don't they?'"

"But that's the biggest lie of all, isn't it? Because everybody definitely doesn't do it. You don't do it, I don't do it, millions of people don't do it. And even if most people were dishonest, does that mean that we have to be dishonest as well? Instead of being true to ourselves and asserting our individuality by doing the right thing, are we supposed to just follow along like a bunch of dumb, blind sheep?"

"But the fact is, and you can't deny it, that the world has gone to hell, and people just don't give a damn any more." Charles shrugged and sighed heavily. "So I've dropped out—that's how I'm asserting my individuality. And why not? What good reason does anyone have today for not dropping out?"

Rodger hadn't even thought of his reply when the words came unbidden from his lips. "Mother Theresa."

"Mother Theresa?"

"Yes, Mother Theresa," he continued, warming to his subject. "When she saw the poor huddled in the slums of Calcutta did she say, 'I can't help these people because there is too much poverty here, too much squalor, too much pain, too much hunger, too much sickness, too much death.'? No, of course not. She did what she could, and eventually gathered others around her who wanted to do the same. She didn't just drop out."

"Well, I'm certainly no Mother Theresa. I'm only Charles Hewitt, and I don't have either the energy or the will to change my life now. I'm happy the way I am, and I'll continue to go on the same way."

Rodger waved an arm, encompassing the shabby living room. "And this is the way."

"Exactly. You see, my answer is simple. But what about you? What do you plan to do about all this extra baggage you're dragging around?"

"I haven't the vaguest idea," Rodger admitted. He gazed at Charles, searching his face for some sign that he knew of some sterling advice, but saw nothing. Aware of the almost certain fruitlessness of his next question, yet still clinging to some dim hope, Rodger asked, "After what I've told you about myself today, and knowing what I believe, what would you suggest that I do with my life?"

Charles' mouth fell open. "You're asking me? After what I've just told you? Knowing what I am, what makes you think that I could possibly have anything to offer you?"

"I was looking for a suggestion from my perspective, not yours."

"Oh." Thinking, he remained silent for almost a minute, then said, "You're still young—only forty. You still have time. Never been like you, but if I were, and believed what you believe, I'd continue searching until I found what I was searching for. Even if it took the rest of my life."

"And if I never find it?"

Charles shrugged. "Then you'll die trying, won't you?"

When Rodger arrived home, he found Claudia in the kitchen preparing dinner.

"Well, what did you get from Charles to further your cause?" she asked. "Nothing, I suppose."

"Nothing from his personal life. He's simply a lonely, bone lazy person, that's all, who wants nothing more out of life, but wants everyone to feel sorry for him because of a back condition he doesn't actually have. Even so, he did give me one piece of sound advise which I intend to pursue."

"Oh?" She laughed derisively. "What possible sound advice could old Mr. Do Nothing give you? Someone who hasn't made even a speck of effort to do anything worthwhile in his entire life."

"Well, I wouldn't exactly say that." Rodger smiled smugly. "After all, he made you, didn't he? And you're certainly worthwhile."

"Now you're just being finicky. Besides, making me hardly required more than a speck of effort, did it. Surely he didn't suggest that you adopt *his* way of life, did he? Although even if you did that you'd at least forget about this...this obsession of yours."

"No, he didn't suggest that. But you'll be surprised at what he did suggest. Frankly, I didn't think he had it in him. When I asked him, given my circumstances, what he thought I should do, he suggested that I go on searching until I find what I'm searching for, even if it takes the rest of my life."

"That lazy bum!" she cried, astonished. "He hates me. Now I know he hates me because of the way I neglect him because I simply can't stand his lifestyle." Anxious, she clutched his forearm with a hand still damp from handling salad vegetables. "What did he say about me? Did he tell you what a horrible daughter I was, that I'd written him out of my life? I'll bet the lazy bum complained long and hard about me, didn't he?"

"No, as a matter of fact he didn't. Your name was never even mentioned. As a matter of fact, I got the impression that he'd written *you* out of *his* life."

"What do you mean?" she demanded angrily, her fingernails now digging into his forearm.

"Well, it's as though you didn't exist for him any more. I'm sure he has photos of you, but there wasn't even one showing in his apartment. I guess right now he thinks more of Sally."

"Sally? Why?"

"Because the only photo in the whole apartment is a nice one of Sally in a fancy frame hanging from the living room wall."

"Of course he has one of Sally," she sneered. "Why wouldn't he, the lazy, useless bum."

"I don't understand. Why would he have a photo of Sally and not one of you?"

She released his forearm and returned to chopping vegetables. "Because Sally gives him money from her allowance now and then. He phones her when he knows Greg isn't around. She refuses to see him, or go near his apartment, afraid Greg might find out and give her holy hell, so she puts the money in the mail and he gets it a few days later. She told me about it, swore me to secrecy. I never told you because I just didn't think it was important enough."

"It isn't. It just verifies what I already knew: that his finances are extremely tight."

"Of course they are, but he made it that way, didn't he? Why should he keep bumming off Sally instead of working more hours, which he probably can." She shook her head. "I don't want to talk about that any more—it just makes me angry." She clutched his forearm again, oblivious of her damp hand, and he could see the concern, almost desperation, in her eyes. "Darling, you're not going to listen to his foolish suggestion about going on and on with this thing until you find what you want, are you? Can't you see what he's trying to do? He hates me because I ignore him, and he knows I disapprove of what you're doing, but he suggests that you go on doing exactly that just to punish me." Her fingernails dug into his forearm and her voice rose. "Can't you *see* what he's trying to do? He's trying to drive us apart, ruin our marriage. Darling, promise me. Promise me that you won't listen to him. Promise me that we'll get back to normal once this mid-life crisis thing is over. Please just promise me that."

"I can't do that. I've already told you that but I suppose you didn't believe me. All Charles' suggestion did was verify my own belief. Nothing has changed."

"But can't you see that our marriage is already suffering. You're ignoring me." She pointed to a window with her free hand. "You spend more time out there hanging around in bars and talking to...to sluts and lesbians than you do talking to me." She flung his arm away from her. "When this all started, I promised that I'd be compassionate and see you through your mid-life crisis, but I *didn't* promise to put up with your endless searching and philandering for the *rest of my life*. Do you *understand*?"

For the first time in ten years her words betrayed a desperate emotion he had never witnessed before. Jealousy. In the past, because he had almost entirely relinquished any personal social life, usually attending social functions accompanied by a watchful Claudia, she'd had no reason to complain, but now he had actually struck out on his own in search of a new life, and she couldn't bear it. Couldn't bear the thought that this new life, should he discover it, would be totally alien to her own beliefs and pull them apart, eventually leading to the disintegration of their marriage.

He said, "I understand that you're upset, and I can understand why. But I need to do this." Aware of her piercing stare, he tried to pacify her without relinquishing his goal. "When all is said and done, it may mean that what I'm searching for just isn't out there. That I'm just whistling in the dark."

"You don't believe that for one moment, do you?" she spat.

"No, I don't, but I can't be certain, can I?"

Amazed, he watched her scowl slowly fade and become a loving smile. She came to him, clasped her arms around him, nestled her cheek to his chest and pressed her body tightly against him. "Darling, I just want you to love me, nothing more," she pleaded. "I want you to think of me every minute and every hour of every day. I want you to forget about everyone else but me. I want you to be obsessed with me. I want you to be mine alone, to live for me alone and no one else. I want you to kiss me and touch me and feel me all over." She raised her head and stared boldly into his eyes. "Do it, darling. Do it *now*."

Still surprised by her rapid transformation from anger to desire, his arms still hung at his sides. He'd witnessed similar scenes many times over the past ten years, but never in the context of such a complete reversal of emotions, and saw her action for what it actually meant: nothing more than another expression of her all-pervading, all-consuming love, a love she now used and would continue to use as a weapon in conjunction with her beauty and her luscious body to obliterate his plans for a different life. She knew his weaknesses and intended to exploit them to preserve the life and the love that she craved. Now, feeling her warm breasts and her warm pelvis pressed against him, breathing in the sweet fragrance of her glistening hair and staring into the bold gray eyes of her lovely face, he felt an involuntary surge of desire rising within him.

She smiled. "We can always eat later, darling."

"Yes, we can," he agreed, certain that he saw a trace of smugness in her burgeoning smile.

11

When Rodger put down the living room phone as they sat at opposite ends of the sofa on the following Saturday evening, Claudia continued to watch her movie on the W channel until a commercial appeared, then removed her headphones and asked, "Who was that?"

Rodger, who had returned to watching his Jays game on the smaller TV, removed his headphones. "It was my father. He's invited us over tomorrow afternoon. Wants us to stay for dinner and maybe a game of Scrabble."

"And you said yes?"

"Yes, I did."

"Without even consulting me?" she accused.

He knew the reason for her tone of voice. The previous evening he'd returned for a second visit to The Kosy Korner in Brampton with his only purpose being to discover whether Vicky had actually listened to his suggestions. He disliked lying to Claudia, and knew the pointlessness of it because a phone call would tell her if he had left the office. Of course, he could always create some innocent story about where he'd been, but this also would be simply another lie. In the end, casting his statement into the flame of her all-consuming love and expecting mercy, he had told her exactly what he intended to do. But Claudia had been merciless, forbidding him to go, and an argument had ensued. Although only a few weeks had gone by, and in spite of initially stating that she would give him some time to pass through his mid-life crisis, she could no longer tolerate his waywardness.

But Rodger knew that he had to go. Until recently, in all the ten years of their marriage, locked in the loving arms of a hedonistic, purposeless, humdrum life, he couldn't recall having even once come to the aid of someone in distress, to actually help another person to become a better person. Claudia had seen to that, and he had succumbed. But seeing Vicky on Friday evening, dressed in beige slacks and a frilly white blouse buttoned almost to her throat, smiling and talking to a clean-cut young man, made Claudia's inevitable nagging when he returned home trivial by comparison. Mary, already well into her alcohol, had only one angry comment as she pointed toward the happy couple: "The little bitch has gone straight as a poker." And apparently she had, for after Rodger had joined them for a drink, met Jerry, and spent a half hour with them, he came away with the immensely satisfying feeling that he had actually done some good, actually helped a fellow human being. And nothing Claudia could do or say would ever change that.

"Are you listening to me, Rodger? Why didn't you even *consult* me?"

He realized by her wounded tone that she now intended to extract her pound of flesh. "You were busy watching your movie, and I didn't want to bother you. Besides, you've never objected in the past. We've been to see my parents many times and you've always enjoyed yourself. You like my parents, especially my mother. And since we haven't seen them for over a month, I thought you'd be happy to go."

"You could have at least *consulted* me," she insisted. "You always have in the past. How do you know I haven't made other plans?"

"What plans?"

She raised her chin proudly. "I'm not totally dependent on you, you know. I do have a career, and that career usually means that I work on Sundays. I don't think I'll be able to go."

"Oh? Why not?

"Because I have an open house scheduled."

"But you have open houses scheduled for every Sunday, and you're usually finished by four o'clock. That gives you plenty of time to come home and change before going to visit my parents."

"I don't think I'll be able to go."

"Why not? You've gone in the past after doing an open house and had no problem, so why not this time?"

"This Sunday...well, my open house is scheduled until five o'clock. I might see more people that way."

He also had an answer for this. "But you've told me many times that it just didn't pay to stay after four o'clock because people were returning home for dinner. Why the sudden change?"

"I'm not exactly *certain* that staying after four won't pay because I've never tried it. I've only been listening to what others have told me. I'd like to try it and find out for certain."

"And it just happens that you want to try it on the very Sunday that I want us to visit my parents."

"Your parents have absolutely *nothing* to do with it," she snapped, her voice rising. "I've already *told* you that I've scheduled until five o'clock."

But he detected the falseness in her objection and saw it as nothing more than the logical culmination of recent events. She wanted to punish him somehow, not only for listening to Charles, not only for seeing Vicky again, but also—and he'd almost forgotten this—for insulting Greg, and now, when he finally asked her for something, she found the perfect opportunity to reject him. He hated this damn niggling, this damn sparring, and even though his mid-life crisis was only a few weeks old, he already found himself longing for a return to the peace his passive acceptance of Claudia's requests had given him during the first ten years of their marriage. Yet he knew that worthwhile changes required worthwhile effort, and that the niggling and sparring would continue and probably even intensify as he continued resolutely on his journey.

"Fine," he said. "If you're determined to stay until five o'clock, I'll simply phone my parents and ask them to reschedule dinner for six. I'm sure they'll agree."

"I still don't think I'll be able to go."

Rodger found himself growing weary of this cat-and-mouse game. Obviously, Claudia still hadn't received her full pound of flesh. "Look, just what is it you want? Just what are you looking for here?"

"That can be summed up in just one word. Faithfulness."

"Faithfulness? I've never been unfaithful to you."

"You've been associating with other women. And that could be the beginning of something far worse. I don't want it to go any further."

"But I've only been interviewing them for the book I'm working on. I haven't been unfaithful, and don't intend to be. For God's sake, Claudia, are you telling me that you're actually afraid that I might try to go to bed with a *lesbian*, or a silly, naive teenager? Do you honestly believe that I'm *that* foolish?"

"No, I don't. But men have a habit of...of losing control, especially after they've had a few drinks, and I don't want that to happen to you."

"But why would it? I'm perfectly happy with you as a sexual partner, so why would I want anyone else?"

"Nevertheless, I don't want you exposed to the temptation because something just *could* happen. That's why I want you to promise me that you won't ever go to that bar in Brampton again."

"Certainly. I have all the information I need and have no reason to go back there anyway. Now, are you finished?"

"Almost. One more thing."

"Yes?"

"Charles is only interested in breaking up our marriage because he hates me. I want you to promise that you'll never go to his apartment again. Ever."

He shrugged. "Fine. Since I've already got all the information I need from him for the book, and transcribed it into my laptop, there's no reason for me to go back anyway. Just one question though."

"And that is?"

"Tell me," he said, grinning, "am I still allowed to say hello to him and discuss the weather if I see him at Wal-Mart, or should I just sneak away like a thief in the night and hope that he doesn't see me?"

"You may still speak to him, if you wish," she replied coldly.

"Fine. Then let's make this official, shall we? He raised his right hand for a mock oath. "I hereby swear that I will never again go to that bar in Brampton or go to Charles' apartment, so help me God. Satisfied?"

"Yes. For now."

But warning bells rang inside Rodger's head. That "For now" left a bad taste in his mouth, making him wonder if his acquiescence hadn't set him on a slippery slope to even further restrictions. Two promises now. How many more would Claudia attempt to extract from him in order recapture the placid, agreeable husband she had fashioned during the first ten years of their marriage?

He said, "Then we'll be going to see my parents. Correct?"

"Yes."

"Can you leave your open house at four instead of five then? Then we could spend more time with them. They do go to bed early."

"No, I can't do that. I've already changed my sign."

But he noticed that she looked away from him as she spoke, her deception as transparent as a freshly cleaned pane of glass, and knew that she had lied, and wondered how often she had lied to him over the past ten years while he placidly and disinterestedly accepted without question almost everything she said.

"Signs can be easily changed."

"No, I don't want to do that. I'll stay until five o'clock."

"You'd probably prefer to stay until eight o'clock, wouldn't you?" he accused. "Then we could just have a quick cup of coffee with my parents and leave. Isn't that what you *really* want?"

Looking away again, she said, "I don't know what you're talking about."

"What I'm talking about is that you really don't want to go at all, and the only reason you're going is because I made two promises. And the reason you don't want me to go is because they, like Charles, might say something to me that'll turn me away from you. Isn't that the truth?"

"That's utter nonsense and you know it. What could they possibly say to you?"

"Well, for one thing, they're religious."

"And? Why would I care about that?" She laughed contemptuously. "When was the last time *you* went to church?"

"And I have no intention of starting to go again. But that's what you're afraid of, isn't it? You're afraid that, because I've told them that I'm searching for a new life, that they *will* convince me to return to church. Well, you can rest easy on that score because that just isn't going to happen. But something else might."

"Something else? Like what?" she asked suspiciously, staring at him.

"I don't know exactly. All I know is that I'll be talking to both of them and looking for suggestions."

"But what kind of suggestions can they possibly offer, other than religious ones? You're forty, and they're in their seventies. You don't even belong to their generation. What can you possibly gain from listening to two people who are thirty years older than you?"

Rodger pursed his lips and shook his head sadly, but moments later found himself wondering whether Claudia's thinking could be so unilateral as to prompt her to ask such a foolish question. He doubted it. He'd always thought of her as a reasonably intelligent person, and therefore her remark probably had been uttered to convince him to refrain from even asking his parents for suggestions.

"Thirty years," he replied.

When they arrived at the tiny bungalow on Edelwild Drive, Rodger pressed a button and chimes sounded inside.

"Who is it?" came Martha's musical voice from an intercom box fastened to the brick wall to the right of the door.

Rodger pressed the intercom button. "Claudia and Rodger."

"Come right in."

The door latch clicked and they pushed inside. Concerned that Martha might fall while trying to hurry to answer the door, Matt, Rodger's father, had had the intercom system installed when they had downsized from their original larger home and moved into the tiny bungalow several years earlier. Also to avoid injury, even though his retirement kept him mainly at home, Matt had equipped her with a small cordless phone with Caller ID which she always carried with her in her ever-present apron as she moved from room to room.

They found Martha, wearing yellow capris and a pink T-shirt, seated at the eat-in kitchen table, her white-socked feet encased in brown Finn Comfort shoes with a brace extending almost to her knee from the left one, her quad cane standing at her side, her limp left forearm cradled in her lap, her cordless phone and a partly finished scenic jigsaw puzzle before her, a puzzle Rodger knew would contain only sixty to a hundred pieces. Many years earlier, Matt had realized that her premature stroke at age thirty-two had diminished her mental capacity to such a degree that she could only complete the simpler, larger-pieced puzzles. Prior to that, she had readily completed puzzles of five hundred or even a thousand pieces. But since then, whenever anyone tried to urge her to concentrate on an even slightly complex subject, she usually countered with, "It gives me a headache."

They exchanged greetings, Rodger and Claudia each bending to give Martha a shoulder hug and a cheek kiss.

"Is something wrong?" Rodger asked pointedly, gazing at the table which held nothing pertaining to food other than condiments and napkins. "I thought we were having dinner?"

"I'm sorry—it's my back. I must have twisted it last night. Trying to get out of bed to go to the bathroom. I can barely walk. We didn't...we couldn't...even go to Mass this morning. We watched it on TV."

"Are you all right, mom?" Rodger asked, concerned, knowing that, unlike Charles, any pains Martha mentioned were legitimate. "Do you think you need to see a doctor?"

"I don't know yet. I'll see how I feel in a few days. Don't worry, I'll probably be fine." She laughed. "I just had a stroke, that's all."

Rodger and Claudia both laughed, but gently, not at Martha but with her.

Claudia smiled and said, "We could always order some dinner in, if you can't—"

"Oh, that's all taken care of, dear. Matt ordered Chinese food. A dinner for four. From Dragon Paradise. It's in the fridge now...just waiting for us."

"Fine," Rodger said. "And where's dad?"

"In the back garden. Weeding."

"I'll see how he's doing." He turned to Claudia. "Coming, dear?"

"No." Claudia put her hands on Martha's shoulders. "Don't get up, Martha. I'll stay here with you and help you to get dinner ready. First, we'll put away your jigsaw puzzle and then—"

"It's so easy," Martha cut in. "You see, it's on a plastic sheet and you just roll it up. It's called a...a...well, whatever it's called, it's easy anyway."

"And then I'll prepare the table and get dinner ready for you." She turned to Rodger. "You go ahead. I'll talk to Matt later."

Rodger found Matt, wearing knee pads and on his knees at the small flower garden, slicing off weeds below ground with a weeder and pulling them out with gloved hands. Years ago, Rodger recalled, there had also been a vegetable garden with neat rows of cucumbers, radishes, tomatoes, carrots, and even potatoes, each row carefully identified with the appropriate sign, all products of Matt's meticulous mind, but as the years went by and Matt grew older, its size gradually diminished until it disappeared altogether and became a neatly manicured lawn. Now, only the small flower garden with its petunias, violets, and pansies remained for Martha to enjoy as she sat on the deck.

But that meticulous mind, except for the odd, brief memory lapse, remained. That meticulous mind, wherein he stored, as in a stringently arranged filing cabinet, the regimented instructions which still guided his life. He represented the best poster boy imaginable for that old but still wise instruction which said, "A place for everything and everything in its place." Even now, he rarely mislaid anything and kept a computerized list containing the whereabouts of items which fell into no particular category. His meticulous mind embraced the use of signs. The hundreds of books in his den library were arranged by subject, each subject having its own printed sign, the titles arranged in alphabetical order by author. A voracious reader of multifarious tastes, he started each day with a few chapters from the Bible, then moved on to other books, mainly nonfiction, although he thoroughly enjoyed the books of the late Saul Bellow, whom he believed to be the finest American novelist he'd ever read. Many years earlier, he'd developed the stringent habit of writing essays for one hour each morning, originally using an old Underwood typewriter but now working with a Hewlett Packard computer into which he'd scanned all his hard copies. Rodger had asked him many times to allow him to read some of his work but Matt had relented only once, allowing him to read an essay on human responsibility for our actions titled *The Responsible Self.* Impressed, and knowing that Matt had written many essays over the years, Rodger had tried to encourage him to collect his favourites into book form and seek a publisher. Instead, fully aware of the very limited audience books of essays had, Matt eventually self-published two volumes and made appearances at local churches where he spoke about the books, read from them, and offered signed copies for sale. He also placed copies in two Orangeville bookstores, including the store Rodger had worked in, where, given their subject matter, the books moved very slowly. Still, if his books were helping even a few people to deal better with their lives, this satisfied Matt.

Especially as reminders for forgetful Martha, red-lettered signs in entwined red rose borders were dotted around the house: "PLEASE REMEMBER TO ADJUST YOUR CLOTHING" on the bathroom medicine cabinet mirror and the full-length bedroom mirror because she often failed to reach around her back far enough with her right hand to completely pull up the left side of her clothing. When he asked her to pull up the lower left side of a garment, she tried by reaching around her back, and if she failed she simply said, "My arm isn't long enough," and Matt, whose meticulous mind disliked seeing things out of place, helped her. On the kitchen cupboard door just above the countertop dishwasher, another sign read "PLEASE DON'T USE THIS AS A SHELF"— because anything there interfered with the door opening—with two large arrows pointing downward to the dishwasher top. Other signs were "PLEASE WASH SINK AFTER DOING DISHES" on the window above the kitchen sink; "PLEASE TURN OFF STOVE WHEN FINISHED" on the wall above the stove. To keep related food and drink items together, signs were also posted just above shelves on the refrigerator wall: BEVERAGES ONLY, LEFTOVERS ONLY, and FRUITS AND VEGETABLES ONLY.

But signs were effective only when their messages were heeded, and Martha often either forgot or simply ignored them. When the refrigerator's neglected leftovers shelf became too crowded, leftovers invariably overflowed down onto the fruits and vegetables shelf, and vice versa. Matt checked the shelves periodically, rearranged them, and invariably subjected soured leftovers and wilting or rotting vegetables to the garbage bag.

While Rodger still lived at home, he sometimes witnessed Matt's breakfast ritual regarding the taking of his medication. Unlike Martha, whose broad gullet handled five pills at once, Matt lined his pills up on the table like soldiers, from largest to smallest. First came General Daily Vitamin, then Captain Gingko Biloba to maintain blood flow to his brain, then Sergeant Vitamin C, then Corporal Vitamin E, then Private Rabeprazole to reduce his stomach acid, and finally Private Proscar to reduce the size of his prostate. One by one, he marched them into his mouth and washed them one at a time down his orange juice gullet slide into his stomach. To your positions, men!

Yes, Rodger thought, that meticulous mind again. That meticulous mind which led him logically to the mathematical exactness of accountancy and from there to make Blackwell Accountants Inc., which he began in Toronto and subsequently shifted to Orangeville, into a highly successful, highly profitable firm which he had hoped Rodger would one day run but, when that failed, eventually sold for a substantial amount upon his retirement. That meticulous mind which even now, at seventy-four, still rarely failed to operate as a well-oiled machine, remembering much, forgetting little. The rigidity remained. Although retired, he still rose each morning at six-thirty and began his daily regimen of low fat meals and a workout on his exercycle. His standard breakfast for many years had been a glass of frozen orange juice and a bowl of whole grain cereal topped with sultana raisins, walnut crumbs, two pinches of wheat germ, a layer of All-Bran, and a teaspoon of dark brown sugar. As a beverage, he disliked milk and poured only enough into the bowl to moisten the cereal. As always, the boxes of his favourite cereals were lined up in alphabetical order on a cupboard shelf—Bran Flakes, Cheerios, Muffets, Quaker Oats, Shredded Wheat, Weetabix—and he consumed them daily in that order, invariably placing the next morning's box of cereal on the kitchen counter before retiring. Rodger had once asked him if he ever varied the cereal order and Matt had simply smiled and said, "Oh, I couldn't do that. That would put me off my schedule." After breakfast, Matt's regimented eating schedule continued: tea at 10 a.m. with either a tea biscuit or a roll; lunch at 1 p.m., a time he'd adopted many years earlier; tea and a piece of fruit at 3 p.m.; dinner at 6 p.m.

In clothing, he believed in a simple, inexpensive wardrobe and enjoyed calling himself "the polyester kid." If he liked a certain pair and colour of socks, he bought three pairs, his favourite colours being navy blue, black, gray, and dark brown; if he liked a certain cotton-polyester shirt, he bought three and changed them daily.

With humour, Rodger sometimes recalled how Matt's attention to detail extended even to the bathroom when he had advised five-year-old Rodger on the proper, efficient use of toilet paper after a bowel movement. Like a teacher instructing a student, he informed Rodger that there were two kinds of toilet paper users: the bunchers and the padders. The bunchers, who simply unrolled a long length of toilet paper and crumpled it before using, he considered wasteful since only a small portion of the toilet paper was ever wiped on. But the padders had it right. They tore off a three-piece section of two-ply paper and folded it twice into a six-ply pad. After using this, they tore off a two-piece section and folded it into a four-ply pad and used this as a final finishing touch. Rodger had apparently found some sense in Matt's advice be-cause he still used the padder's method even today.

Healthwise, Rodger admired Matt's condition. With his stomach acid and prostate under control, Alzheimer's disease represented his main fear, which was why he took Gingko Biloba twice daily (which he also made certain Martha took) to increase the blood flow to his brain to promote better memory and clearer thinking. Yet he also knew that his brain resembled a muscle which continued to function best when regularly exercised. To this end, as had been his practice throughout his adult life, he performed daily mental drills by completing word puzzles, especially crosswords and anacrostics, and doing at least two hours of reading, at least one hour of which would be devoted to mentally stimulating prose.

As a retired accountant, he still dabbled at the profession by doing his own, now greatly simplified, bookkeeping and accounting and preparing his and Martha's annual joint income tax return, the burning desire to account legally for every last cent still strong within him.

In the realm of fathers, Rodger knew that Matt had been a mild, capable, intelligent, and just one, and remembered his childhood as being relatively happy, possibly because he had no brothers or sisters to contend with and received the full attention of his parents. He'd been taught right from wrong, that to live a fulfilled life you had to expand yourself, reach out beyond the inhibiting boundaries of your own egotism and become that person which you were meant to become. Only, Rodger thought sadly, he hadn't become that person. Instead, he left his father's influence behind when he left home, like a valuable book forgotten on a dusty shelf, and instilled himself into the mass-market world outside. A mass-market world supervised by Claudia.

Now, leaning his elbows on the deck railing and feeling a distinct twinge of guilt—even though he hated gardening of any kind—for allowing the vegetable garden to disappear because he had not offered to help when his father's age had prevented him from continuing, he called, "Need any help?"

Matt looked up. "Sorry, I didn't hear you come out. No, that's it for today. My hiatus hernia has started acting up." After packing the cut weeds into a green garbage bag, he tried to get up.

When Rodger saw him struggling, he came down the steps and gave him a hand.

White-haired, brown-eyed, almost six feet tall and still lean at one-seventy, Matt rose and they shook hands warmly. "I've been on my knees too long," he explained. "The old knees aren't what they used to be, or the back."

Looking into Matt's tanned face, Rodger felt again, as he always did, that he was looking into the face of an older version of himself, but took the family resemblance as a compliment for he had always admired and respected Matt. Still, as in his own face, he could see little in Matt's face, except the aging boyishness, which would have people say that he resembled Robert Redford.

Squinting, Matt gazed up at the clear blue sky. "Another dry, sunny day. No rain again, for a change. I heard on the news the other day that this is the wettest summer we've had in Orangeville in about twenty-five years. The flowers hate it, but weeds seem to flourish in any kind of weather. Let's sit down and take a breather. Is Claudia inside?"

"Yes. She's getting the dinner ready for mom. Is mom okay? She said she hurt her back and can barely walk."

"She'll probably be fine in a few days," Matt care-fully placed the gardening tools into a red plastic pail labelled GARDENING TOOLS and heaved a heavy sigh of relief as they seated themselves. "This has happened before. She strained her back trying to get out of bed in the middle of the night. I was asleep when she called for help."

"She doesn't seem to be losing any more weight. That would help."

"She's lost over twenty pounds in the last two years, but now she's stuck around the one-eighty mark. I do all the shopping and make sure that I don't buy her any junk food, but it's hard for her to lose weight when you consider how she lives. Be-cause of her condition, she lives a sedentary life, spending most of her time watching movies on television, especially the older ones, which she loves. Otherwise, she might do the odd jigsaw puzzle or work on a colouring book or do a paint-by-number painting. And that's about it. She can't do handcrafts because they require two hands and her left arm is practically useless. I bought a few wraparound weights a while back and have her exercise her legs and good arm to try to keep her in shape and keep the weight down. Even so, her balance isn't what it used to be."

"I haven't seen you two for a while. How's she doing otherwise? Can she still handle some of the housework?"

"Well, I'm around most of the time to help, but she does her best. She still washes and dries the laundry and I help her put away; she still cooks the meals and does the dishes and does a bit of baking now and then. When I bring home the groceries, she helps to put things away. But she's afraid of falling and won't touch the vacuum cleaner any more, so I do that. And she can't go into the yard any more on her own—her balance just isn't good enough." Matt paused, as though hesitant about what he intended to say next, then continued. "I know Martha wouldn't approve of me telling you this, but she'd never tell you herself because it's, well, a personal thing, but you're our son and I believe you deserve to know about her health. Just don't let on that you know or she'll know I told you."

"What is it? Is it serious?"

"We don't know yet. She's incontinent at times, not during the day or in public, just overnight. She can go normally during the day, about every four hours, but overnight she's up every two hours and sometimes can't even go. She takes these Detrol pills twice a day, which are supposed to control incontinence, but sometimes she wets herself overnight. Maybe it's just because it takes her so long to reach the bathroom, even though it's right beside our bedroom. She's slow to get up out of bed, and for a while it was pretty bad. She'd try to get up by using the little wooden handrail at the side of her bed, but sometimes it took her fifteen or even twenty tries to make it to her feet, and she was too late. And she'd never wake me for help. Then I decided that she needed an easier and quicker way to get up out of bed. To do this, I bolted a metal grab handle vertically to a drawer of her dresser which faces the right side of her bed and put a wing nut at each end of the drawer to hold it closed. Then I fastened the back of the dresser near the top about six inches from the wall with hooks and rope. I didn't want to take a chance that the dresser might topple over on her when she pulled on the grab handle. Anyway, this has certainly helped—she's usually up in just a few tries. But the other problem is that she walks very slowly because of her condition, taking tiny steps, so I get up and help her now. And that has helped a great deal because she gets to the bathroom faster.

"She's had bloodwork done, and a urinalysis, and last week I took her to Headwaters for a pelvic ultrasound. In about two weeks she's going back to Headwaters for a cystoscopy. Then the urologist, Dr. Singh, will assess the results and decided what needs to be done."

"Well, I'm sure she'll be okay, and I certainly hope her back feels better in a few days. By the way, have you been watching the Jays games?"

"Yes, I have, but there isn't much to watch, is there. Even with Leonard, there still only a five hundred team. Besides, I'm sick of the hypocrisy."

"Exactly what hypocrisy do you mean? There's so much of it around these days. Are you talking just about baseball, or sports in general?"

"Sports in general. Don't get me wrong, I still love baseball, basketball, and tennis. To me, there are few things in life more exciting than watching two great teams battling it out, or watching two great tennis players in action. It's the hypocrisy of sport that I deplore. Things like the steroid scandals where players lie through their teeth when they're caught and only own up to the truth when they're cornered and have nowhere else to go. Things like the same mouldy old bullshit players dish out to reporters. When Southam signed a contract with the Jays in 2007, he was given an up-front payment of several million dollars and a contract for several million more. And when he was being interviewed by reporters, the same dumb platitudes came up, and that mouldy old question came up again: 'Hank, why did you decide to play for the Bluejays?' And, of course, instead of telling the truth, instead of stepping around the bullshit, Southam waded right through it when he answered with the inevitable and predictable mouldy old platitude: 'I just wanted to help the team, and felt that I could contribute to its success.' Well, you and I both know that South-am's statement was nothing but a big load of crap.

"Lydia Bingham cramped up at the 2006 Wimbledon, and did a supreme acting job while lying on the court and trying to extend her time there as long as possible so that threatening rain would start and the match would be postponed. Finally, she rose and was taken to her chair for treatment. When her medical break time ran out and she was forced to either play or retire, she did play but played poorly. But then the rain did start and the match was postponed—her stalling had achieved its purpose. When the rain stopped, she returned and won the match. Later, when reporters interviewed her at a press conference, asking the same dumb platitudes they always asked, the inevitable mouldy old question came up again: 'What kept you going after you had the cramp? What gave you the courage to actually come back and win that match?' And, of course, instead of telling the truth, she answered with the inevitable old, predictable platitude: 'I told myself that I couldn't quit, I couldn't stop, I just *had* to try as hard as I could to keep going, etc., etc., etc.'

"Sports interviews are filled with this type of hypocrisy. Reporters ask the same platitudes and know what the answers will be before they are even given because the answers are always the same. They know that the answers will be nothing but bullshit because none of these athletes has the guts to speak the truth because they're afraid of what the public might think of them once they actually know the truth. And that truth could have been spoken in two simple words. The two winners at Wimbledon, male and female, would receive about 1.4 million dollars each, and the Bluejays paid Hank Southam several million dollars as a signing bonus. When a reporter asked Lydia Bingham what kept her going after the cramp, and another asked Hank Southam why he decided to play for the Bluejays, the truth could have been spoken in two simple words. It would be extremely heartening, when a reporter asks his dumb platitude, to hear an athlete answer truthfully and courageously with those two simple words: 'The Money.' Because that's what it's all about today. There's no team loyalty or truthfulness any more; it's all about the big bucks."

"True. But what about—?"

Rodger stopped as Claudia appeared and summoned them to dinner, greeting Matt with a smile and a hug and a cheek kiss before returning to the kitchen.

"We'll talk later," Rodger said. "There are a few things I need to discuss with you."

"Fine."

They went inside, Rodger to the kitchen table, Matt first to the bedroom to change into beige twill slacks, a short-sleeved tan shirt, and brown deck shoes. Claudia had tastefully arranged the Chinese food in bowls and serving plates along the centre of the table, a feast of egg rolls, sweet and sour chicken balls, sweet and sour pork, ja-doo chicken wings, chicken mixed vegetables, beef chow mein, chicken fried rice, and, of course, the inevitable bagged fortune cookies, with a cold glass of Garden Cocktail beside each person's plate.

As they filled their plates, Claudia placed them singly into the microwave oven for two minutes each and returned them hot and steaming to the table before seating herself.

"Thanks loads," Martha said.

Claudia nodded and smiled.

After they had eaten in silence for a few minutes, Matt suddenly asked, "Now, what was it you wanted to talk to me about, Rodger?"

Surprised at first, after a few seconds Rodger realized that Matt had simply exercised his "privilege of age," that habit of the elderly to say whatever they desired whenever and wherever they wanted. Rodger saw life as a circle which began in diapers, progressed to perfectly honest speech which later deteriorated to chicanery and lies when the ugly reality of the real world broke through, became righteous again if a person eventually managed to decry and prevail over the evil surrounding him, returned gradually to perfectly honest speech as age advanced (the "privilege of age"), returned often to a childish state (Alzheimer's disease), and closed the circle by returning to the diaper state (Depend underwear).

"I thought we could talk about it later," Rodger said lamely. "After dinner. In private, while the ladies are cleaning up the kitchen."

Matt said, "Later, nothing. You said you had a few things you wanted to discuss with me, so why not right now?" He stared boldly at Claudia. "You haven't had anything to discuss with me for about ten years, so let's get it out into the open. Is there some reason why the ladies can't hear what you're going to say?"

Rodger gazed across at Claudia and met her stony stare. "Well, no...it's just that—"

"Do we really need to bother with this at all," Claudia interrupted. "Right now Rodger's going through his mid-life crisis and he's going around asking all kinds of people, even women, what they think life is all about. Because he thinks there's something wrong with his own life. With our marriage. But I'm sure he'll be over it soon and we can get back to living sensibly again."

Rodger had a sudden vision of the man who, while courting his girlfriend and eventual fiancee, found that she laughed at everything he thought funny, cheerfully agreed with everything he said or suggested, but once married, once entrapped, found that the laughter and agreement had suddenly vanished. Was he that man? For ten years, had he been nothing more than Claudia's willing and passive dupe instead of asserting himself? And now, as he fought to free himself from the rubble of his manhood, he knew that Claudia would be fighting equally hard to maintain her position by heaping more rubble upon him.

"A mid-life crisis?" Martha said, turning to Rodger and adding accusingly, "Why didn't you tell us? We haven't seen you, heard from you for several weeks."

"I'm sorry. I've been busy. I'm—"

"You're always busy. Too busy to even bother talking to your own mother."

"I'm writing a book."

"A book? What kind of a book? Are you still writing that book you started many years ago?"

"No, I gave up on that. It just wasn't worth continuing with."

"Why not?"

"It wasn't important enough. I thought it would be just a waste of time."

"You see, Martha, " Claudia said, "Rodger wants to write a book about how other people conduct their lives to see if he can find some inspiration in their lives which he can use to improve his own life." She stared pointedly at Rodger. "Apparently he's not happy with the life he has now. I'll be glad when he gets over this mid-life crisis so we can return to a normal, sane life."

"Funny," Martha said. "I don't recall that Matthew ever even *had* a mid-life crisis." She gazed fondly at her husband. "Did you, dear? You never ever mentioned anything to me."

Rodger saw the conversation becoming interesting. He reached into his slacks pocket, removed his digital recorder, switched it on and placed it near the centre of the table. "I'd like to start recording this. There might be something I can use in my book."

During the conversation, like a surgeon deftly performing a delicate operation, Matt had been carefully quartering a chicken ball and eating it piece by piece. Swallowing the last piece, he said, "It seems to me that mid-life crises belong to people who feel that there already are crises in their lives. I personally never felt that. And if you feel that you've been reasonably successful in leading a decent and productive life, and believe that you're still doing so, there isn't any reason to have a mid-life crisis, is there? You simply continue doing what you've been doing all along."

"Tell that to Rodger," Claudia said sharply. "Because all his mid-life crisis has done is told him to question and even reject the good things he already has."

"But my dear," Matt replied. "Don't you see that the reason Rodger feels that way is because he feels that there actually *is* something wrong with his life and he wants to change it?"

"Nonsense," Claudia spat, angrily jabbing her fork repeatedly into her beef chow mein. "Rodger has a wonderful life—he just doesn't know how to appreciate it, that's all. Can't we get off this silly subject and move on to something more pleasant?"

Ignoring her, Matt turned to Rodger. "Is this what you said you wanted to talk to me about? How to conduct your life?"

"Yes. Definitely."

Matt turned back to Claudia. "Then I'm afraid I can't get off what you call 'this silly subject.' For about ten years, my son hasn't asked me for any advice, and now, finally, he's here doing exactly that, and I don't intend to ignore him." He paused, thinking, then said, "Tell me, my dear, have you ever read Plato's writings on Socrates?"

"No, but I've heard of him. He lived a long time ago, didn't he?"

"Yes, a few centuries before Christ. He was a Greek philosopher, and like Christ he never wrote a word himself. Where Christ had his Matthew, Mark, Luke, and John, Socrates had his Plato to write down his words. And Socrates said something which is just as true today as it was in his time. He said, 'An unexamined life is not worth living.' I've examined my own life many times over the years, and have even occasionally made changes, sort of bringing myself up to date, but these changes were usually small, which is why, I suppose, that nothing significant actually happened when I reached the mid-life crisis age. It was merely like a blip on a computer screen when the lights go off for half a second. And now Rodger's time has come. And to him it's apparently far more than a mere blip on a computer screen. And I'm not so sure that it's simply a mid-life crisis either, and that this whole desire to discover a new life will disappear a few months or a year from now. I believe that after ten years of living mainly for himself, Rodger has finally honestly realized that there is a better, more productive life."

"And how do you propose that he do that?" Claudia said. "By going to church every Sunday?"

Rodger detected the obvious sarcasm in her voice but ignored it. Turning to Matt, whose face registered only a benevolent smile, he asked, "What do you think I should do, dad? How do you think I should change my life?"

"In order for me to recommend changes, I first need to know what your life is like now. I think I know, and how you feel about it, but I need to hear it from you."

Rodger told him of his feelings of profound waste and emptiness since the morning of his tenth wedding anniversary, of his struggles to find an answer, of his futile interviews with men and women who had even more problems than himself, which produced for him nothing more than lessons on how *not* to live.

With lips pursed, Matt nodded repeatedly as Rodger spoke, as though he had heard the same complaints a hundred times before, then said, "In reality, life is simple, and the rules for a good life can be simply stated, though of course not easily followed. The problem is that we make life complicated by the myriad actions we use to avoid that simplicity." He carried a forkful of chicken fried rice to his mouth, arranging his thoughts while he chewed slowly and methodically and finally swallowed, then rose. "Excuse me. I'll be right back."

He returned a few minutes later carrying several paperback and hardcover books, placed them in a pile beside his plate, and reseated himself. "Because, you see, we have hundreds and hundreds of self-proclaimed gurus out there telling us that life can't possibly be that simple because we *need* what they have to sell in order to make our lives happy and successful. So they write best-selling books, and make videos, and appear on daytime talk shows and PBS plugging their wares, and are probably paid thousands of dollars per night for making public appearances and spouting their gospels." He held up a copy of *The Seven Spiritual Laws of Success.* "Yes, we have our Deepak Chopra telling us all about karma and the benefits of reincarnation." He held up a copy of *Healing the Shame That Binds You.* "We have our John Bradshaw taking a page from Freud and telling us that we all need to reach back into our lives, even into our childhoods to discover and deal with the shame which is responsible for our unhappiness." He patted the remaining books in the pile. "We have our Wayne Dyer with his own twist on how to live better spiritual lives; we have our Robert Fulghum with his homespun philosophy, telling us that all we really need to know we learned in kindergarten; we have our John Gray warning us that we must first realize that men are from Mars and women are from Venus; we have the late Leo Buscaglia telling us that love is the answer." He held up a paperback copy of Buscaglia's *Living, Loving & Learning* and read from the back cover. "Buscaglia tells us that 'the loving person must return to spontaneity—return to touching each other, to holding each other, to caring about each other....Hugs are good, they feel nice, and if you don't believe it, try it.' And the book market is flooded with *Chicken Soup for the Soul* books, all expounding the same sad, repetitious, teary stories. We have our Richard Carlson telling us not to sweat the small stuff.

"Now don't get me wrong—I believe that there are some good points in all of these books—but it seems to me that it's totally unnecessary to read all the books by these authors because they quickly become repetitious. After all, as publishers and authors know only too well, 'If it isn't broken, why fix it?' If you've had good success with one book, why change the formula? You can't jump to the other side of the fence; you have to continue to expound your philosophy because if you don't the reading public will lose faith in you, stop reading you, and believe that you're mainly in it for the money. Which of course you are. So your future books must expound your philosophy again...and again...and again. You just have to try to keep expanding your readership. So, after publishing *Men Are from Mars, Women Are from Venus,* John Gray churns out stuff like *Mars and Venus Single Again; Mars and Venus in Love; Mars and Venus Together Forever; Mars and Venus in the Bedroom; Mars and Venus on a Date.* All expounding the same basic philosophy.

"Richard Carlson's books deal mainly with happiness and stress reduction. His big bonanza book was, of course, *Don't Sweat the Small Stuff...and It's All Small Stuff.*" Matt held up a recent reprint and referred to a list. "Here are some of his other titles: *Don't Sweat Guide to Entertaining; Don't Sweat the Small Stuff for Teens; Don't Sweat the Small Stuff Treasury, A Special Treasury for Fathers; Don't Sweat the Small Stuff Treasury, A Special Selection for Friends; Don't Sweat the Small Stuff Treasury, A Special Selection for Mothers;* and *The Don't Sweat the Small Stuff Guide to Golf.* All expounding the same philosophy.

"But the books which take home the publishing world's Oscar for a series of books run amok is the *Chicken Soup for the Soul* series. The first book dealt simply with 'the Soul,' but by now there must be about *twenty* books available." Matt referred to a list. "Here are some of the many souls that they're concerned with: Preteen, College, Golden, Teacher's, Sister's, and the Soul of America. Teenagers are particularly well represented: we have the Teenage Soul, the Teenage Soul 2, the Teenage Soul: On Love and Friendship, and the Teenage Soul on Tough Stuff. Women are also well represented: we have the Woman's Soul, the Woman's Soul 2, the Mother's Soul, the Nurse's Soul, and the Mother and Daughter Soul. These books offer a perfect example of how much money can be made by presenting the same simple, teary, emotional stories over and over and over again." He held up a copy of *Chicken Soup for the Teenage Soul on Tough Stuff* with the back cover facing them. "But the vital difference here is this: on the back cover of each book it states that a portion of the proceeds from the sale of every title in the series is donated to charity. No percentage is mentioned, which made me suspicious, but when I went to their website for confirmation I was in for a pleasant surprise. Since the first Chicken Soup book was published about fifteen years ago, over three-and-a-half million dollars has been donated to a very long list of charities. This is a perfect example of a publishing venture actually making a difference."

"I don't get your point," Claudia said, growing impatient with Matt's teacherlike dissertation. "Where are you going with all this?"

Matt raised a pacifying hand. "Patience, my dear, patience. I'm coming to the point soon, and you'll see that my preamble was necessary." He took a long, slow sip of his Garden Cocktail and continued. "Go online to any major book dealer and key in the words 'self-help' and see what comes up. I went on amazon.ca last week and did that and over 57,000 listing came up; I also went on chapters.ca where over 7,000 listings came up. Go to amazon.com and over 89,000 listings come up. Go to any major bookstore and you'll probably see shelves and shelves crammed with hundreds of self-help titles, most of them claiming that they have the ability to solve life's difficulties. The sheer number of books is in itself daunting. And because the knowledge we ingest from these books is fragmented, each supplying only a part of the solution, the more authors we read in search of a complete solution the more conflicting the books become." He sliced into a fresh chicken ball, carefully quartered it, deep in thought as he slowly ate all four pieces, and finally continued. "The main problem is like having a pair of slacks full of holes and we patch some of them, say, with red patches, which soon run out. We then resort to blue patches, green patches, brown patches, but the slacks keep getting older and more and more new holes keep appearing and we never seem able to patch them all and make the slacks whole again. Just as we never become whole again.

"Fulghum states many of life's solid truths in his simple little essay at the start of *All I Really Need to Know I Learned In Kindergarten.* He was told to share everything, to play fair, to not hit people, to not take things that aren't yours, to say you're sorry when you hurt someone, to stick together when you go out into the world, to be conscious of wonder. Children learn these values very early in life, from teachers and from good parents, but often forget about them as they grow older and become confronted by a selfish, mercenary, and hedonistic world. Fulghum shows that his creed for living can be stated on a single page. It's a good creed, but it isn't complete. My creed for living, written thousands of years ago, can also be written on a single page, and comes from the only book you need to read to learn how to live a good, productive life: The *Bible.*"

No one at the table could fail to hear Claudia's heavy sigh, and Rodger knew that she had to be thinking something like "I knew it would end like this—all about religion."

Undaunted, Matt turned to her, smiling benevolently. "Yes, my dear, The *Bible.* Specifically the four gospels which depict the life of Christ. Learn from his life, a life which followed the ten rules listed in the *Old Testament.* The ten rules of life which can be listed on a single page. Those ten rules?" He pointed to a large, ornate print of "The Ten Commandments" hanging from the kitchen wall.

Irritated, Claudia said, "Are you trying to tell me that I've been sitting here listening to your entire…your entire presentation just to be told that all I need to do is to practise The Ten Commandments?"

Mention of The Ten Commandments, and seeing Claudia waving her right arm for emphasis as she spoke, made Rodger notice the cheap Ten Commandments bracelet on her wrist, the one he'd bought at Dollarama because he couldn't find one anywhere else, with the commandments represented by small metal scrolls. When she finished speaking and lowered the arm to the table, he noticed a wider gap between two of the scrolls, indicating that one of them had either fallen off and possibly been lost, or had been deliberately removed from the flimsy bracelet.

"No," Matt answered calmly. "Actually I wasn't speaking to you at all. I was directing my comments toward Rodger, who specifically asked me for direction in his life. But if you *were* to ask me for direction, I would certainly tell you exactly the same thing."

"I don't need any direction," Claudia said gruffly. "I'm doing quite well as things are, thank you."

"Don't be too sure," Martha said. "You never know what to expect next. I keep saying that."

Claudia continued, still addressing Matt. "And I don't need you trying to tell Rodger how to live his life either." All he needs is to get through this mid-life crisis and everything will be fine again."

"But I *asked* him to," Rodger objected. "And I'm interested in what he has to say." He knew now why Claudia had finally consented to come to visit his parents: to sabotage his efforts to gain information from his father because she feared that Matt's suggestions might turn him against her. Also, he felt that she still harboured resentment toward him and still sought revenge for the way he'd insulted Greg. He knew that she felt threatened, saw the authoritarian rule she had enjoyed over the past ten years beginning to yield, and would gladly throw a monkey wrench into the works to damage the machinery. He had no desire to side with Claudia, but felt that he had to speak the truth, at least a watered-down version of it. He had no intention of admitting to Matt that he had issues with God, issues so serious that they often made him wonder if they could ever be resolved, knowing that any mention of these would be greeted by Matt with shock and dismay. He had no intention of opening up that can of worms—at least not yet. Instead, he turned to Matt and said mildly, "I don't think The Ten Commandments are what I'm looking for. Something else is missing. Besides, I already keep them…well, most of them."

Matt asked, "What about honouring your father and your mother?"

"I think I do that, don't I?"

"Not really," Martha accused. "You haven't even phoned us for over a month. Ignored us. What do you call that?"

"Well, I guess I'll have to work on that, won't I. But I don't steal, I've never killed anybody, I've never committed adultery, I don't spread malicious gossip, I don't covet my neighbours goods or his wife or his attractive daughter because I already have all the material possessions I'll ever need or want, and I have the best sex life with Claudia that any man could ever want." He made this last statement in the hope that Claudia would be pleased enough to retreat from her argumentative position, but when he observed her he saw no change in her grim expression.

Claudia said, "This is nothing more than an exercise in futility because Rodger will soon be through this phase and revert to his normal, sensible life. Why don't we get onto a more pleasant subject?" She turned to Martha. "Have you lost more weight, dear? You look much slimmer than the last time I saw you."

"Yes, a few pounds. It helps with the walking."

But Matt insisted. "Surely you're not trying to say that the way you and Rodger have lived for the past ten years is sensible, and that his desire to now change his life is foolish, are you? Can you give me even one concrete example of anything truly worthwhile that the two of you have done during the past ten years?"

"Like what?" Claudia spat. "Like going to church every Sunday? Like handing your hard-earned money to spurious charities that spend most of it paying their own staff? Like donating tons of food to the food bank so that bums who are too lazy to work can continue to sponge off others? Is that what you call worthwhile? Until now, we've been happy for ten whole years—and that's the main thing. That's the only thing that matters."

"No, my dear, it isn't," Matt replied calmly, shaking his head. "And I doubt that you've ever actually experienced true happiness. Because true happiness has nothing whatever to do with amassing more and more material possessions, amassing more and more money, and enclosing yourself in your own private, selfish little world while neglecting and locking out everything and everyone outside it that doesn't contribute to that world. None of us is put on this earth to isolate himself or herself from humanity. It isn't enough to simply do *something* with your life—you must do something *good*. And to do this we must strive to discover that good which will expand our lives and allow us to live beyond the constrictive frames of ourselves. We're not put here on this earth simply to accumulate money and possessions and wallow in our own personal creature comforts. No, we're put here for a noble purpose, and that purpose means moving beyond our own egos and expanding our horizons and achieving something worthwhile with our lives. We were put on this earth to serve, not to be served. And this can't possibly be done if our lives are eaten up in a constant search for more ways to embellish our own self-aggrandizement. Instead, we need to dis-cover our own personal noble purpose and begin acting on it."

Matt turned to Rodger. "You said earlier that The Ten Commandments are already part of your life, but to what extent? The *Bible* cautions us that you can't serve two masters, money and God. Are you not serving the money god more?"

"Maybe I am," Rodger admitted. "And that's exactly why I'm here talking to you. I'm tired of it all; I feel as though I'm drowning. I want to move my life onto some higher plane but I don't know how."

"But isn't that what The Ten Commandments are all about? As I said earlier, the instructions on the proper way to live a happy and productive life are not complicated, they're simple, and they can be listed on a single sheet of paper. But they are difficult to keep. So many of us seem to have forgotten these instructions, perhaps because they go back thousands of years and we think they're now out-dated. But they're not—they'll never be outdated. They are ten rules for living the way God wants us to live by avoiding those mistakes which can only lead to discontent, misery, and continual unhappiness."

Claudia said, "But today's Catholic church doesn't give you much incentive to do so, does it? Is it any wonder that so many people don't go to church any more when all you hear about on the news are stories of priests and even bishops being charged and convicted as pedophiles, many of the cases going back twenty years or more? Recently I heard that the Catholic church has paid out almost three hundred million dollars in damages to these people." She jabbed a forefinger at the framed "Ten Commandments." "How do you equate such a horrible scandal to that?"

Matt replied calmly. "Your faith is weak, my dear, and it shows. Probably thousands of people, like you, have fallen away from the church because of this scandal. But let me ask you this: If you discovered that the Canadian government was corrupt, which it sometimes is, would you stop voting, or move to another country? Or if you discovered that big business management is sometimes corrupt, as the recent Enron case proved, would you stop buying the products produced by *all* big businesses? Or if you discovered that a prominent charity spends eighty percent of its donations on its own staff and promotions, and only twenty percent on its recipients, would you stop donating to *all* charities?"

"No, of course not. That would be just silly."

"But aren't you doing exactly that when you condemn every Catholic church in the world because a small percentage of these churches contained pedophiles?"

"But it's not the same thing," Claudia insisted. These men are *priests* and *bishops!*"

"Yes, they are, but they're also human beings. And just because they're priests and bishops doesn't rule out that a tiny percentage of them may become pedophiles. No sector of our society, either male or female, can be pure white—it's simply impossible. Most of us, regardless of how hard we try, are varying shades of gray. Personally, I don't believe that the case against pedophiles in the Catholic church is even nearly as wide as the public has been led to believe. When the media pounds away at these stories for weeks and months on end, they achieve a prominence which they may not deserve. I personally don't believe that there are nearly as many legitimate cases, many of them going back twenty years or more as you said, as the media have reported. After all, if you have a legitimate case why wait twenty or twenty-five years to complain? What began as a trickle rapidly became a river of complaints as God knows how many men ran to their lawyers claiming fraudulent sexual attacks by Catholic clergy as they tried to cash in on their so-called pain and shame.

"Priests are intelligent men—they're highly educated. It generally takes five to seven years of intensive study in a seminary after leaving college, or nine years after leaving high school to become a diocesan priest. So I wonder how many men would be willing to go through that rigorous training with the idea that *nine years later* they'd be in a position to molest children. That makes no sense to me what-soever. In the meantime, some rotten apples have been removed, but I'm left to wonder how many innocent priests have been condemned."

"Well, I have to say," Claudia said smugly, "that this is exactly the reaction I expected from you. After all, you are a staunch Catholic, aren't you?"

"Yes, I am, and have been all my life. But I didn't say what I said just because of that. Priests are not God—they are only messengers of God. And just because they sometimes wear white vestments does not necessarily mean that the souls beneath those vestments are lily white, nor do I expect them to be. Most of them are probably lighter shades of gray than we are, but they are still shades of gray. I attend church to practise my faith, to adore God, not because of the priest. And although I find this pedophile scandal disgusting and deplorable, it hasn't dampened my faith." He took a sip of his wine, then continued. "But something has certainly dampened yours, and Rodger's, for ten years, hasn't it? I'd be interested in knowing what."

Claudia said, "For me there's never been anything to dampen because there was never anything there to begin with. I think you know by now that I only married in the Catholic church to please Rodger because I knew that he wouldn't marry anywhere else. Churches, Catholic or otherwise, have never been an important part of my life. I don't feel that I need their preaching to be happy. And now, especially with what's gone on lately, I'm beginning to wonder if *any* of the main teachings of *any* Christian church are even valid any more."

"Are you still talking about the priest scandal?"

"No." Rodger watched as a smug, triumphant smile spread across Claudia's lips and knew that another round was about to begin. "I'm talking about *The Da Vinci Code*."

"Ah. But you are aware that the book is a novel, a work of fiction."

"Yes, I am."

"Are you saying then that you believe some of it to be fact?"

"Yes. It makes me doubt Christ's role."

"Yes, the book was written to do exactly that. Tell me, have you ever wondered at the timely release of the book?"

"Timely release? I don't know what you mean." But Rodger saw that she had looked away from Matt.

"One of the main creeds of clever publishing is to strike while the iron is hot. You might remember that when Princess Diana was killed books about her rapidly flooded the market. Publishers fell over each other in their haste to get a piece of the action. So, too with the publishers of *The Da Vinci Code*. When the book was published in 2003, the Catholic church was already in the throes of trying to defend itself against pedophilia accusations. Eureka! What a perfect time to release a book which could cast doubt on Christ's celibacy in millions of minds and therefore on the entire Christian faith. And that's exactly what happened, isn't it? *The Da Vinci Code* creates confusion in readers' minds, I believe deliberately, especially readers who will grasp at anything to condemn the Christian faith. On the copyright page, the book shows the standard disclaimer which informs the reader that this is a work of fiction. Yet a few pages later we see a 'FACT' page which informs the reader that *some* of the so-called 'facts' mentioned in the book are actually *true*, which probably leads many readers to believe that they actually *are* true. But here again Brown subjects this information to his creative imagination and distorts history when writing about the Holy Grail and the Priory of Sion. The legendary Holy Grail was supposedly Jesus' cup at his last supper, and had nothing whatsoever to do with Mary Magdalene. Brown states that the Priory of Sion, a secret society, was founded in 1099 and included Botticelli, Newton, Victory Hugo, and Leonardo da Vinci as its members. But Leonardo da Vinci, or any of the others, couldn't possibly have known about the Priory of Sion, or belonged to it, because it actually wasn't founded until 1956, 437 years after da Vinci's death. This may be interesting fiction, but fake history."

"But what about the theory that the person sitting to Christ's right in the Last Supper painting isn't John but Mary Magdalene? Doesn't this person look more like a woman than a man?"

"If you mean because he was clean shaven and had a boyish face, yes. But let me ask you this: If there was no so-called secret society called the Priory of Sion in da Vinci's time, where and how did he get the information that Jesus and Mary Magdalene were married, or even not married, and had a child? Are you saying that da Vinci belonged to some *other* secret society?"

"I'm not sure, but maybe he did," Claudia persisted stubbornly. "Yes, maybe that's where he got the information. Secret societies are plentiful, you know."

"Ah, yes, they certainly are. And the reason so many exist is because down through the ages there have always been hateful people who are so miserable that all they want to do is condemn even the worthy, moral beliefs in life. And they do it anonymously, hiding away in their secret holes, hating, gutless, afraid to reveal themselves and stand up for their fraudulent 'truths' because of the avalanche of criticism they know will follow. Is that all you have to fall back on in defence of your lack of religious belief?" Without waiting for Claudia to answer, Matt continued. "You've seen copies of da Vinci's *Last Supper*, haven't you?"

"Of course."

"Good. Now let me ask you this: How many total people are depicted in the painting?"

"That's easy. Thirteen."

"Yes, thirteen. And who were they?"

"Well, Jesus, and his apostles...and...and..." Claudia reached quickly for her wine and took a large gulp, almost draining the glass.

"And Mary Magdalene? But that would make fourteen, wouldn't it?"

Fumbling for an answer, Claudia finally blurted out, "Judas was already gone—there were only eleven apostles."

"No, my dear, there were twelve. Excuse me a moment." Matt rose, went into his den, returned a few minutes later carrying a *Bible* and opened it at the table. "Da Vinci's *Last Supper* depicts the very moment after Jesus has accused one of his disciples of betraying him. The disciples are reacting in horror at the thought that anyone at the table would betray their master.

"Chapter 26 in Matthew reads: 'When it was evening, he sat at table with the twelve disciples; and as they were eating, he said, 'Truly I say to you, one of you will betray me.' And they were very sorrowful, and began to say to him one after another, 'Is it I, Lord?' He answered, 'He who has dipped his hand in the dish with me, will betray me. The Son of man goes as it is written of him, but woe to that man by whom the Son of man is betrayed! It would have been better for that man if he had not been born.' Judas, who betrayed him, said, 'Is it I, Master?' He said to him, 'You have said so.'" Matt closed the *Bible* and put it aside. "So you see, my dear, there was nothing mysterious about da Vinci's painting, nothing secretive, no hidden message. Da Vinci was a great painter merely exercising his art by depicting an important moment in history from the *Bible*. Nothing more, and certainly nothing less."

Rodger gazed at Claudia and received an icy stare in return, but his tiny smile clearly informed her that she'd been foolish to lock religious horns with a man who read voraciously and had studied religion for over sixty years.

Claudia, already feeling the effects of too much wine drunk too quickly, reached for her half-filled glass and drained it in a few gulps before extending it toward Matt. "I want another glass of wine," she demanded.

"Certainly," Matt said, filling her glass.

Out of spite, Claudia immediately took a sip before returning the glass to the table. The wine had loosened her tongue, strengthened her irrational stubbornness, and forced her to persist. "Regardless of what you say, I don't have to believe what you say just because you say it, and I don't have to believe the *Bible* either."

"No, of course you don't, but remember this: Kahlil Gibran, a very wise man, once wrote that 'a tree grown in a cave does not bear fruit.' Is that how you're living your life?"

"Of course not. I've got a very good life which is bearing plenty of fruit. I've got a good home, a late model car, no money worries, and a husband I love and who loves me. And all I want to do is to go on loving him. Does that sound like I'm a tree growing in a cave?"

"You misunderstood. Gibran was writing about *spiritual* fruit."

"I don't need spiritual fruit—I've got my own life."

"Yes, you've just told me so. Tell me, my dear, do you recall why you left the church to pursue your present life?"

"Because I simply found it totally boring. The same priest saying the same boring things and preaching the same boring things week after week, month after month, year after year. I just didn't believe it and couldn't take it any more."

Matt nodded several times. "Ah, yes, the perpetually bored person, the person who has a habit of dozing off during the priest's homily until he or she eventually becomes *so* bored that he or she leaves the church altogether. The list of frivolous reasons people can concoct for leaving the church is truly amazing. Some say they just don't like the priest, or the deacon, or the other parishioners, or even the appearance of the church itself. Oddly enough, they never seem able to locate a church that satisfies them, and eventually even give up the pretense of even trying. Amazing. Others, like the late novelist Brian Moore, who left Ireland because of the religious intolerance there and came to Canada, still never returned to the church and became an agnostic. Even so, he appeared to spend the rest of his life pursued by his faith. In many of his novels, he grappled with its transcendent aspects. Some of Moore's work is so detailed that it can almost be used to explain church dogma.

"The list is almost endless. Many years ago I had a friend in Toronto who'd been raised as a Catholic but never attended church after he became an adult. He did, however, constantly listen to Billy Graham on the radio and never missed Graham's television programs. He admired the man and talked about him constantly. Apparently he had found his own particular brand of faith. But that all ended when he learned one day that Billy Graham owned a large colour television set. His admiration suddenly vanished and he never listened to Billy Graham again. You see, he saw Billy Graham only as an evangelist, a spokesman for God, and he wasn't allowed to own any fancy materialistic possessions like a colour television set, or a nice car, or a nice home. Being a follower of Christ, he should live like a pauper with sandals on his feet and donate practically every cent he earned from his broadcasts to the poor and the downtrodden. Yes, those who begin seriously looking for excuses to desert their faith can easily find them in the unlikeliest places.

"When a Canadian author, who died in April, learned that her twenty-year-old son had been killed in a tragic motorcycle accident, she went into a church one afternoon to try to return to her religion. But she couldn't pray, couldn't talk to God, and God didn't talk to her. The church was empty, and all she heard was silence. She left, and never entered a church again. How frail, how presumptuous is such a faith. Although she hadn't attended church for many years, because she was grieving she was presumptuous enough to believe that perhaps she'd hear angels singing and God would suddenly speak to her when even some of the world's greatest mystics hadn't even earned that privilege.

"A few weeks ago, a black Supreme Court judge admitted that he left the Catholic church in 1968 after Martin Luther King had been shot and he heard a priest say, 'I hope the black S.O.B. dies.' Just *one* priest, not the entire Catholic church, made a hateful racial comment and that immediately turned him away from the Catholic church. I could go on and on with examples, but the main point I'd like to make is this: The people mentioned here all seem to possess the same failing, a frail, lacklustre faith which was determined to use any excuse to get out of the church."

"Do you honestly expect people to continue practising a religion they no longer believe in?" Claudia demanded doggedly.

"I think you need to truthfully assess the reason or reasons why you left the church and then honestly ask yourself whether they are valid. And if the only reason you can think of is that you want to spend the time pampering yourself, or seeing how much more money you can make so that you can eventually buy a million-dollar home, then I believe that you need to think seriously about reconsidering your decision because you're living only for yourself instead of for God."

"I feel exactly like that most of the time," Rodger admitted guiltily, aware that Claudia had flinched at the words 'million-dollar home' and given him an enigmatic glance, a mere flick of her eyes. Why? Did the words remind her unpleasantly of the million-dollar Caledon East real estate sale? But why unpleasantly when the sale had netted her a huge commission? Did her glance indicate some feeling of guilt, or simply her suspicion that he had betrayed her by deliberately leaking the details of the real estate sale to Matt, which she had specifically warned him to keep secret from his parents? Which he had. But did she suspect that he hadn't? Or, even after three years was some other detail of the sale still nibbling at the edges of her mind? Even now, he had to admit that he had never been completely satisfied with her explanation.

Matt said, "Then you need to do something about it, don't you? You said that you obey most of the commandments, but what about the first?"

"The first?" Rodger replied foolishly, aware that his very words admitted his ignorance.

"Yes, the first: 'You shall have no other gods before me.' You need to ask yourself what other gods you have created within your own life which are preventing you from finding your true self in a fellowship with God."

"That's the main reason I came here today—to get your advice. Of course, I also wanted to see you both, but I'm confused and I need your advice. I'm perfectly aware of all the activities you do to fulfill your own life. You're heavily into church work. You read at Mass, you usher, you serve on the parish council, you visit and comfort the sick. You belong to the Knights of Columbus and participate in their projects, and were even a Grand Knight back in the nineties. You support worthy charities and sometimes go out of your way to help people with legitimate problems or needs. Fine. Wonderful. I'm proud of you and even envy you because I know that what you do has brought you peace and contentment and happiness. But that just isn't me. I've thought about all of your many good deeds, and tried to envision them applied to my own life, but it's like trying to squeeze a wooden block into a round hole—it just doesn't fit. And it doesn't fit because it just isn't me."

"Well, the last thing I'd ever want you to do would be to become a carbon copy of me just because I'm your father, or for any other reason. That would be a serious mistake because you must find your own road to salvation. But let me ask you this: Have you ever thought that you might simply be running?"

"Running? From what?"

"From yourself, of course. Tell me, since you started this campaign to find your true self, where have you actually looked?"

Matt's question forced Rodger to mentally review the objects of his search and he suddenly realized how banal and trivial they actually were. Sheepishly, he told Matt about his discussions with Claudia, Ray, Penelope, Katherine at the restaurant, Mary and Vicky at the Kosy Korner, and Charles.

As though he had heard such stories many times before, Matt kept smiling and nodding knowingly until Rodger finished, then said, "Don't you think that your search thus far resembles that of a monkey looking for a banana in a coconut tree?"

"Maybe it does, but it's all material for the book, isn't it? I look upon them not as lessons on how to live, but as lessons on how *not* to live and would describe them as such in the book and point out why they should be avoided. Don't you think that such a book would serve a very worthwhile function?"

"Yes, I do. But right now you don't know why such wasteful lives should be avoided, do you? You say you don't believe that your answer lies in the spiritual life, but what else do you have to fall back on? It's fine to critique other people's lives, but unless you can offer them a more sensible and viable alternative you're simply wasting your time. My opinion is that the only true answer is a spiritual one. You disagree." Matt shook his head several times. "The old cliche says that 'the acorn never falls far from the tree,' but you have, haven't you, Rodger? You're a far different person than the one who left here, newly married, about ten years ago. I noticed the change soon after your marriage." He glanced at Claudia, then shook his head. "No, that's not exactly true—I noticed the beginning of this change soon after your engagement. And I've seen it take a firmer and firmer hold over you as the years went by. But I've never mentioned it, mainly because you've never asked me for advice, and I never offer advice to a man, which I believed you were, unless he asks for it. But also because I believed that you were mature enough to handle the situation. But you weren't, were you? Until now. And apparently the only reason you're looking for direction now is because you're suffering from mid-life crisis. And now that you've come and asked me for advice, I'm giving it to you.

"To achieve its true destiny, the correct path for the male heart is this: First, a boy attaches himself to his mother; second, he breaks free from his mother and finds his father; third, he breaks free from his father and finds himself, and becomes a man; fourth, after finding himself he is now ready to confidently unite in matrimony with a woman. But this didn't happen with you. As so often happens, when you left this house you left only because you were getting married. As a result, you were immediately thrust into a new situation which didn't allow you either the time, or the inclination, to find yourself. Until now. The lesson to be learned is this: In order for the male heart, mind, and soul to mature and achieve its own manhood, it cannot remain permanently lodged in the female heart."

Good God, Rodger thought. Haven't I been thinking exactly that since the morning of our anniversary? That I had consistently lived under Claudia's influence, mainly doing what she expected of me, living the way she wanted me to live while forfeiting my own manhood?

"Besides, Claudia," Matt continued, "you tell me that you've spoken to four other women about this problem of finding yourself. Have you not wondered why you asked a total of five women for help but only two other men besides me? In other words, why would you expect the answer to your male problem to more likely come from a woman rather than a man?"

Now Rodger felt backed into a corner. He hadn't told Matt that the real reason he had spoken to so many women was to determine if he could locate one who, unlike Claudia, believed in a simple, straightforward, unmaterialistic, worthwhile life. He knew Claudia wouldn't like what he had to say, and tried to sanitize his words. "I was simply looking to see if there were any women out there who believed that there were more important things in life than material possessions, and what exactly did they believe in if they did believe that."

But Matt, who rarely held back his opinions, refused to let him off the hook. "And if you had found such a woman? What then?"

"Well, I..." Rodger grappled for words, "...I guess if I admired her I'd try to change my life so that it reflected hers."

Claudia, with eyes now glassy, her excessive drinking having driven out all sense of decorum, blurted out, "And then I suppose you'd desert me and go and live with *her* and make love to *her! In a tent!*"

"No, I just—"

"And then the two of you could get up in the morning and go into the bushes in your bare feet and pick wild raspberries for your breakfast. Isn't that what you want to do? *Isn't it?*"

Martha, who had been busily consuming her food, looked up suddenly and said, "Simply delicious, this Chinese food is. Claudia, don't you think this Chinese food is *simply* delicious?"

"Yes, Martha, *simply* delicious," Claudia replied, waving a dismissive arm at Martha without even bothering to look at her. "*Deeply* delicious."

Before Claudia could continue her tirade, Matt tried to diffuse the situation by quickly breaking in. "You never have to worry about having to force Martha to eat. She loves food. When someone puts a plate of food before her, she gives it her complete attention. And she isn't fussy either, eats anything, not like some people. I sometimes kid her about that, telling her that she'd even eat a fried rat's nest if someone placed it in front of her. She says that we can't throw anything out because there are millions of starving people in the world. To which I usually reply, 'What are we supposed to do with our leftovers then? Package them up and put them on a plane to the Third World?' And she's so appreciative when she's served food. On the few occasions when we eat out, and the waitress asks about the quality of the food, Martha always has the same answer: *Simply* delicious. Give my compliments to the chef.'" He smiled lovingly at Martha. "And we may have only eaten spaghetti and meatballs!"

"Well, I do love to eat," Martha admitted. "But I do watch my portions. And you rarely seem to buy me the junky food I keep asking for. And I *have* been losing weight, haven't I?"

"Yes, you certainly have, dear. Keep up the good work."

Sulking, Claudia had retreated back into her chair, using the pretence of studying her nails as an excuse to ignore everyone.

Matt said, "You've been looking for a mentor, Rodger, but you've been looking in the wrong places and asking the wrong people. You can't expect women, or men who haven't found themselves, to instruct you on how to find yourself and become a man. But when you left here, after breaking free of your mother and I, you reverted to looking for answers in women because you went directly into a marriage which you became deeply involved in, and never gave yourself time to examine your own personal interior life to see where you stood as a man. And now you've reverted back to me for answers. We've never spoken about this since you left because I don't believe in offering a grown man advice unless I'm asked for it, but tell me, how much time have you spent over these past ten years seriously examining your inner life and trying to find yourself, trying to locate the real you and dis-cover the real reason why you were put on this earth?"

"Very little," Rodger admitted. "And obviously I didn't come up with any answers or I wouldn't be here. Most of the time I just went along with Claudia's suggestions. It was a comfortable life so I didn't object much—I just let her call the shots and went along with her because I loved her." Claudia laughed derisively, but Rodger continued. "We both earned good money, had a nice home, traded in our cars for new ones every few years, could afford to buy what we wanted and eat out whenever we wanted, took expensive vacations and cruises together. Like I said, it was a comfortable life."

"Yes, comfortable," Matt agreed. "But totally self-centred. Apparently never reaching beyond the boundaries of your own selves and expanding outward and upward onto a bigger and higher plane. To do this you actually need to question your hedonistic lifestyle and, perish the thought, even *give up* some of that lifestyle for the greater good and become part of the larger picture." He paused for several moments, reflecting, then continued. "When

Martha and I went to your home for dinner several months ago, you took me into your den and I glanced over some of the titles on your bookshelves. I saw there a number of books I'd given you when you were in your late teens. Books like *Seeds of Contemplation* and *No Man Is an Island*, by Thomas Merton, *Walden*, by Thoreau, *Essays*, by Emerson, *The Imitation of Christ*, by Thomas a Kempis, and *Pascal's Pensees*. Although at that age you couldn't possibly have understood much of what these authors had to say, you were interested and did try to read them, and frequently questioned me about ideas in the books. And this interest continued, perhaps not quite as intensely, until you were married. But tell me, when was the last time you opened any of these books?"

"I…I don't remember. Not lately." Rodger tried to save face. "But I guess I've looked into them now and then."

"You don't sound very sure, which leads me to believe that they've been gathering dust on your shelves for years. You're a grown man—I can't order you to do anything. I can only suggest; I can only advise, but you've apparently rejected my advice. Earlier, I thought of suggesting that you meet with our parish priest and get his opinion, but since you've rejected the spiritual solution I doubt that he could offer anything further. But let me tell you this: In order for you to ever find contentment and peace, you must descend into the darkness of your own soul and continue to keep questioning relentlessly until you bring forth light. And when this light appears, you will recognize it as *your* light, *your* true destiny, and the only possible road you can follow. But in order to do this you need time to reflect, a place to reflect, a place where you can be alone without being disturbed, a place where you can search for answers and place your life in God's hands. I believe that the best way you can do this is by going on a retreat."

"A retreat? But I've never been on a retreat in my life. I wouldn't even know what to do."

"Don't worry, you'll be told what to do and when. You're given an agenda, but whether you follow it or not is your own decision. If you prefer to remain alone in your room to reflect, that's fine. The Saint Augustine Retreat Centre near Newmarket is a good place to go. I've been on retreats there many times with the

Knights." Matt opened one of the books on the table, withdrew a small slip of paper, handed it to Rodger. "Here's the name and phone number. Give them a call."

Rodger gazed dumbly at the slip of paper, then stared incredulously at Matt. "You *knew*." he accused. "You knew all along that I wouldn't be easy to convince and you had this ready."

Smiling benignly, Matt said, "No, I didn't know, I only surmised. I surmised that a person who has been away from the spiritual life for ten years could be difficult to convince to break old habits. And being an old Boy Scout I still believe in being prepared. Will you phone them?"

"I'll think about it." Rodger inserted the slip into his wallet.

Martha said, "Matt thought we could have a nice game of Scrabble after dinner. But Claudia does seem a bit under the weather."

"Going home," Claudia muttered, her head lolling to one side, eyes half closed, her body leaning heavily on an arm of the chair. "Going home." But she made no move to rise.

"Maybe another time," Matt said, turning back to Rodger. "If you do decide to go on retreat, I hope you take some of the books I mentioned with you, for inspiration."

"I'll think about it."

"Wait a minute,"Matt said. "Haven't you forgotten something?"

"Forgotten what?"

"You've asked me all kinds of questions, but you still haven't asked your mother what she thinks a good life should be all about. Don't you think that she also deserves to give you her opinion?"

"Well, sure, certainly...I—"

"My opinion doesn't matter," Martha said. "It isn't really important."

"No, dad's right," Rodger insisted. "I'm very interested in hearing what you have to say, mom."

"Well, all right, but it's really very simple compared to all the fancy things your father had to say. I think we just have to try to be good people, generous and considerate of others, and try to help other people whenever we can, instead of hurting them. We just need to have more love in the world. I'm sorry, I guess that's just simplifying everything, but that's what I feel."

"Maybe so," Matt said. "But what a wonderful world it would be if only people could be exactly like that: giving instead of taking, generous instead of greedy, loving instead of hating."

Rodger agreed. "Yours may be the simplest explanation, but in a way it's also the most profound. Deep down, most of us probably want to be exactly the way you said, but somewhere along the line we get sidetracked. Just like I've been sidetracked."

"But you're only sidetracked because you want to be," Martha said. "Nobody forced you into it."

No, Rodger admitted, nobody had forced him into it, not even Claudia. He had voluntarily gone along with her, allowed himself to be sidetracked, but now the time had come to return to the main line.. "I know," he said miserably. "I know, mom."

As Rodger rose to leave, Claudia began struggling to her feet. After giving Martha a hug and a cheek kiss, and shaking hands with Matt, Rodger went to Claudia's aid, but she slapped his hand away angrily and cried, "No!" But she'd been sitting for a long time and when she finally managed to stand the full force of her excessive drinking dizzied her, causing her to grab for the table with both hands as she lurched against it. When Rodger started to reach for her again, he noticed Matt's upraised hand as Matt moved quickly around the table and firmly gripped Claudia's arm. "Come, my dear," he said gently. "I'll help you to the car."

Claudia gazed glassily up at him, and Rodger could see that she wanted no help from either of them but realized that her condition prevented her from being independent.

"Going home," she muttered, releasing the table and sagging against Matt. With her back to Martha, she waved an arm over her head as they moved jerkily toward the door. "Bye, Martha."

"Goodbye, dear. You go home now and have a nice rest."

When Matt finally succeeded in helping Claudia into the car, he walked around to the driver's side and Rodger rolled down the window.

"Sorry about that," Rodger said. "She's rarely ever like this. It's just that she was—well, upset."

"I understand. Before you leave, there's one wonderful Emerson quote from his essay titled 'Self Reliance' which I read you many years ago. This one paragraph contains the key to finding yourself and becoming a man. I've read it countless times over the years. So many times, in fact, that I memorized it many years ago. It goes like this: 'There is a time in every man's education when he arrives at the conviction that envy is ignorance; that imitation is suicide; that he must take himself for better or worse as his portion; that though the wide universe if full of good, no kernel of nourishing corn can come to him but through his toil bestowed on that plot of ground which is given to him to till.—"

"The power which resides in him is new in nature," Rodger continued, "and none but he knows what that is which he can do, nor does he know until he has tried.'"

"You remembered. Then think about it."

"I will. I promise."

Driving home, Rodger noticed that Claudia sat pressed against her door, sitting as far away from him as possible, her lower lip thrust outward in an angry, sulking pout, and he knew from past experience that she'd say nothing until they arrived home, and then...well, then, providing that the excessive wine would still allow her to function, her anger and frustration would boil over and she'd let him know how she felt. Normally, she knew how to pace her drinking so that this rarely happened, but Matt's incisive rejoinders had made her so defensive and frustrated that she responded in the only way she knew how: by drinking so excessively that her responses eventually became mere pointless stubbornness.

After she staggered away from the car, she allowed him to help her into the house, shaking him angrily away when she reached the support of the living room sofa and fell heavily into it.

"Need another drink," she said.

He knew she'd say that, and wondered how much of this she'd remember in the morning. Was she now living in some dim alcoholic haze which would leave no lasting memory, or actually aware enough to know that asking for another drink would make him angry, and relishing the thought? He couldn't tell. Only tomorrow morning would provide the answer.

"You don't need another drink," he advised. "You've had enough to drink. You'll put yourself out if you have any more."

"Need another drink," she said loudly.

He toyed with the idea of doing exactly that, giving her another drink, letting her swallow it in a few gulps, and hoping that it *would* put her out and possibly ward off the accusations he knew were about to come. But he immediately ruled out this tactic as being cruel and unfair.

"I'll get my own drink," she muttered, struggling to rise.

"No, don't bother. You just relax and I'll get a glass of wine for you."

He had decided what to do. He went into the kitchen and half filled a wine glass with white wine from the refrigerator, topped up the glass with cold water, and stirred, effectively reducing the wine's alcohol content from twelve percent to six percent, barely stronger than a good bottle of beer. He doubted that such a mild drink could do much further damage, and only hoped that she failed to detect his tampering.

She apparently suspected nothing, barely taking a sip before placing the glass on the coffee table, her mind possibly on other things, causing him wonder if her excessive drinking had begun to make her stomach queasy. But her sudden smirk told him otherwise: She probably didn't want the wine at all, and was merely congratulating herself for being able to convince him to do something against his will. Punishing him, no doubt, for his earlier conduct at his parents' house. This led him to believe that, in spite of the drinking, her sensibilities were still in reasonable working order.

"You deserted me," she whined.

He sat down at the far end of the sofa. "Deserted you? How?"

"At your father's. You hung me out to dry, didn't you? *Didn't* you? You didn't come to my defence once. Not even once. Just hung me out to dry. Left me blowing in the wind."

"Did you ever think that the reason I didn't defend you was because I didn't believe what you were saying?"

"I don't *care*," she moaned, her voice filled with self-pity. "I'm your *wife*—you should've defended me regardless of what I said."

"Sorry, I just can't do that. I can't lie just because you're my wife. I've told you many times never to get into discussions with my father, especially about religion, because he's far more knowledgeable than you and you'll always lose, but you never listen. And then you're miserable, like now. Besides, I think that many of my father's ideas are quite relevant to my own life right now."

"You're not saying that you're returning to church, are you? Or going on that silly retreat he mentioned?"

She seemed to be recovering somewhat from the wine, making him wonder if her previous "drunkenness" had been at least partly manufactured by Claudia to free her from a bad situation. "Returning to church, no, but going on retreat, maybe. I don't see anything else on the horizon, so I might as well try it. It certainly can't do me any harm. I need to get away by myself to think things through."

"And leave me here alone. Desert me again, just like you did tonight. Is that all I mean to you? *Is it?*"

"You mean a great deal to me, and I'm not deserting you. I'm merely going away for a weekend to think things through. After all, when was the last time we spent a few days away from each other. I can't even remember."

"Then you're determined to go? Even though you know I don't want you to?"

"Yes, I've just decided, I am going. I need to go; it's vital that I go."

"Then to hell with you!" For spite, she picked up her glass of wine and drained it in a few gulps, then stretched out on the sofa and closed her eyes, kicking at him as her feet encountered his body.

"I'll help you to bed," he offered, rising. "You'll be more comfortable."

"I don't *want* to go to bed," she said, her eyes remaining closed. "Especially not with you."

So that was it—the cold shoulder. Being such a docile husband over the past ten years, rare were the occasions when he'd experienced this type of rejection, but he felt convinced that they would now become more frequent because, drunk or sober, the patience she had promised just a few weeks ago had already evaporated, leaving behind a jealous, demanding, angry wife.

Watching her, he saw that the combination of drinking another glass of wine and lying down were too much for her—in a few minutes she fell asleep. Gently, he removed her shoes, placed a cushion under her head, and turned out the lights.

12

Overnight, Rodger kept to his own side of the bed, half expecting Claudia to desert the discomfort of the sofa and join him, having grown accustomed over the years, as they both slept together on their sides spoon fashion, to having her warmth either in front of him or behind him. But he felt no disturbance, and when morning came he noticed that no head had touched her pillow.

He found the spare bedroom empty, the bed still made, her clothing from the previous evening slung carelessly over a chair. As he returned to the master bedroom, he heard from the kitchen below what sounded like a spoon clicking against a coffee mug as coffee was being stirred.

At the kitchen table, he discovered a haggard, morose Claudia, obviously brassiereless, wearing nothing more than a peach housecoat and white, backless slippers, her blonde hair messy, her gray eyes slightly bloodshot. She'd managed to remove her makeup, exposing an ailing, almost white face, obviously a result of last night's drinking. With her face now naked, he could see the beginning traces of aging that over twenty years of almost daily cosmetic use had left: crow's feet at her eyes, a few lines across her forehead, wrinkles at the edges of her lips. Although still a very attractive woman, even without makeup, he knew that as the years passed the cosmetics she still wore mainly to enhance her appearance would become the mask she wore to hide the remorseless, ever advancing signs of age.

On the table, empty of plates or food, a teaspoon lay beside her barely touched mug of coffee. At this point of each day, she usually asked him what he wanted for breakfast, but he knew that he could expect nothing more than a cup of drip coffee this morning.

He sat down opposite her and sipped his coffee, waiting for her to mention his proposed retreat, which would prove that she remembered last night.

"How did you sleep?" he asked.

"Terribly. And now I've got a splitting headache. I won't be going in today."

"What about a bite to eat? I'll make you some breakfast."

"No. That's the last thing in the world I need. And you'll have to get your own—I feel like I'm going to throw up any minute."

"Maybe just a glass of juice?"

"No."

"How about a Bromo then?"

"No, nothing. I'm going to bed soon." She raised her mug toward her mouth, made a face, put it down again, the smell alone making her nauseous. "You've decided then, have you? About deserting me for a weekend?"

"I'm not deserting you. And yes, I have decided—I'm definitely going and I'll be phoning today to make a reservation."

"I see."

Without another word, she rose and left the kitchen. He heard her climbing the stairs and several seconds later the sound of a door slamming. When he went up later to shave and prepare for work, he found the spare bedroom door closed.

Although his past passive behaviour had given Claudia little to complain about, she had com-plained enough through ten years of marriage to familiarize him with what her "I see" actually meant. It meant that, when he came home that evening after having phoned her at noon hour to tell her that he'd be leaving on retreat a week from Friday, he found no dinner waiting and was told icily that there were TV dinners in the freezer and whether she ever prepared another decent dinner for him depended entirely on him. In an attempt to convince him to reconsider his decision to leave on retreat, she had begun an intense vocal campaign, one he knew only too well, one by one pulling various ploys from her magician's hat of feminine wiles. She continued to sleep in the spare bedroom and refused all physical contact: "Why should I let you touch me when you won't even show you love me by giving up your silly idea?" She constantly belittled his endeavour: "You're just wasting your time on such foolishness. You'll see, nothing will ever come of it and you'll simply revert to your old self once you come home. You're just wasting your time so why bother. Why *bother*?" She tried to play on his pity: "You don't love me any more, do you? If you did, why would you leave me here all alone, why would you desert me? How can you possibly be so terribly cruel and thoughtless? After ten years of faithful marriage, I thought I knew you, but I don't, do I? I see now that you're nothing more than a selfish brute who doesn't care for anyone or anything but himself." And finally, reaching deeply to the bottom of her magician's hat, she produced the feminine last resort: copious tears combined with pitiful wailing and the repeated accusation, "You don't love me… you don't love me…you don't love me…"And with her magician's hat of ploys empty, she repeatedly invaded the sanctity of his lockless den, where he sought privacy because he had recently begun to read again, and attacked his reading with blatant insults and ridicule: "How can you read this horrible trash. It's all nothing but a bunch of legends, fairy tales, and lies. You're a fool, that's what you are. A poor, deluded, stupid fool! One of these days, when you're not around, I'm going to take every damn book in this room into the backyard and build the biggest bonfire you ever saw..

For his part, Rodger saw clearly through her transparent motivation and generally maintained a stoic indifference to her tirades, having been subjected to her desperate anger on a few past occasions. Nothing had changed. Her self-pity, her whining, her jealousy, her derision, her insults, her sexual refusal—all were simply her feminine wiles in action, mingled with the unspoken threat that her present conduct could become permanent, to convince him to take pity on her and relinquish his desire to leave on retreat. Although the thought of her burning all his books horrified him, he seriously doubted that she would do anything so drastic. He knew Claudia to be an intelligent woman, and even though the retreat situation had never happened in the past, he doubted that she would allow her present conduct to continue indefinitely when she knew that it could only drive him even further away from her. Although she now made his life tense and miserable, past history told him that this would probably change in a few days. Being unloving and uncharitable weren't in Claudia's nature—she was the exact opposite. She needed love and attention too much, almost desperately at times, and her present bitchy conduct only served to deprive her of both. He knew also that the fear he saw in her eyes represented the main driving force behind her present conduct. An intense fear that this retreat, just one weekend away from her giving him plenty of time to reflect, could drive a permanent wedge between them.

And, as he suspected, exactly this happened. When he arrived home at his usual time on Friday evening, she greeted him wearing only red, backless slippers and a sheer, flaming red negligee, all new, and when she escorted him into the dining room he found a lavish dinner waiting complete with glowing candles and chilled wine, the table replete with a platter of lean, thickly-sliced rump roast, serving bowls filled with creamy mashed potatoes, baby carrots, plump green peas, wax beans, and broccoli, all hot and steaming, with the end of the table holding two fattening, high-calorie desserts: pumpkin cheesecake and black forest chocolate cake, both his favourites.

As he seated himself, an old cliche popped into his mind: "You can get more with honey than you can with vinegar." He smiled inwardly. Women were like chameleons, weren't they? One day they were completely alienated from their husbands; the next day they simply changed their colour and embraced the old relationship again. Their lives seemed to have no solid rudders guiding them, no definite, hardrock cores producing ingrained resoluteness, only the ever-changing fluctuations as they flitted back and forth from one side of the brain to the other, and whose sole motivation for their actions, regardless of the consequences, was an attempt to achieve whatever they wanted.

Claudia insisted on pouring the wine and filling his plate, and when she came behind him and reached forward and placed his plate before him, she pressed against him, wrapping her arms tightly around him, kissing the side of his neck, moulding her plump, warm breasts against his back while his nostrils eagerly inhaled the redolent muskiness of her perfume.

"Darling, I've been an idiotic fool," she said softly. "Can you ever forgive me for behaving the way I have for these past few days?"

"Right now," he admitted, "you're doing a damn good job of making me forget."

"Then I'll just keep on doing exactly that. This *is* lovely, isn't it? Isn't this the way it should be between you and me all the time?"

"Yes, it is. And this is more than lovely—it's incredible."

And the following days and nights leading up to his Friday departure were even more incredible. From the living hell of the previous week, she now devoted her attention to making his life a living heaven. Her regular lovemaking during that final week became more demanding and frenzied than he'd ever known, swallowing him completely in its intensity. "Love me, darling," she begged hoarsely, throwing her body against him. "I need you. Please love me as you've *never* loved me before," and, swept into the flames of her desire, he tried willingly and valiantly to match her own raging passion.

Having booked no evening real estate appointments for the week, she pampered him endlessly, never disputing anything, complimenting him on even his most trivial statements, bringing him his slippers and coffee when he arrived home from work, constantly asking him if everything was all right, if he wanted anything, if he felt comfortable, if he needed anything at all, and continued to serve him excellent dinners, even one evening treating him to a sumptuous dinner and wine at the One 99 Restaurant, followed by a comedic farce at Theatre Orangeville. On other evenings, at her insistence they sat together on the sofa with a glass or two of wine while she kissed him frequently, her warmth nestled against him, her probing hand exploring his body as they watched saccharine movies on the W channel.

She bought him gifts for the retreat: two new shirts, two new ties, a gold Cross pen, and an alligator skin briefcase to hold the books and note paper he intended to take with him.

Although completely aware of her motivation, that her actions represented a battle between what she could offer and what the retreat could offer, warning him that *this* is what he'd be missing if he chose another way of life, he said nothing, initially basking in her pampering. He found himself vacillating, telling himself that his marriage had been good in the past, but never this good. Would it be so harmful to continue on like this? But would it be this good permanently if Claudia won? He doubted it. How long would it be before he returned placidly and humbly to their previous uxorious relationship? He knew that she was pulling out all the stops, doing everything in her power to convince him that, although her way of life may be hedonistic and selfish, it was certainly more physically enjoyable than anything he could envision. Yet, even recognizing this, he still couldn't completely rid himself of that ache deep inside himself for something more worthwhile, more rewarding on a larger scale, something less hedonistic and selfish and more righteous. And he also knew that if the retreat failed to provide an answer, and Claudia knew that she had entrapped him again, the attention she now showed him would definitely begin to wane. But would that be so bad? Disregarding the fantastic lovemaking, her constant, loving attention had already begun to pall and become intrusive, leaving him with sparse private time to think or reflect. She always seemed to be by his side, intensely attentive and rarely out of sight, causing him to feel boxed in, almost claustrophobic. But as Friday approached, he felt his anxiousness lifting in spite of Claudia's constant closeness as he contemplated the release and privacy the weekend ahead would certainly bring.

Recognizing Rodger's easily aroused sexual desire as her greatest ally, and her greatest stronghold, she used Thursday, the final evening before his departure, to give him her body with vigorous intensity, using every weapon in her arsenal to instill an indelible memory of this night in his mind to counteract the influence of the retreat.

Early Friday morning, before leaving for work, Rodger retreated to the den to pack a few books to take with him on retreat. As he drew out Merton's *No Man Is an Island*, two folded, printed sheets came out with it, having been concealed between books. When he unfolded them, he saw that they were a computer print-out dated 2003 which he had neither relegated to the filing cabinet or to the shredder, probably because he intended to reread the pages one day but had totally forgotten about them once they had disappeared from view, which told him the astonishing truth that he hadn't even opened *No Man Is an Island* in at least five years. Could he blame Claudia for that, when he could have escaped to the sanctuary of his den any time and buried himself in these books? Hardly. The sad truth assailed him again that for the past ten years he had been her willing dupe, sinking with a contented sigh ever deeper into the hedonistic lifestyle she continually offered him.

He saw that the sheets were an e-mail which had been forwarded to his father from a fellow parishioner, and which his father had then forwarded to him. Had he deliberately hidden the sheets so that they would become "out of sight out of mind"and be neglected? Then why had he not simply destroyed them? Because, he thought, he must have believed at the time that they were too important to destroy and had kept them in deference to Matt, whose heading read, "I thought you might find this prayer thought provoking." The e-mail continued:

OPENING PRAYER—NEW YORK STATE SENATE

I thought you might enjoy this interesting prayer given in New York at the opening session of their Senate. It seems that prayer still upsets some people.

When Minister Jesse White was asked to open the new session of the New York Senate, everyone expected the same banal generalities, Instead, this is what they heard:

"Heavenly Father, we come before you today to ask your forgiveness and to seek your guidance and direction. We know that Your word says, "Woe to those who call evil good," but this is exactly what we have done. We confess that:

We have lost our spiritual equilibrium and reversed our values.

We have mocked the absolute truth of Your Word and called it Pluralism.

We have rewarded abject laziness and called it Welfare.

We have murdered our unborn and called it Choice.

We have exploited the hungry and the poor and called it the Lottery.

We have failed to discipline our children and called it Building Self-esteem.

We have coveted our neighbor's possessions and called it Ambition.

We have abused power and called it Politics.

We have polluted and poisoned the air with pornography and profanity and called it Freedom of Speech.

We have ridiculed the time-honored values of our forefathers and called it Enlightenment.

Search us, Oh, God, and know the contents of our hearts today. Cleanse us from every sin and set us free. Guide and bless these men and women, who have been sent here to lead us to the center of Your will, and we beseechingly ask these things in the holy name of Your Son, the living Savior, Jesus Christ. Amen."

The response to Minister Jesse White's words was instantaneous. A number of the legislators walked out in protest during the prayer. But in five short weeks, Nazarene Christian Church, where Reverend White is pastor, logged over 5,000 phone calls and only 49 of these responded negatively. The church is now receiving international requests from Korea, Africa, and India for copies of this prayer.

Paul Harvey aired this prayer on his radio program, "The Rest of the Story," and received a larger response than any other program he has ever aired. With the Lord's help, may this prayer flood our nation and genuinely become our powerful desire so that we can again be called, "One nation under God."

God bless gutsy Reverend Jesse White!

When Rodger turned the sheets over, he saw that he had scribbled a note on one of them which read: "How is it even remotely possible to solve these enormous problems? Maybe this is what God actually WANTS." Those issues again. Those interminable issues with God which hung in his mind like a malignant tumour, which had grown appreciably since his marriage and would continue to plague him until they were resolved. And they *would* be resolved, he promised himself, *had* to be resolved this weekend on retreat, one way or another.

When Friday evening came and he prepared to leave, Claudia gave him a long, hungry kiss, smiled radiantly, and simply said, "Do what you must, darling—but remember me."

13

When Rodger arrived at the Saint Augustine Retreat Centre near Newmarket, he checked into 104, a cool, single-windowed seven-by-nine foot room with stippled white walls and old-fashioned, brown, nine-inch floor tiles. The single bed, of brown metal piping and with a hard mattress, held two heavy blankets and a small crucifix hung on the wall above it. In a corner sat a firm, maroon, faux leather armchair with bare chrome arms, and against a wall a straight-backed wooden chair and a writing table holding a thick, worn paperbacked Jerusalem Bible and a tiny desk lamp, an unframed colour print of a cathedral on the wall above it. In a corner, a small, dated sink with two separate taps, with a wastebasket beneath it and a mirror, a light fixture, and a small glass shelf holding a water glass and a tiny cake of soap above it, came with two white towels and a washcloth. Clothes were to be hung on two double-pronged metal hangers fastened to the door, for which a few wire hangers were supplied.

Although clean, the room had absolutely no odour, as though—even when Rodger knew the room's age—everything in it was still sterile and no one had ever stayed in it before, making him feel almost afraid to touch anything, to contaminate the room with his fingerprints, with himself. Did he even belong here? he wondered.

The weather report called for a cool night, yet the heating register beneath the window felt cold. Could no heat be the reason for the two heavy blankets? He noticed a small drawer in the writing table and opened it out of curiosity. Inside were several religious leaflets left by previous occupants and a twelve-inch wooden crucifix. As he removed the crucifix and held it up, Christ's image swung sideways and hung by one arm because the nails holding the legs and one arm were missing. Apparently the crucifix had been placed into the drawer and forgotten—just as his faith had been forgotten. While checking in, the Filipino at the desk had told him that refreshments and snacks were avail-able in the basement dining room. After unpacking and pinning his name badge to his shirt, he went there, made himself a hot chocolate in a Styrofoam cup, chose a few chocolate chip cookies over a muffin, and joined three men at a table.

A fat, balding man with no neck and thick lips named Herbert Cliburn seemed only interested in being the centre of attention while talking about himself, his religious life, and his religious "achieve-ments." "Yes, I'm very generous with my donations to the church," he bragged loudly. "I won't say exactly how much I give—I wouldn't want to embarrass you boys." He snickered. "But, believe me, it's substantial. Quite substantial. And I never miss Mass either. I'm there seven days a week, praising the Lord, even though during the week the church is almost empty. But I'm there, the Lord can depend on me *every day.* How many of you can say that?" he challenged loudly. "How many of you can say that you go to Mass *every day?*" He went on and on in this bragging, self-centred vein until Rodger, finally realizing that he had no other vein, tuned him out. He found the man boring and revolting, and wondered how any man could so mistake the purpose of a religious retreat as to come to one merely to blatantly showcase his own pompousness.

When Herbert finally relinquished the floor, Jerome Riddle, still slim and handsome in what Rodger took to be his mid fifties, stepped in. "Me, I don't have time to go to Mass every day because I'm up to my ears trying to keep up with the demands of the people around me. My boss is a slavedriver who keeps me running all day long, just can't stand to see me sit down for even a minute, and when I get home at night all I want to do is flop in my chair and be left alone. But I can't even do that because then my wife is on my case with all of *her* demands. She needs this, and she wants that, and the kids are being rowdy, and *'you've got to do something!'* No rest, ever. Except when I come here for a couple of days. This is the only place I ever get any rest."

When Jerome finally wound down and lapsed into silence, Rodger turned his attention to Edgar (Rocky) Rockford and only one thought came into his mind: *What the hell is this guy doing here? Did he think he was coming to a rock concert?* Seated and looking to be in his late twenties, Rocky appeared taller than the rest of them, possibly six-foot-two, a tall string bean with a perpetual sneer frozen to the thin lips of his anonymous face, which he'd tried to distinguish from other faces with rings through a nostril and an eyebrow, his total image one of blackness. Black, greasy-looking, shoulder-length hair, black T-shirt, black leather vest, black jeans with a wide black belt with a large buckle displaying a black skeleton head, and black cowboy boots. Tattoos of snakes, dragons, naked women, and swastikas covered his skinny arms.

Gaining Rocky's attention, Rodger asked, "Do you have a bike outside?"

"No. We came in my old man's car."

"We?"

"Yeah. My friend Lyle and me. My old man told me he'd kick me out of the house if I didn't come. Do you think I'd come to this crappy joint for any other reason?" He raised his chin proudly. "But I got the last laugh. I said I'd come if he let me bring my friend Lyle along and a two-four of Labatt's Blue. He's chilling the beer right now. I'll be going up there soon to guzzle a few with him."

Rodger disliked arrogance in anyone, but especially in a person who apparently did absolutely nothing to even earn it. "So that's the only reason you're here?"

"You got that right, buddy. But we got the beer. Me and Lyle'll party all night, so we'll be okay."

"Tell me, Rocky, do you work?"

"Right now I'm between jobs.

"And you still live at home."

"Got to, don't I? With no money coming in, I'd be out on the street, wouldn't I? Or looking for welfare. That'd be pretty stupid, wouldn't it, when I can stay at home and let the old man pay all the bills."

Rodger wondered how much of this bravado talk he'd hear if Rocky's father were present. "But does he give you any money?"

"Sure. It ain't much, but I get enough out of him each week for smokes and a few beers and a few rounds of pot. And I can party it up with my friends on weekends. It helps when I tell him I need money for the subway and carfare and lunch and coffee and donuts at Tim Hortons while I'm looking for work."

"And are you actually looking for work?"

"Sure. Sometimes. Do you know what it's like tryna find a job in Brampton? They take one look at me and say, 'Don't call us, we'll call you,' or they tell me to come back after I've put on a long-sleeved shirt and taken the rings out of my face. And it's only some crappy job paying about eight bucks an hour."

At this point, Herbert and Jerome saw that Rodger and Rocky were into a long discussion and that they would no longer be centres of attention, so they decided to leave, Herbert yawning and saying that it was time to retire and Jerome agreeing, adding that they had to be in the chapel early in the morning.

When they were alone, Rodger continued. "So what kinds of jobs have you been applying for?"

"Mostly filing clerks in department stores."

"Do you not think that an employer who is paying you money has the right to insure that his employees, who are in the public eye, present a good image to that public?"

"They're just prejudiced, that's all. I got rights too. I should have the same rights everybody else does, but they're against me because of the way I look. And for a lousy eight bucks an hour."

"Have you ever thought of looking for a job in a shipping department, where you're not exposed to the public?"

"No, I don't want that—that's heavy work. I want light work, like stocking shelves. Why should I slug my guts out for a lousy eight bucks an hour?"

"Then why don't you set your sights on earning a higher wage?"

"How? You tell me."

"Go back to school and learn something that will *qualify* you to earn a higher wage."

Rocky laughed. "Are you nuts? Is that all you got to offer? I've been out of school for six years now and I ain't got no intention of going back—ever. School is for idiots and morons."

Rodger also wanted to laugh, aware that by leaving school far too early, and apparently learning nothing valuable since, Rocky had certainly classified himself with the idiots and morons. "Then I'm afraid, Rocky, that you're on a slippery slope that can only take you even lower. Tell me, have you ever lived away from home? When you were working, I mean."

"No. Because the jobs usually never lasted more than a couple of months. And I never had enough time to save enough money to rent a furnished room. I did some light assembly work in a few factories for a while. But they didn't want workers, they wanted slaves and the cruddy slavedrivers held a whip over your head all day long. I got better things to do with my life than put up with that crap."

"And did you pay your father room and board while you were working?"

"Hell, no, why should I? He's my father!"

Rodger duly noted that Rocky had used 'father' instead of 'the old man' for the first time. Apparently there were times when his father still deserved to be treated as a human being, as when he generously supported a lazy, useless son. "So what do you intend to do, Rocky? Spend the rest of your life living off your parents without even paying them a cent?"

"No, I'll be paying them back plenty when I become a success. I'm not exactly loafing around all day—I'm working on my music, my songs, and some day I'm gonna be famous, wait and see."

"What Music? What songs?"

"Rap music, that's what. And I write the words too. Some of these guys make millions, so why shouldn't I when my stuff is just as good as theirs. Maybe even better. I just gotta make the right connection to get me started and then I'm on my way to the big money."

"And do you write the same kind of lyrics that the other guys write? I've listened to some rap music and found that most of it's hateful to women. It insults women, degrades women, sings about beating them and raping them and sometimes even killing them. Is that the kind of garbage you're writing?"

Rodger knew that he'd expressed the truth when he saw the sudden look of surprise on Rocky's face.

Rocky said, "Chill out, man. What difference does that make as long as you're making money. The way you make it ain't important. I read about these guys. Some of them own half a dozen big cars and a few big houses and got money coming out of their ears. That's for me; that's all that counts."

"And *do* you actually hate women?"

"Hell, no, it's only a job. It's just a way of making a buck, that's all. What difference does it make how you make it, as long as you get rich."

"So, if you become successful, you don't believe that you're doing any harm by performing rap music which promotes hatred and rape and violence against women."

Rocky shrugged. "Look, man, it's just music, just enter*tain*-ment, just a way to make a living. It don't need to have nothing to do with whether I believe it or not, does it?"

Rodger felt stunned because he suddenly realized that Rocky could have been speaking about him, and that his admonitions to Rocky were also admonitions to himself about his own job, his own life. "Let me tell you a little story, Rocky. I once knew a man who took a job with an advertising agency and worked there for several years because the money was good. He had a beautiful wife, a well-paying job, a nice house, a nice car, and all the money he needed. Then one day, when he was forty years old, he woke up one morning after ten years of marriage and asked himself what he had done with the first half of his life. And the answer that quickly came back was this: absolutely nothing worthwhile. He'd done nothing for the past several years but write commercials for asswipe and pussy pads and toothpaste for people with twelve-year-old mentalities, and he hated it, and he hated himself for doing it. Sure, he and his wife had more than enough material possessions, but they'd detached themselves from humanity and only lived for themselves and their own comfort. And when he realized this he told himself that he couldn't possibly go on like this because he was meant to be part of something far bigger than himself, and he had to do something about it."Rodger stopped talking and simply kept staring at Rocky until Rocky became nervous and began shifting in his chair.

Finally, Rocky said, "I don't get it, man. What are you tryna say?"

"What I'm trying to say is this: We need to do more with our lives than merely accumulate money and personal possessions. We need to find out who we are and give something back to the world. Other-wise all the money in the world and all the material possessions in the world won't make us happy because we're only living selfishly for ourselves."

"You tryna tell me that if I make it big doing rap music that I ain't gonna be happy?" He laughed. "Think again, man. Throw a pile of dough in my lap and I'd be as happy as a pig in s-h-i-t. No problem."

"Oh, you might think you're happy for a while, because you haven't had any money before. After all, money can buy a lot of things, but money alone certainly won't make you happy—you need much more than that." Rodger shrugged. "In any case, it's all immaterial because I don't see you making any real money in rap music."

"Why not?" Rocky demanded.

"Because I think that your interest in rap music is merely a front for your own laziness. You're just using it to show your father that you're actually trying to do something, try to make something of yourself. Tell me, how much does he know about rap music? Have you ever shown him any of your lyrics?"

"No." Rocky hesitated, finally continued. "He ain't interested."

"No? Are you sure it isn't something else? Are you sure he hasn't seen them because you know he'd be horrified if he ever saw what you've written?"

Rodger needed no answer to his accusation; he only had to look into Rocky's wide-eyed face to know that he'd spoken the truth.

"He ain't interested, I said." Rocky insisted lamely.

For the first time, Rodger studied the tattoos on Rocky's forearms and noticed one of interest. "So how is Jane doing these days?"

"Jane? Whuddu you know about Jane?"

"All I know is that you've got a tattoo of a red heart on your arm with her name inside it."

"Oh, yeah." Rocky looked at the tattoo, as though noticing it for the first time.

"Some young people make the mistake of having a tattoos of the names of persons they're having hot and heavy relationships with put on, thinking the relationships are never going to end because they're madly in love. And then they do end, and they're left with tattoos they don't want any longer. Is that what happened to you, or are you still seeing Jane?"

"Still seeing each other. Been seeing each other for over two years. We'll be getting engaged and set a wedding date once the money from my rap music starts rolling in."

"Ah, yes, the rap music. Tell me, have you ever sung any of your rap music songs to her?"

Rocky looked horrified. "Are you nuts? She'd walk out on me and never talk to me again if she ever heard any of my songs. Besides, she don't have to know nothing about them. All she's gotta do is enjoy the money once it starts rolling in."

"So you're writing rap songs about degrading and doing violence to women, but you're going steady with a woman you expect to marry someday. That's hypocritical, and makes me wonder which is the real you. How do you treat Jane?"

"Just fine. I treat her just fine."

"Do you ever degrade her sexually, insult her womanhood, slap her around, beat her, anything like that?"

"No! What the hell do you think I am?"

"Well, we've already established that you're a hypocrite. I was just wondering what else you might be."

"Well, I ain't *that*. I ain't never been that with Jane."

"Good. I'm glad to hear that. And speaking about Jane, what kind of a person is she? Does she have a job?"

"Sure, she works as a waitress in a restaurant in Brampton. Been there for about three years now. Does pretty good in tips too."

"Does she still live at home?"

"Yeah. And her parents don't even ask for room and board. They just like having her around."

"So she has a bit of disposable income. Have you ever borrowed any money from her?"

"Now and then," Rocky answered, looking away.

"Much?"

"What business is that of yours?"

Rodger shrugged. "None, really, but I do have a point I'd like to make. But if you're afraid to answer, that's fine with me—we'll just forget about it."

"I ain't afraid to answer! Jane knows that a creative guy like me needs time to get established. So she slips me a few bucks now and then—so what? And she won't even let me pay her back either. That's how good she is to me."

"Yes, you're a lucky man, aren't you? And I guess your father has slipped you a few bucks now and then, too, hasn't he? As a matter of fact, over the years he's probably slipped you a lot more than a few bucks, hasn't he?"

"Maybe he has. So what—he's my father, ain't he? And since the time I left school and started working he's kept track of every nickel he ever gave me. It's a loan, not a gift, he tells me, and its gotta be paid back someday. And I'll pay him back when the time comes."

"And what about your friends, the guys you hang out with. How many of them have you borrowed money from over the years, to support your creative talent, and never paid back?"

"They all know that they'll get their money back someday. When I'm a huge success."

"But will they, Rocky? Will they? Especially if you never become a huge success. May I tell you another little story?"

"I'm tired." Rocky said, looking at his watch. "I'm going upstairs to crash."

"This will only take a few minutes," Rodger assured him. "And it may help you a great deal in the future."

"Okay, okay, go ahead, but make it snappy—I'm tired." Rocky said impatiently, folding his tattooed arms tightly across his chest.

"You remind me of a man I once knew. He was about your age. He came to Orangeville from Winnipeg with his parents and lived with them because he had no job and no money. He was waiting for a cash court settlement from Winnipeg for a minor injury he received when hit by a car. A few months later it comes—a $6,000 cheque. He quickly leaves home, rents an old house, spends a few thou-sand dollars furnishing it, and proceeds to use it as a party hangout for he and his friends, where the booze flows freely and the pot stinks up the place.

"Well, soon he's broke and without a job. But work is just about the last thing he's interested in—all he wants to do is party—so he borrows from his father, borrows from his friends and never pays them back, and goes on welfare. He keeps borrowing more money from his father, who eventually cuts him off. Desperate, he takes a job driving cab, but gets kicked off welfare when he fails to claim his income.

"He takes a job with a man who drives around Ontario peddling Chinese T-shirts and pullovers and track suits. Meanwhile, his friends are pestering him for the money he owes them, and the landlord is pestering him for back rent. He manages to save up enough money for the first month's rent on a decrepit old house just east of Orangeville which has been vacant for almost a year, and moves again, leaving the back rent unpaid.

"So he finds new friends and the partying continues. A few month's later he gets a decent-paying factory job in Orangeville. But the work is too strenuous, not for him, so he starts searching for a way to make some easy money without having to work for it. A few month's later, he goes on compensation, claiming carpal tunnel syndrome, has an operation on his wrist, and tells me that he may be getting a $15,000.00 buyout from compensation. But he doesn't get it and they eventually take him off compensation for his repeated refusals to return to work, claiming that he still has wrist problems.

"He finds a job doing light packaging for a small manufacturing firm. He moves again, this time west of town, leaving debts behind. He has no phone now because of all the bad debt he's run up with Bell. And his time in Orangeville is running out. He can't take it any more—things are getting too hot. His old party friends have tracked him down and want their money, some even threatening to beat the crap out of him if he doesn't start paying up, and some of his old landlords have also found him and are threatening to take him to small claims court to get their money.

"The last time I spoke to him, a few years ago, he said he was moving to Guelph, and I guess that's where he is now. Sometimes I think about him and wonder how much partying he's doing now."

"And?" Rocky said angrily. What're you tryna say? That I'm like that?"

"No, but you could well be in the future. It sounds like you've got yourself a good girl in Jane, but it also sounds like your just using her right now for your own ends. It seems to me that you're just using your rap music as a front, trying to convince her that you're doing something productive when all you really want is to have her keep dishing out money to you indefinitely."

"Like hell!" Rocky leaped to his feet. "She's my girl and we're gonna get married!"

"Oh, are you? When? After you make your first million as a rap singer and she finds out what you're really singing about? I don't think so. Once she finds that out, I don't think she'll want to be within ten miles of you. You don't lie to people you love. If you really love Jane, the first thing you'll do is tell her the truth about your music, then you're going to tell her that you're going to stop doing it because you really don't hate women and were only doing it for the money. And if she doesn't walk out on you, then you're going to make Jane proud of you by getting off your butt and either finding a respectable job or going back to school to learn something which will allow you to earn a decent living. If you tell me you're going to do all that, you probably will eventually marry Jane. If you don't, you might as well kiss her goodbye right now. And if you don't mature and start accepting some responsibility for your actions, you might as well also kiss your life goodbye."

Rodger rose and met Rocky's angry stare. "One more thing. All the boozing and pot smoking in the world, all the face and tongue jewellery, all the black clothes, all the tattoos won't make a man of you. It's what's in here and here that counts," he said while tapping his chest and his head. "So what's it going to be, Rocky?"

But even before he replied, Rodger could see that the anger in Rocky's face had only intensified, and knew what his answer would be.

"Who the hell are you anyway?" Rocky spat. "I don't need you to tell me how to live my own life. I'll do as I damn well please."

"Yes, I'm afraid you will. I'm deeply afraid that you will."

"The hell with you!" Rocky turned away and marched out of the room and up the stairs.

Disappointed with his initial encounter with other re-treatants, Rodger returned glumly to his room. Were the other retreatants going to be no more inspirational than the three he'd just met? He began to wonder if he'd made a mistake in coming on retreat simply looking for answers from other retreatants, or even from priests or speakers, but then decided that he was being presumptuous in expecting answers after having spoken to only three men, and even in expecting others to do his own work. After all, as he'd just told Rocky, in the end his answers had to come from searching his own mind and heart, not from only searching the minds and hearts of others who were in many ways different from himself.

On Saturday morning, he studied the agenda and decided to go to the prayer service in the tiny chapel which he found less than half full and would have been filled to overflowing with only eighty people. Carved into oak and lining both white side walls above the oaken wainscotting, hung the four-teen Stations of the Cross; a large oaken crucifix with several Latin words above it dominated the wall behind the altar. Years ago, when he still attended Mass regularly, he could have translated the words, but now he had forgotten. He slid silently into a pew halfway down the aisle, suddenly recalling the days when he used to be an ardent Catholic and always sat near the front of the church where, except when the church was jammed, there always seemed to be plenty of space, and used to say to himself, C'mon down, folks. Plenty of seats here. Don't worry, you won't be contaminated.

Although he had to admit that most of the men here—some Knights of Columbus members and many Filipinos—appeared reverent, at least while in the chapel, and seemed to be much better adjusted and happier even though he hadn't yet spoken to any, Rodger adamantly refused to feel anything even remotely resembling a spiritual experience. As a person who hadn't been inside a church for years, he felt like an alien, as he would had he mistakenly walked into a beauty salon, and now asked himself the same question he would have asked had that happened: *What am I doing here?*

As the more than three dozen men in the tiny chapel lustily sang the entrance hymn, *Amazing Grace,* the oaken walls almost throbbing from the penetrating loudness of their voices, Rodger remained silent, his attention wandering as he gazed around him. He saw Rocky just across the aisle staring at him, mouth clamped firmly shut, eyes bloodshot, his friend and his grim-faced father beside him, and that accusing stare said only one thing: If you're so damn high and mighty, why aren't you praising the Lord by singing? To impress Rocky, Rodger tried to sing, but his pathetic croak was easily drowned out by the others, and Rocky gave him a sardonic sneer before turning triumphantly away.

One of the Filipinos rose and delivered a reading from the Bible, but Rodger barely heard and paid little attention, and later read dully, paying little attention to the meanings of the words as men on either side of the aisle read prayers alternately. He could generate no interest in what was being said. His years of absence from church had left him feeling cold and alien toward it. To bolster this rejection, he deliberately resurrected distasteful memories of being forced to attend church as a child, kneeling for long periods on hard kneelers, listening to long, boring sermons, and being pushed into becoming an altar boy and joining the choir when he would have preferred to remain in the background. But by contrast other memories forced their way into his mind. He recalled how, as he knelt to pray with head bowed after communion and had finished praying, he would pass the time and try to take his mind off his aching knees—Matt always sat at the front of the church and never rose from his knees until everyone had received communion—by observing the feet of the parishioners as they passed by his aisle seat on their way to receiving communion. Especially during warm summer Sundays, when many parishioners wore either sandals or open-toed shoes, he was surprised by the large number of women who painted their toenails, but foot imperfections were his real search. A few older women actually had their big toes permanently lapped over their second toes from many years of wearing pointed shoes; others had second toes longer than big toes. Others had ugly, gnarled toes; others had toenails which looked as though they had been chewed down to the quick, making him wonder, if this were actually the case, how the foot had reached the mouth. At first, when-ever he spotted a pair of bad feet, he quickly looked up so that he could put a face to the feet and smugly said to himself, Oh, so *she's* the one with the overlapping big toe, or, Oh, so *he's* the one with the ugly, gnarled toes. But his smugness soon evaporated when Matt asked him what he was doing and he finally admitted the truth. Then Matt whispered, "Remember your humility. You may look at the feet, but don't look at the faces. Then you won't know who they belong to, and won't have anyone to criticize."

Just as Mass started on another Sunday, Rodger found himself staring out through the glass fire door at the side of the church as he watched for parishioners coming across the parking lot, invariably arriving late for Mass, and silently criticizing them for their lateness.

When Matt noticed, he whispered, "What are you doing?"

"Nothing," Rodger whispered back.

'Then why are you staring out the door?"

When Rodger realized that he had just lied, and in church, he admitted the truth.

Matt whispered, "Don't criticize others—we all have our faults. Be humble, and just try to keep your own life in order. That's far more important."

Another time, when Rodger saw the married couple Henry and Florence Higby entering church and walking down the centre aisle to their pew, he whispered to Matt, "I heard that Florence is having a relationship with another man."

Matt replied, "I'll talk to you when we get home."

And when they arrived home, Matt asked, "Who told you that Florence was having a relationship with another man?"

"Somebody in church. He told me not to tell any-body his name."

"I asked you a question and I want an answer. *Now.*"

"It was Lloyd. Lloyd Graham."

"And who did Lloyd hear the story from?

"I don't know—he wouldn't tell me."

"I see. And how old is Lloyd now."

"Sixteen."

Matt nodded. "Tell me, do you think he likes Florence?"

"No, I guess not. She once caught him marking something on the side of the church and reported him to Father. He's told me other bad stuff about her in the past."

"And did you believe him?"

"Well, I—"

"There's an old striped feather pillow in the linen cupboard. Bring it to me and a pair of scissors."

When Rodger did so, Matt led him outside to the centre of the backyard and said, "Now cut the end of the pillow open and shake the feathers out."

"I don't understand. I—"

"Just do it."

"But it's windy and—"

"Just *do* it."

And when Rodger did, the wind caught the feathers and blew them in all directions."

"Now," Matt said, "I want you to pick up every feather."

Rodger stared at him. "I can't do that. Most of them are gone. It's impossible."

"Yes, it is. And it's just as impossible to stop the spread of gossip once it starts. So don't you ever be the one to allow it to start. And don't you ever be the one to spread it."

As the years passed and he grew into manhood, Rodger found countless opportunities to exercise and practise Matt's wisdom, for he soon discovered that most of us prefer to search for and dwell upon people's faults rather than their admirable points. While in his early twenties, he read an essay by Eleanor Roosevelt which stated that "Great minds discuss ideas, average minds discuss events, small minds discuss people." Sage advice, but extremely difficult to follow strictly.

Now, as he glanced around the tiny chapel at the intent, prayerful men before him, he asked himself, Where is that humility now? He had refused to sing until goaded by Rocky, and merely mumbled the prayers. With his future life at stake, had he merely come here to close his mind and pompously shut out whatever the retreat had to offer? With nothing else going for him, he had to at least try!

As he entered the basement dining room for breakfast, Herbert waved him to a table where he, Jerome, Rocky and his father, and Rocky's friend sat. and Rodger unwillingly joined them, afraid they'd think they were being shunned if he did otherwise. Now, with his father beside him, Rocky had little to say and sat sulking like a child who'd been refused a piece of candy, and Rodger realized that, even in his late twenties, Rocky still carried the baggage of that hate relationship with his father that most men have left behind several years earlier.

Rocky's friend, Lyle, a puny little man in his early twenties who appeared to barely break five feet, also wore face jewellery and his arms and the sides of his neck were tattooed mainly with serpents and dragons in full colour. But his blonde hair and milky skin indicated that he rarely ventured into the sun for fear of burning, causing the jewellery and the tattoos to look extraneous on him, like apples on a pear tree, almost as though Rocky had convinced him against his will to have them done to make himself appear more manly. And af-ter hearing Lyle speak, Rodger quickly became convinced of the truth of this because Lyle spoke with that soft, velvety cuteness reserved for some gays. Now, the reason for the compulsory adoring looks Lyle kept giving Rocky, and Rocky's misogynous rap lyrics, all became perfectly clear. It becomes far easier to degrade and despise women when you no longer require them for your sexual pleasure.

This new information left Rodger confused. Would the real Rocky please stand up! Was Rocky gay, straight, or bisexual? If gay, he was using Jane and playing her for a fool; if straight, he was using Lyle and playing him for a fool; if bisexual, he was using them and play them both for fools. As he glumly ate his corn flakes and sipped his orang juice, Rodger suddenly felt tired of trying to understand the dark corridors of Rocky's convoluted life and decided, since his time here was so short, to turn his attention back to the real reason he came on retreat: to discover how to proceed with his own life.

Meanwhile, Herbert and Jerome were like broken records, continuing in the same boring, complaining vein as the previous evening.

Rocky's father, Peter, a portly, balding man in his late fifties with a neatly trimmed beard, spoke sternly and demandingly to Rocky about his behaviour while on retreat, and Rocky simply kept nodding absently, aware that away from his father he could live his own life and be content with the knowledge that he'd gotten his pound of flesh by bringing Lyle and the beer along. In spite of himself, Rodger couldn't let go. He now saw the situation as possible material for his book and wondered if Rocky's rebellion and prolonged hatred for his father could be blamed on Peter's condescending attitude toward him. Was his homosexuality actually genuine, or, even in his late twenties still just his continued retaliation against a stern and rigid upbringing? For that matter, was even his misogyny genuine, or merely another way to scandalize his father and possibly some day bring in the income which would allow him to leave home permanently and persist in an amoral field merely for the sake of making money.

Rodger tried to stir the pot by questioning Peter about Rocky's behaviour, expecting to expose a tyrannical father. Instead, he found an extremely tolerant one who believed that he could only lead by example and Rocky must find his own way in life. Rodger tried to probe Peter regarding Rocky's musical taste, and even hinted at the gay relationship between Rocky and Lyle, but Peter refused to swallow the bait, closing down the conversation by firmly stating his conviction that Rocky would eventually find his way.

At 9:30 a.m., Rodger attended a session in the lounge/library with about three dozen other men. When Mark, the spiritual advisor conducting the session, asked each man in turn how he had spent the past year and what he had achieved spiritually and otherwise, most of the men spoke frankly on subjects like losing loved ones, problems and achievements with their marriages, with their children, with their jobs and their employers, and with their faith, but when it came to Rodger's turn he felt nervous about exposing his current marital and identity problems to strange men and could only say that it had been an ordinary year at his and Claudia's jobs and that there were no important changes.

Mark had a few retreatants pass around several coloured sheets to each man. When Rodger looked at a blue sheet, his eyes widened and it grabbed his attention because the two headings at the top of the page were "False Self" and "True Self" and in the column below each heading were listed the ten characteristics of each. He immediately found a personal connection here, for hadn't he been living inside the body of a False Self for over ten years? And hadn't he been searching for his True Self since the morning after his tenth anniversary? Directly below False Self were two separate circles beside each other, the larger circle almost twice the diameter of the smaller circle, slightly above it, and containing the word "SELF," the smaller circle containing the word "ego." Directly below True Self were also two circles with the smaller circle joined near the bottom of the larger circle, the larger circle exactly twice the diameter of the smaller circle and containing the word "GOD," the smaller circle containing the word "ego."

Before Rodger could study the sheet further, Mark took the floor and began to speak. "Gentlemen, we are now going to study the blue False Self-True Self sheet," he said, holding up the sheet. "Please follow along. Under False Self, we see by the position and size of the two circles, and that the word SELF is in capitals and the word ego is in lower case, that SELF, not ego, controls this type of person.

"Number 1: This type of person is characterized by *separateness and self sufficiency*. He, not God, is going to be in complete control of his life.

"Number 2: The disconnected self. This state represents a loss to God because we have lost our true selves which are a part of God.

"Number 3: he must keep manufacturing and concocting himself because his whole world revolves around himself instead of around God.

"Number 4: He must constantly reinvent himself, constantly keep trying to develop his personality to cope with the demands of the world.

"Number 5: He needs to constantly justify and validate himself.

" Number 6: He needs to constantly assert himself in his drive for achievement and power.

"Number 7: He needs to protect himself, and has immense security needs because he alone has made himself responsible for all of his actions.

"Number 8: He is inherently needy and fragile because he knows that if *he* loses, *everything* is lost. Because of this constant pressure, he is prone to addictions to satisfy himself.

"Number 9: Because his pressurized and demanding world is closed within himself, he must look outside himself for happiness.

"Number 10: Because he has renounced God, in sin, he constantly feels lost and alienated.

"Now," Mark continued, "let's explore the characteristics of the True Self and note the differences. Here we see that the small circle, "ego," is connected to the large circle, "GOD," because this person's life is centred around god's will and living the religious life.

"Therefore, Number 1 states that the True Self is characterized by *contentment and communion with God.*

"Number 2: The re-aligned self. This state is like the grain of wheat which has died to its restricted boundaries to become the Large Self, the God Self, the Christ Self. The man who has discovered this state has found enlightenment.

334 LESLIE G. SABO

"Number 3: No concocting, no manufacturing—this man only needs to discover himself.

"Number 4: No reinventing because he is already original and whole.

"Number 5: His faith has already justified and validated him.

"Number 6: No need to constantly assert himself because he is naturally humble and non-violent.

"Number 7: Nothing to protect because his faith makes him impenetrable and indestructible.

"Number 8: He is inherently joyous and satisfied.

"Number 9: He finds happiness within *and* without.

"Number 10: He is constantly partaking of the banquet of life, the true wholeness available to each one of us, the free gift of God."

As Rodger listened, he could clearly see that he fitted snugly into most of the ten descriptions of the False Self, and into almost none of the True Self, which failed to surprise him considering the life he had led for the past ten years. But could he be absolutely certain that all his problems simply stemmed from not following his religion? Of course not. There had to be something else… some other way.

Yet why are you here? What did you expect to find by coming here? What other answer can there possibly be in a monastery? Did you actually expect some different solution?—or are you merely hoping.

After the first segment of Mark's presentation, he reminded the group that Father Luke would be hearing confessions in the chapel starting at 11 a.m. A discussion period followed where many of the men participated, revealing personal details and problems of their lives, but again Rodger refused to discuss his own problems publicly and waited for the session to end before approaching Mark and asking to speak to him privately.

But Mark refused to offer the panacea that Rodger wanted to hear. After Rodger explained his marital and personal problems, Mark simply said, "Even though you may want to better your life, your life is still being largely controlled by your False Self.

You're looking for a solution to your problems, but you seem to be only interested in solving your problems on your own terms, without making any sacrifices. I know you want me to give you something else, something more to your liking, but only the church's teaching can bring you back to your True Self, and I can't give you any better advice than that. I'm not a marriage counsellor, but you seem to have some deep problems there. In any case, you're far better off to talk to a priest about them instead of me."

No help there. No exceptions. No coddling. Nothing but the long, hard religious road to fulfilment. With still almost an hour until lunch, Rodger returned sullenly to his room to brood about his condition, diligently searching his mind for a solution, any solution outside the church which would guide him to his True Self through another door, some unknown back door which he could sneak silently through and there, suddenly, come face to face with his True Self. But what door? And where? The more he scoured his mind the more frustrated and deflated he became. Perhaps, he reasoned, he didn't actually need to rid himself of *all* the failings listed on the False Self list. Perhaps he only needed to rid himself of one or two to achieve his goal. For example, instead of sitting in the church's front pew, perhaps he only needed to step inside the church's back door, and stand there, and simply breathe in the atmosphere, and that would be sufficient for him to find his True Self. In other words, maybe he could merely hang around the fringe of the church, attached to it only by a few tenuous threads, and that alone would be enough. After all, he still had issues with God and His church, didn't he? Serious issues, deep doubts, unanswered questions which he hadn't even admitted to Matt but which, in spite of all his early reading in religion and theology, still haunted him. He fully realized that from the moment he entered the retreat centre he had been vacillating, rationalizing, making excuses for himself instead of clearly accepting his faith. Still, he refused to surrender, knowing that somewhere along the line there had to be a showdown between him and his God. And he knew that this showdown had to happen soon, before he returned home tomorrow. To Claudia.

He glanced at his watch. Eleven-fifteen. Father Luke had already been listening to confessions for fifteen minutes. How long would it take him to hear the confessions of about three dozen men? Probably no longer than an hour, especially if most of the men had little to report. Would he go and make his first confession in more than ten years and begin by telling Father Luke that he'd missed Mass more than five hundred times since his last confession? His pride advised him to stay away. Lacking the humility required to confess his sins, he'd always hated confession. As a child enrolled in a Catholic school, when he knew that the priest would be attending the school regularly to hear students' confessions, he always tried to behave so perfectly between the priest's visits that he'd have little or practically nothing to confess. But not today. Today he'd have to admit that he'd missed Mass more than five hundred times—and he balked at the idea. But, as much as he hated the idea, he eventually softened his stance by telling himself repeatedly that he would feel much better later because his confession would lift a huge weight from his soul. Yet he couldn't help envisioning the look on Father Luke's face after hearing Rodger's admission.

As he entered the chapel and blessed himself, he saw several men seated in the pews awaiting their turns. To his right were the three doors of the confessional box, the centre door for the priest, the two side doors for the penitents. One of the Filipinos emerged from the sacristy to the right of the altar, closed the door, knelt in the first pew and made the sign of the cross. Another man seated near the front entered the sacristy. Rodger studied the silent confessional box and noticed that the centre door was slightly ajar. He opened it quietly. The interior had been gutted and converted into a storage closet. To his dismay, he realized that confessions were being heard in the new manner: face to face in the sacristy. He would be deprived of the dark anonymity of the confessional box and be forced into the light of the sacristy where he'd be required to sit facing Father Luke and look him straight in the eye while confessing his sins. For a moment, Rodger thought of turning away and simply returning to his room and forgetting about the whole thing, but eventually slid silently into a pew. Pride.

Foolish pride clinging to us all like Velcro. When he managed the bookstore, one of his customers told him that when she asked a woman acquaintance who had to be well into her eighties how old she was, she looked down her nose at her and replied coldly, "No one knows how old I am, and no one will ever know, not even after I'm gone, because my age won't even be in my obituary, or on my gravestone." Foolish pride. He once saw a woman in her early eighties attest to that pride at an Orangeville polling station where the ballots were being cast on the second floor. When asked if she'd prefer to take the chairlift to the second floor, she asserted proudly, "No! I'm not 102 years old! I'm perfectly capable of climbing the stairs, thank you!" And after she'd finished voting and someone asked if she'd prefer to take the chair-lift down, she snapped, "No! I'd sooner fall down the stairs than take that chairlift down!" That foolish pride—where would it take her in the future when a bad hip forced her to walk with a cane or a walker or ride in a wheelchair? Would she then say, "No! I'd sooner *die* than show people that I'm wearing out and growing old!" and then commit suicide because she refused to face her own mortality? Still, these women didn't have his problem to contend with: confessing his sins to a priest, which he hadn't done for over ten years.

But he needn't have worried. Father Luke turned out to be a thin, bearded, balding priest who appeared to be in his mid-seventies, his expression remaining calm and passive as Rodger confessed, as though he'd heard the same thing hundreds of times before. And even when Rodger admitted that he no longer remembered the Act of Contrition, Father Luke calmly said it for him. But the priest had no qualms about the severity of Rodger's sins and gave him a complete rosary to say as his penance. Knowing that Father Luke still had other confessions to hear, yet wanting to discuss his marital situation with him, he asked if they could meet for a private discussion after the two p.m. Mass. Father Luke agreed that they would meet in the sacristy.

After lunch, Rodger returned to his room with about an hour to spend in reflection before Mass. Idly, he opened Thomas Merton's *No Man is an Island,* a book he hadn't opened since his marriage, and the dedication on the front flyleaf surprised him, largely because he'd forgotten all about it, and felt a twinge of guilt as he read, "To my son, Rodger, on his 21st birthday. May this book inspire you to great things in God's name.Dad."

He'd read the book at that time, and been deeply moved by certain chapters, pencilling in marginal brackets in areas which impressed him the most, but now, after the book had sat gathering dust for ten years on a bookshelf in his den, he remembered little. As he turned to Chapter 1, "Love Can Be Kept Only By Being Given Away," and began searching for sections bracketed as relevant, he suddenly sat bolt upright as he came upon a paragraph which read: "To love another is to will what is really good for him. Such love must be based on truth. A love that sees no distinction between good and evil, but loves blindly merely for the sake of loving, is hatred, rather than love. To love blindly is to love selfishly, because the goal of such love is not the real advantage of the beloved but only the exercise of love in our own soul. Such love cannot seem to be love unless it pretends to seek the good of the one loved. But since it actually cares nothing for the truth, and never considers that it may go astray, it proves itself to be selfish. It does not seek the true advantage of the beloved or even our own. It is not interested in the truth, but only in itself. It proclaims itself content with an apparent good: which is the exercise of love for its own sake, without any consideration of the good or bad effects of loving."

Was this Claudia? Did she love him selfishly, for no other reason than to gain her own ends? Troubled, he read the next bracketed paragraph: "The first step to unselfish love is the recognition that our love may be deluded. We must first of all purify our love by renouncing the pleasure of loving as an end in itself. As long as pleasure is our end, we will be dishonest with ourselves and with those we love. We will not see their good, but our own pleasure."

He read further, the book now clenched in his hands: "A selfish love seldom respects the rights of the beloved to be an autonomous person. Far from respecting the true being of another and granting his personality room to grow and expand in its own original way, this love seeks to keep him in subjection to ourselves. It insists that he conform himself to us, and it works in every possible way to make him do so. A selfish love withers and dies unless it is sustained by the attention of the beloved. When we love thus, our friends exist only in order that we may love them. In loving them we seek to make pets of them, to keep them tame. Such love fears nothing more than the escape of the beloved. It requires his subjection because that is necessary for the nourishment of our own affections.

"Selfish love often appears to be unselfish, because it is willing to make any concession to the beloved in order to keep him prisoner. But it is supreme selfishness to buy what is best in a person, his liberty, his integrity, his own autonomous dignity as a person, at the price of far lesser goods. Such selfishness is all the more abominable when it takes a complacent pleasure in its concessions, deluded that they are all acts of selfless charity."

Did these sentences not perfectly describe Claudia? And did they not prove that her so-called love over the past ten years had been nothing more than a cruel farce, that she only sought her own selfish ends and didn't really love him at all? He had to have it out with her, had to force her to confess the truth. And if she did, then what? His muddled mind groped for answers. Could he continue to live with Claudia in a ludicrous marriage? The questions accumulated, but no definite answers came. Maybe Father Luke could help.

At Mass in the tiny chapel, something strange happened. Just before Mass began, Father Luke went to the side tabernacle to retrieve the hosts for communion and place them on the altar. To unlock the golden tabernacle door, he turned a key on a thin, beaded chain from which hung, laminated inside clear plastic, a rectangular bright red image on white of Christ as The Sacred Heart. After removing the golden ciborium containing the hosts, he turned the key back to the locked position and left it there. Rodger noticed that this motion had caused The Sacred Heart to begin swinging back and forth like a pendulum. He saw this as normal and turned his attention to the Mass, expecting The Sacred Heart to stop swinging at any moment, but when he looked again, minutes later, the swinging still hadn't stopped or shown any sign of even diminishing. Looking for a sensible explanation, he told himself that something within the chapel kept causing The Sacred Heart to continue swinging. A draught from the small side window about five feet away? But he could see that no draught could come from a fixed window which couldn't even be opened. A fan somewhere, perhaps on the ceiling? But there were no fans anywhere. Unable to find an explanation, he became anxious, disturbed, his stare probing The Sacred Heart and refusing to turn away, his mind willing it to stop swinging. But it swung on, taunting him. In desperation, he laughed inwardly, and told himself that the entire incident was ludicrous. *Something* in the chapel *must* be keeping The Sacred Heart swinging. But what? He brushed aside as silly the vain idea that it could possibly have anything whatsoever to do with him, and looked around hungrily to see if someone else, who could possibly be the recipient of some secret message from God, stared at The Sacred Heart, but anyone close enough to see appeared intent on the Mass. He realized suddenly that he now actually believed that the swinging Sacred Heart held some secret, spiritual meaning, but again he laughed inwardly, knowing the absolute foolishness of believing that God would ever communicate with him, and jerked his attention back to the Mass. But the swinging Sacred Heart kept luring him back again and again, swinging...swinging...until he actually hurled his humility to the winds and began to believe that all this *had* something to do with him. He found himself thinking indignantly, *What do You want from me? Damn it, stop swinging and leave me alone! I have issues with You and I don't intend to let You off the hook until they're settled—do You hear me?—I have serious issues with You!*

After he walked up the aisle and received communion, he had to pass directly in front of the tabernacle to return to his seat. Was it merely his distraught imagination, or had The Sacred Heart actually *swung harder* as he passed before it? His mind now in shambles, he couldn't be certain.

After Mass, on his way to the sacristy to speak to Father Luke, the swinging Sacred Heart still taunted him. Alone now in the chapel, he felt a sudden urge to reach out, grab it, stop its incessant movement, but his hand froze, then began to tremble as it neared the tabernacle and a deep, shivering chill rushed through his body. What if, after he stopped the swinging and released The Sacred Heart, the swinging started again? With no one else in the chapel, wouldn't that prove that the spiritual message was meant only for him? And what could that message be but a severe criticism of the past ten wasted years of his life? Afraid, he pulled back, laughing inwardly again, telling himself again that the whole incident was ludicrous, that something within the chapel kept causing The Sacred Heart to keep swinging, but his laughter had become weak, pitiful, no longer derisive, and as he drew away the warmth returned to his body.

The sacristy door opened and Father Luke stepped out. "Oh, you're here. I thought you might have forgotten our appointment and left."

"No." He thought of telling Father Luke the truth, but quickly decided against it, feeling that even a priest might think it all laughable. "No, I was just admiring The Sacred Heart," he lied, following Father Luke inside.

"Now, what can I do for you?" Father Luke asked as they sat facing each other.

"It's my wife, Father. I believe that she doesn't love me and wonder what I should do about it."

"How long have you been married?"

"Ten years."

"And how long have you believed this?"

Rodger hesitated, reluctant to admit the truth, but finally said, "Just since I came here. I brought along a copy of Thomas Merton's *No Man Is an Island*. I'm sure you've read it."

Father Luke smiled benignly. "Yes. I'm quite familiar with the works of Father Louis. Go on."

"Well, I was reading the first chapter: 'Love Can Be Kept Only by Being Given Away.' The description he gives there fits my wife perfectly. She doesn't love me—she's only using me to attain her own selfish pleasure."

"And how does she go about doing that?"

"She doesn't want what's good for me, even though she pretends to. She only wants what's good for herself and she doesn't care how she gets it. She loves, not because she loves me, but merely for the sake of loving. It doesn't matter who she loves—it could be any man she's physically attracted to. And then she'll enslave him, just as she has enslaved me for over ten years."

"Do you mean to say that you've been married for ten years and haven't suspected anything? That sounds incredible."

"I guess I've been a pretty passive husband," Rodger admitted. "I've trusted her because I love her, and simply went along with her most of the time. Of course, I've had a few doubts over the years, who hasn't, and even questioned her about one of them, but it's only during the last few weeks that I've begun to seriously examine our relationship. I guess it's because I'm going through my mid-life crisis and feel the need to do something worthwhile with the rest of my life, and I wanted to know if she felt the same desire with her own life. And when I began to question her I discovered that she didn't."

"I see. Has she ever given you any reason to believe that she's been unfaithful to you?"

Rodger's mind flashed back to Claudia's million-dollar real estate sale in Caledon East. "No...I mean I'm not absolutely certain. There was an incident about three years ago which has never been completely resolved to my satisfaction."

"And you've never brought the problem to a head?"

"No. I've discussed it with her a few times over the years but she always denies everything."

"Perhaps she has good reason to deny everything. Perhaps she's innocent."

"Perhaps, but I'm doubtful, and if she doesn't even love me...?"

"Before you make any hasty decisions, you must investigate further by confronting her and be absolutely positive that she doesn't love you, and be absolutely positive that she has committed adultery, and if your accusations are true, then you must decide whether you can continue to live with her. But you must first make a supreme effort to try to save your marriage."

"And if can't? If I find that everything is true, what are my alternatives?"

"An annulment is one solution, but that should be considered only as a very last resort, and it takes years to finalize. Before taking such a drastic step, you must do everything in your power to save the marriage. Does your wife attend Mass?"

"No. Never."

"Are there any children?"

"None. She didn't want any."

"Ah." Father Luke nodded knowingly. "This is one of the common preferences of...of controlling and ambitious women. Does your wife have some type of career?"

"She's a real estate agent, and works hard at it. She's a very materialistic person, always wants to keep moving up in the world."

"I see. And did you want children?"

"Yes. Actually I wanted two, a boy and a girl."

"But she convinced you otherwise, because she felt that her career was more important than raising a family."

"Yes," he admitted sheepishly. "It was just a few weeks ago, on our tenth wedding anniversary, when I began to delve more deeply into our relationship that I began to realize just how controlling she's been throughout our marriage, and how passive and understanding and forgiving I've been."

"I see. Is she a very attractive woman?"

"Yes. Very."

"Ah. Very attractive women are often quite capable of making men, especially their husbands, do things which they would rather not do, confident that their physical attractiveness combined with a healthy serving of women's wiles will get the job done. And what about you? Since you've confessed nothing, am I correct in assuming that you've never been unfaithful?"

"No. Never."

"Do you love your wife now, without the proof of her fidelity?"

"Yes, I...I think I do."

"You sound doubtful. Just how strong is your love? Would you continue to love her if you found the proof?"

"I...I don't know if I could. Ever since our tenth anniversary I've become suspicious of her, which I never was before because I was so passive and trusting. When I was reading about selfish love in *No Man Is An Island*, it seemed to describe her perfectly. And if that's true, she's only interested in what she can get out of me, using me in any way she can. Knowing that, I doubt that I could continue to love her."

"Regardless of that, you must do everything in your power to save your marriage," Father Luke said firmly. "I have, of course, read *No Man Is An Island*, and also know that Father Louis doesn't recommend a breakup in such a marriage. He even provides guidelines for turning selfish love into unselfish love. If, in fact, your wife is as you seem to think she is, then you must first attempt to transform her love by using these guidelines."

"And if that fails? Annulment aside, what's my alternative then?"

Instead of answering, Father Luke gazed at the wall and remained silent for what seemed to Rodger to be a long time. Finally, he asked, "My son, why did you come here this weekend?"

"Well, to find myself. To discover the real me. I feel as though I've been living a false life for the past ten years. I thought that if I came here and closed myself in my room and kept thinking about my problem that I'd eventually arrive at a suitable alternative. But now I'm just confused."

"Ah, yes. Of course you're confused. You're confused because of your 'suitable alternative.' Suitable to whom? To you or to God? Because only those suitable to God are worth following. It strikes me that you're trying to escape your true destiny. You came here thinking that you'd close yourself in your room and search your heart for a suitable alternative to your present, unfulfilled life. But now, after listening to Brother Mark's presentation, and reading Father Louis, and listening to me, who all keep telling you to listen to your *soul* instead of your heart, you're confused. But in truth there is nothing to be confused about, is there? Follow your soul instead of your heart, instead of your own personal desires, and it will lead you to the peace and fulfilment you're searching for."

"And how do I do that?"

"I can't tell you that. Your soul must give you the answer."

As Rodger left the sacristy, his gaze fastened on The Sacred Heart as though drawn by a magnet, and he was astonished to see that it had stopped swinging. But his astonishment quickly became complacency. So, he thought smugly, it had all been nothing more than a draught somewhere after all, nothing more than the outside wind entering through a crack or a hole, which had now subsided,. Still, he felt tense and nervous as he gazed at The Sacred Heart because he also knew what else the stillness could mean. From the edge of his mind, he could hear a deep, masculine voice saying, "I've delivered the message. Now I'm waiting for you."

With still about a half hour before Mark's afternoon session, he returned morosely to his room and sat dejectedly in the darkness. He felt a growing tension, a growing frustration and anger because after weeks of searching he now felt no closer to a solution than he had when he began. Yet he knew where the answer lay. Knew it but had been pushing it to the corners of his mind for years because he feared to confront it. Knew that he couldn't possibly move ahead until he had resolved his issues with God. Unanswered questions which haunted him could no longer crowd his mind, crying out for answers which never came, were never found. God had plenty to answer for, and he wouldn't make it easy for Him. And only if He answered satisfactorily could he possibly believe again as he had in his childhood.

Seeing the retreat inexorably coming to an end, and with his mind filled with his own concerns, Rodger paid little attention at Mark's second session, which devoted itself mainly to further exploring and deepening the attributes of the False Self and the True Self, and wondered why he hadn't remained in his room. Instead of listening, he found himself rehearsing what he would say to God when the time came. He couldn't mumble or be indecisive like some callow schoolboy; he had to know exactly what he wanted to say and say it like a man. At this thought, he looked down and saw that his hands were trembling.

At dinner, sullen and silent, he barely tasted his food and left half of it on his plate, ignoring the conversation of those at the table, intensely jealous of those men around him in the dining room who had apparently found the peace and contentment in their religion which still eluded him after weeks of searching elsewhere.

Angry, frustrated, vengeful, he stopped at the main entrance on his way back to his room and looked out through the glass doors. Dark clouds were rolling in; it would soon be dark. He heard a faint clap of thunder in the distance.

Inside his room, he picked up *No Man is an Island* and tried to read, but only managed a few paragraphs and even those passed blankly through his mind. He tossed the book onto the bed and paced the small floor restlessly, his hands balled into angry fists. Back and forth, back and forth, fuming, castigating himself, castigating others, castigating God, pounding his fist repeatedly into his open hand. He looked out the window and saw that it had grown very dark and the rumbles of thunder were closer, louder, more frequent. He didn't give a damn. He had to get out! He had to vent his frustration , had to have it out with Him! Grabbing his jacket, he left the room, left the retreat centre, started walking away along a path into the gusty darkness. Finally, he found himself at the edge of a grassy hill which led down to a small lake, well out of earshot of the retreat centre.

Now it's between You and me, he thought. Just You and me.

He raised his arms and pointed toward the blackened sky. "We know *nothing*," he shouted. "We understand *nothing*. We clutch at You, but as we squeeze we realize that You're nothing more than a handful of mercury which drains away between our fingers. You feed us crumbs from Your table, but refuse to feed us the meal. Not one of us knows for certain where we go after we breathe our last and leave this earth because You are a total conundrum. Even the vast, brilliant mind of St. Thomas Aquinas couldn't explain You in almost two thousand pages of *The Summa Theologica*. In the end, defeated, all he could murmur was a humble, 'It's all straw.' Even his great mind couldn't penetrate Your dark secrets because You hold all the cards and play only a few of them. You are the Head Honcho, the Grand Poobah, the Big Boss who tolerates no disobedience from His slaves.

"I bring You anger. I bring You *rage*. I vilify You. Do You understand, I *vilify* You. You are a secretive God, an angry God, a cruel God, a vengeful God, a sadistic God, a merciless God. You, who have the power to change whatever You wish, bring us pestilence, AIDS, floods, hurricanes, typhoons, tsunamis, raging fires. You kill millions with a mere snap of Your almighty fingers."

The wind grew, swirling in all directions, whipping at his body, but he only growled and leaned forward into it, as though leaning against the force of God Himself, and shouted even louder.

"It's said in *The Bible* that You make us in Your own image, but You give us free will which won't allow us to retain that image. By exercising that free will, we become Hitlers, Mussolinis, Stalins, Husseins, other dictators, murderers, thieves, rapists, and adulterers. Even Your own Popes slaughtered heretics in the Middle Ages. Is this what You wanted by giving us free will? To see millions upon millions of innocent people, created in Your own image, slaughtered for Your own pleasure? Is this the kind of beastly God You are? Admit it, You made a mistake here. Because even God can make a mistake, can't He? You thought that it would work, didn't You? You thought that all You had to do was give everyone free will and everyone would automatically do the right thing, behave morally, responsibly, generously, lovingly, unselfishly. But it didn't work, did it? But why, when You could have stopped it, did You not? But surely even God needs to rest. Were You asleep for centuries? Did You not *smell* the sickening stench of burning flesh as mil-lions of Jews—men, women, children—were roasted in the ovens at Auschwitz? Did You not *hear* the horrifying screams of millions of men being slaughtered in countless wars, and millions of innocent people being slaughtered by animalistic tyrants and dictators? Did You not *see* the battlefields swimming in blood and littered with the guts of the uncountable dead? Did You not *feel* that something had gone horribly wrong with Your plan?

"Tell me, God, where is our soul? Is it between the liver and the kidneys? Between the heart and the stomach? Tucked in behind the pancreas? Nestled between the lungs? Clinging to the appendix? Perched atop the intestines? Where? Wouldn't it have been better if You had allowed us to see our souls on CAT Scans or X-rays, ranging from black to white to denote their moral condition, so that we actually knew that we had them? Wouldn't it have been better if everyone *knew* that they had souls and *knew* that because of these souls they had life everlasting? Wouldn't that have made the world a much better place to live in? And wouldn't it have been far better to have simply created a race of fundamentally *good* people? People who lived lovingly. People who were honest. People who trusted each other. People who didn't have to live behind locked doors. But that wouldn't do for You, would it, Mr. Grand Poobah? Because if all human beings were born good and *knew absolutely* that they would remain so because they had no free will to do otherwise, and *knew absolutely* that they had souls, and *knew absolutely* that they were all bound some day for an eternal heaven, then what would be the point of all the gruelling struggles of living? So You gave us free will, and beasts instead of human beings, and the deaths of millions of innocent men, women, children, and infants. Is it just a matter of space with You? Do You see Your battered and bruised old world bulging at the seams with humanity? Is that Your only rationale for the mindless wholesale slaughter which You knew had to come?

"Tell me, how far does Your universe extend? How many galaxies? How many millions of miles? Or is it billions of miles? Do even You know the answer? It can't go on forever, can it? Everything must have an end *somewhere.* If this is true, then is the universe itself encased in some gigantic box or sphere? And if so, beyond that box or sphere—what? You are a secretive God who gives us no answers, only more and more questions.

"Faith faith faith, that's all we're ever given. We're told that we must have faith, that we can't possibly understand Your ways because Your ways are not our ways. That's all You give us to go on. So we try to keep building up our faith, keep shovelling more coal into the furnace to keep building up the fire because faith alone isn't much and the fire keeps dwindling or dying. Is that all You can give us? That and the infamous handout of will power? *It isn't enough!*

"You tell us to obey the commandments, to be humble, generous, loving, unselfish, and if we are our reward will be eternal life in heaven, but answer me this: Isn't seeking eternal life in heaven as a reward for living a good life the most ultimate selfishness possible? Could anyone possibly be *more* selfish? And if a person actually finds *joy* in being humble, generous, loving, and unselfish, where is the sacrifice?"

The wind grew even stronger and swirled angrily around him, his pantlegs flapping wildly like flags, and the thunder, now booming and frequent, had come much closer. Light rain began to fall. "I'm not afraid of You!" he yelled at the top of his voice, jabbing his forefingers at the black sky. "C'mon, bring it on! Blow me off the face of the earth! Rip my clothes off with Your wind! Here, I'll help you!" He yanked off his jacket and flung it aside, tore open his shirt and threw it into the wind, toppled to the damp grass in a heavy gust of wind as he tried to remove a shoe. Sitting there, he yanked off his shoes and flung them skyward one by one, yelling, "Here! *Here!*" Casting his socks aside, he pulled off his slacks and underwear, struggled to his feet and heaved them skyward. "*Here!*" he shrieked. "This is what You want, isn't it? You want to see me stripped down to the bare nothingness that I am in Your eyes. The bare nothingness, the basest grains of sand that we all are in Your eyes. Damn You. *Damn* You!" A violent clap of thunder burst the black clouds above and a deluge of cold rain pounded down, totally drenching him in seconds. "Dear God," he pleaded. "What do You *want* of me? What the *hell* do You *want* of me? Tell me. *Please tell me!*" He raised his face toward the black sky and allowed the cold rain to wash over him, his hands now clasped above his head as though in prayer, tears flowing freely and mingling with the rain. "Dear, dear God, in God's name, in Your name...please... I'm begging You...please...please wash me clean of this polluting will which forces me to doubt everything instead of accepting You completely."

Exhausted, sobbing uncontrollably now, he fell to his knees as the angry wind drove him forward and he began to rock back and forth like a wounded animal, his head bowing deeply forward, an agonizing, open-mouthed wail bursting from him each time his head struck the soggy grass as he felt his body dryly regurgitating his many years of doubt and disbelief and hollowing it out of him, until he gasped, "Jesus...Jesus...*Jesus!*"

14

When Rodger arrived home at two o'clock on Sunday afternoon, he barely had time to put his bags down and close the door before Claudia came rushing toward him and into his arms, crying, "Darling, I'm so glad you're home! I've missed you so terribly!" She kissed him hungrily, feverishly clutching him to her. But he knew definitely now that it was all a game, a game in which Claudia only honestly cared about one winner, herself, and he could only muster a lukewarm response to her greeting.

Concerned, Claudia drew away. "Is something wrong, darling?"

"Yes, something is very wrong."

She studied him closely. "Are you all right, darling? You look pale. Did they treat you well? Did they feed you properly?"

"Yes, they treated me very well," he said flatly, unable to keep the coolness from his voice. "And I'm all right. Perfectly all right for the first time in ten years."

"What does that mean?" she asked suspiciously. "Have you made some sort of decision?"

"Yes, I have, but right now I don't know what I'm going to do about it, or where I'm going with it. If I'm going to pursue this thing, whatever it is, I'm going to have to do something tomorrow, and I'm still not sure that I can do it. And if I can't do it, the whole thing is nothing but a charade and I might as well just continue living my life exactly the way it is now."

"And what is this thing you intend to do? Or not do?"

"I can't tell you now. I'll tell you tomorrow, after the fact. And if I don't do it—well, there's really no reason for me to tell you at all, is there?"

"I'm your wife, Rodger," she said indignantly. "Don't you think I have a right to know?"

"You will know. Tomorrow."

"But if you don't tell me what you're thinking of doing, and you don't do it, I'll never know, will I?"

"That's probably best."

She stared at him suspiciously. "You're not going to do something *foolish*, are you?"

"No. I think it'll be one of the most brave and sensible things I've ever done in my life."

As usual, Rodger arrived at Drummond's on Monday morning at 8:45, fifteen minutes early, in time to deposit his briefcase on his desk and perform his usual chore of starting a carafe of morning coffee, normally hearing the soft drone of the exercycle as he passed by Drummond's closed office door. Instead, this morning he stopped at Drummond's door and reached out, his raised fist halting only inches from the door as he reflected on the repercussions this decision would cause in his life—if he followed through with it. When he found himself wavering, he steeled himself, shoved the thought resolutely from his mind, and knocked three times.

"Come in."

His suit jacket draped over the back of his desk chair, Bart Drummond continued cycling as Rodger entered, a light sheen of sweat on his forehead. "Only a few minutes to go. Sit down, Rodger, sit down. I'll be with you shortly."

"Thanks, I prefer to stand."

"Oh-oh. This sounds like something serious." But Drummond continued cycling.

"It is."

Drummond turned to look at him for a few seconds, but refused to leave the exercycle until a bell on the machine rang telling him that the session had ended. As Drummond approached his desk, Rodger observed him, a small, sturdy, slender man a few inches over five feet. Like most of Drummond's employees, Rodger knew all about the elevator shoes which added two inches to Drummond's height, making him look about five-foot-six. He also knew that short people often tried to compensate for their shortness by striving mightily to succeed, thereby proving to the world the fallacy of the stigma attached by so many to short people. Because of this, women rarely became attached to men shorter than themselves, which coincided perfectly with the intrinsic North American obsession with appearance rather than sub-stance. Rodger had sometimes wondered if this could be the main reason why Drummond had never married. For a while, because he had never seen or heard of Drummond ever going out with a woman, Rodger had thought that he might be gay, but had never witnessed anything to prove that either.

Although in his late fifties, Drummond's black hair remained thick and had barely begun to recede. Too black for a man in his late fifties, Rodger had often thought, suspicious that Drummond regularly used a dye. His small, deeply tanned head was mounted on a thin, wiry neck. Smallness dominated his face: dark brown eyes with eyelids that barely cleared the pupils, giving him a sinister Asian appearance, a curved, hawkish nose, thin-lipped mouth, compact ears—all seemed to have been created in miniature. The tiny cleft in his pointed chin could barely be seen unless examined closely. Even his teeth, still all his own, were smaller than normal, like a child's first set of teeth. But Rodger knew from experience that Drum-mond's small stature was more than augmented by his relentless drive for business success.

Drummond drew a Kleenex tissue from the box on the desk and wiped his forehead before slipping into his gray suit jacket with the pearl gray hand-kerchief in its breast pocket and the red rose in its lapel and seating himself at his desk. In a way, Drummond's red rose reminded Rodger of Trudeau, who always seemed to wear a red flower in his lapel. Impeccably dressed, as usual, Rodger thought. White shirt, striped tie, dress shoes polished to a high gloss. In all the years he'd worked for Drummond, he'd never once seen a wrinkle in the man's clothing.

"Sit down, Rodger, sit down," Drummond invited again. "Why are you being so formal?"

"I'd rather stand."

"You're not ill, are you? You look rather pale around the gills. You're getting a bit paunchy, aren't you? And are you losing your hair?"

Just like Drummond, Rodger thought, always commenting negatively on other people's health because he felt so confident and secure in his own health regimen which included daily sessions on the exercycle, a vegetarian diet, nothing to drink except pure fruit juices, herbal teas, or bottled water. Junk food and pastries were like poison to him, his only desserts being fresh fruit. A bottle of Vita-Vim 50+ vitamins, which he took regularly for extra energy, always stood on his desk. In excellent health, he regularly bragged to his employees about his low blood cholesterol and rarely missed an opportunity to warn those employees with pot bellies or spare tires to either get into shape or expect to live shortened lives. This tunnel vision regarding health sometimes went even further. Over his years with the company, Rodger could recall two occasions when overweight employees were dismissed be-cause Drummond felt that they were "presenting an unhealthy image to our clients."

"No, I'm okay," Rodger said. "But I need to talk to you."

Drummond raised a hand. "Just hold on a minute or two. Because what you intend to tell me can't possibly be more important than what I'm going to tell you. I was thinking of telling you in December, but I'll do it now because I'm anxious to tell you the good news."

"The good news?"

Drummond smiled. "Sit down, Rodger. Because after I tell you what I've got to say you'll want to sit down anyway."

Shrugging, Rodger sat down, placing his briefcase on the carpet beside the chair. "I don't understand."

"You will. Rodger, you've been with this company for a long time, several years. Work-wise, I've watched your production over the years closely, and I've been impressed. Idea-wise, you're always coming up with fresh material and unique copy. I believe that you're the best writer we have on staff, even better than Ray, and that's why I've decided to do what I'm going to do. Earnings-wise, you've been a great asset to this company, Rodger, and I want to show my appreciation for your stalwart effort over the years."

Rodger thought he understood the message now and said, "If you're going to give me a raise, I—"

"A raise? Is that what you've been thinking about?" Drummond laughed. "Oh no, Rodger, it's much more than that. Much, much more." He straightened in his chair, interlaced his fingers on the desk, raised his chin and said proudly, "At the start of next year, you'll be signing a partnership agreement in the company which will entitle you to forty percent of net profits."

Stunned, Rodger's throat became suddenly dry and tight, making him speechless, and even if he could have spoken he wouldn't have known what to say because he found himself plunged into a turmoil of indecision. Thankfully, Drummond quickly filled the void.

"You look completely shocked. Well, I can't say that I blame you. I'll bet you never expected anything like *this*, did you? But remember this: don't think it's going to be a piece of cake work-wise. Of course, I still want you to continue writing commercials, but I also want to start breaking you into the management aspects of the business, and once I see that you're on the right track I want to step back a little, leisure-wise, and enjoy life, spend more time on the golf course and on the tennis court. And maybe some day, if and when I decide to retire, I might even give you the opportunity to buy the business from me."

Rodger still struggled to find his voice. Before entering Drummond's office, he knew what he intended to say, but this...? As he tried to sort out his thoughts, to buy time, he said weakly, "Are you ill?"

Drummond laughed. "Ill? Don't be silly. You should know better than that by now. Health-wise, I'm as fit as a horse."

"Then why? I don't understand. You've run this business for many years—why give it up now?" Rodger saw now the direction in which his thoughts were leading him. He was actually trying to *discourage* Drummond from making him a partner. Long familiar with Drummond's finicalness, he knew how tightly any partnership agreement written by Drummond's lawyer would be worded. Drummond would still be the boss. Breathing room would be scarce in the straitjacketed work environment that such an agreement would create. Long hours, home-work, and six-day weeks would be common, and Drummond's browbeating, now that Rodger would be sharing in the net profits, would be more prevalent and intense than ever when work failed to be completed on time or when he considered work second-rate. In short, Rodger knew that every drop of energy would be squeezed from him in trying to maintain the demands of the job. And in so doing, would he have even a minute to devote to changing his life and developing himself into a valuable human being?

Drummond said, "I didn't say I was giving it up—I said I might. Look, I want you to understand that everything we say here this morning is completely confidential. Everything about the partnership, and everything about what I'm going to tell you next. No one in this office knows a thing about any of this, and I don't intend to tell them until the proper time because plans are still up in the air. Do you understand? *No one* is to know *anything* about what we discussed here today."

"I understand perfectly."

Drummond rose, paced back and forth several times behind his desk, finally stopped and rested his hands on top of the chair as he faced Rodger. "I'm almost sixty years old, Rodger, and during that time I've known a few women. As a young man, I sowed a few wild oats, like most of us, but nothing serious ever became of any of it. And after I started this business, I just never had the time or even the inclination to pursue that facet of my life. And on the few occasions when I did, it just never worked out: I didn't want the women who wanted me, or vice versa. I've always wanted a wife. No children, but a good wife to come home to." Gripping the chair, Drummond paused, as though trying to decide whether to continue, then relaxed and said, "You see, Rodger, I've met someone." He quickly raised a cautious hand. "Oh, there's nothing definite yet, but she likes me very much and I feel exactly the same way about her. And we have a great deal in common. We're like two peas in a pod, you might say. Engagement-wise, I haven't asked her yet, but intend to very soon and I'm certain that she'll accept. So, marriage-wise, it looks like I'll probably soon be a husband. And I know it's not just the money because she's pretty well off herself, having spent most of her adult life as a secondary school teacher. The main point is that after we're married we're going to want to spend as much time together as possible to make up for lost time. She wants it that way, which means I'll eventually want to sell the business. And if you shape up the way I expect you to, it could be to you."

"No," Rodger said.

"What?" Drummond stared at him incredulously, his knuckles suddenly whitening as his fingers clutched at the top of the chair. "What did you say?"

"I said 'no.' You've been so wrapped up in telling me about the partnership agreement and selling the business that you haven't even bothered to ask me why I came here. Aren't you even the least bit curious?"

"Look," Drummond said angrily. "I've just offered you a way to make a hell of a lot of money and maybe even own your own business. What the hell could you have to say that's more important than that?"

"The reason that I came here this morning."

"And that is?"

"That I'm leaving, Bart."

"Leaving? Leaving what?"

"Leaving Drummond's. As of this morning, I don't work here any more."

"What the *hell* are you talking about?" He sat down and leaned menacingly forward across his desk. "Wait a minute— you're not just putting me on, are you?" he asked suspiciously. "You haven't approached Kendall's, have you? Is that what this is all about? They haven't offered you more money, have they? With a partnership here, I guarantee you that you'll make a hell of a lot more than they can ever offer you. How much are they willing to give you?"

Rodger raised a hand. "They haven't offered me anything because they haven't approached me and I haven't approached them, and I don't intend to. It's nothing like that because I'm getting out of advertising for good. Tell me, does everything have to come down to money for you? Do you think that every person in this world is only interested in how much they're worth?"

"Don't sneer at money—it can buy you a hell of a lot."

"Sure, material things, but not the important things. Not love, true friendship, or self-respect. Or a productive and worthwhile life. Because you have to earn those qualities."

"Then if it isn't the money, what is it? Why are you leaving advertising, a field that has paid you very well for several years?"

"I'll tell you why. Because over the years I've developed an intense abhorrence for the uselessness and frivolousness of a job which writes commercials for twelve-year-old mentalities about ass-wipe and pussy pads and toothpaste and shampoo and hair colouring. I'm sick to death of wasting my life writing trash for the masses."

Drummond's face reddened. "You thankless anus! You've been working here for several years, taking home big chunks of my money every week, and now you decide, *after several years*, that you're too damn good for the job. You lousy hypocrite!"

Rodger smiled inwardly. Over the years, he'd often been amused by some of the descriptive euphemisms that Drummond, who never swore, used, like calling him a "thankless anus" instead of using the term most men would have used: "thankless asshole." He said calmly, "Claudia thinks I'm going through the mid-life crisis, and maybe she's right, but it's more than that. A lot more—it's become a permanent problem that I now know is never going to leave me until I resolve it. I'm not a hypocrite. For weeks now, I've been trying to find myself, trying to find even a crumb of something, anything, that would give my life some lasting and moral value, and it's only since then that I've realized how abysmally empty it is. And how totally useless my work is."

"Useless?" Drummond shouted. "Do you call it useless when we write commercials for toilet tissue? You tell me, where would we be without toilet tissue and facial tissue? I'll tell you where we'd be: we'd be still wiping our anuses with Sears catalogues and blowing our noses with rags. You tell me, where would women be without sanitary napkins and tampons? I'll tell you where they'd be: they'd be still covering their vaginas with rags which they kept washing in the laundry. You tell me, where would we be without deodorant and antiperspirant? I'll tell you where we'd be: we'd be up to our eyeballs in stinking humanity and forced to look at dozens of people every day with those horrible sweatrings under there arms. You tell me, where we'd be without toothpaste and denture cleaner and mouthwash? I'll tell you where we'd be: we'd be back to brushing our teeth with our fingers and be subjected to halitosis from every person we spoke to at close range. How would you like to live in *that* kind of world? Yet you sit there and claim that our work here is useless. Well, thank God that other people, people in the know, don't think that." He swivelled his chair to the side, sprang to his feet, rushed to the wall and jabbed his forefinger at three large plaques that hung there. "I don't give a damn about your opinion—*these* are the opinions that *I* care about. The opinions of the C.A.I.O., who honoured me by presenting me with these three annual awards in recognition of the excellence of our work. They voted Drummond's the best in Ontario—the *best*.

"And *that's* what I care about. Business-wise, these awards give us publicity, let the public know that we do quality work which will bring them more business, and that in turn brings us more business and improves our bottom line. I'm proud of Drummond's, and proud of the work we do, and proud of the way our work stimulates the Canadian economy and helps to create jobs for thousands and thousands of Canadians." Drummond returned to his chair, sat down, placed his arms on the desk, leaned forward menacingly and glared at Rodger. "But you, the thankless anus who thinks he knows it all, in your profound ignorance believe our work here is useless."

Rodger ignored the insult. "But it's all for money, isn't it? And that's where the problem begins for me. Don't get me wrong, I have nothing against democracy or free enterprise—people need to earn a living. And I'm sure that over the years our commercials have helped to improve the bottom lines of giant conglomerates like Procter & Gamble, Colgate-Palmolive, Unilever, Weston's, and a number of others. Fine. Great. My personal concern is with the *methods we are forced to use to produce those bottom lines.* Because the big boys know what they want, and tell us, we are usually forced to work to their general or specific guidelines. After all, they're the ones who are paying us, aren't they? But these guidelines, especially if we're writing TV commercials, inevitably involve us pandering to a mass market with the IQ of a twelve-year-old. Although there are many millions of intelligent TV viewers, our commercials are certainly not written for them.

"If a young female pop singer, who I knew had a third-rate voice, bragged to me that she was worth twenty million dollars, the first question I'd ask her would be how she earned that money. And when she answered with something like, "Well, I just scream it out as loud as I can, and the music pretty much drowns me out, and I just keep wiggling my ass and wiggling my tits, and ramming my pelvis at the crowd, and grabbing at my crotch, and that's how I made all that money," then her money means absolutely nothing to me. If a movie star tells me that he's paid millions of dollars for every movie he makes, and I know that each one of his movies is merely a carbon copy of the one before, an empty, predictable piece of garbage in which the shootings, the car crashes, and the explosions never stop and you've lost count of the corpses before the movie is even half finished, then his money means absolutely nothing to me. Such people are completely without moral fibre. They are on their hands and knees pushing peanuts with their noses. And that's all we're doing around here: pushing peanuts with our noses all day long."

Drummond sneered. "And getting paid damn good money. How many tens of thousands have I paid you over the years? If you're so bloody high and mighty, why don't you return some of it to me then?"

"Well, I did earn it, didn't I?" Rodger countered. "I earned it in spades, spending years at a job I hated. If I'd enjoyed it, I wouldn't be here now, would I?"

"So now you're giving it all up. Packing it all in and getting out of advertising. For what? Career-wise, what do you plan to do next?"

"That's just it," Rodger admitted sheepishly, "I just don't know. I know that, one way or another, I'm going to publish this book I'm working on, which would prove helpful to anyone who reads it and applies the suggestions to their own lives, but beyond that I just don't know. The only thing I do know is that whatever I decide to do it'll be because I'm certain that it'll make some kind of positive difference in the world. Not only that—it'll be be-cause I'm certain that it's the one reason I was put on this earth for. You see, every one of us has been given a purpose for being here—we just have to find it. And it's a noble purpose, which has nothing whatsoever to do with material possessions, money, power, sex, or any of the other countless forms of self-indulgence. I don't want to go to my grave believing that I've just wasted all my time here, do-ing absolutely nothing for anyone else but me and mine."

A twisted sneer spread across Drummond's lips. "I suppose you've reverted back to the childish idealism of your youth and think you're going to save the world. Well, I've got news for you. Read history, the world went into the sewer many many centuries ago and has never come back up, and never will, and you'll be lucky if the piddly little bit you can do is even going to make a mis-erable crumb of difference."

"Maybe so. But when you put millions of miserable crumbs together, they become many loaves and do make a difference. Be-sides, each person is an individual. As Emerson wrote, each person has his or her own row to hoe, and I've learned over these past few weeks that no one else can instruct me on how to hoe mine. Yes, I'm concerned with the way the world is going down the drain, but my major concern isn't what *other people* are doing about it, but what *I'm* doing about it. I don't cheat on my income tax because some cheat tells me that 'everybody does it.' We are not here sim-ply to follow the herd when the herd is leading us over a cliff. Each one of us is given an individual responsibility to do something pro-ductive and worthwhile, in a noble sense, with our lives."

"Are you saying that my business isn't productive?" Drum-mond snapped. "I worked my posterior off for years and years to get here, often sixteen hours a day, and you come in here and tell me that it hasn't been productive? *Bullcrap!*"

"I'm talking about being productive in the noble sense; you're talking about being productive in the material sense."

"But the material sense is what makes things *happen.* Money is the *catalyst* which makes things happen. Philanthropy makes things happen. Cash donations by millions of individuals make things happen. If it weren't for all these, the world would be far deeper in the sewer than it already is."

"True, but writing cheques is easy, especially if you have the money. But too often the people who write these cheques feel that their job has been done once the cheques are mailed. Then they can pacify themselves by saying, 'Well, I've done my part. Now you can do yours.' I don't want to be like them; I want to *do* something.

"Most of the men who made the greatest positive changes in the world had no money. Christ and his disciples had no money, Gandhi had no money, Thomas Merton had no money, Socrates had no money, Albert Schweitzer had no money, and precisely because they had no money they were able to concentrate on the important values of life. Few of the saints were wealthy; most of them were simple, ordinary men and women. And maybe I ought to become as simple as they were. Maybe I ought to see if I can get a part-time job as a greeter at Wal-Mart."

Drummond laughed. "That's idiotic and you know it. Just listen to yourself—how low are you going to go? You're giving up the chance of a lifetime and you haven't even got a clue how you're going to replace it." His voice suddenly became calm and soothing. "Look, Rodger, there's nothing for you out there—you're just wasting your time. You've already found your proper niche and it's right here with Drummond. You're a valuable asset to this company, and would be a valuable asset to any company in this field. You're intelligent, creative, reliable, and for several years you've faithfully served as the true backbone of our writing staff. Please reconsider, for the good of the company. With you gone, too, you'd be putting me in a real bind. First Ray, now you—"

"Ray? What about Ray?"

Drummond looked puzzled. "Haven't you spoken to Ray lately? I thought you two were buddies."

"I was away on a retreat for the weekend. He told me that last week he'd be away on vacation. What about Ray?"

"Oh, I thought you knew the truth, but maybe I'm the only one who knew. I thought maybe he was the one responsible for making you want to leave. You see, Ray's gone."

"Gone?" Rodger felt a sudden cold chill run down his spine and shivered involuntarily, then shook off the negative thought. "Do you mean he's gone to work for the competition?"

"No."

"Then what?"

"You're not going to like this, Rodger, but there's no easy way of saying it. Ray is in Headwaters. He's been there since last Monday."

"All he told me was that he was taking a week's vacation—I guess he didn't want me to know." He hesitated, almost afraid to ask the inevitable question, but finally said, "Do they know what's wrong with him?"

"Yes, they know. And he knows. But I'd rather he told you himself. He asked me not to tell anyone."

"Just one question, then. Will he be coming back to work here?"

"Only if he wants to."

"That doesn't exactly answer my question, does it?"

"I didn't mean it to. You'll have to ask Ray what he intends to do."

"I'll visit him at Headwaters after I leave here and find out what this is all about." His voice softened. "Look, Bart, I'm deeply sorry about Ray leaving, but I'm leaving, too, and that's final. I've got to. I can't possibly work here any longer. But I wasn't aware of Ray's situation, and I don't want to leave you in the lurch, so I'm quite willing to give you two weeks' notice to give you some time to find replacements."

"I don't want your damn notice," Drummond snapped, and Rodger could see that he'd finally given up the battle and the real Drummond he'd known for several years emerging, the Drummond who couldn't gracefully accept no for an answer, especially from those he considered his underlings. "Do you think I want to keep someone here who hates his job, who thinks our work is petty and useless, who thinks we're writing for a bunch of twelve-year-olds? Do you think I want to keep a person like *that* around here for another *two weeks*, demoralizing the rest of my staff?" He jabbed a forefinger at the door. "Clear out your desk and get out.

And leave your work in progress there. Your severance pay will be in the mail this week."

"Bart, I didn't want to leave this way. I thought—"

"*Did you hear me?*" Drummond yelled, his arm now as stiff as a ramrod, the forefinger pointing rigidly toward the door. "*I said get out!*"

After obtaining a ticket from the machine, Rodger pulled into the parking lot at Headwaters Health Care Centre on Rolling Hills Drive. Although he knew that this building, Orangeville's new hos-pital, had been in operation since May, 1997, and that the old hospital on First Street had been sold and converted into the Lord Dufferin Centre, a seniors' residence, neither he nor Claudia, remaining healthy, had ever been inside Headwaters as patients, and the only member of their families who had ever been a patient there was his mother who'd had a breast lumpectomy performed in 2002 and had completely recovered. They had visited her regularly during her stay. But as far as ill clients or acquaintances were concerned, they only rated get well cards and, possibly, flowers or fruit baskets.

Their visits to his mother had been rigidly structured: enter the hospital, buy a gift at the Gift Shop, visit for a half hour, and leave. They had no idle time to spend exploring and evaluating the hospital or its grounds. Still, Rodger knew that Headwaters featured state-of-the-art equipment and had received two awards: the 3-M Health Care Quality Team Award in 1999 for its services, and the Ontario Architectural Design Award in 2000 for its design. Now, as he entered the spacious lobby, he felt a strong desire to make a closer examination of the facility, knowing clearly that the honest reason for his interest stemmed from his reluctance to see Ray and discover the true nature of his illness.

After aimlessly wandering the halls, and reading many of the donors' names of individuals and businesses on various-sized plaques on a long wall, he decided to prolong the inevitable even longer by visiting the Gift Shop, telling himself that he had to buy Ray a little gift. As he browsed idly, the short, stick-thin saleslady—wearing a pale gray dress which ran from her neck to well below her knees, with a shifting wattle sagging beneath her chin and an osteoporotic hump below the back of her neck, wearing too-red lipstick and thick-lensed glasses that magnified her pale brown eyes—approached him and asked if she could be of assistance.

"Just looking," he said. "I'm visiting a friend."

"Male or female, dear." Despite her physical appearance, he found her voice both cheerful and silken. "Adult or child."

"Adult." He read the name badge on her shapeless chest. "It's a man in his mid-fifties, Phyllis."

"Well, the male gifts are in this area," she instructed, leading him to the opposite side of the shop. "Does he expect to be in hospital for some time, or just having some minor procedure done?"

"I really don't know. I haven't been told yet."

She smiled sympathetically, showing a perfect set of dentures marred by a fleck of too-red lipstick on one of the incisors, and patted the back of his hand. "Well, I'm sure it's nothing serious, dear. After all, if he's only in his mid-fifties—well, that's only middle age, isn't it? When my Henry, God rest his soul, died three years ago, he was seventy-five, so I know what losing someone close to you means. We married very young—he was twenty and I was only eighteen. We'd been married for fifty-five years when he died...." As she continued to speak glowingly about her marriage, Rodger realized that she had just divulged her age as seventy-six. Had it been inadvertent, or intentional? A very old cliche stated that a woman never liked to divulge her age, yet he recalled that when he worked at the bookstore, where customers sixty-five years and older were allowed fifteen percent discounts on their purchases, that women readily offered the information, sometimes even stating their actual ages when he asked those he considered borderline if they were pensioners. Some, perhaps those with little cash to spare, offered the information merely for the fifteen percent discount, but many who actually stated their ages did so proudly, as though they were to be personally congratulated for having lived so long. "...and he always treated me so well," she was saying. "Never once in all those years did he ever strike me. A perfect gentleman, my Henry was." She shook her head sadly, her voice no longer cheerful. "It's such a shame that he had to die. Nothing has been the same since. Sometimes I wish that I'd gone first—that way I wouldn't have to suffer the way I'm suffering now, without him."

"What do you think would be a suitable gift for my friend?" he asked.

"Oh, one of those boxes with two decks of cards in it would be nice," she replied, pointing. "He could play solitaire and pass the time. Do you ever play solitaire, dear?"

"Sometimes. In my computer."

"Oh, I don't have a computer. I wouldn't have the faintest idea how to work one. Henry never had one either, but he always had time for me. I only get two days a week here at Headwaters; the rest of the time I'm pretty much alone in my apartment because most of my friends have died...." His thoughts drifted away as he recalled that his grandmother on his mother's side, who he used to visit in a nursing home in Toronto many years ago, had exactly the same habit: She went on and on about her own problems, mainly her health and her loneliness, until she saw that you showed signs that you intended to leave, then asked you something about yourself to encourage you to stay. Your life and your problems were her second choice, but she'd rather have you talk about yourself than be left alone. He felt resentful then, feeling that his grandmother was only using him for her own selfish purposes, but now, listening to Phyllis blatantly profess her own deep loneliness, he suddenly felt empathy, not pity, for her, and listened also because, although anxious to see Ray and learn about his illness, conversely he felt reluctant to hear any bad news from him.

As he listened further to Phyllis lamenting her loneliness, his empathy forced him to envision her pain by placing himself in her position. He asked himself gloomily: Was that all growing old meant? Assuming he lived that long, was that all he had to look forward to in his seventies? A lonely, desperate search for companionship, even from strangers, for a few hours two days a week? And how did she spend the rest of her time? Sitting alone in her apartment with only the radio or the TV for companionship? Keeping one or the other on constantly because she couldn't bear the voiceless silence of a life without her Henry? Living vicariously through the happier, more exciting lives of others as she watched TV movies, picturing herself as the heroine, still young and vibrant and desirable and needed? Or did she spend some evenings playing euchre or bridge in the building's recreation room with other elderly tenants, contributing her share to a mindless sea of incessant nattering? He felt a sudden claustrophobic choking at the very thought of being straitjacketed into such a state of purposeless emptiness and an intense sense of urgency engulfed him.

Before it's too late, I've got to do something that's worth something!

"I said I see you're married," Phyllis said loudly."

"What?"

She smiled indulgently. "Your mind must have been wandering." She pointed to his left hand. "The wedding band—I see you're married."

"Yes. Yes, I am."

"And you probably have a beautiful wife, don't you?"

"Yes," he admitted. "Yes, she's quite beautiful; her name is Claudia."

"Would you believe that I was once beautiful, too? Maybe even as beautiful as Claudia?"

He knew that she wanted only one answer and gave it to her. "Yes, I do believe that, " he said, appraising her with his eyes. "I believe that you were once very beautiful. As a matter of fact, in some ways I think you're still beautiful. You have a beautiful voice. Have you ever done any radio or TV work?"

He couldn't be certain, but he believed that under the makeup on her cheeks she actually blushed. "Oh, stop it," she said, tapping his hand, feigning anger but pleased. "My Henry would never allow me to do anything like that. My Henry believed that a woman's place is in the home, and that's where I stayed. And I loved every minute of it because my Henry was the best, most considerate and loving husband a woman could ever have. But now my Henry's gone, and nothing will ever be the same. Now everything has changed. Now...."

As Phyllis enumerated the failings of her present life, Rodger's thoughts drifted away to a dream he'd had on his final night on retreat. In it, he sat on the grass and leaned against the wall at the back of what appeared to be an apartment building. Several feet away, he saw a brown, furry seal and wondered what a seal could possibly be doing there. Fearing that the seal might bite him, he drew away, but the seal waddled up to him and quietly laid its head in his lap. When he realized that the seal only wanted love, he began petting the top of its head and down its back. His fear gradually subsided and he began enjoying the petting, and the seal seemed to enjoy it as well and eventually moved away, satisfied, not waddling any more but walking on newly formed legs. The dream meant nothing to him when he awakened on Sunday morning, but now, as Phyllis continued to bemoan her fate, he understood its significance. She, and other unfortunates—the lonely, the sick, the poor, the destitute, the deserted, the battered, the raped—represented the seal struggling along on its flippers that came to him for help, for hope, for comfort, for encouragement, and his stroking of the seal's head and back represented all these virtues, allowing the seal (the human being) to cast off its crawl and sprout the legs it needed to walk off smartly and bravely to confidently face the world.

He wasn't so vain as to presume that the Lord infiltrated his dream with this message. Yet the dream had come to him and he now saw clearly that all his weeks of searching for answers to the problems of his own life—his conversations with Claudia, Ray, Penelope, Katherine in the Brampton restaurant, Mary and Vicky at the Kosy Korner, and Charles—were truthfully not that at all. Yes, he earnestly desired to change his own life, but the true reason why he spoke to these people was because he felt empathy for them and *wanted to improve their lives*. From this empathy, and not from his certainty that he could never find solutions to his own problems anywhere but inside himself, emerged the idea for the book. Even his angry outburst against Greg, although it relieved the mounting tension of years of harassment, had meant more than merely a character assassination of a man whose lack of ethics he despised. It had also been meant as a warning that Greg was headed for a severe downfall unless he tried to salvage his reputation by improving those ethics.

The retreat aside, Rodger could now truthfully admit that the only two persons he went to visit with the sole purpose of gaining inspiration from them were his parents. He deeply admired their selfless, generous natures: their joint sponsorship through World Vision of three children, one each in Indonesia, Ethiopia, and Colombia, their regular donations to the church, Matt's positions as lector, member of the parish council and of the Knights of Columbus, Martha's regular donations to dozens of charities concerned with funding research into various diseases, with special emphasis on cancer research because of her own successful bout with the disease. But as much as Rodger admired and respected his parents, he failed to envision himself duplicating their roles. Yes, with his retreat experience still fresh and vivid in his mind, and acknowledging his revitalized craving for faith in his life, he would certainly return to the church either with or without Claudia's approval. Still, Emerson's instructive words flashed warningly through his mind: "No kernel of nourishing corn can come to him but through his toil bestowed on that plot of ground which is given to him to till." And he saw his "plot of ground" as a hands-on mission to bring comfort and encouragement to the lonely, the poor, the sick, the hungry, and the destitute. Worldwide, the task appeared formidable, gargantuan, but he had to do whatever he could—one person at a time, one life at a time, one soul at a time.

He gazed at Phyllis—the shifting wattle beneath her chin, the osteoporotic hump below the back of her neck, the thick-lensed glasses—and said, "Yours must be a lonely life."

"Yes, it is," she admitted readily, surprised and pleased that someone had actually recognized that she had a problem. "*It is!*"

The next words were out of his mouth before he even had a chance to reflect on them. "I'll come and visit you."

"Visit me?" Incredulous, she stared at him, her magnified pale brown eyes suddenly glistening. "No one *ever* visits *me.*"

"Well, I will. What other day do you work here?"

"Friday. I work Mondays and Fridays. But you don't have to—"

"I'll visit you on Wednesday then."

"That would be wonderful. But what about your job, your work?"

"Actually, I'm no longer working. I've decided to restructure my life and rethink my priorities. Will noon be okay?" He reminded himself to take his digital recorder along. "We'll discuss things—I'll try to help you."

"Yes, yes. Yes, that would be fine." Phyllis became animated, waving her arms excitedly. "Do you like apple pie?" she asked eagerly.

"I'm crazy about apple pie."

"Then I'll bake you one," she said, clapping her hands together excitedly. "I'll bake you the best, the most delicious apple pie you ever tasted."

"I'm sure you will."

Rodger wrote her address and phone number into his pocket notebook, paid for the playing cards, and left her. Reluctantly, he inquired at Information for Ray's room number, still hesitant, still afraid of what Ray would tell him and feeling a twinge in his stomach each time he thought about it. He gazed longingly toward the snack bar, telling himself that he felt hungry and that a coffee and a bran muffin would see him through until lunch time, then shook his head, certain that he was only deluding himself and trying to postpone the inevitable.

His stomach churning, weakness gripped him as he grabbed the handrail and slowly descended the stairs to the lower level patients' rooms. Unable to contain his curiosity as he walked shakily along the hall, he paused at open doors and peered inside, pretending to be looking for a certain person, as though seeing other ill patients would prepare him for seeing Ray. Some of the rooms simply contained two patients lying in their beds, many of them old, some asleep. As he gazed at them, he felt a deep empathy and again reflected on the vast enormity of pain and suffering and asked himself: How many like this, lonely or suffering or both, were in this hospital, how many in Orangeville, in Ontario, in Canada, in the world? And which bed would he be lying in, perhaps waiting for death, ten years, twenty years, thirty years from now? Would the disease responsible for his own death be cancer, heart disease, diabetes, kidney disease, liver disease, lung disease, AIDS, or any of the countless other diseases known to man? And who would come to visit him, talk to him, comfort him in his sickness, or in his dying? And when that time came, and nothing productive could any longer be achieved with his life, would he have anything whatsoever to show for it?

I've got to do something!

As he stopped at a door and looked inside, he saw a small, frail, elderly woman in a mauve gown, alone in the room and barely awake, engulfed in an armchair that could almost hold two of her side by side, a walker standing beside it, but her tiny eyes widened as she saw him looking at her and smiling gently, as though surprised that anyone other than the staff, especially a stranger, would ever pay even a crumb of attention to her.

"Come in," she begged in a tiny, high-pitched, girlish voice. "Please come in."

He took a chair and moved it next to hers and sat down. "You look like you could use a little company."

"Yes. I rarely see anyone except the nurses now and then."

He noticed that her fingers were bare; he extended a hand. "My name's Rodger." If his eyes had been closed, he would have thought that he was shaking the hand of a ten-year-old as she placed her trembling hand into his.

"Millicent," she said softly.

"I'm pleased to know you, Millicent. But don't you have any relatives or friends who came ind visit you? Brothers or sisters?"

"When you get to be my age," she confided grimly, "most of your relatives and friends are gone, or they've moved away and you've lost touch with them. I had two brothers who never married, like me, and now they're both gone." She reached out and touched his hand for an instant. "I'm so happy that you're here. It's so nice to meet someone who can take the time to talk to you."

"I'm glad to be able to keep you company. If I'm not being too nosy, may I ask why you're here. I mean, you're not in bed, you're sitting up and..."

"I had a right hip replacement done a week ago. They don't waste any time here—they started me on physiotherapy two days after my surgery. I'm just waiting for the volunteer to come and wheel me over there." She tapped the walker. "I can manage to get around with this, but it's still awfully painful. The nurses try to help by giving me pain killers. It's not like the old days—they don't keep you in hospital very long now. Since I live alone, tomorrow they'll be discharging me to a rehabilitation centre for a few weeks, maybe even months, for further therapy. The doctor won't allow me to go home until I can get around well on my own. I don't want to go home and be alone unless I can take care of myself."

"You'll be all right," he assured her. "You have the advantage of being light—you won't be putting much weight on your new hip. I even wonder how you ever reached this point. You don't even weigh a hundred pounds, do you?"

"No, I don't." She searched his kindly face, as though trying to determine how much to reveal, then nodded in approval and continued. "I wasn't always this slender," she admitted. "Before I started having hip trouble, I was...well, quite a bit heavier. My doctor told me that I needed to lose weight, but I guess I waited too long. My hip was already in poor condition by the time I lost the weight."

A burly, bearded volunteer arrived pushing a wheelchair. "Well, Millicent," he said pleasantly, "it's time for your ride again."

"Karl," she said proudly, "I want you to meet my friend Rodger. He's been visiting with me. And...and he's going to come and visit me in the rehabilitation centre, too, aren't you, Rodger?"

"Why...yes," he said, rising to leave, shaking Karl's hand. "Of course I will." He wrote the information she gave him into his pocket notebook. "I'd better be moving along now. I'm visiting a friend just a few doors away."

Astonished, he asked himself: Is it possible that my true earthly mission is something as utterly simple as this? Comforting one person after another? Nourishing one soul after another? Does it all come down to this utterly simple humbleness, and has all my futile, pompous searching for some monumental, world-shattering enlightenment been nothing more than an extension of my own inflated ego?

He thought of Matt, who had so often told him that a good, productive life was simple, not complicated, and felt like someone who'd been searching vainly for enlightenment for weeks and weeks in the basement of a house when he should have been searching in its attic.

When he arrived at Ray's room, he hesitated, took a deep breath, stepped cautiously inside. With the head of his bed raised, Ray lay asleep on his side, wheezing, his hair dishevelled, his face above the scraggly beard pale and thinner, as though starving for blood. An old man, small and shrivelled, lay asleep in the other bed, his weak, sporadic moans apparently prompted by a distressing dream.

Rodger sat down quietly in the chair beside Ray's bed and decided to wait a few minutes to see if he awakened.

Ray soon stirred, a deep, racking, liquid cough that worried Rodger jarring him awake. When the coughing finally subsided, he reached for a Kleenex. "What are you doing here?" he asked testily. "How long have you been...sitting there watching me?"

"Just a few minutes—I didn't want to wake you. I saw Drummond this morning and he told me you've been here since last Monday."

"Did he tell you...*why* I was here?"

"No. He told me I'd have to find that out for myself. That's partly why I'm here. You told me you were going to be on vacation last week. Instead, you've been here. What's wrong with you?"

Ray folded his arms tightly across his chest. "Look, there's nothing wrong with me...that a few days of...rest won't cure," he wheezed. "They're discharging me this afternoon...and I'll probably be back to...to work by next week."

Rodger's previous reluctance in seeing Ray now became deep concern. "Listen, Ray, you and I've been friends for a long time, so don't lie to me. When you woke up a few minutes ago, you were coughing so hard that I thought you'd bring up a lung. And even though you tried to hide it, I saw the red stain on the Kleenex you carefully folded and carefully placed in your waste bag. And that red stain doesn't mean bronchitis. And your shortness of breath doesn't mean asthma. So don't bullshit me, Ray—we've been friends too long for that."

"Drummond told you, didn't he?" Ray accused.

"No, he didn't tell me anything, but I'm not blind. I can see that you're really sick."

"Get the hell...out of here, Rodger. This isn't your fight. Go out and enjoy life...while you can."

"So you at least admit that you've got a fight on your hands. It's the smoking, isn't it? Forty years of smoking has finally caught up with you."

"No...I—"

"For God's sake, Ray, admit it. It's your lungs, isn't it?"

"Get out of here, Rodger—I don't need you here. It's nothing...I'll be fine...they're giving me treatment."

"It's more than nothing. What do you think friends are for? To desert you as soon as you've got a problem? Stop trying to be the big, strong man for a change."

"Get out of here, Rodger!" Ray reached for the nurse call button. "Get out of here or I'll call the nurse!"

"You won't call the nurse and you know it. Because we're friends. If you're sick you're sick, that's all. Let's do something about it, together. What did the doctors say?"

"Get out, Rodger," Ray pleaded weakly, his voice hoarse. "*Please* get out. I can handle this on my own."

"What did the *doctors* say, Ray?"

"Jesus, you won't bloody well leave me alone, will you?" Sighing heavily, he unfolded his arms and lowered them to rest limply at his sides, his hands open with palms turned upward. He shrugged helplessly. "The news isn't good. My lungs are shot." And as though on cue, he grabbed a Kleenex and broke into a paroxysm of deep, fluid coughing which shook his entire body. Finally finished, he wiped his mouth, disposed of the Kleenex, and lay back, exhausted. Laughing hoarsely, he gasped, "Shit, I thought... one of my nuts...was coming up then."

Rodger recalled how he'd reacted to Denny's lung cancer four years ago, merely visiting him occasionally, perhaps playing cards or watching sports on TV instead of remaining closer and offering support during the dying days of a terrified atheistic friend who believed that he had to look forward to was total nothingness. And why? Because he, Rodger, had issues with God himself and because of these felt no desire to even offer Denny the possible comfort of an afterlife which he himself had difficulty believing in. So they played cards and watched sports on TV, and avoided even mentioning Denny's imminent death. But he couldn't let that happen again—he had to do something!

Rodger asked, "What kind of treatment are they giving you?"

"They can't operate. They've set me up for a long series of... chemotherapy...starting tomorrow. And they'll be using radiation." Ray shrugged. "I guess it'll help a little, maybe stave off the inevitable for a while...but probably just for a while."

"But you've got to try to maintain a positive attitude, Ray. You can't give up hope."

"I haven't done that. You'll see me back at Drummond's in a week or two....I promise."

"But I'm afraid I won't be there. I quit this morning."

"What? What the hell for?"

"I felt that I was just wasting my life away there, writing commercials for twelve-year-olds. I'm taking my life in a new direction—I want to do something productive, something meaningful. Drummond even offered me a partnership."

"A *partnership*? And you turned him down? You must be *nuts*. What did Claudia say when you told her? She must've blown her top."

Rodger saw that Ray felt relieved in turning the conversation away from himself and his illness, and continued. "She doesn't know yet. I wanted to make sure that I had the guts to leave Drummond's before I told her. I've already told her that I'll explain everything tonight."

Ray shook his head. "You poor bugger. I can just imagine... how she'll take the news. Probably kick your bloody ass out of the house."

"I doubt that, but we'll see. I can't go into it right now, but there are a number of issues we need to discuss, and I don't know yet where that's going to lead us."

Ray nodded. "I get the picture. And right now the picture I get...is that your life is in...one hell of a mess. Look, you had it made at Drummond's—how could you ever turn down a *partnership?* Go back and tell him you'll take it. Even beg him if you have to. You just can't pass up this kind of an opportunity."

"No, that phase of my life is finished for good. And with or without Claudia, my life is going in a whole new direction."

"What direction? Providing that you get things...straightened out, what are these great plans...of yours for the future?"

"Do you really want to hear about them? Or are you just waiting to pounce on me after I tell you?"

"I really want to hear them. I want to hear what would prompt a man...to say no to a partnership at Drummond's...and even think about getting...on the outs with a beautiful wife...like Claudia."

Even though Rodger realized that Ray's beliefs were not his own, that he spoke to a resisting audience, he felt an urgent need to defend himself and express his feelings. "Something morally productive. Something valuable for the betterment of society. In the past few weeks, talking to people and gathering material for my book, most of the people I met were just frittering their lives away on trivialities, doing things which won't make even one brush-stroke of difference to the big picture because most of them are mainly concerned with the minute pictures which are themselves. They refuse to move outside the box. And the worst of it is, most of them are miserable. And they are miserable *precisely because* they are obsessed with their own lives. Beyond the high walls of their minuscule lives, the world outside means nothing.

"I also met people like this when I worked in the bookstore: women who read voraciously and brought in bags of books to trade, who lived vicariously by frittering away their lives with their heads buried in frivolous romance novels, frivolous mysteries, or frivolous modern fiction, reading the same formula stories over and over and rarely finding even a drop of nourishing drink, perhaps getting fat as they ate pastries or chocolates while they read, interested only in their own comfort, their own hedonism, and contributing absolutely nothing to society. One middle-aged, overweight woman, who came in with a shopping bag full of read books almost every month, said she wanted to pick up a few books because she was going to Florida for a three-month holiday. I wanted to ask her, but didn't, why she needed a three-month holiday when her *whole life* was one long, book-reading holiday.

"Such books are not literature, they're mere entertainments—shallow mass market fiction produced to cater to every conceivable whim of the readers, many of them badly and sloppily written in simple language which can often be easily understood by most fourteen-year-olds. The demands on the reader are minimal and superficial—we wouldn't want them to actually start doing a little *thinking*, would we? But true literature makes us do exactly that. It plunges us into *life*, where we may even find ourselves as we *really are* and may even, God forbid, actually *learn* something about ourselves. Try reading Norman Mailer's 'The Man Who Studied Yoga' and you'll immediately see the difference. He keeps adding one layer after another to the work. He's writing about life, and his work can tell you something about life, while mass market fiction is merely writing about entertainment.

"Men, and I'm one of them, spend thousands of hours every year watching sports on TV but contribute nothing to society, contribute nothing to the betterment of the world. Until recently, how much time during the last ten years have I actually spent doing anything, *anything whatsoever*, for anyone but Claudia and myself? Did I help to support the church? No. Did I contribute to any worthwhile medical or humanitarian charities? No. Did I help the destitute, visit and comfort the sick and the lonely? No. Did I even donate groceries now and then to the food bank? No. Did I make even one sacrifice for anyone other than Claudia, perform even one selfless, generous act? No. But I did other despicable things which came very easily: I accepted an extra ten dollars change from a weary cashier at Zellers without saying a word; I stood in the express lane at Zehrs behind an old woman buying a few cans of stew and pasta and baked beans who found herself thirty-five cents short after emptying her battered purse, and turned coldly away when she gazed at me pleadingly; forcing her to leave one of the precious cans behind; I ignored ragged, winter beggars on

Broadway, rationalizing my heartless actions with the flimsiest of excuses as I said to myself, "If I can do it, why can't they? Exactly when did I become part of this what's-mine-is-mine-and-what's-yours-is-also-mine-if-I-can-get-my-hands-on-it generation? Was it when I fell under Claudia's spell? When I look at myself, it sickens me. What kind of abominable creep have I become?"

Ray shook his head sadly. "So now you want to become some kind of martyr...is that it?"

"No, not a martyr. It wouldn't be anything like being a martyr—I'm too cowardly for that. I just want to do *something good* with the rest of my life. I'm forty now. When I'm fifty or sixty or seventy, I don't want to be looking back at the same thing I'm looking back at now. I haven't just talked to several women these past two weeks—I've actually tried to *help* them because I could see that they were unhappy." He paused. " And speaking of women, has Rebecca been to visit you?"

"Once. She hates hospitals...hates being around sick people...maybe because of what's happened to Penelope."

"So she hasn't offered to take care of you after you're sent home?"

Ray laughed hoarsely. "Are you nuts? That's just about the last thing she'd ever do. If it was her mother, maybe...but even then I'm not sure. And she certainly doesn't want to be taking care of a sick *man.* Just the thought of handling a sick man...would probably horrify her."

The words flowed easily from Rodger before he even had a chance to reflect on them. "But it wouldn't horrify me."

"You?" Ray gave him a piercing stare. "What the hell are you talking about?"

"I'm talking about coming to stay with you so you'll have someone to talk to, and someone to take care of you if you can't take care of yourself."

Ray folded his arms tightly across his chest. "Hell, I don't need anybody to look after me—I'll be back to work in a week or two anyway. You'll see. Besides, they'll be sending a sexy nurse around...every couple of days to look in on me." He looked away. "So you're talking crazy. Real crazy."

But Rodger's empathy drove him on. He pictured Ray at home in his apartment, sick, alone, afraid, seeing his life inevitably and inexorably winding down, with no one to talk to but an occasional nurse who, since he was a man, he could only present with a brave front. "Ray, listen to me. You're a good friend, and I want to help you in any way I can. I mean that—*I want to help you. I need this. I need something vital to hold on to, something to tell me that I'm here in this world for some useful and moral purpose instead of being just another useless tit on a bull."

"Forget it—I'm okay. Stop trying to change the way of the world. Go home to Claudia and try to straighten out...your own mess. And go back to Drummond...beg him for your job back. Jesus, what the hell's...the matter with you? How stupid can you get? Can't you even see...when you've got it made? You've got a helluva beautiful wife, you've still got a chance at a terrific job, and you're trying to blow it all. Straighten out your own mess...and leave me alone."

"And what if I can't straighten it out? What then?"

Ray turned away. "Just straighten it out, that's all."

Rodger's voice softened. "Look, I know you're a man, Ray. And I know that you're manly. You wear a beard, and cowboy boots, and a black leather jacket, like to drink beer and ride around on your Harley and pick up women. And you've probably been to bed with more women than I can count on my fingers and toes. So you don't have to prove to me that you're manly, that you're tough—I know that. But even tough guys can get sick. Even tough guys can need help sometimes. And I think you need it now, or soon."

"No. It's because I'm still a man that I don't need anybody to coddle me. Go home to Claudia, Rodger. I'm okay. You'll see, I'll be riding the Harley again, and picking up more women."

"Yes, you probably will still be doing that—for a while." Rodger knew what he wanted to say next, but he had to squeeze the words out of himself. "Because, like you said, the chemotherapy or the radiation or both should help. Temporarily. You said yourself that they can't operate. So what happens when the treatments no longer help? When that time comes, do you want to be alone most of the time with your suffering, with only a nurse or Rebecca visiting you occasionally. Alone and afraid and—"

"Damn it, I'm *not* afraid. I've had my innings, all nine of them, and enjoyed every one of them. And now it's payback time. Old Omar said it well: 'While the rose blows across the river brink, With old Khayyam the ruby vintage drink: And when the angel with his darker draught draws up to thee—take that, and do not shrink.' Like I said, I've had my innings...and there'll be more before I go, but I know damn well that the 'angel' he mentions... didn't come down from any heaven. Because I know that there's only one place I'm going, and it's the same place we're all going. Into black nothingness." He shook his head, as though to shake out the thought and discard it, and when he continued Rodger could barely hear him. "But I'm not afraid...I'm not afraid..."

But Rodger knew better. He knew that virtually everyone, from the most religious person to the most confirmed atheist, feared the vast, final unknown of death, from which no one except the phoney voices in seance rooms and the silly "ghosts" in TV fantasies ever returned to verify the existence of the afterlife. We can have all the faith in the world, but no one can truly *know*. Which, he knew now, is as it should be. Because if we could simply reach inside ourselves and draw out our souls and hold them up to the light and actually *see the visible proof* of our afterlives, what would be the purpose of living? And what would be the purpose of even having free will to decide if we either believed or disbelieved if we had no use for it? Ray had made his decision—at least for now, and although he refused to admit it, he was afraid. Even those who believed in heaven and the afterlife were afraid because they knew that even they could be wrong, and that the essence of God's truth would always remain impenetrable.

We were all afraid.

Rodger said, "All right, you're not afraid. And you're going to face the inevitable like a man. But do you want to do it alone? Have the doctors told you what it's going to be like after...after the chemotherapy and the radiation no longer work?"

"No," Ray snapped, looking away. "They haven't told me a damn thing. All they do is try to soft-pedal everything."

But when Ray replied so quickly, and his eyes shifted away from him as he spoke, Rodger knew that he was lying. "Did you insist on knowing the truth and force them to tell you? Is that what happened?"

"No, I told you, they—"

"Don't bullshit me, Ray. You *made* them tell you, didn't you? And they did, because they knew that you had a right to know."

Ray rolled onto his side, turning his back to Rodger. "Go away, Rodger," he said hoarsely. "Go away and leave me alone."

"What did they tell you, Ray. I'm your friend—I deserve to know the truth."

Ray continued to speak to the wall. "Okay, they did tell me the truth, and the truth sucks. I've got small-cell carcinoma, the kind that grows quickly, and I'll be lucky if I last a year. I asked them...to lay it on the line and they did. Here's what I've got to look forward to: a horrendous cough, sometimes with bloody sputum...wheezing and shortness of breath...hoarseness, chest pain... shoulder and arm pain, fever on and off, fatigue most of the time, a loss of appetite which eventually leads to weight loss....Later on my face will swell up, and the lymph nodes in my neck, making it difficult to swallow....I can still us a puffer to open up my lungs, but later on I'll need oxygen to help me breathe—I can just see me now, chained to one of those damn portable oxygen tanks and wheeling it around—and all the time I'll keep growing weaker... and thinner because I can hardly eat anything. And in the end it's back into the hospital...sucking on oxygen and being fed through a tube...until even the oxygen doesn't help." Ray turned back to Roger and glared at him. "You silly bastard, is that what you want?" he demanded. "To live with a helpless, dying man? To feed him when he can no longer feed himself? To bathe him when he can no longer bathe himself? To give him oxygen when he can no longer breathe? To put on another diaper after he pisses himself? To wipe his ass when he can't even do that? Is *that* what you want?"

"Yes yes *yes,* that's exactly what I want. To take care of you whenever you need something; to look after you in every way I can for as long as you need me. That's why I'm here in this world, to help others—I realize that now. I realize now that the only possible way I can ever feel complete, feel as though my life has been worth something, is by doing exactly that. For God's sake, Ray, let me *help* you!"

Ray turned away again and closed his eyes. "I'm tired," he said weakly, his voice hoarse. "Extremely tired. Leave me alone. I need to get some sleep...before they come to discharge me."

"You're just trying to get rid of me, aren't you?"

"Yes, I am."

"Then I'll go."Rodger rose and gently squeezed Ray's shoulder. "Just remember what I said."

When Ray remained silent, Rodger started for the door, but just as he was about to leave, Ray said, "Rodger?"

He turned to see Ray still lying in the same position with eyes closed.

"Yes?"

"Call me. Call me tonight....I'll be home....Let me know how you made out...with Claudia."

"I'll call you."

15

When Rodger reached home, he changed into a fresh shirt and wandered aimlessly around the bedroom thinking about what he would say to Claudia when she arrived. Aware that she'd probably object to his recording their conversation, simply from spite if he told her he'd be leaving, he decided against using the digital recorder, confident that, if he intended to use her in his book, he now knew her motives well enough to write them from memory.

He noticed the cheap Ten Commandments bracelet on her vanity, the one he'd bought for her at Dollarama because he hadn't been able to find one elsewhere. To pacify him, although he knew that she disliked the bracelet, she'd worn it a few times when meeting with clients, and even now still wore it occasionally, most recently when they'd visited his parents, always leaving it on her vanity so he wouldn't think she'd forgotten about his little gift. What had motivated him to purchase the bracelet for Claudia in the first place? He'd never seriously considered the question. He knew that her loveliness certainly made her extremely attractive to her male clients. Concerning these same clients, had he felt a latent fear that she might be tempted to stray from her marriage vows, and that wearing the bracelet during these meetings would act as a kind of defence mechanism, constantly warning her to avoid adultery?

Idly, he picked up the bracelet, and again, as he had at his parents' house, noticed the wider gap between two of the scrolls, which he'd never later questioned Claudia about. There were only nine scrolls. Again he reasoned that she could have lost one, the bracelet being only a flimsy piece of costume jewellery. Yet when he opened her jewellery box he saw the missing scroll there and his eyes widened in surprise when he read the inscription: "Thou shalt not commit adultery." Had the scroll simply fallen off, and if so, why had she not asked him to replace it as she normally would since she knew herself to be all thumbs when it came to handling tools? Or had she deliberately removed it, and if so, even though she considered her vanity off limits to him and had often told him so, why would she blatantly display the bracelet for him to see if she had something to hide? But the nagging question still mocked him: Why had she deliberately kept the adultery scroll separated from the rest of the bracelet instead of asking him to replace it? He wondered when it had become detached. The only time he could recall her ever wearing the bracelet without the adultery scroll was when they had recently visited his parents. Had she actually removed the adultery scroll because it no longer pertained to her because she had been unfaithful to him? Many questions, but no answers. Yet the answers to these questions were vital to their marriage.

His suspicions aroused, he remembered their discussions about her faithfulness regarding the million-dollar real estate sale in Caledon East. That tiny seed of doubt had lingered with him ever since the sale, tucked away in a corner of his mind. That tiny seed of doubt which had never germinated and grown until it crowded his mind with suspicious doubt, but remained, refusing to die, like a small, dormant sebaceous cyst waiting for the bang or bump which would bring it into festering life.

Rodger sat at the kitchen table toying with a half eaten cheese sandwich and a half empty mug of coffee, neither of which he wanted, when Claudia arrived home for lunch at twelve-thirty.

"What are you doing home?" she asked, surprised, her brow knitting. "You never come home for lunch." She eyed the sandwich. "You can't eat just that—I'll prepare something for you."

"Don't bother, I'm not hungry," he said flatly.

"You look pale; is something wrong? Are you ill?" She touched his forehead. "You don't have a fever."

"No, I'm not ill, I'm just not hungry." He pushed the sandwich away and turned to face her. "Claudia, we need to talk."

"Have you made a decision about what you spoke about yesterday?"

"Yes, I have, and we need to talk about that and many other things. We need to try to clear the air and find out where this marriage is going."

"Well, that certainly sounds serious." She filled a mug with black coffee and sat down opposite him. "Now you've managed to put *me* off my lunch as well."

Wanting to adopt a superior position, he rose and pushed the chair in, gripped the top of it and leaned over its back. "First, I'll tell you the decision I've made," he said firmly.

"Yes?"

"I've quit my job."

Her mouth and eyes widened in astonishment. "You've *what*?" The mug of black coffee, halfway to her mouth, no longer interested her. With a shaking hand, she returned it noisily to the table.

"I said I've quit my job."

"Do you mean that you've found something that pays even better? Are you going to Drummond's competitor?"

"No, I'm taking my life in a new direction. I'm getting out of advertising for good so that I can do something more rewarding with my life."

"And what have you found to do?" she asked suspiciously.

For a moment, he thought of mentioning Ray's condition and their recent discussion at the hospital but quickly dropped the idea when he recalled that her jealousy toward Ray made her dislike him. "Nothing definite yet," he admitted. "But it'll probably be something in the charitable line. I'm tired of taking and never giving."

Incredulous, she jarred the table and spilled some of her coffee as she jumped to her feet and leaned over the table, staring at him wide-eyed, her chin jutting belligerently. "Are you absolutely *insane*? Do you mean to tell me that you left a eighty-thousand-dollar job and now you tell me that you have 'nothing definite yet'? How could you be so stupid? I want you to phone Drummond *right now* and *beg* him for your job back. Do you hear me?"

"No, I don't hear you because I don't intend to do that," he said calmly. For ten years, he had succumbed to her demands because he found most of them trivial in the larger scheme of things, but now, when it mattered, even her insults seemed to come from another time, another life, and were like feathers trying to move a mountain. Still, her false love rankled and he relished the reaction his next words would bring. "Even if I don't work, my savings and investments will see me through for years if I'm careful. Maybe I'll see if I can get a part-time job as a greeter at Wal-Mart to bring in a few dollars."

"A greeter at Wal-Mart!" she shrieked. "You gave up a job at Drummond's that paid you eighty-thousand dollars a year to be *a greeter at Wal-Mart*? You bloody fool!"

"I don't think so. It may teach me a little humility, which has been sadly lacking in my life, and help to start me along the road I want to travel. You meet people, you talk to people, you become part of the human race again. You listen to them, listen to their problems, maybe even try to help some of those you believe are truly worthy of help. It would at least be a beginning."

"A beginning for what? A trip to the poorhouse? Do you intend to squander the money we've been saving for our new house on people who can't even fend for themselves? Because that's what's going to happen, isn't it? Then what's going to happen to our new house, the one we've been dreaming about for years?"

"You mean the one *you've* been dreaming about for years.'

"But...but you never disagreed with me whenever I mentioned it."

"No, of course I didn't, because I was simply trying to pacify you, as I've been trying to do for the past ten years. I never wanted a new house, *you* wanted a new house. This house is finally paid for and is perfectly satisfactory—why do we need to start paying off another mortgage?"

"Why?" she snapped. "Because I want to *do* something with my life, *get* somewhere, that's why." Her voice suddenly softened, became throaty and sensuous. "Darling, don't you understand, we're a *team*. We've always been a team, and teams need to support each other to succeed. We're like...like two halves of the same circle, and without each other we're simply arcs, incomplete, unfulfilled. We *need* each other to be fulfilled and succeed. Can't you see that?"

"I can see that you need me, but there are problems with our marriage which need to be discussed before we can move on."

"Problems? What problems?" she challenged. "What are you talking about?"

"Earlier today, while I was waiting for you to come home, I was in the bedroom and happened to notice the Ten Commandments bracelet I gave you a few years ago on your vanity. One of the scrolls was missing, the one that said 'Thou Shalt Not Commit Adultery.' What—"

"You were snooping around my *vanity,* when I've told you never to touch my things? Would I ever paw through the things on your dresser?"

"No, you just tried to create a whole new wardrobe for me," he said with relish. "Don't try to evade the question. What happened to that scroll, Claudia?"

"That bracelet wasn't made to last and you know it. It just fell off, that's all."

"How long ago?"

She shrugged. "I don't know. Maybe...maybe about six months ago."

"But why wouldn't you have asked me to replace the scroll when it would have only taken me a few minutes?"

"I didn't think it was important because I hardly ever wear the bracelet anyway. It looks too cheap."

"But you have worn it without that adultery scroll, haven't you? As a matter of fact you wore it recently when we went to visit my parents. Why would you do that, especially visiting my parents, when you could have asked me to repair it? I guess the only reason Martha didn't take a closer look was because she'd seen the bracelet before. Because if she had, she might have asked you the same questions I'm asking you now."

"What are you trying to say?" she demanded.

Rodger leaned over the back of the chair until their faces were only several inches apart and stared into her eyes. "What I'm trying to say is that maybe you deliberately removed the adultery scroll because you had a guilty conscience."

"*What?* Are you insane? Are you actually accusing me of... of..."

"I'm not accusing you of anything—I said 'maybe.' But I'd like to remind you that you never did satisfactorily explain your million-dollar real estate sale in Caledon East. And if you tampered with the Ten Commandments bracelet—"

"I didn't tamper with anything!" she shouted. "You know as well as I do that you bought it at Dollarama. It's just a piece of cheap costume jewellery that wasn't made to last and one of the scrolls fell off, that's all. It could have been any one of the scrolls."

"Then why did you hide it away in your jewellery box, as though it was an object of shame that you didn't want to be reminded of? If you didn't feel any guilt, then why didn't you ask me to replace it?"

Claudia slammed her fist down against the table. "You went into my jewellery box?" she shouted. "How *dare* you."

"I dare in retaliation for the way you've tried to control my life for the past ten years. I dare because I absolutely refuse to cater to your whims any longer. Now, answer the question, unless you have something to hide. Why didn't you ask me to replace the scroll?"

"I've already *told* you—I just didn't think it was that important."

"You don't think *adultery* is that important?"

"I didn't mean that—you're twisting my words. I meant that I didn't think it was that important to replace *any* of the scrolls if they fell off because I rarely wore the bracelet anyway. Do you honestly believe that if I had a guilty conscience I'd be foolish enough to feed it every time I opened my jewellery box and saw the scroll there? Of course not. If I actually did have a guilty conscience, which I don't, I would have disposed of the scroll a long time ago and simply told you that I'd lost it." She glared at him. "You never have completely forgotten about the Caledon East real estate deal, have you?" she accused. "It's been festering inside you all these years, hasn't it, because you still aren't completely sure if I told you the truth? And the bracelet's missing scroll is just another excuse to keep it festering, isn't it?"

"*Have* you told me the truth, Claudia?"

"Of course I've told you the truth," she blurted out. "The problem is that you stubbornly refuse to believe the truth when you hear it. Good God, must we go through this *again?*"

"Yes, we must, because the conversation we're now having is going to determine whether or not our marriage is going to continue."

"What are you saying?" she asked, frightened, her hands suddenly balling into tight fists. "What's the *matter* with you? Are you trying to tell me that our marriage is in trouble?"

"I'm telling you exactly that. I need to know the truth—now. Did you sleep with the guy who bought that million-dollar house in Caledon East so that you could close the deal and get a huge payday?"

Claudia laughed, moved around the table to his side and turned him toward her. "Darling, don't be ridiculous." She wrapped her arms around him and nestled her head on his shoulder. "I've already told you, many times, that he was a despicable, egotistic creep and I wouldn't have gone to bed with him for *any* amount of money. Because you're my husband and I love you, love you more than life itself." She took his hands and pressed them against her buttocks. "And your the only man I ever want to go to bed with."

Gently, he squeezed the familiar, curvaceous warmth of her buttocks, the same exquisite buttocks he had fondled hundreds of times and marvelled at for over ten years, but now they exerted no more passion within him than warm, pliant putty because he knew the falseness of her 'love.'

"Love," he said, angrily pushing her away. "You don't even understand the meaning of the word. You bastardize love. You're not in love with me—you're merely in love with love. In love with the very act of loving. And that act can be performed with me, or Joe Blow, or any man you choose to practise your so-called love on. But deep down the man doesn't mean a damn thing to you; all you're ever interested in is *your* pleasure, without any regard whether or not it gives *me* pleasure. You give love only for the selfish reason of having your so-called love returned instead of giving it without conditions. Your so-called love is selfish, nothing more than a cruel ruse to keep me showing my love for you again and again and again. Because you're not *in* love, you're just loving. Going through the motions. Trying to make me believe that you truly love me, but actually only trying to make me continue to love *you* by using every trick, every lie, every deception you can think of."

And as he stared at her, studying her reaction, he saw, even though he expected it, what he hoped to God he would never see: that the dagger of his words had driven straight into the heart of her selfish love and brought forth blood, and her shocked surprise at finally being found out, something she thought would never happen, brought from her the reflex actions which sealed her guilt before she could even control them. The message conveyed, involuntarily and only momentarily, by her suddenly gaping mouth, widening eyes, heavy sigh, her fists relaxing and unfolding, all told him that he'd been speaking the truth and she knew it.

Still, hoping he had failed to recognize or understand the signs, she quickly erased them and stubbornly persisted. "No, darling, you're wrong, completely wrong. I need you. I need you every day of my life, every minute, just like I've always needed you, just like you've needed me all the years of our marriage. I need you to touch me and hold me and kiss me and make love to me. I need you to tell me I'm beautiful. I need you to tell me you love my whole body—my feet, my calves, my thighs, my clitoris, my buttocks, my breasts, my face, my lips, my nose, my eyes, my hair. I need you to be sweet and gentle and romantic, all the time. Darling, don't you understand, I *need* you."

"You you you. Everything is you. And the man is supposed to be nothing but some love slave who feeds your love affair with love. Not a person in his own right—you certainly haven't allowed me to have my own identity—but just some lackey to have around whenever you need him to feed your unquenchable thirst for loveless love. Our marriage has been nothing but a sham all along, hasn't it? One big lie—at least on your part. While you pretended to love me to get what you wanted out of me, I gave you whatever I could because I sincerely loved you. But now that I realize that my love was never honestly reciprocated, that your love was simply an act, I can't go on with this charade another day."

"Darling, please," she pleaded, moving toward him. "I need you. *I need you!*"

As she tried to put her arms around him, he pushed her aside. "Need me? You need me only in the same way you would need any man who appeals to you physically. You're beautiful—that'll be easy for you to do. As for me, I can't live this lie any longer. I'm leaving. I'll pack a few clothes and some books and you can pack the rest of my things. I'll send someone for them later. I'll take my laptop and my disks and my briefcase—I'm going to finish my book and publish it and see if I can help some other people."

"Are you insane?" She laughed derisively, a laughter tinged with fear. "You can't just *leave* a ten-year marriage. Where will you go? How will you survive? You've lived under my wing for ten years and now you think you're going to strike out on your own and everything will be fine. Well, it won't be, count on it. Because I'm the one mainly responsible for any success you've had. I'm the one who has controlled and directed your life for over ten years, and without me you're nothing and you know it."

"What I know is that without you to influence me I have a chance to become something worthwhile, but with you I have no chance."

"Without me, the only chance you have is to become again what you were when I met you—a nothing, a nobody. Now that you've stupidly decided to leave Drummond's, how long do you think your savings are going to last? Do you honestly believe that just going around and helping people who are incapable of helping themselves is going to support you? Hardly. They're just waiting for an idiot like you to come along. Do you honestly believe that publishing some silly book, and working at Wal-Mart, is going to support you after they've drained you dry of every cent?" She laughed derisively. "How stupid can you be."

He recalled how often in the past she had similarly mocked his efforts to gain some form of individuality. Years ago, when he had told her that he thought of joining the Knights of Columbus to help others, her angry rhetoric soon convinced him that they needed nothing more than each other for happiness. Whenever he tried to develop new male friendships, or simply spend the odd evening hanging out with a few guys from the office, her jealousy quickly raised its ugly green head. She especially disliked Ray because Ray had taken him away from her more often than anyone else. And her excuse for constantly restricting his life was always the same: their love meant that they only needed each other, and that no one should ever be allowed to interfere with that love. And he had eventually believed her. But no more. Now he knew that from the beginning her so-called love had been nothing more than an elaborate act to fulfill her own selfish desires.

"I'll survive," he said defiantly. "I'll survive and flourish. I'm going to the den now to pack a few things, and I need to make a phone call."

"Why can't you phone from the living room?" she snapped. "Are you afraid I might hear?"

"No, it's not that. It's just that I'm not sure where I'm going yet, and the phone call will tell me. If you're interested, I'll be glad to tell you when I come back."

"Go, then," she said, waving him away as you would a trailing dog and turning her back on him. "And don't hurry back." Suddenly, she swung back and faced him. "Do you really want to know the truth about what happened between Harry Denker and me?"

"Yes, I do. Because I haven't heard it yet, have I?"

"No, you haven't."

Not certain whether to continue, she twisted her hands together nervously. Still, he couldn't help wondering if what she said even now, after all these years, would finally be the truth.

"Then let's hear it," he encouraged.

"I don't know whether I should. You may get the wrong idea—about me, I mean."

"Try me."

"All right," she said doubtfully, her voice shaking. "We went to the property in Caledon East. Denker took a long look around and liked it. But before signing the offer, he said he needed one little favour from me. When I asked him what it was, he said he found me very attractive and first needed to have sex with me. After that, he'd be glad to sign the offer. I told him no, I was a married woman and just couldn't do that. In answer, he grabbed me and tried to kiss me and started pulling at my clothes. I tried to resist, honestly I did, but he had a knife and threatened to *slice my face open*. I had to give in, I just *had* to. He used the knife to hack off my panties, and held the knife only an inch from my cheek as we had sex, and when it was over he threw the fancy pair of panties at me that he'd brought in his briefcase. I had to put them on because I had nothing else to wear. Then he signed the offer and threw it at me and left. He... he raped me, Rodger," she managed hoarsely, tears beginning to trickle down her cheeks. "He *raped* me!"

Ah, the women's well, he thought disdainfully. That final resource, those pockets of reserved tears women had tucked behind their eyes, always filled, always replenished, always ready to spring to the surface on command and expose themselves whenever necessary to gain a point. But her tears no longer impressed him; too often in the past he had found them closely related to the crocodile—phoney, griefless emotion used only to achieve her own selfish ends. Even so, in the past he had usually given in—because he loved her. But now...

"If he raped you," he demanded, "why didn't you tell me when you got home? Why didn't you tell me so I could call the police?"

"I was...I was too ashamed—I didn't want the police to know. I didn't want anybody to know, not even you. I didn't want it to become public knowledge, be taken to court and put on a witness stand and asked to describe everything that happened." The tears flowed freely now. "And what about my real estate career? Do you honestly think that people would come flocking to me to buy homes because I'd been raped? They wouldn't. They'd probably call someone else before calling a rape victim. And how many would avoid me because they believed I was lying and actually invited Denker to have sex with me just to get the $30,000.00."

"Well, didn't you?"

She stared at him incredulously and moaned, "How can you say that? I'm your wife; how can you possibly believe that I'd ever jeopardize our marriage by willingly going to bed with another man? He *raped* me, Rodger. I've told you the truth—what possible reason could you have for believing otherwise?"

"I have thirty thousand reasons, one for every dollar you were paid. All Denker had to do was dangle that carrot in front of your greedy nose. He's a prominent Orangeville businessman, a highly successful commodity trader who's even published a best-selling book on the subject. He's prominent in the community and regularly associates with Orangeville's elite, a position that his vanity obviously treasures. Why would he be foolish enough to endanger all that by raping you?"

"He swore me to secrecy!" she shouted. "He swore that if it ever became public that he'd raped me he'd come and slash my face to ribbons!"

"Nonsense. Do you even know what truth is any more? You know as well as I do that you weren't raped and that the only incentive you needed to have sex with him was the money. How did you manage it in that big, empty house? Bare floors can be very uncomfortable. Did you at least find some plush carpet to do it on?"

"No! I *told* you, he *raped* me! He would've *disfigured* me if I'd resisted! Is *that* what you wanted?"

He moved toward her, intending to grab her biceps and shake her, but as he drew closer she began to back away, fear in her tear-filled eyes. He stopped, amazed at his new power. In all the years of their marriage, he had never once known her to be afraid of him, but instead of exhilaration he felt only a keen sense of failure and dejection. Fascinated, he studied her face, the once smooth, perfect cosmetic mask now marred by several wet streaks, like rain tracks tracing their way down powdery beige sand, running from her eyes to the edges of her nostrils, then turning inward to the peaks of her prominent philtrum before continuing downward to wet her lips. *Don't pity her!* he warned himself. Don't weaken your stance by giving in to her crocodile tears and feeling sorry for her and making up and stepping back on the same worn, hollow treadmill when you know from experience that she's lying.

Still, his voice softened, almost pleading as he said, "In God's name, Claudia, tell me the *truth*. This is over, finished—there's no reason to lie any more."

Sniffling, she stared at him, saying nothing, and he could almost hear the gears of the machinery of her mind turning, grinding away...searching...searching, and he knew that she still hadn't surrendered.

"Yes," she agreed, "since you're going anyway, I might as well tell you the truth." She turned away and walked into the living room and sat on a sofa with her back to him. She plucked a piece of Kleenex from the box on the coffee table and began raising it to her face, then thought better of it, crumpling it as she lowered her hand.

He felt certain that the only reason she refused to improve her appearance by dabbing at her damp eyes and cheeks and lips was because she wanted to continue looking her worst, still determined to elicit his pity and reverse his decision. When would this incessant acting stop? What further lies would she attempt to inflict upon him now? To hear better, he moved closer to her and stood behind the sofa.

She sighed heavily and bent forward in a submissive attitude, like a person suffering some internal pain, and as she spoke her words were a listless drone, as though Rodger had left and she spoke only to herself. "Denker insisted on taking his own car, his BMW, to the Caledon East house, and also insisted that I take mine. I found out why later. It was his third viewing of the house, and he said it would be his last before making his decision. But I wasn't worried because I saw that he definitely liked it. But he soon let me know that he wasn't going to sign the offer until he had his pound of flesh. And I was to be that pound of flesh. He said he thought I was beautiful and was strongly attracted to me from the first time we met, and promised to sign the offer if I agreed to have sex with him. Those were the exact words he used: 'have sex.' Not 'make love.' Which made me wonder what kind of sexual depravity he had in mind. I could have refused, but I knew that if I did he would have refused to sign and would have simply made an offer for the house with another broker.

"There was no furniture in the house. I asked him if he planned to do it right there, on the shag carpet, but he just laughed. Oh no, we'd go to his home in Cardinal Woods and have a few glasses of champagne and then have a one-hour session of sex, and if I performed satisfactorily he'd sign the offer. And I'd be $30,000.00 richer. I didn't like that word 'satisfactorily'—what did he intend to do to me? But he refused to tell me, no matter how much I begged him, only promising that no one would ever know."

She buried her face in her hands. "So I eventually agreed. We went to his four-bedroom house in Cardinal Woods and drank champagne, and I got a little drunk because I was afraid of what he might do and I didn't want to be completely sober. He...he...I can't even tell you what he did, except to say that he debased and degraded me as a woman. But I agreed to it all. And when it was finally over, he gave me the fancy panties to wear home because mine were ruined, then signed the offer and told me to get out." She raised her head and turned her tear-stained face toward him. "You don't understand, do you?—you've never ever understood. You don't understand that I did it for us, so that we could more quickly move up in the world, get a bigger and better house, associate with a better class of people and become a part of Orangeville's elite. I wanted that right from the start, but it's something you've never ever wanted. I already knew that when I arrived home with the signed offer in my briefcase, knowing that I was $30,000.00 richer. I knew that I couldn't possibly tell you what actually happened because you, with your stringent upbringing, would've reacted exactly the way you're reacting now. You would've wanted to leave me. And knowing that, yet still knowing that I wanted more out of marriage than you were willing to give, I decided to actively pursue Denker, an eligible bachelor, not for the kinky sex, which I abhorred, but for the prestige he could bring into my life when I moved into his circle and became part of the elite. I had visions of even making him fall in love with me, even marrying me once I'd obtained an annulment from you. I knew that he traded commodities by computer from his home, and that the markets were usually closed by about three o'clock. After the deal closed, I gave him a few weeks to settle in at Caledon East, then went to visit him one afternoon at about three-thirty. I'd put on some nice clothes, revealing but not too revealing. There were two cars in the driveway: his BMW and another smaller car. For a moment I thought I'd leave, thinking that he had company, perhaps a business acquaintance, but soon tossed out that idea and rationalized that the smaller car belonged to a servant or a cleaning lady. But when I rang the chimes, Denker himself answered. He looked shocked, as though he never expected to see me again. 'What the hell do *you* want?' he snarled. I told him that I just wanted to talk to him, that I wanted us to be friends. But he just laughed. 'Friends?' he said. 'Don't be bloody ridiculous. I don't associate with whores.' And he slammed the door in my face!" She stared pleadingly at him. "Rodger, he called me a whore. A *whore!*"

He felt a sudden sense of deep relief. He knew that after all these years she had finally spoken the truth, and that the suspicion which had lingered tenaciously in the back of his mind during all that time, refusing to be eradicated, had ultimately been laid to rest. Still, he felt no exhilaration over her confession, only a profound resentment that she had been lying to him all these years, and couldn't resist speaking the words that rose like bitter bile from his throat. "And what would you call a woman who sells her body for thirty thousand pieces of silver? A saint?"

"You didn't have to say that, didn't have to hurt me that way. What I did happened a long time ago, years and years ago. I've never been unfaithful to you since."

"No, I don't think you have, yet isn't even once too much? But in the end, now that I know the truth, and as much as I despise what you did, I think I could still forgive you and move on with our marriage, if that was the main problem. I think I could even forgive you for the incessant materialism which rules your life; I could at least try to live with that and try to prevent it from affecting my own goals, if that was the only problem, although in the end I know it probably would. But the third problem, the knowledge that you don't even love me, that you're only in love with the state of being in love, only in love with taking instead of giving, which you can do with any man who is gullible enough to be your love slave, as I was, makes it impossible for me to continue with this marriage. A true marriage depends on reciprocal love; without that, it's meaningless, like a man with only one hand trying to clap. Your innate selfishness, apparently inherited from your stepfather, has destroyed this marriage, but I won't allow it to destroy me. Because I need more than this charade we've been living for the past ten years. I'm moving on to a better life, a more productive life, a more moral life, something I can look back on when I'm an old man and be able to tell myself that my life hasn't been entirely wasted in digging my arms up to the elbows into the world's bodily pleasures and grabbing everything I can. That I was put here for a noble purpose and that I've at least tried to achieve that purpose by reaching beyond myself and making my life productive and worthwhile."

"You sanctimonious *bastard!*" Claudia shouted, snatching several pieces of Kleenex from the box on the coffee table and wiping them furiously across her wet cheeks, smearing her makeup and causing her to look worse than ever but oblivious in her fury. As Rodger stared in amazement, the tears in her eyes receded, disappeared into their pockets as though a tiny vacuum behind her eyes had sucked them back out of sight. "Do you think your shit doesn't stink? Do you think you're something special, something better than me? Well, let me tell you this—you're not. And if you leave this house, leave me, the big, bad world out there will gobble you up and chew you into mincemeat and spit you out into the gutter. Because *I'm* the one who's been supporting you all these years. You were absolutely *nothing* until you met me, pathetic. Working at miserable dead end jobs and going absolutely nowhere. *I'm* the one who kept after you until I forced you out of your simplistic, naive fantasy world and made you see it as it actually is: greedy and grasping and filled with people who don't give a damn about anybody but themselves. But to win you've got to play the game; we've all got to play the game. And I played the game well with you. Because *I'm* the one responsible for your job at Drummond's, your juicy bank balance, your healthy investments, everything. I only married you because I thought I could make something out of you. And I did. And now you want to give it all up, throw it all away, throw our marriage away. Greg was right about you when he called you Rodger the Dodger because that's all you are. Giving up and running away instead of facing up to things. Rodger the Dodger," she sang, taunting him as malicious children would taunt a child in a schoolyard. "Rodger the Dodger, Rodger the Dodger, Rodger the Dodger."

He saw more clearly than ever the absolute futility of continuing the argument, of ever freeing her from Greg's influence and convincing her that no one forced you to play the game but yourself, and that there existed a better, more humane ways of life which many people, in spite of the world's current prevalent hedonistic philosophy, still followed.

Sighing heavily, he simply said, "Yes, you and Greg are certainly two of a kind, aren't you? He made you everything you are today."

"Yes, he did," she said proudly. "But soon we'll only be one of a kind, at least in Orangeville. They're leaving."

"Leaving?"

"They've bought a house in Listowel and will be moving there in two weeks. He's opening up a real estate office there, where nobody knows him. Apparently too many people here have said too many things to too many people and his business has dropped off drastically. But I suppose you're delighted to hear that news, aren't you? Delighted to know that you were right, that what you told him would happen actually did happen. And probably also delighted to know that now I'll be left here all alone. That must make you *very* happy."

His eyes probed her face for some confirmation that she'd spoken the truth and not simply used the information as another ploy to gain his pity, but her expression revealed nothing. Yet why would she lie when she knew that he could phone Sally to verify the truth?

"Why didn't you tell me before that they were leaving?" he asked.

"Why would I want to do that after the way you insulted him the last time you saw him. I'm only telling you now so you'll know... so you'll know before you decide to desert me and leave me all alone."

"You'll never be all alone, Claudia. Never. You're too beautiful for that. Once the men around here discover that I'm gone and you're available they'll be swarming around you like bees to a honeycomb."

"I don't want other men—I want you."

"Instead of thinking about me, you'd be far wiser to start thinking about advancing your career, because that's been your main concern all along, hasn't it? Making more and more money in real estate. And now that Greg's leaving, it's your perfect opportunity to do so, isn't it? Now's the time to start up on your own."

"I'll be doing exactly that. I've already registered for The Broker Course," she said smugly. "And I've already inquired about renting an office."

"Fine." He saw no further reason to continue the conversation and turned away. "I'm going to the den to make an important phone call."

"Am I a bad person, Rodger? Is that why you want to leave me?"

"No, you're not a bad person, just mediocre. As a matter of fact, we're both mediocre. We've made each other mediocre over the years by kowtowing to the erroneous, hedonistic Great Canadian Dream which states that accumulating more and more material possessions is the road to happiness. Lies. And that's why we're now having this discussion. For the past ten years we've been gorging ourselves on our own selfishness. Over the years, your frivolous, tempting, but hollow philosophy has rubbed off on me and made me frivolous, too. Over the past few weeks, that fact has come through to me loud and clear. That life is now over. Finished. I have now officially started my new life. And that new life will be a life which has some meaning, some value, while continuing to live with you will only perpetuate the pointless life we've been leading for the past ten years. And why would I continue to do that, why would I be that foolish, especially now that I know that you don't even love me."

Insulted, she waved him impatiently away with the back of her hand, as you would a dog or a cat. "Then go, Rodger the Dodger, go," she snapped. "Get out of my sight."

But as he reached the top of the basement stairs, her caustic voice stopped him. "I suppose you're going to phone mommy and daddy to tell them that their darling boy is returning home," she sneered. "That Rodger the Dodger needs their precious support because he's too weak and frightened and insecure to deal with his new world. That he wants to sponge off them until he *finds* himself. That he wants to attend church with them again, like a good little boy, and associate with a bunch of boring, back-slapping do-gooders who only compliment others so that they too can be complimented. Isn't that what you're going to do?"

"No," he said. "I have no intention of returning home. What I'm actually going to do is phone Ray Foley."

"Ray Foley? Why on earth would you want to phone *him*?"

"I'm going to ask him if I can come and live with him."

She appeared more bewildered than ever. "But why?" Her brow furrowed and her eyes betrayed a suspicious look. "You're not…you're not…?"

"Gay?" He laughed. "How can you even think that after the sex life we've had for the past ten years?"

"Then why? What other possible reason could you have for wanting to live with Ray Foley?"

He noted that she still called him "Ray Foley," always adding the surname. From past experience, he knew that she only called people by their complete names when she disapproved of them, as she always had with Ray because of his lifestyle.

Suddenly, as though she had discovered the truth, she laughed scornfully. "Oh, *now* I see what's going on here. Your wanting to leave me has nothing whatsoever to do with some high-flown idealism that makes you want to change the world. You're going to live with Ray Foley for the most common and crass reason imaginable: to join him in his boozing lifestyle of going to bed with any woman who'll have him. Isn't that really what this is all about? You're leaving me so that you can pull out all the stops and play the field because you're afraid that your time is starting to run out, the most common symptom of mid-life crisis. Can't you see that? But no matter what you do, you'll never ever find any woman as good in bed as me. Tell me the truth—isn't that what this is *really* all about?"

"Wrong again," he said, unable to keep the victorious tone from his voice. "I'm going to live with Ray because he's suffering from inoperable lung cancer, and I want to do whatever I can to help him to maintain his quality of life during whatever time he has left."

Claudia's mouth fell open, and slowly closed. "You should have told me," she accused, embarrassed. "Did it give you pleasure to listen to me make a fool of myself? Is that why you're only telling me now?"

"Maybe it is," he admitted. "Maybe I'm just being so petty because I'm trying to get even for ten years of being used and lied to."

She ignored his comment. "That news is awful, and I'm deeply sorry for Ray Foley. But does he being terminally ill mean that you must go and *live* with him? It just doesn't make any sense to me."

"No, it wouldn't. Being who you are." He sighed heavily, acutely aware of the complete hopelessness of ever softening or diluting Claudia's egocentric obsession with control. Even now, when she knew that he intended to leave, she still felt compelled to attempt to control his actions. This being so, he simply turned away and went downstairs.

At his desk in the den, with the door closed, he phoned Ray's number. After six rings with no answer, he hung up, knowing that Ray had no answering machine but did subscribe to Caller ID. Yet he wondered at and worried over Ray's not answering and found himself envisioning several different possibilities. If at home, why had he not answered? Was he for some reason unable to reach the phone on time? Perhaps using the bathroom? Or asleep? Or simply refusing to pick up because he saw Rodger's name on the Caller ID and had changed his mind about accepting Rodger's help? No, that didn't sound reasonable—Ray would face the situation, as he had in the hospital, instead of running away from it. Then why hadn't he phoned back? What if something even worse had happened? What if he had suffered some kind of attack and even now lay unconscious and helpless on his apartment floor?

Trying to control his negative emotions, he phoned again. Still no answer. He told himself that Ray may not even be at home, that for some medical reason, perhaps a relapse, he may not have been discharged and may still be in the hospital. He phoned Headwaters and was told that Ray had indeed been discharged earlier that afternoon. He phoned Ray again and let the phone ring several times. Still no answer. Fearful, he decided to go to Ray's apartment to investigate, but at the top of the stairs he heard the phone ring once and knew that Claudia had answered on an extension.

The empty living room told him that she had gone upstairs and answered in the bedroom. In case it was Ray, and wanting to speak privately to him, he hurried back to the den and picked up quickly, hoping that Claudia hadn't yet had a chance to start questioning or browbeating him.

"It's Ray Foley," Claudia said flatly, and he heard the click as she hung up.

"What took you so long to call back?" Rodger demanded. "Where have you been?"

"You sound like my late mother. Already."

"Sorry. It's just that I became worried when you didn't answer your phone. I thought maybe…maybe something had happened to you."

"Don't worry, I'm okay. I had to take a cab home from Headwaters…because I left my car here when I went in. When I checked my fridge, I found that some of my food had gone bad, so I went to Zehrs and picked up some groceries. I just got back. What's up?"

"Did Claudia question you?"

"No. All she had a chance to say before you picked up was, 'Oh, it's *you*.' I know she doesn't like me…because of my lifestyle… but her voice could've frozen the balls off a brass monkey. It sounds like things went badly between the two of you this afternoon."

"No more badly than I expected. We're finished, Ray. I'm leaving."

"Did you tell her about me? Does she know about…?"

"Yes, I told her about your condition and that I hoped to go and live with you and help take care of you. That's probably why she sounded so cold on the phone."

"She must hate my guts. Because she probably feels that I'm the one largely responsible for breaking you two up....What's with you two anyway? You've been married for ten years, and suddenly everything falls apart. I'm not going to be responsible for breaking up your marriage, unless there's a damn good reason. Is this just your mid-life crisis talking, which will soon pass, or is there actually something seriously wrong with your marriage?"

"There's something seriously wrong—and it can't be fixed." As he spoke, Rodger listened intently for the telltale click warning him that Claudia had picked up on the extension. He told Ray the details of Claudia's million-dollar Caledon East real estate deal and her sexual encounter with Harry Denker.

Ray said, "What's the big deal? If I was a real estate salesman, and some woman buyer came along and told me that...I'd have to have sex with her...before I could earn a thirty grand commission, I'd jump at it, even if she was ugly."

"That's you, Ray. You'd jump at anything female, any time."

"Okay, maybe I would. And I'm not married either. But that's a hell of a lot of money for a one-nighter. When did this happen?"

"About three years ago."

"Hell, millions of women are cheating on their husbands every day. Had she ever been unfaithful before that? Or since?"

"Not that I know of."

"So Claudia cheated on you once in ten years. I don't think I want to be responsible...for breaking up a marriage just for that."

"It's not just that—I've already forgiven her. And I can also forgive her for being a grasping, hedonistic, egocentric, materialistic person and try to live with it and keep our marriage together while going my own way. But when the most vital part of any marriage is missing, what else can you do but leave."

"But you've always told me that your sex life is great."

"You dopey bugger. You've been reading too much *Omar Khayyam*, living too much below the belt. I'm talking about love. Claudia's innate selfishness makes it impossible for her to love anyone but herself. She's in love with love, not with me. She goes through the motions to make it look good, puts on a good show, but it has everything to do with her own personal satisfaction and nothing to do with love. Everything to do with any schnook, which I was, who she finds physically attractive and can continually mould and manipulate until he becomes her perfect love slave. Is that the kind of relationship you expect me to continue with? Marriage means much more to me than that—I just can't do it."

"My friend, you're a romantic," Ray advised. "You want the whole ball of wax, and I guess I envy you for that. But I can tell you from experience that you've got…one hell of a tough row to hoe if you ever expect to find…that idealistic relationship which, as one poet said, is 'like two hearts beating as one.' You might think I'm nothing more than some aging Casanova, but in truth I've been looking for the same thing all my adult life. But it just never happened. The gears never actually meshed; that elusive, reciprocal magic was never there. Whenever I met a woman I thought I could become seriously attached to, I could see that she looked upon me as just another one-night stud. And the women who were becoming serious about me, I saw as nothing more than delectable sex objects. The only time a relationship ever became reciprocal was on the sexual side. Which in many cases was pretty damn good. But not the whole ball of wax. Never the whole ball of wax. And I guess, even now, I'm still looking and hoping, but almost haphazardly, and never with the same fervour as in my naive youth. Because I know how rare and elusive real and honest love…between two people actually is."

"So you agree with me then. You agree that it's pointless for a man to persist with a loveless relationship, and that it would be far more worthwhile for me to leave and spend my time helping you instead."

"Hold on. You're asking me to agree to too much here. I agree that for *you* the right thing to do is to leave, because you're Rodger Blackwell. But I *don't* agree that it'd be the right thing for *me* to do. If I had a woman like Claudia, assuming that she didn't hate me and we had a great, reciprocal sexual relationship, I'd stay with her until Big Ben bonged thirteen."

"Then you believe that I'm making the right decision, given the way that I am."

"Yeah."

"Then the only question we need to answer is wether or not you want me to help you by coming to live with you. Is that right?"

"Yeah. But are you absolutely sure that that's what you actually want? I don't want you coming here...just because you feel it's your duty, because we're friends. And I certainly don't want you coming here...just because you pity me. I can't stand pity—not even now."

"I'm not going to pity you. Pity is a useless emotion, which may assuage a person's conscience, but does absolutely nothing to help the person being pitied. The reason I want to be with you, help you, is because recently I feel as though I've wandered out of the dark cave I've lived in for the past ten years and emerged into bright sunlight. And that sunlight has made me see that I'm not just here to spend my life imprisoned in my own private little hedonist world, obsessed with fulfilling my own material and sensual pleasures. No, God put me—every one of us—here for a definite purpose, and I know now that it's only in recognizing my purpose and fulfilling it that I can ever be truly happy. And right now my purpose is simply this: to help anyone in authentic need in any way I can. Because we're all in this together, all part of the same human family, all inextricably attached to each other by some gigantic, invisible umbilical cord. Every human male is my brother; every human female is my sister. And that's why I want to help you."

"I'm well aware of your Christian upbringing, and that it looks like you've returned to your roots, because you've just been expounding Christian principles. And I guess Christian philosophy makes a lot of sense—if you believe in the afterlife. But it's not for me. And even if it were it's too late for me to change now anyway. I've read the *Rubaiyat* since I was eighteen, and lived by it, because that's what I believe.

> "'Oh, come with old Khayyam, and leave the wise
> To talk; one thing is certain, that life flies;
> One thing is certain, and the rest is lies;
> The flower that once has blown for ever dies.'

"To me, there's no returning, no coming back for another ten or fifteen lives while we try to perfect ourselves, which none of us ever seems to do. And no gigantic, eternal paradise in the sky either. There's only death, and after that, nothing. But I now do accept that as time goes on…I'm probably going to need more and more help, and I do believe that your offer is sincere, and I thank you for it. But I'll only allow you to come and live with me under two conditions."

"Name them."

"Number one: that you leave, if I ever ask you to, with no questions asked."

"Done." Rodger doubted that Ray, as his health failed and his need for help increased, would ever ask him to leave.

"Number two: no religious discussion whatsoever. I don't want you to try to convince me of the superiority of your philosophy over mine."

"Only if you ask."

"Don't worry, I won't."

Brave words, Rodger thought, and he believed that Ray probably meant them—now. But what about three months down the road? Or six months? Or nine months? How many men, accepting imminent death as they grew weaker and weaker, would not be terrified at the thought of facing a black nothingness and at least hope for an afterlife?

Rodger said, "I have a bit of packing to do before I leave. I can be at your place in about an hour."

"Fine."

As he reminiscently browsed the books on the shelves, recalling the importance they had once held during his early manhood, Rodger felt that a vital piece from the core of his life, now found again, had been missing for the past ten years. Now, his life had gone full circle, from regularly attending church with his parents since early childhood, to the discovery under his father's encouragement of the writings of Thomas Merton, Thomas à Kempis, Pascal, Emerson, and Thoreau, to ten years of ignoring and even reviling the church's teachings and living under Claudia's mercenary, hedonistic influence, and now back to believing in the tenets of his religious beginnings.

Opening his briefcase, he began packing the books: Merton's *The Seven Storey Mountain, Seeds of Contemplation, No Man Is an Island,* Kempis' *The Imitation of Christ,* Emerson's *Essays,* Thoreau's *Walden and Other Writings,* and Pascal's *Pensees,* the various studies which had represented the backbone of his reading during early manhood. To these he added a large writing pad on a clipboard and several computer disks, including the backup disk for his book, and placed his laptop computer into its zippered carrying case.

As he left the room, he stopped and turned in the doorway and took a final look around, conscious that he would miss this room which had been his only true sanctuary in the house for the past ten years. Here he could close the door, think his own thoughts, do his own thing, be his own man, escape Claudia's constant need for attention when it became too demanding. Too smothering. But even here, he had to admit, with countless opportunities to do something constructive and worthwhile, in the end what had he actually achieved? Until his recent retreat, he hadn't even opened any of the books he had loved and cherished as a young man. Yes, he had tried to write a novel, which he recently discarded in disgust when he confirmed it to be nothing more than another miserable example of mass market pap, lacking even a drop of originality, a pathetic carbon copy of a book which had been written thousands of times before. And what else had he done here in this room for the past ten years? Played thousands of games of FreeCell solitaire on the computer? Read thousands of newspapers? Read hundreds of trite, threadbare novels that would probably descend into oblivion within five years? Listened on CDs to countless hours of music? Without even a drop of nourishing nectar for the mind or soul except for a few dozen pieces of literature, all these were merely pure entertainments to him, while he scrupulously avoided the soul-expanding books gathering dust on the shelves. But now that would change, he thought almost reverently as he patted the briefcase containing the seeds of his future life. Now he would try to become the man that God had destined him to be.

Leaving his briefcase and laptop computer near the front door, he saw no one as he hurried past the living room doorway and upstairs to the bedroom to pack, vaguely conscious of a faint musky scent in the air, half expecting Claudia to still be there, perhaps curled up in a miserable fetal ball dabbing at her eyes in one last attempt to elicit his pity.

But the empty bedroom puzzled him. Could she actually have had the audacity to leave? Snub her nose at him by beating him to the punch? He doubted it. And to make certain, he looked out the front window and saw her car still in the driveway. He decided that she must be either in the kitchen or in the backyard. After packing several changes of casual clothing, he carried the suitcase downstairs and placed it near the front door.

As he entered the living room in search of Claudia, he saw no one at first, but a sudden chill ran down his back as the potent, unmistakable musk scent assailed his nostrils, warning him that Claudia lurked somewhere nearby and making him suddenly aware that she only used musk scent for one purpose.

Oh my God, he thought incredulously. *Oh-my-God!*

"I'm over here, darling," Claudia purred.

Stunned, his gaze drifted to the back of the sofa, where he saw snaking out across the sofa arm a foot in a toeless and heelless red wedgie slipper, the painted toenails like brilliant drops of blood, and then a shapely calf in glistening nylon. Her toes began to curl and uncurl rhythmically, causing the slipper to slap against her heel.

Slap-slap-slap-slap-slap…

The final temptation. He should have known that there had to be one final temptation.

As he approached, musk scent attacking his nostrils and almost dizzying him, he gazed down at beautiful, smiling Claudia lying languidly across the sofa, her makeup flawless again, her radiant hair deliberately splayed out around her head like a large blonde halo, her pink robe lying on the sofa arm, wearing nothing but the red slippers, thigh-high red nylons, and a flaming red negligee wrap. She raised a half empty glass of red wine in a silent toast and took a generous sip. He noticed that the wine bottle on the coffee table, apparently newly opened, had already been well used.

"You're absolutely incredible," he gasped.

"Yes, I am, aren't I," she replied, totally mistaking his meaning, and before he could say another word she put down her glass and rose only a few feet away and stood facing him, her feet spread in a dominant pose, a confident, self-satisfied smile curling her lips as her blood red fingertips reached for the edge of the red negligee. "This is what you *really* want, isn't it, darling?" she taunted as she pulled open the filmy negligee and allowed it to slip to the floor behind her. She cupped her hands beneath her plump breasts and hefted them, their swollen brown nipples jutting provocatively. "These are what you really want, aren't they? Soft, and smooth, and warm. To lay your head against, to fondle, to kiss, to suck, to love them as you've loved them hundreds of times before. Isn't that what you *really* want?" She turned her back to him and bent forward, thrusting her shapely, jutting buttocks toward him, gripping them with her blood red fingertips and wiggling them. "And aren't these what you *still* want? Aren't they just as soft and warm and lovely as they were ten years ago? How many hundreds of times have you stroked them and squeezed them and kissed them? How many times, darling?" She turned back to him, ran her hands down her sides to her shapely hips, brought them together to cover her triangle of black pubic hair. "And how many hundreds of times over the years have you touched me here, gone into me here, and had your juice drawn from you here inside my beautiful vagina?" Like a stripper presenting her nakedness for approval, she raised her arms, crossed them momentarily, spread them wide and raised her hands high. "Isn't this what you *really* want?"

"You're absolutely incredible," he murmured miserably, staring, rooted to the spot and barely able to speak, for now he knew that he did mean it the way she had first assumed.

"*Isn't* it, darling?" she said, smiling smugly, supremely confident as she moved forward and wrapped her arms around his neck and squeezed her nakedness against him, rubbing her pelvis into him, mercilessly massaging his burgeoning hardness. "*Isn't it!*"

"I...I..." Tormented by doubt, he found it impossible to speak, for the absolute truth of their marriage descended upon him like a dense, black, polluted cloud, enveloping him and choking off his speech. Even as Claudia's blood red lips clung like a leeches to the side of his neck, draining him of his resistance, the smell of her wine-soaked breath mingling with the potent musk scent which rose between their straining bodies, a small, pleading voice cried out inside him that right from the very beginning this was all their marriage had ever meant. To both of them. He'd always thought of himself as living on a higher level than a purely sexual plane, and even after Claudia had admitted that she didn't love him, he still believed that at least he had loved her. But now he realized that their marriage had always been nothing more than a complete sham. This...this purely physical attraction—her obsession with being wanted and desired, his obsession with possessing her lovely body—had been the mutual lie they had both lived under for ten years. And the only tenuous glue holding their marriage together during all that time had been the mingling of his semen with her genital lubrication. Even now, she would have been far easier to resist if she'd remained fully dressed, but the sight of that incredibly lovely nakedness which had tempted him relentlessly for ten years made him almost senseless with rampant desire. He groped through the wreckage she had inflicted on his mind for a handhold, for something to shore up his crumbling defences, anything that would lead him back to his original plan, to his future, and finally dredged up Ray, a dying Ray coughing out his life and needing him, but Rodger cursed inwardly and castigated his miserable weakness when even this failed to smother his raging lust. Groaning, his hands still at his sides, he felt an overpowering urge to surrender, to reach back and crush her warm, soft buttocks between his fingers, yank her against him, and rub into her. And did so. Immediately, her clinging lips left the side of his neck and moved to his ear.

Then he heard it.

A tiny, teasing, victorious laugh. A laugh that told him that he had failed again, that she still held him a sexual prisoner, that there would be no other, more rewarding life for him because he lacked the strength necessary to escape her sexual domination. At that moment, although he couldn't recall ever hating anyone except perhaps Gunderson, he hated her, and hated himself for his weakness. And as his hatred for her boiled up inside him, he pushed her savagely away and shouted, *"No!* It's over. There's nothing more here. Nothing."

She laughed loudly, derisively. "Nothing more?" She pointed toward his crotch. "Just look at yourself. Does *that* look like there's nothing more here?"

As he gazed down helplessly at his jutting manliness, he recalled a girl he'd gone out with while in his late teens who ended everything she said with a silly laugh, making him wonder if she'd even laugh if they were in bed together. And she had. She giggled whenever he kissed her, giggled when he fondled her breasts, laughed when he ran his hand between her legs, and laughed uproariously and never stopped laughing when he slid into her. Taunting him. His erection had quickly vanished, and from that day onward he believed that nothing could bring death to a man's sexual potency more surely than a woman's derisive laughter.

And Claudia still laughed at him, and as she continued to laugh he felt his sexual desire draining away in disgust.

Staring at her boldly, he said, "I'm leaving now. You'd better get dressed—I'll be opening the front door. Some man might pass by and see you naked."

"And maybe it'll be a real man," she said sarcastically, making no move to pick up her negligee. "Someone who knows how to make love to a beautiful woman and take care of her."

"You'll certainly have no problem finding that," he admitted. "They'll be lining up once they know that you're available. The problem is they won't know what they're getting into."

"Go ahead, open the door," she challenged, proud-ly thrusting out her full breasts. "Let's see who's out there."

But when he opened the door wide, she hurriedly pulled on the negligee and slipped into her pink robe.

"Yes, that's better," he said, leaving the door wide open as he turned back to her. "You wouldn't want to jeopardize your reputation in Orangeville, would you? You never know when another guy might come along who wants to buy a million-dollar house."

"Oh, there will be others," she said haughtily. "Plenty of others—now that *you're* gone."

"Yes, I'm sure there will be. Plenty of others."

He turned away, picked up his bags, started out, then turned back. "Just tell me one thing, truthfully. Knowing what I now know about Denker, if I had decided to stay and another million-dollar deal came along, and the buyer refused to close the deal unless you first went to bed with him, would you do the same thing again?"

Claudia hesitated barely an instant before defiantly thrusting her chin upward and replying. "Yes. Yes, I certainly would. Because money, and what money can buy, is more important to me than anything else in the world."

He nodded several times, already knowing her answer even before he had asked the question, but wanting to hear it confirmed from her own lips.

He said, "Yes, even more important than love. Even more important than your own soul."

Rodger turned away and walked out.